Large Print - Romance   SW

STOCKTON-ON-TEES BOROUGH LIBRARIES

A fine will be charged if this book is returned after the
due date. Please return/renew this item by the last date
shown. Books may also be renewed by phone or
internet. Replacement charges are made for lost or
damaged items.
www.stockton.gov.uk/libraries

D1349774

0043114547

Deborah Challinor is a freelance writer and historian. *Union Belle* is her fourth novel, set in the Waikato coalfields near to her birthplace of Huntly. She now lives in Whakatane, on the east coast of the North Island of New Zealand.

UNION BELLE

When the first effects of the 1951 waterfront workers' strike ripple through the country, Ellen McCabe — wife, mother, union supporter — is happy with her life in Pukemiro, a coal-mining town in Waikato. Even when her husband's union strikes in support, and making ends meet starts to wear her down, she's still prepared for leaner times . . . But when Jack Vaughan arrives, something inside her shifts. Jack, a friend of her husband, is a handsome, charismatic war veteran. Suddenly everything changes irrevocably, as the turmoil and divided loyalties amongst the townspeople threaten to tear her apart . . . This is a story of love, duty and passion during the strike that turned friends into enemies, shattered communities and almost brought New Zealand to its knees.

Books by Deborah Challinor
Published by The House of Ulverscroft:

TAMAR
WHITE FEATHERS
BLUE SMOKE

DEBORAH CHALLINOR

UNION BELLE

Complete and Unabridged

CHARNWOOD
Leicester

First published in 2005 by
HarperCollins*Publishers (New Zealand) Limited*
Auckland

First Charnwood Edition
published 2006
by arrangement with
HarperCollins*Publishers (New Zealand) Limited*
Auckland

British Library CIP Data

Challinor, Deborah
   Union Belle.—Large print ed.—
Charnwood library series
1. Coal miners' spouses—New Zealand—Fiction
2. Strikes and lockouts—Stevedores—New Zealand
—Fiction 3. New Zealand—Social conditions—
20th century—Fiction 4. Love stories
5. Large type books
I. Title
823.9′14 [F]

ISBN 1–84617–392–2

Published by
F. A. Thorpe (Publishing)
Anstey, Leicestershire

Set by Words & Graphics Ltd.
Anstey, Leicestershire
Printed and bound in Great Britain by
T. J. International Ltd., Padstow, Cornwall

This book is printed on acid-free paper

This book is dedicated to Tiny Brown,
who died in October 2004.

Acknowledgements

Pukemiro is a real town, and most of what happens in this story regarding the Waikato coalminers' strike, from late February to the beginning of July 1951, actually did happen. But other aspects of the story are completely fictional. None of the characters in this story are real, either, except for those whose names already appear in the history books, and any resemblance to actual people is a genuine coincidence and certainly not intentional.

But to make the story as historically accurate as possible, I interviewed various people who were involved at the time of the strike, in one way or another. So thank you to Fred Rix, Tom and Rita Hunt, Noel Tregoweth, and Betty and the late Tiny Brown, and to the other, anonymous, interviewees, and also to Dora Janssen for providing me with a list of people to talk to.

I also consulted archives relating to the strike, and to what life in Huntly and Pukemiro was like then. So thanks also to Linda Wigley, Director of the Waikato Coalfields Museum, and her staff, for access to photographs, mining manuals and other documents, and Rosemary Marshall, District Librarian at the Huntly branch of the Waikato District Library, and her staff, for access to the *Huntly Press*. Also very useful was a collection held by Hamilton City Libraries, called *The Huntly Coalfields Oral History Project*, and a book researched and compiled by Gwyneth Jones, called *When Coal Was King*.

A final thank you, too, to Lorain Day and the team at HarperCollins*Publishers*, for their support and encouragement, and to Anna Rogers, for another excellent editing job.

The darkness is a-closing
I can hear it, I can see it

Leo Fowler, 'Entombed',
Pit Poems, 1939

Prologue

She stops the car at the top of Joseph Street, gets out and leans against the warm bonnet. It's late June and noticeably crisp now that the sun has dropped behind the hills, and her breath is making small foggy clouds in the air. She can hear birds in the nearby bush, a trio of small boys arguing in the school playground, their school bags abandoned on the asphalt, and from somewhere down the street the faint but unmistakable beat of ZZ Top's 'Velcro Fly' — the house she passed with the Norton motorcycles parked reverently on the front verandah, perhaps.

She narrows her eyes, trying to imagine what the little township might have looked like fifty-three years ago when there were a handful of shops, and a post office, and the miners' hall was still standing. There were around 400 people living here then, mostly coalminers and their families, many of them Geordies and Lancashire-men, or Fifers and Irishmen and Welshmen, originally from the coalfields of the UK. Although enough of the old homes still seem to be occupied, down abbreviated side streets she has seen empty and derelict houses, bleached paint flaking off warped weatherboards and front porches lurching at precarious angles. The streets

1

are named Joseph, Edward, James, Robert, John and Bernard, suggesting that the town planner may have come from a family with lots of boys.

There are no shops at all in Pukemiro now, but it's quiet, and has a certain shabby charm, and the houses are probably a cheap buy for young families. As for the older residents, if you'd lived all your life in a tiny community like this, why would you want to move away from the beautiful, rich coal seams that gave you a livelihood for all those years? And the mud and the septic tanks and the isolation, and the bitter winter cold forever looking for a home in old bones. Maybe there are good reasons for moving out, she thinks after a moment.

She can smell the coal. It's in the air in the smoke from sitting-room fires and kitchen ranges, and raw in the ground beneath her feet, damp now with recent rain. The underground mines out here closed decades ago — Pukemiro in 1967, Glen Afton and McDonald two years later — but there will be pockets of coal left behind.

What a bright little community Pukemiro must have been before then, though — close knit, insulated but still aware, and clean because the hill between the mine and the township kept the fine black grit from the railway and the coal screens at bay. At the height of its production Pukemiro Collieries employed 800 men, who brought 700 tons of coal to the surface every day, but those days are long gone. Now most of the older miners are dead, or retired somewhere else, their families grown up and moved on,

2

leaving the town to doze like a scruffy old dog.

She checks her watch — time to get back into Huntly for her appointment. Near the bottom of Joseph Street she drives past a man on a ride-on mower, cutting the strip of grass between his house and the road. She waves at him and he gives her a blank look.

★ ★ ★

Huntly West now, and still that smell of coal.

The low winter sun almost blinds her and she squints to read the numbers on the letter boxes. She stops the car outside a compact, semi-detached state house, and checks the address in her notes. This is it.

It'll be another frosty Waikato evening as soon as the sun goes down properly, and already the garden path feels slippery with half-formed ice, so she places her feet carefully. She doesn't want to arse over, especially not if anyone happens to be watching through the window.

Three concrete steps lead up to a tiny porch, the tongue-and-groove panelling of its interior painted an insipid mint green. A mat made out of wavy black rubber strips underlines the door sill, and a mesh screen fits over the opaque glass door behind it.

Clearing her throat nervously, she smooths her hair and presses the round white buzzer. This is the bit she likes least, the introduction; it always makes her feel uncomfortable, and a bit invasive.

After a moment the glass door opens, and she is momentarily confused — the face peering out

3

at her through the mesh definitely doesn't belong to an eighty-four-year-old woman.

'Hello,' she says, hoping she isn't about to make a fool of herself. 'I'm Cathy Martin, from the university. I've got an appointment to interview Mrs Ellen McCabe. Is this the right address?'

The young man in the doorway has very dark brown, unsmiling eyes and curly black hair. He nods. 'My grandmother.'

He's a nice-looking bloke, but she senses he isn't particularly pleased to see her. Still, his deliberate move to one side invites her into the house.

She opens the screen door and steps into a narrow, galley-style kitchen smelling faintly of roast meat. A television is on somewhere. Against the window wall is an oven, and a sink set into a red Formica bench; the opposite wall is lined with a bank of cupboards painted lime green, and a big, late-model refrigerator.

On top of it sits a large birdcage housing a scrofulous-looking grey parrot with crimson tail feathers. Down one white-enamelled side of the fridge is a small lahar of fresh bird shit. As if to make sure she knows how it gets there, the parrot hangs its bum out of the cage and lets go with another lot.

'Cold out there?' it squawks.

Cathy doesn't know whether to answer it or not.

The young man shakes his head and calls out, 'Gran, this bloody bird of yours has shat down the fridge again!'

4

A disembodied voice replies tetchily, 'Well, clean it off then.'

The man mutters 'Christ,' and opens the cupboard under the sink, letting out a waft of disinfectant and damp.

'Is that Mrs McCabe?' Cathy asks, wanting to laugh at the crapping parrot but deciding she'd better not.

'Yep, hang on.' He takes out a faded, neatly folded tea towel and walks past her. 'Come through,' he says over his shoulder.

She follows him out of the kitchen, past a compact dining table — more Formica — and through to a small, overheated sitting room that smells of furniture polish and old lady.

The long curtains are drawn and a portable gas heater glows orange in front of them, although the tiled fireplace is empty. The carpet is old, burnt ochre and swirly, the wallpaper a faded, patterned, celery green. Positioned directly in front of a television is a La-Z-Boy chair. As Cathy regards the back of it, a blue-veined hand holding a remote control emerges from its depths and points towards the TV; the sound goes off, leaving Judy Bailey yapping energetically away in silence. The chair swivels slowly around.

'It's the girl from the university, Gran,' the young man says. He's still holding the tea towel.

Cathy bends forward so the old lady doesn't have to get up, and extends her hand. She feels absurdly as though she's being presented to the Queen.

'Hello, Mrs McCabe. I'm Cathy Martin, I

rang you the other day about the 1951 strike? Thank you for agreeing to see me.'

'You're welcome, dear.' She doesn't sound at all tetchy now.

Ellen McCabe is quite small. Her hand feels dry and smooth, although the back of it is discoloured and shiny with age spots. Her hair is white and thick, as are her eyebrows, and a pair of startlingly dark-blue eyes twinkle beneath them. Her dentures are unnaturally even and also very white. Still visible under the loose, wrinkled skin of her face is the elegant bone structure that must have made her a very attractive woman in her younger years.

'Sit down, dear, make yourself comfortable,' she adds, shifting in her chair and adjusting the crocheted rug draped over her knees. Nothing is visible beneath it except a glimpse of thick support hose and a pair of fluffy purple Warehouse slippers.

Cathy settles herself in a black vinyl armchair with a tan-coloured squab and begins her usual, slightly nervous, spiel. 'If possible, I'd like to tape this interview. Then I don't have to worry about taking notes. Will that be all right with you?'

She's found it's better to set up her tape recorder as soon as possible. Sometimes, if she mentions too early the sorts of questions she wants to ask, the interviewee will start answering them before she's even got it out of her bag.

'Whatever suits you, dear.'

The young man demands, 'Does she have final say over what you end up using?'

'Yes, she does,' Cathy says. 'I'll send you a

copy of the tape, Mrs McCabe, and you can veto anything you might not be happy about after you've had a listen to it.'

'Thank you, Matt,' the old lady says. 'Why don't you put the kettle on? You could clean up Fintan's mess while you're waiting for it to boil. I'm sure Miss Martin could do with a cup of tea.'

'Fintan?' Cathy asks.

'The parrot. He can be very mouthy and two-faced, for a bird.'

Matt reluctantly goes back into the kitchen, and turns the tap on.

'My grandson,' Mrs McCabe says in a loud whisper. 'He's a good boy but very protective of me. Thinks talking about it might upset me.'

Cathy gets her tape recorder out and sets it up on the coffee table in front of her, plugging in the microphone and inserting a blank tape. An enormous, coal-black cat is stretched out under the table; it barely moves even when Cathy inadvertently pokes it with her boot.

'Will it, do you think?' she asks. 'Because if you do have any upsetting memories, you don't have to talk about them if you don't want to.'

The old lady waves her hand dismissively. 'Oh, not after all these years, it won't. What did you want to know?'

'Well, what it was like, really. What life was like in Pukemiro in 1951, how the miners felt about going on strike, what it was like for the wives and the children, what you did to manage — all those sorts of things.'

Mrs McCabe contemplates the worn gold

7

wedding band on her left hand. 'I can certainly tell you about what it was like for the women,' she says eventually. 'I can give you a good idea of what the men thought about it, too, and what they did, but some of that's only from hearsay and my own observations. My husband died quite a while ago, but he would have had some good stories for you. He was on the union committee at the time.'

Matt comes back with the tea things, and sets them out on the coffee table. He moves a small end table over to his grandmother's chair, pours her a cup of tea and adds milk and two sugars, then passes Cathy the teapot.

'Will you be all right, Gran?' he asks.

'Of course I will, love.'

'I'll pop back later, if you like.'

Mrs McCabe sighs. 'Only if you really want to.'

'I do want to.'

While this interchange is going on, Cathy studies a collection of framed photographs on the wall, including a portrait of a couple she assumes are Ellen McCabe and her husband on their wedding day, a less formal photograph of them with two young boys, and various other pictures of adults, babies and children, some quite recent, some clearly taken decades ago. Ordinary family photos, but precious all the same.

A little apart from these pictures is another photograph, of Ellen McCabe as a young woman sitting on the steps of a porch, smiling widely at the camera, her heavy, shoulder-length hair

8

blowing across her face and her eyes almost closed. To her left, up on the porch itself, a well-built, dark-haired man is leaning on the rail, ignoring the camera and gazing down at Ellen. He's also smiling, but it's abundantly clear that she's the only thing he's interested in looking at. Cathy's eyes flick from the wedding photo and back to this one. No, it's definitely not the same man, although he does look vaguely familiar.

As Matt is leaving, the old lady follows the line of Cathy's gaze. 'That one with my boys Neil and Davey was taken at the end of 1950. We had a very happy Christmas that year, despite everything that was going on. That was just before the strike started, that photo.'

Cathy takes a sip of her tea, then switches the tape recorder on. 'How did it start, Mrs McCabe, from your point of view?'

'May I ask you a question first, dear?'

Cathy nods. 'Shall I stop the tape?'

Mrs McCabe looks at her, her gaze suddenly sharp and shrewd. 'No, it's all right. Now, do you want to know the story of the strike, or do you want to know my story? Because it makes a difference, you see. A big difference.'

Cathy feels the hairs on her arms start to rise. 'Your story, please, if you want to tell it.'

Ellen McCabe nods and, with contemplative slowness, straightens the rug over her knees. 'Yes,' she says, 'I think I do.'

1

The heavy tread of Tom's boots on the back porch was Ellen's usual signal to put the frying pan on the coal range, and give the fire smouldering inside it a good jab with the poker.

'You're home early,' she said over her shoulder as her husband stepped into the kitchen, still carrying his rucksack and his crib tin. When he didn't answer, she looked around and noticed the expression of barely concealed triumph on his face. 'What's happened?'

'We've gone out,' he said, dropping his bag on the floor. 'Where are the boys?'

'Down at the creek looking for crawlies.' She opened the refrigerator, took out a bowl of sausages and laid four in the pan. Poking them with a fork to rupture the skins, she added a scrape of dripping and broke in three eggs as well. 'Because of the watersiders?'

Tom sat down at the kitchen table. 'More or less. We worked most of the shift, then came up and voted to go out in support of them, and in protest against the emergency regulations. It was unanimous.'

'Are all the Waikato miners out?'

'All the underground jokers. Thompson's is staying open to supply the hospitals, but the other opencasters have all walked off. It's not on,

11

bringing in emergency regulations, not in this country. Typical Holland, what a bastard. Worst bloody prime minister we've ever had.'

Ellen tucked thick strands of russet hair behind her ears, leaned against the bench and crossed her arms. Her husband was a good-looking man — fit and rugged, as miners tended to be, and tall too, not always a bonus underground — although his eyes could be hard and his face darkly belligerent when he was angry.

'Was it a secret ballot?' she asked.

'No, just a show of hands — we didn't have time to fuck about with secret ballots. Sorry, love.' Tom normally refrained from swearing too coarsely, as he didn't hold with bad language in front of women, except in dire circumstances. It was tricky after a day at work, though; the swearing down the mine was shocking. 'West Coast and Taranaki are out too, and so are the freezing workers, the hydro-electric jokers, Portland and Golden Bay cement, and most of the drivers and railway workers. Nearly all the TUC affiliates and a fair few of the FOL unions too, as of yesterday and today.'

'The Southland and Kamo miners as well?'

Tom's mouth set in a hard line of disapproval. 'Not yet, but they won't be far behind, they'll come into line.'

'It'll still slow the country down though, won't it, even with just half the pits out?' Ellen sighed. 'Well, at least we knew it was coming.'

And they had, this time, unlike the miners' strike of 1942 and the countless stoppages that

12

had come after that. In '42 no one had been prepared, and the strike on top of the war rationing had meant hard times for nearly everyone. She and Tom had only been married a year, and she'd been pregnant with Neil.

Back then, the Pukemiro men had gone out because ten of them had been paid less than the minimum wage by Pukemiro Collieries, the private owner of the mine, and within a week all Waikato miners were out in sympathy, although no miners elsewhere in New Zealand downed tools. The government, panicking because of the effect the coal shortage would have on the war effort, had come down hard on the strikers. Every Pukemiro man was served a summons for illegal striking and 182 of them sentenced to a month in prison. But after a round of intense meetings, and at the very last minute, the government announced it would take over control of the mines for the duration of the war and that the prison sentences of the Pukemiro men would be suspended, providing they went back to work. They did.

Ellen had been sick with worry at the thought of Tom in jail. She spent the day before they were all due to leave mending his suit so he wouldn't have to go to prison looking tatty, and had burst into tears of relief when news of the reprieve came. Tom thought it all a great joke, but Ellen had been rather less amused, despite her support of the men's demand for the minimum wage. But they'd survived then, and she expected that they would survive this time too.

When the trouble with the Auckland watersiders had started a few weeks ago, she'd gone into Huntly to the Co-op and stocked up on tinned food and other bits and pieces they might need. But it was worrying — money was fairly scarce at the best of times. They were still paying off the mortgage on their house, and now there was her new refrigerator as well, her pride and joy even though it was only one of the smaller models, on hire purchase from Farmers. It was an extravagance, but her mother had given her the money for the deposit and she'd pestered Tom until he'd finally given in and said she could have it, even though they couldn't strictly afford it. Since its delivery just before Christmas she'd marvelled every day at how she'd ever managed without it, but she might just have to again if they couldn't keep the payments up and it had to go back. Which could be very embarrassing as well as disappointing, as just about every housewife in Pukemiro had been around to admire it.

It could also be very likely, now that the coalminers had gone out in support of the watersiders, locked out of the Auckland ports en masse a week ago. At face value it was over a pay increase, but people were starting to realise now that it went deeper than that, that Holland and his Tories were gunning for the wharfies, and through them the country's other openly militant trade unions. But Ellen knew they weren't the only ones who might be facing trouble — if they were to find themselves in financial strife, so would plenty of other families.

She turned back to the range and gave the sausages a gentle nudge so they wouldn't catch. 'How long do you think you'll be out?'

Tom shrugged. 'Depends on the watersiders, I suppose. Not long, if Jock Barnes gets his way.'

Ellen pulled a face, but made sure Tom couldn't see it. She didn't particularly like Jock Barnes; he might be the national president of the Waterside Workers' Union, and a founding member of the new Trade Union Congress, but in her opinion he was loud-mouthed and overbearing. Toby Hill, Barnes' right-hand man, wasn't much better. But the watersiders revered Barnes, and the miners had always supported the watersiders, so you couldn't say a word against either man. And she agreed wholeheartedly with Barnes' convictions. There was nothing wrong with a bit of good, organised industrial militancy to rattle the government's dags.

She arranged the sausages on a plate and placed the fried eggs next to them with exaggerated care. Tom hated it when the yolks broke and, because he did, so did Neil and Davey, so she had become very skilled at keeping them in one piece.

As Ellen set Tom's plate in front of him, he grabbed her and pulled her down onto his knee. She was nine inches shorter than him and nearly five stone lighter, and he could easily pick her up and carry her, which he sometimes did if he was feeling particularly playful.

She sniffed his short light-brown hair, fluffily clean and smelling of soap from his recent

15

shower at the mine bathhouse. Beneath the hair, and out across his right temple, ran a jagged line of coal tattoos ground into his skin after the face he'd been working at four years ago collapsed and almost killed him. The marks had never faded, and neither had the mental scars; he still had nightmares and cold sweats from time to time, although he would never admit this to anyone but Ellen.

His big hands settled on her waist and he gave her a gentle squeeze.

'Don't, the boys will be in soon,' she said, although she was giggling. 'Eat your eggs before they go cold.'

'They won't be in for ages.'

Ellen knew that, but she also knew she had to start the dinner; the sausages and eggs were only Tom's afternoon tea, and he'd be hungry again by half past six.

'Let me up, love,' she said, 'we'll have a cuddle tonight if you like.'

He pushed her reluctantly off his knee, gave her backside a friendly pat and turned his attention to his plate while she rinsed the frying pan in the sink.

Halfway through his third sausage, he said suddenly, 'Oh, the committee's coming over after tea, to talk about the strike. Could you rustle up some supper?'

Ellen sighed inwardly. There was a perfectly good miners' hall just down the street, why couldn't they meet there? Neil and Davey would be awake half the night with the kitchen full of rowdy men.

'Probably,' she said, 'but I'll need to pop down to the shop.'

Ellen took her apron off and fetched her walking shoes from their bedroom, but when she came back Tom seemed lost in contemplation.

She was almost out the back door when he said, 'Ellen?'

'Mmm?'

'Don't worry, love. I don't think it'll go on too long, this one. We'll be all right.'

Ellen looked at him for a moment. 'I know,' she said, then went outside.

★ ★ ★

Under a bright blue sky bulging with the heat of a relentless summer afternoon, it was even muggier than it had been in the kitchen, and Ellen felt sweat trickling down from her armpits before she reached the front gate.

She glanced at her neighbour's house as she walked past, wondering how poor Dot was taking the news about the strike. Badly, probably, given her chronic nerves. There were five children in the Sisley household, all under the age of ten. Dot's husband Bert was a good, steady bloke, but even he was hard-pressed to manage when she was having one of her bad spells.

Across the dusty street the little primary school was silent and empty now that the school day had ended. Cicadas shrilled and rattled raucously in nearby trees, but over the racket she could still faintly hear the shrieks and howls of children as they played and swam in the stream at the bottom of the gully below the town. She envied them; floating in the cool shade of a bush-canopied creek was surely the best place to be on a day like this, although she doubted there'd be crawlies within a mile of the place by now.

She turned into Joseph Street and began the trudge down the hill to the shops. By the time she'd stopped several times to exchange the latest news and speculate on how long the strike might last, whether Barnes would back down over his demands, and whether or not that bastard Fintan Walsh from the Federation of Labour would come to the party and support the watersiders, she had to hurry the last few yards before Fred Hollis the grocer closed his shop.

On her way back home she made a short detour to say hello to her parents. Climbing the steep wooden steps at the rear of their house, she rapped on the open back door and called out, 'Mum? Anyone home?'

Silence for a moment, then the measured walk of her mother as she appeared out of the gloom of the hallway.

'Hello, dear,' she said. 'Come through, I'm in the lounge.'

Ellen followed her mother down the hall and into the sitting room. Gloria Powys never entertained in the kitchen, not even her own family. As far as she was concerned, the only appropriate room in which to receive visitors was the lounge. Not the sitting room, the lounge.

Ellen flopped down in an armchair and

slipped off her shoes, waggling her bare toes in the slight breeze from the open window. 'Where's Dad?'

'Where is he normally?' her mother replied, sitting down on the matching couch opposite.

'At the pub?'

Gloria's sour expression said it all.

Ellen's father, Alf Powys, was a bit of a drinker. Having retired from the mines several years ago, he had contrived ever since to spend as much of his time as he could manage in the pub or the workingmen's club in Huntly, or at the Glen Afton club, known to locals as the Blue Room, or at the Waingaro hotel — anywhere in fact that Gloria either couldn't go or wouldn't be seen dead. Ellen knew that if he was at the Huntly pub this afternoon, he wouldn't be back until well after six when the last train from town pulled into Pukemiro Junction, at which point he'd get off and stagger the rest of the way home past the Pukemiro mine and over the hill everyone called Gentle Annie. She was disappointed — she'd wanted to talk to him about the strike. He loved to discuss union business, and he missed dreadfully the daily comradeship of the men he'd worked with for decades.

Throughout much of her adult life, Ellen had pondered the mystery of why her mother had ever consented to marry her father, and at the age of thirty-one she still hadn't come up with a decent answer. They were as different as coal and gold: her father was without doubt the coal, while her mother was absolutely convinced she was the gold. Ellen had done the arithmetic

19

years ago and worked out that her older sister Hazel had been born well after her parents had married, so that hadn't been the reason. Surely then there must have been love between them at some point? But Gloria maintained steadfastly even now, and especially after a couple of sweet sherries, that she'd been tricked into believing she was marrying a man well on his way up the ladder, a man destined to become a mine manager at the very least, but had realised far too late that Alf Powys was going to fall well short of that mark.

Alf, on the rare occasions that Ellen could recall him bothering to defend himself, insisted that Gloria had been sadly mistaken, that he'd only ever been one for shovelling the coal, not managing it, and that he'd never had ambitions to organise anything other than himself. And the men in the union he belonged to. The social aspirations had always been Gloria's, not his, and if he'd disappointed her then he was sorry, but he couldn't do much about it now. Pass the beer. He was a very decent man, Alf Powys, respected and well liked, but age and life with Gloria had also made him extremely stoical.

As compensation, or perhaps revenge, Gloria had over the years demanded the best of everything — the latest in household gadgets and furniture, the best quality clothes for her daughters, the smartest house in Pukemiro. Alf had worked his fingers to the bone, almost literally, to earn the money to pay for it all, but these days, while he had his many mates, his popularity and his memories, all Gloria had was a new lounge suite and a house that didn't have paint peeling off the outside.

And although she hadn't understood at the time, Ellen could see now why her mother had been so against her marrying Tom McCabe. She'd been frightened that Ellen, her precious younger daughter, would be confined to a dreary life in a small mining town, making packed lunches day after day for a man who would always have coal dust ingrained in his skin and under his fingernails, and who might, with nothing more than a premonitory subterranean rumble or a sudden whiff of gas, leave his wife a widow well before time.

It was true that Ellen did make Tom's lunch every day, and his breakfast and his dinner, but she loved him and did that, and everything else they shared in their lives, willingly. She enjoyed living out at Pukemiro, unlike her mother who was on at her dad at least once a week to move into Huntly, and she was comforted by the closeness of the small community (except, sometimes, for the never-ending gossip) and the industry that made them such a unique little group.

Ellen was definitely her father's daughter: she loved the coal, she loved the life, and like him she regarded the trade union almost as a religion. Without the union there would be nothing for the men who risked death underground every day, and nothing for their families should they not come back up. And because the union had voted to go out in support of the watersiders, she would do

21

everything she could to help.

'Have you heard?' she asked her mother.

'About the strike? Yes, I've heard, they've been talking about nothing but all afternoon up and down the street.'

Ellen knew her mother didn't have much time for striking miners, regardless of their reasons for going out, but whether it was simply because her father had been a lifelong union man himself, she had never been sure.

'What do you think about it?' she asked.

'What I think is you'll be very sorry if it goes on for much longer than a few weeks,' Gloria said. 'How will you pay your mortgage? And what about Neil and Davey? They can't go to school on empty stomachs, you know. Do you want a cup of tea or a cold drink?'

'Cold drink, please. They won't go to school on empty stomachs, Mum, you know that. There's plenty in the vege garden, and the union will rally around, they always do.'

'I don't know why you didn't marry someone from outside, like Hazel did,' Gloria said, shaking her head ruefully. 'Look at her now, lovely house in Auckland, three beautiful children, husband making lots of money.' She stood up.

Ellen sighed — not this again. 'I've got a lovely house in Pukemiro, with two beautiful kids and a husband earning all we need.'

'Not after today, he won't be,' Gloria said as she went out to get the drinks.

Ellen loved her sister, but she was sick to death of hearing about how marvellous her life

22

was compared with her own. Hazel was eleven years older and had married very auspiciously, if you thought that sort of thing was important. And good for her, but Ellen had never once envied Hazel's big house in Remuera, or her husband's admittedly substantial income. She had Tom, she had her boys, and that had always been enough.

Gloria came back carrying two glasses of home-made lemonade on a tray set with a perfectly pressed placemat, and handed one to Ellen. 'Look at you, you look worn out. And where are your stockings?'

Ellen sipped her drink gratefully. 'It's too hot to wear stockings, Mum. And who puts stockings on just to go down Joseph Street to the grocer's?'

'I do.'

'Well, I'm not you.'

Gloria ignored her. 'At least your father will be pleased about the strike.'

'He will, won't he? It'll give him something to sink his teeth into.'

'Only if he puts them in.'

'Oh, Mum, why do you always have to be on about him?'

Gloria swirled lemonade around in her glass, watching the pips form a lazy arc then disappear beneath a lemon slice. 'I really don't know,' she said eventually. 'Force of habit, I suppose.'

Ellen said, 'You'll drive him away one day, you know.'

Her mother looked up sharply, then laughed. 'I doubt it. He's sixty-eight years old, where on earth would he go?'

Ellen didn't know what to say to that, and didn't even want to contemplate it. She couldn't bear the idea of not having her father around.

'The union committee's coming over tonight,' she said, changing the subject. 'I thought I'd do sandwiches and pikelets.'

'They'll all bring beer and smoke their heads off and leave your house smelling like a billiard hall.'

'Probably.'

Gloria regarded her daughter with a sort of resigned sympathy. 'I've got a nice bit of ham you can have, if you like.'

'Thanks.'

★　★　★

The men began to arrive at eight o'clock, knocking on the back door and greeting Ellen politely as they came in. They weren't supposed to be meeting like this, according to the newly imposed emergency regulations, but no one was particularly bothered. They weren't allowed to picket, display or distribute posters or subversive literature, or organise protest marches either, but all were topics on tonight's agenda.

By a quarter past eight, six members of the Pukemiro Mine Workers' Union committee were crowded around the kitchen table; the president Pat Wickham, Frank Paget, Bert Sisley, Vic Anscombe, Lew Trask and Tom. As union secretary, Tom would be chairing the meeting and recording the resolutions.

'Where's Jack?' he asked as he wrote the date

24

and time in the record book.

'Saw him up the street,' Pat Wickham replied. 'Should be here in a minute.'

Tom checked his watch. 'Well, we can't wait,' he said, and declared the meeting open.

Several of the men lit cigarettes and Ellen placed an ashtray in the centre of the table. Neil and Davey were in bed, but she knew they would both be lying awake in the dark, eyes wide with the excitement of it all.

She rearranged the damp tea towels draped over the plates of supper waiting on the bench, and was on her way out of the kitchen when there was another knock on the back door. Tom got up, so she continued on into the sitting room, where she planned to finish reading the latest *Woman's Weekly*, then do a bit of sewing. She was making herself a new dress to wear to young Dallas Henshaw and Carol Selby's wedding this coming weekend, and still had the hemming to go, which she always preferred to finish by hand because it looked so much neater. The dress, made from material she'd gone all the way to Pollock & Milne in Hamilton to buy rather than the fabric shop in Huntly, was in a dark-blue taffeta with a low back and a snug waist. The material had been an end-of-bolt, which was why she'd been able to afford it, and its length meant that the skirt wasn't as full as she would have liked, but it was still a new dress.

She left the windows and curtains open because of the heat and, although only the standard lamp was on behind her, the moths and mosquitoes soon arrived. But the insect killer was in the cupboard under the kitchen sink, and as she didn't want to interrupt the meeting she resigned herself to an evening of slapping and scratching.

Tom stuck his head around the door an hour and a half later, just as she was putting the finishing touches to the hem.

'Can you make us a pot of tea, love? We've finished and we're having a few beers, but Frank's having a cuppa.'

Ellen nodded and put her sewing to one side. Frank Paget had sworn off the booze a year ago, and not before time as far as his wife, Ellen's best friend Milly, was concerned. Frank had always been the last person to leave social events, and was always legless when he finally did, tripping and staggering and swearing his way home, more often than not arriving to a locked door and his pyjamas biffed out onto the front lawn. It had been quite funny for a while, but had become less and less amusing as time went on, especially for Frank's family. Eventually he'd started smashing windows to get into his house, then one night he'd smashed Milly, resulting in a visit from the local doctor to tend to her broken nose and split lip.

Milly and the kids had moved out after that and gone to stay with her parents in Taupiri, and Frank had really hit the skids for a couple of months. Ellen had wanted to go and talk to him about sorting himself out, but Tom had told her to keep out of it; according to him, Frank would come right in his own time. But then Milly's father had been seen banging on Frank's front door one night, and Frank turned up at work the next day with his own split lip, telling anyone who'd listen that he'd decided to take the pledge. And he did, too: not a drop of alcohol had passed his lips since. Milly and the children moved back home (their return observed with empathy and interest from behind net curtains by various Pukemiro residents), and Frank transformed himself. He'd always been a good bloke — well, until the booze had got to him — and Ellen admired the way he'd pulled himself together, so tonight she was more than happy to make him tea.

She stood up. 'I'll just check on the boys first.'

The boys' bedroom was marginally cooler than the sitting room, the wide open windows catching a hint of the night breeze coming down off the hills. Neil's eyes glinted in the darkness as he watched her open the bedroom door.

'Still awake?' she whispered.

He nodded and grumbled, 'It's too hot, I can't sleep.'

Ellen tiptoed across the room and laid a hand on his damp forehead under the light brown hair that fell perpetually into his eyes. 'I know, love, we're all feeling sticky. Here, take your cover off and just lie under the sheet. Better?'

Neil nodded, and Ellen bent and kissed his cheek.

'Have they decided?' he whispered.

'Who?'

'Dad and them.'

'Decided what?'

'I dunno.'

'I don't know, either. I've been in the sitting room since after tea.'

Unsatisfactory as it was, the answer seemed to satisfy Neil, and he rolled onto his side and thrust his feet out from under the sheet. ''Night, Mum.'

''Night, love.'

Ellen hovered for a moment over Davey's bed but he was fast asleep, his mouth open and a thread of dribble dampening the pillowslip. She kissed him too, and smiled as he stirred slightly.

She adored her boys, and sometimes when she looked at them, the sensation of love she felt in her chest physically hurt.

As Gloria had predicted, the air in the kitchen was blue. Ellen blinked through the haze at the men around the table, littered now with tobacco packets and open beer bottles. And then her heart stopped. Only for a moment, but the gap where the beats should have been caused her to sway and reach out a hand to clutch at the bench.

Tom saw. 'You all right, love?' he asked.

Ellen nodded. 'It's smoky in here, I'll open the door.'

She turned away quickly, because sitting next to Frank was someone she hadn't seen before, a young man with dark hair that curled down almost to his collar, and eyes the colour of deepest lignite. He had smiled at her, just at her, a smile of such intensity that for a moment she had felt distinctly light-headed.

★   ★   ★

28

'Who was that new bloke?'

They were in bed, the kitchen door and windows left wide open to let in the fresh night air.

Tom rolled over and slid his hand across the firm curve of Ellen's stomach, rubbing gently but insistently in the way that told her he wanted sex.

'Jack Vaughan, came up from Ohura about ten days ago. Seems a reasonable sort of joker. Bad timing, though. Mind you, Ohura's out too, so I suppose it doesn't make a lot of difference. Why?'

'Just wondered, I haven't seen him around. Why is he on the committee already?'

Tom wriggled closer. 'Well, we've been one short since Ken had his heart attack, and Jack was the union secretary at Ohura for two years, so it made sense to ask him on.'

Ellen waited a second or two, then said, 'If he's just moved up here, then perhaps we should invite him and his wife around for tea one night.'

Tom moved his hand up to her breast, his rough thumb stroking the tender underside beneath the nipple. 'Don't think he's got a wife.'

For some reason, this piece of news disturbed Ellen, but she pushed it out of her mind. Moving to face her husband, she slid her leg up and over his hip, and guided him into her.

2

March 1951

The Henshaw women and the Selby women slaved all Friday preparing the Pukemiro miners' hall for Dallas and Carol's wedding reception the next day, and it was generally agreed that they'd made a lovely job of it. It was a shame, though, that the newlyweds would be embarking on married life together without an income, because Dallas was a miner and out on strike. But his mother had none too subtly let it be known that he had a few bob tucked away, so no doubt all would be well for them, at least in the meantime.

The walls of the hall were festooned with jade-green ponga branches from the bush, each one decorated with a large white crepe-paper bow. Trestle tables, a vase of sweet-smelling honeysuckle in the centre of each, lined both sides of the hall, leaving a good space in the middle for dancing. Below the stage sat the wedding party's tables, spread with snowy tablecloths and a spectacular floral centrepiece arranged by Carol's mother. The wedding breakfast had been served, admired and enjoyed, although there was still a substantial supper to come later on, and the guests were leaning back in their seats, lighting cigarettes and refreshing drinks before the band started.

While Tom prised the lid off another beer,

Ellen looked around for Neil and Davey. No sign of them; they were probably outside somewhere running around with the other kids. The sun wouldn't go down for another hour, and anyway they could see in the dark, those two. She sipped her shandy, wishing it was whisky. She liked a tot of whisky — something else she'd inherited from her father — but Tom disagreed with women drinking hard liquor. Occasionally, at a 'ladies' afternoon' at the house of one or another of her friends, she would indulge and waft home afterwards feeling as light as a feather and seeing bright new colours in everything, then proceed to burn the tea or cook the vegetables without peeling them. Tom would be less than amused, but the boys would dance around the kitchen trumpeting, 'Mum's been on the jar, Mum's been on the jar!' until their father clipped them across the ear.

On one memorable occasion, when the boys had been very young, she had carefully pushed their pram home from her friend Val's house in Bernard Street, diligently avoiding every pothole and large stone on the road so as not to wake them, only to discover to her absolute mortification when she got home that the pram was empty; she had forgotten to put them in. But those afternoons with the girls were infrequent, and just as well, really. So this evening she was sticking to her shandies, and perhaps a sherry for the toasts at supper time.

She felt content, and tonight the strike seemed miles away. The men had only been out a week, and the novelty of having Tom at home most of the time was still fresh. It would soon wear off, according to Gloria, but at the moment Ellen was enjoying his company.

The hall was becoming even more crowded as additional dance guests arrived. Soon there would barely be room for everyone to sit down, but when the band started, that wouldn't be a problem; Pukemiro people enjoyed a good spin around the dance floor.

'Ladies'?' she mouthed to Milly, sitting opposite her across the table.

Milly nodded and grabbed her handbag, leaving Frank to nurse his bottle of Lemon and Paeroa.

The toilets were occupied, so the women joined the queue.

'Your dress came out well, didn't it?' Milly said.

'I thought so,' Ellen replied, feeling a small flush of pride.

'It's gorgeous — the colour matches your eyes perfectly. I've always said you should sew professionally.'

'Actually, I've been thinking about getting a job at Berlei, but I doubt Tom would let me. And I'd have to be back home by the time the boys got in from school.' Ellen pulled a wry face. 'Imagine what Mum would say, though, a daughter of hers sewing bras and knickers.'

'That's true. I forgot about your mum and her high horse.'

Ellen leaned towards the mirror above the handbasin and applied fresh lipstick. 'You're lucky, she never lets me forget it.'

Milly had heard Ellen's moans about her mother too often to bother acknowledging the comment. 'Carol looks lovely, doesn't she? Her dress must have cost a fortune, all that satin and lace. I love the high collar. Not sure about the train, though. It'll be filthy by the end of the night.'

Ellen pressed her lips together to set her lipstick, then said, 'It comes off.'

'How do you know?' Milly asked, examining her own reflection and pushing her energetic curls back into place.

'The flower girl stood on it when Carol was coming down the church steps.'

'That's a clever idea. Not standing on it, I mean, having it detachable.'

By the time they'd returned the band was warming up, and there was a rush to see the new Mrs Henshaw and her husband waltz a circuit of the dance floor. Ellen felt her eyes prickling as everyone cheered and she recalled her own perfect wedding day.

It seemed such a long time ago now, but it wasn't really, only ten years. They'd had a bit of an 'austerity' wedding because of the rationing — a pale-blue suit for her instead of a wedding dress because she couldn't get the material, and a sponge cake instead of fruit — but there had been compensations. Because Tom was in an essential industry he'd been exempt from military service, so she'd not had the misery of being parted from him so soon after getting married. He could have just taken off and joined up like a few of the younger miners, but he'd

33

chosen to stay at home on the coal. But now and then she wondered if he regretted not having gone, although he'd never said anything. She also wondered whether, as a sort of compensation, the union had become Tom's army and the government the enemy, especially now that the Tories were in. Perhaps he was getting his taste of war after all.

She sat down and stretched towards him so he could hear her over the noise of the band. 'Dallas looks pleased with himself.'

'I expect he would, with a bride like young Carol. I was pretty pleased myself on our wedding day, if I remember rightly.'

Ellen smiled, and lowered her head to drop a light kiss on his shoulder, then stopped as she realised her lipstick would mark his good shirt.

'Jack!' Tom exclaimed suddenly, and reached around Ellen with his hand out.

She swivelled in her seat and found herself staring directly into the face of Jack Vaughan.

He nodded and shook hands with Tom, although his eyes never left hers. 'Evening Tom, Mrs McCabe. I didn't get a decent opportunity to introduce myself the other night. Jack Vaughan,' he said, offering her his hand.

She took it, feeling the strength and roughness of his miner's fingers.

'Yes, I know. Hello, Jack,' she replied, astounded at the steadiness of her voice, given that her heart was suddenly pounding so violently. 'It's very nice to meet you. Please, call me Ellen.'

Jack's face creased into a slow, wide smile, and

34

his dark eyes sparkled. Ellen's stomach did a slow flip.

'I'd better check with Tom first, he might not appreciate me being so familiar,' he said with an earnestness Ellen couldn't be sure was real or not.

'What's that?' Tom said, leaning across the table and knocking over a half-full bottle of beer in the process. 'Bugger.'

'Your lovely wife has just asked me to call her Ellen. No objections?'

Tom righted the spilled bottle. 'None at all, mate. Call her anything you like, just don't call her late for dinner. She likes her food, does Ellen.'

Ellen felt a twinge of annoyance. She was accustomed to Tom's teasing, and normally didn't mind it, but he could have refrained from doing it tonight. In front of Jack Vaughan.

Jack seemed to sense her discomfort. 'Would you like to dance?'

Ellen glanced at Tom, who shrugged amiably. There were several unopened bottles lined up in front of him and Bert Sisley had settled himself on his other side, clearly wanting a chat.

'Yes, thank you Jack, that would be lovely.'

She placed her hand in his and let him lead her onto the dance floor as the five-piece band launched into a brisk and rather loose rendition of 'Begin the Beguine'.

He was a good dancer, economical of movement but deft and confident. She looked back at Tom but he was deep in conversation, a skinny cigarette wedged into the corner of his mouth.

Steering her towards the back of the hall, away from the noise, Jack said, 'Your eyes really are navy blue. I've never seen that before.'

Ellen blushed and stared straight ahead; he was shorter than Tom and her eyes were level with his throat. He had a five o'clock shadow, but she could clearly smell the scent of shaving cream on his skin. Perhaps he needed a new razor.

Deliberately redirecting the conversation, she said, 'Tom says you've just moved to Pukemiro.'

Jack nodded. 'A week or so ago. I had five years down at Ohura before that.'

'And before then?'

The band cranked up the volume.

'Sorry?'

Ellen raised her voice. 'Where were you before then?'

'Overseas.'

'With the army?' It was where most young men had been six or seven years ago.

'Mmm.'

Ellen awarded herself a mental tick; she'd suspected he was a veteran. The tilt of his shoulders said there was more to him than met the eye, something tempered and a little unyielding. He was a very good-looking man, too, although the heaviness of his brow would always save him from being called beautiful.

'Have you always been a miner?' she asked.

He moved back slightly so he could see her face. 'Since I was sixteen. It's in the blood, I suppose. My dad was on the coal his whole life, in the Rhondda and then here.'

'But you were born in New Zealand?'

'Only just. Mum was eight months gone when they arrived — I was born at Blackball. Mum's still down that way, in Westport, although Dad died a few years ago.'

'Tom has always been a miner, too. So was my father, before he retired.'

'I know, he told me. Tom, I mean.'

'About Dad?'

'Mmm. He said you're a chip off the old block.'

Ellen grinned. 'Dad's a miner through and through. He was always big in the union, he lived and breathed it. Still does, really. Twenty-six years he was down the pit.'

'Pukemiro Collieries?'

Ellen nodded. 'He started there when the mine opened in 1915.'

Jack sidestepped another couple, taking Ellen neatly with him. 'So what does he do now, your dad?'

'Props up various bars, whenever he can get away from Mum.'

'She doesn't like him drinking?'

'No, she thinks it's common and working class.' Ellen wondered why she was telling Jack all this.

'Begin the Beguine' came to an and, and the band slid into a waltz.

'Another one?' Jack suggested.

Tom still had his head down, with Pat Wickham now, so Ellen nodded. Jack eased her closer, but she made sure their bodies didn't touch. She began to worry that he might notice her hand was getting sweaty in his, then it occurred to her that she was probably breathing shandy fumes all over him, speaking so loudly and forcefully over the band, and she ducked her head. They danced on in silence for several minutes, until she found their lack of conversation embarrassing.

'What made you come up here?' she asked.

Jack shrugged. 'Needed a change, I suppose.'

'Isn't the inside of one mine the same as the inside of any other?' She thought for a moment, and answered her own question. 'No, I suppose it isn't, is it?'

'Not really. And it's always good to get to know new people.'

Ellen glanced down as she felt a tug on her skirt; Neil hovered behind her, his best shirt hanging out of his shorts and his shoes and socks nowhere to be seen.

'Davey's spewed up,' he announced.

'Has he? Where?'

'Outside, on the steps.' Neil shot a look at Jack. 'Who's this?'

'Don't be rude, love. This is Mr Vaughan, a friend of your father's. I'm sorry,' Ellen said to Jack, 'I'll have to sort Davey out.'

Jack smiled ruefully, releasing her as she turned away. 'I'll wait,' he said to her departing back.

Outside, Davey sat on the hall steps looking very small, his knees drawn up to his chin, arms folded across his stomach. Ellen bunched her skirt around her legs, sat down next to him and felt his flushed cheeks.

'What have you done to yourself, sweetheart?'

'Spewed up.' Davey's eyes were watering and his face was pale.

'Why, do you think?'

Neil said, 'Three helpings of trifle and cream, probably.'

'Thank you, Mr Know-It-All. Did you have three puddings, Davey?'

Davey nodded, blinking back tears of fright and self-pity.

Ellen smoothed damp hair back from his forehead. 'Is there any more to come up?'

Her younger son nodded again, leaned sideways and opened his mouth. A last weak, watery squirt of trifle came up, followed by a loud burp, then nothing. A tea towel appeared on the handrail next to him.

Jack, standing on the top step, said, 'I thought you might need something to clean him up. I couldn't find a proper towel.'

Out here, where it was quieter, his voice was rich and warm and slightly gravelly, with a hint of the accent West Coasters often had. It wasn't a particularly deep voice, but Ellen was shocked to note the disconcerting effect it was having on her. She felt every syllable he uttered, every vowel and consonant that came out of his mouth, stroking her skin, seeping into her pores and filling her with something she hadn't felt since she was a girl.

She folded the tea towel and gently wiped Davey's mouth and chin.

He grimaced. 'Yuck, Mum, it smells like sick already.'

She sniffed. 'Pooh, it does, too. All right now? Good, go and wash your hands and face then, there's a good boy.' As Davey ran off, evidently recovered, she called after him, 'And don't eat anything else, all right?'

He nodded, his blond hair flopping, but didn't look back.

Jack held out a hand to help Ellen to her feet. 'Nice-looking kids. Do you just have the two?'

'Yes, and they're enough of a handful some days.'

'You never hoped for a daughter?'

Ellen smiled wistfully. 'A little girl would have been nice, but no, we're more than happy with Neil and Davey.'

'You are, or Tom is?'

It was on the tip of Ellen's tongue to say to Jack that Tom did think two children were enough, and that she would have liked at least one more, but she stopped herself: she didn't know Jack Vaughan well enough to be divulging that sort of confidential information. Tom would be ropable if he thought she was going about telling *anyone* their personal business.

Jack must have seen something in her face, because he held out a placating hand. 'Shall we?'

'Sorry?' Ellen was mildly startled.

'Shall we go back in, Tom might be wondering where you are.'

'Oh, I doubt it. He likes nothing better than to sit with a beer in one hand and a smoke in the other talking union business with his mates.'

Jack laughed. 'Typical miner, then. Well, I'll take you back to your table.'

40

Inside the band was having a break. Ellen sat down next to Milly, whose eyes were glazing over. Milly had never been one for the finer details of union matters, although as a miner's wife she'd always faithfully supported Frank's decisions regarding his employment, whether she understood them or not.

Tom, one eye closed against the smoke from his cigarette, was in full flight. 'So I said to Tony Prendiville, if those bastards bring in emergency regulations and honest men get sent to jail just for helping a striker, or even a striker's family — his *kids* — then it's a bloody black day for New Zealand.' There were general rumbles of agreement from the men around him. 'And he says, 'Don't worry, Tom, that'll be the last thing they'll do.' And what have they done? Christ, I never thought I'd see the day in New Zealand. We didn't go to bloody war just to put up with that sort of bullshit.'

Vic Anscombe, who actually had served overseas, said, 'You didn't go to war at all, Tom.'

'No, but we knocked ourselves out day and night shovelling coal so other buggers like you could.'

Vic nodded in agreement and raised his bottle in a silent toast; coal production had been essential to New Zealand's war effort, and it was a very unwise person who suggested that the miners hadn't pulled their weight, regardless of the strike in 1942.

Milly leaned over to Ellen and whispered,

41

'Who's Prendiville again?'

'National president of the United Mine Workers' Union.'

'Doesn't Tom like him?'

Ellen shook her head. 'Or Fred Crook, the secretary. Thinks they're too soft because they've started pushing the wharfies to arbitrate, but Barnes and Hill won't do it, especially now Holland's deregistered their union.'

Milly nodded. She wasn't always up with the play, but she did know who Jock Barnes and Toby Hill were; Frank went on about them often enough.

'If Tom had his way,' Ellen said, lowering her own voice, 'they'd be out tomorrow.'

'Barnes and Hill?'

'No, Prendiville and Crook.'

'And will he have his way?' Milly asked, draining the last of her shandy.

'I doubt it,' Ellen said, 'but there's been a fair bit of complaining about the pair of them.'

The band started up again and Ellen sat back, not at all keen on sharing her views about national union leaders at the top of her voice. She let her gaze wander down the table to where Jack Vaughan was sitting, and immediately felt herself blush as she caught him staring at her. He gave that intense, dazzling smile, and raised his bottle to her. The gesture reminded her that her own glass was empty, and she pushed it across the table towards Tom, hoping he would take the hint and fetch her another. He didn't, but Bert did, signalling that he would also replenish Dot and Milly's drinks while he was at it.

Ellen risked another glance at Jack, but he was talking to Andrea Trask now, Lew Trask's pretty nineteen-year-old daughter who was reputedly on the lookout for a husband. Or rather, Andrea was talking to him; in fact she was almost draped over him, her long dark hair touching his face and her hand on his arm. When they got up to dance, Ellen frowned and looked away, annoyed at herself but not sure why.

Bert set her drink on the table, and she smiled up at him, grateful for the distraction.

'I shouldn't have any more after this one,' Milly said. 'Frank says it doesn't bother him but, well, you know, I don't like to rub it in.'

'How is he getting on?'

'Great. It's been over a year now and he hasn't touched a drop. Things are ever so much better at home.' Milly frowned. 'I just hope this strike doesn't upset him too much.'

'Why would it upset him?'

'Well, not the strike itself, it's just that we don't have much money put aside, and if it goes on for too long we could really be in the cart.' She paused. 'Actually, we don't have any money put aside.'

'I know what you mean,' Ellen said. 'We aren't exactly flush either, but it's too early to worry. And if the worst comes to the worst, the union will look after us.'

'I know, but I still worry.'

They were interrupted then, by a loud cheer from the dance floor. A wide circle had formed around two dancers, Jack and Andrea Trask. Jack had taken off his sports coat and was leading

Andrea in an energetic cha-cha, spinning her this way and that, their hips moving in unison as they danced around each other. Andrea was laughing, throwing her head back to swing her hair, and moving her rump so her full skirt flicked up and out. Jack was grinning too, and Ellen could see he was enjoying himself.

'They're very good together, aren't they?' Milly said, raising her eyebrows at Ellen. 'Perhaps she's finally about to nab that husband she's been after.'

'Yes, wouldn't that be nice,' Ellen said.

The band finished the number with a flourish of drums and the crowd erupted in a spontaneous burst of applause. Andrea whispered something to Jack, but he shook his head and took her elbow, escorting her off the floor, much to her rather poorly concealed chagrin. He gave Ellen a tiny wink as he went past, then sat down with the men and opened another bottle of beer.

Pat elbowed him in the ribs and lowered his voice in deference to Lew, who was sitting further down the table. Lew's wife had died eight years ago, and since then he had been very protective of Andrea, although it hadn't done much good. 'You could be in there, lad, if you play your cards right,' Pat said. 'Could do a lot worse for yourself. She's a cracker, that Andrea.'

Jack grinned but said nothing.

At supper Tom didn't bother getting up, content to drink and smoke. Ellen bought him a plate anyway, piled with sausage rolls, club sandwiches and a raspberry lamington bulging with cream, usually his favourite treat. He ate half a sausage roll and the lamington, then pushed the plate aside and rolled another cigarette.

Ellen was debating whether to eat his club sandwiches when she glanced up and saw her mother waving at her from across the hall. She waved back and went over.

Her father was there too, his face cheerful and flushed. 'Ah,' he said, 'here she is, the belle of the ball.'

Ellen pecked him on his slightly bristly cheek. 'Hello, Dad. I came around to see you the other day but I missed you.'

Alf's eyes twinkled and he tapped the side of his nose. 'Out gathering intelligence.'

Gloria snorted. 'Out gathering hangovers, more like.'

'What do you think about the strike?' Ellen asked.

'Could be a good one,' Alf said. 'Can't see Holland backing down. They say he's out to clobber the watersiders this time, teach them a lesson.'

Ellen nodded. 'They also say that Barnes is out to teach Holland a lesson.'

'That, petal, is why it could be a good one.'

Ellen could see her father was clearly chuffed with recent events; he'd always loved a good strike. 'How long do you think it might go on, Dad?'

'Who knows?'

'Tom says they shouldn't be out for more than a couple of weeks.'

Alf's face became serious for a moment. He reached for his beer. 'I wouldn't be too sure about that, love, with all due respect to Tom. Holland means business. He's brought in the emergency regulations, and the military to man the wharves, and he's banned the papers from printing anything in favour of the unions. Mind you, the *Herald*'s always been firmly up the government's arse — nothing new there. But he's never done that before. Why, are you worried?'

Ellen considered lying, but her father had always been able to see straight through her. 'A bit. I'm sure the union will see us right if it comes to that, but, well, we don't have much put away.'

Alf stifled a burp. 'Is it the mortgage you're worried about?'

Ellen nodded.

'Well, don't be,' Alf said. 'Your mother and I aren't completely destitute. I expect we could probably help out.'

Ellen didn't really feel any better. 'Thank you, Dad, very much, but I can't see Tom being too keen on the idea. You know what he's like with his pride.'

Gloria said sharply, 'Pride will be the least of his worries if he doesn't get back to work and a regular pay packet soon.'

Alf rolled his eyes in exasperation and turned to talk to someone else across the table.

'Oh, Mum,' Ellen said, 'not everything in life is about money.'

Gloria changed tack. 'I see that new lad Jack

Vaughan is making a bit of a splash with the ladies.' She nodded towards the dance floor where Jack was dancing with yet another girl. 'Good-looking bloke, isn't he?'

'I suppose so.'

'You suppose so? He's fit and gorgeous with a smile that would turn any woman's head, and he's single. There'll be a stampede for him, you mark my words.'

Ellen was a little embarrassed, but then her mother sometimes said things like that. Beneath her coiffed hair and smart clothes, and her insistence that propriety and the social niceties of life always be observed, ran a rich vein of worldly knowing and earthiness that tended to pop up from time to time, usually without warning.

'I also see Andrea Trask's doing her best to stake her claim,' Gloria added. 'The look on her face when he walked her off the dance floor before supper! She's never been backwards about coming forwards, that one. I expect it's because she doesn't have a mother to tell her how to behave. She'll frighten him off if she's not careful.'

Sometimes Gloria's gossip got on Ellen's nerves. 'They were only having a dance, Mum.'

'Really? She looked to me as if she was eyeing him up for his wedding suit already.'

Ellen sighed. She loved her mother, but how her father put up with her sometimes was beyond her. She envied his ability to turn himself off whenever he felt like it. But she conceded Gloria's point — Andrea Trask was certainly a piece of work.

'Have you seen Neil and Davey?' she asked.

'I haven't seen Neil, but Davey was over by the supper table about fifteen minutes ago shovelling down sausage rolls. I suggested he might want to go easy on them, given that he's been sick already tonight. He told me all about it in gory detail.' Gloria smiled fondly. 'He's a very talented storyteller, that child.'

Ellen checked her watch. 'I suppose I should think about getting them home, it's nearly eleven.'

Gloria glanced across the hall. 'Thomas looks like he's settled in for the night, you might have a job dragging him away. Oh look, Jack's dancing with Meg Thomasson now. I'd be very cautious there, if I were him.'

Meg Thomasson was a widow, a New Zealand-born woman originally from Southland, left with three very young children several years ago after her Scandinavian husband was killed underground at the Pukemiro mine. They'd been happily married and since his death Meg had not fared well, taking her comfort wherever she could find it. But the children were reasonably well looked after and she was considered by most in the community as harmless, although a handful of Pukemiro's less charitable residents referred to her as the town bike. And she wasn't a stealer of other women's men, preferring to go with unattached males — hoping, it was generally assumed, to find a new husband and a father for her children.

Ellen didn't know her very well, only enough to say hello at the shops, but she didn't approve of the fact that Meg was sometimes the butt of jokes and looked down on just because she was lonely and sought company. It was true, she was a bit of a tart, but surely that was her business? She didn't think though, that Meg would be Jack's sort of woman.

Tonight Meg's brassy blonde hair gleamed as she whirled, her smile wide and the lightweight fabric of her pale-blue dress clinging to her ample curves.

'Meg's all right,' Ellen said, 'leave her alone.'

'Yes, she probably is,' Gloria replied, 'but she doesn't do herself any favours putting herself about the way she does.'

Ellen shrugged. 'That's up to her, isn't it?'

'It is, but you can't be a tart in a small town and not expect to suffer for it one way or another.'

'I think she probably does suffer, Mum.'

'Oh, I expect she does, and I'm not saying I'm not without sympathy for her, but she does ask for it.'

Ellen gave up because she'd lost track of the point she'd been trying to make. 'Well,' she said, pushing her chair back from the table, 'I'm off home. Tom can find his own way when he's ready.'

She rounded up Neil and Davey and told Tom they were going. He squeezed her hand, tearing himself away from the conversation only long enough to tell her he'd be home soon himself.

Outside the air was finally cooling; perhaps she should have brought a cardigan after all. The boys were yawning hugely, despite their insistence that they weren't tired and it was too early

49

to go home. She took their hands and stepped onto the street.

'Ellen?'

Jack was standing on the steps of the hall, his form silhouetted against the bright lights inside. 'Would you like me to walk you and the boys home?'

Ellen smiled. 'Thank you, Jack, but it's only up around the corner, we'll be fine.'

He came down the steps. 'Are you sure? It's on my way home.'

'Where are you staying?' Ellen was curious.

'I'm renting a house in Robert Street.'

She laughed. 'Then you're going in completely the opposite direction to us. Thanks anyway, but I've got Neil and Davey to look after me, haven't I boys?'

The boys nodded and pulled on her hands, anticipating their pre-bedtime cup of cocoa.

Ellen thought it was very considerate and rather charming of Jack; Tom had not offered her an escort since their courting days, no matter how many times she had left an event early to take the boys home. But then Pukemiro was a very safe little town, and nothing ever happened to people walking its streets, alone or not.

'Goodnight, Jack,' she said.

He raised a hand. 'Goodnight, Ellen.'

★   ★   ★

She was spooning tea leaves from the caddy into the pot when Tom finally appeared in the kitchen the next morning. She'd been up since seven to get the boys their breakfast before they disappeared outside. The Sunday roast was on and she'd make a start on the vegetables as soon as she'd seen to Tom's breakfast — providing he had an appetite.

He sat down, put his elbows on the table and held his head in his hands. His hair stuck up in all directions and the smell of beer was still coming off him. He seldom allowed himself to get really drunk, but obviously he had last night. He hadn't come in until after one, and had banged about the bedroom for what seemed like ages trying to get his socks and trousers off before finally collapsing into bed. Then he'd asked her four times if she was awake, and when she finally answered him, he'd said, 'Sorry, love,' and fallen asleep.

'Bit of a head this morning?' she asked.

'*Why* did you let me drink all that beer?' he moaned.

She laughed; he said this to her every single time he drank too much, ever since she had first known him. 'Do you want something to eat? It might help.'

He slid his hand over his mouth. 'Nothing fried.'

'Two Aspro and a couple of poached eggs on toast?'

He nodded, then winced. 'And a big glass of water.'

'Dry horrors?'

He nodded again, cautiously this time. Ellen fetched his drink and he sat sipping it in silence while she made his breakfast.

51

'What time did everyone leave?' she asked eventually.

'I don't know, but I wasn't the last. It was a good bash.'

'It was,' Ellen agreed, although still not regretting that she had come home early. 'What time did Dallas and Carol get away?'

'Didn't notice. I don't think they're off until today anyway.'

Ellen buttered some toast. 'Auckland for a week, isn't it?'

Tom shrugged — details like the destination of honeymooning couples didn't normally capture his interest.

'Well, I hope the weather stays nice for them,' she said. Then, to avoid any misunderstandings, she added, 'Jack Vaughan offered to walk me and the boys home last night.' She set Tom's breakfast in front of him.

'I know,' he said, rupturing his eggs with a fork and grimacing as the bright-yellow yolks spilled out. 'He told me. Good joker, Jack.'

Ellen left Tom alone while he ate, starting on the dishes and watching through the kitchen window as birds fought over the stale crusts Davey had scattered on the lawn. The sparrows might have to go without soon, though if the strike kept on, they'd be eating the crusts themselves.

Tom burped, said pardon, aligned his knife and fork in the middle of his empty plate and stood up. 'That does feel better, thanks, love,' he said, bringing the plate over to the sink. He smelled of beer and eggs now, but Ellen thought he had a bit of colour back.

'What did you talk about all night?' she asked, although she had a fairly good idea. 'You all had your heads down with Bob Amon for long enough.'

Bob Amon was president of the Waikato Miners' Union central council.

Tom said, 'The council's setting up a strike-relief committee, to work in with the watersiders' committee in Auckland. There'll be a Puke women's auxiliary as well, to organise the food and all that at this end. I've put your name forward.'

Ellen nodded; she'd expected that he would. The central council included union officials from each of the seven local underground mines, and it would be mainly their wives serving on the women's auxiliary.

She pulled the plug out of the sink and reached for a tea towel. 'Will you be on the relief committee?'

Tom nodded.

'When's your first meeting, then?'

'Tomorrow afternoon, town hall at two.'

Ellen didn't bother asking whether the women were invited, because they never were. 'Well, find out what you can about what we're going to need to do. Who else's name was put forward?'

'Milly, and Rhea Wickham, and Lorna Anscombe, for the Puke auxiliary. Not sure about the women from the other mines.'

'Dot?'

'No, Bert thinks she'll have enough on her hands.'

What he meant, and they both knew it, was that Bert was worried about Dot's mental health. She didn't manage well in a crisis, and had a difficult enough time looking after her kids as it was, so asking her to serve on a committee when the pressure was on was out of the question.

'Probably for the best,' Ellen said.

'Bert thinks so.'

Bert Sisley loved being a coalminer, and he delighted in his five young children, but above all he adored his wife and was very protective of what he termed her 'delicate nerves'. She'd been a bright and pretty girl when Bert had started courting her just before the war, and they'd married a few months before Ellen and Tom. They'd seemed a blessed couple, but then their first child had arrived and suddenly everything had changed.

Marrying a decent man and having a family had been all that Dot had ever wanted out of life. Along with various household items for her glory box, she had quietly collected the things she would need for a new family — tiny knitted baby clothes, packets of nappies, a bassinet set — and when she fell pregnant only a few months after she and Bert were wed, they were both thrilled. The pregnancy was uneventful, and watched with enthusiastic anticipation by the rest of the community, but when Ellen visited Dot in the maternity home soon after the baby arrived, it was clear that something had gone horribly wrong.

Instead of the radiant young mother Ellen had anticipated seeing, Dot was curled up on her

54

bed, white-faced and silent. She seemed unable to respond to anything Ellen said to her, and when the nurse brought her new daughter in for feeding, Dot had reluctantly taken the infant onto her lap, looked at her briefly, then burst into hysterical tears and thrust the baby back at the nurse.

Pregnant herself at the time, Ellen had been thoroughly shocked by Dot's behaviour. So had poor Bert, who had never in his worst nightmares imagined that his wife would reject their first child, whose name he'd had to choose by himself: April, for the month of her birth. He told Ellen after her first visit that the doctor said it wasn't unheard of, and that it should just be a matter of time until Dot became accustomed to being a mother, but that he'd also warned that things could be a little rough until she did.

And it had been rough. Dot had done her best, but it was almost a year before she managed to struggle out of her severe depression, and by then she was pregnant again. She gave birth to twins, and this time spent six months in Waikato Hospital, much of it in the psychiatric ward. The babies were kept with her, as the doctors believed it would be best for them, but when Dot finally came home she was a changed woman: still pretty, and still the love of her husband's life, but with something vital missing from her spirit. Bert and his mother had cared for April, but with the arrival home of the next two babies he was almost at his wits' end.

But they managed, with the help of family and neighbours, including Ellen, and life seemed to have resumed on an even keel when Dot found herself pregnant again. Some observers noted at that point that as the Sisleys weren't Catholic they must simply be out and out careless, but no one ever said this to Bert or Dot.

It was twins again, which was a mystery because there was no history of twins on either side of the family, but this time Dot was fine with the new babies. It was a huge relief to both her and Bert, but the whole experience of motherhood had robbed her of her self-confidence and left her nerves in a permanently tattered state. She had learned to love all her children, but even so still succumbed to intense and very black depressions from time to time. Ellen wondered if the trauma of the first three babies had affected her mind permanently. Women did occasionally abandon their children, she knew that, but she thought it must be so much worse when it wasn't through choice — when a mother wanted to love her babies but simply couldn't. There had been no more pregnancies for Dot since, thank God, but if she'd had some sort of medical procedure to prevent it during her last stay in the hospital, she never talked about it.

The children were all quite young and still a handful for Dot, and it was no surprise that Bert went out of his way to protect her from any unnecessary stress. Ellen knew Bert had thought long and hard about going on strike, but in the end his principles and loyalty to the union had won and he'd voted to go out, despite what it might do to his family. Tom hadn't even been critical of him for wavering. Privately, Ellen believed Bert hadn't actually had much choice — you just couldn't be a union delegate and on the committee and vote against striking.

She hoped Bert wouldn't live to regret his decision. She hoped none of them would.

3

Ellen put her cup down and touched a serviette to the corners of her mouth to collect any stray jam or cream from her scone. They were in the polish-scented sitting room of Rhea Wickham's house halfway down Joseph Street, four of them — Milly, herself, Rhea and Lorna Anscombe — meeting to discuss their contribution to the Huntly Women's Auxiliary.

Rhea, Pat Wickham's wife, was a big woman, in her fifties and quite formidable with greying hair swept back off a face that was still handsome, and large breasts that formed a single, solid shelf. As hostess, she was smartly dressed and wearing a marcasite brooch that matched her earrings, and Ellen was glad she had bothered to change out of her shorts and blouse before she'd come out.

The obligatory cup of tea out of the way, it was time to get down to business. Ellen knew this because Rhea had produced an exercise book and a pencil, and was waiting expectantly for Milly and Lorna to stop chatting. When they had, she began.

'As you know, ladies,' she said in her rather deep voice, 'we are in the midst of an extremely serious strike.'

Ellen couldn't be sure, but she thought Milly might be working hard to suppress a giggle. Rhea Wickham was president of the local branch of the Country Women's Institute and a respected and influential woman in her own right, but her bearing and rather formal approach to everything she did could be daunting, and occasionally not entirely warranted. The strike was a serious matter, certainly, but there was probably no need to state it like Michael Savage announcing that war had been declared against Germany.

'Therefore,' Rhea went on, 'we must make arrangements to ensure that every striking family has food and anything else that might be needed. Money will soon become tight in many households,' she added unnecessarily.

Lorna, Milly and Ellen all nodded; the men had only been out for ten days and already the Friday pay packets were sorely missed.

'As discussed at the meeting in town on Monday, the men are making arrangements to buy vegetables in bulk from the market gardens at Pukekohe, and anywhere else we can find a decent supply. The produce will be collected by truck and brought back to be distributed.' She looked up. 'That, ladies, is where we will come in. The goods will be given out on Tuesdays from the town hall for the Huntly miners, from the club at Glen Afton, the hall here at Pukemiro and so on, along with any meat we can obtain. We, and the women from the other branch auxiliaries, will be required to man those distribution centres.'

Ellen knew all this, and so no doubt did Lorna and Milly; their husbands had also been at the Monday meeting.

'And there will be plenty of other work, too.'

59

Rhea paused, as if searching for the right words. 'During previous strikes, especially those of longer duration, some . . . well, no, let's be honest, ladies, a lot of men came under pressure from their wives to go back to work.' She peered over the top of her spectacles. 'Now, I know what you're all going to say, and I'm not advocating that we go around all the wives in Pukemiro bullying them into standing firm behind their husbands. That's the sort of tactic the government is so fond of, and we won't stoop to that level. I've raised a family myself during troubled times, and I know what it's like to worry day and night about how on earth to feed them when the cupboards are almost empty, what to do about the mortgage and how to pay the doctor when someone gets sick. It's hard, it really is, but of all the women in this town, you must know what's at stake.'

They all did, even Milly. When the Tory government had come to power in 1949, Holland had vowed to crush the nation's militant trade unions. The Auckland wharfies' latest industrial action was a direct and deliberate challenge to Holland, and the day of reckoning had finally arrived, but failure of the miners' unions around the country to stand strong would seriously weaken the watersiders' position.

There was also the matter of the emergency regulations, which Ellen believed should have had every decent New Zealander up in arms, regardless of whether they had any personal affiliation to, or sympathy for, the trade union movement.

The government now had unlimited powers, and funds, to counteract strikers and their unions' activities. Striking, or encouraging a strike in any way, was a serious offence, as were pickets and marches, addresses at public meetings by the WWU, and printing or distributing strike-related material. For any of these you could go to jail. And the police could enter any premises to enforce the regulations. To make matters worse, the Minister of Labour, Bill Sullivan, could appropriate the funds and records of any striking union at will. Therefore strikers and their families could be starved back to work, and their homes could be invaded by the police without warning or permission at any time of the day or night. New Zealand had apparently suddenly become a totalitarian state.

Ellen knew that the unions would get around the regulations one way or another, but the fact they had been brought in at all shook her to the core, and she knew she wasn't the only one who felt that way. This was New Zealand, for God's sake, not Nazi Germany.

'Where will our meat come from?' Lorna asked.

'We'll buy some in,' Rhea replied, 'despite nobody being allowed to sell it to us, and we've already had offers from local farmers, providing we organise the butchering ourselves. Has anyone been to the shops?'

She was asking had anyone been forced to enquire about credit yet, but was too polite to say this openly.

There was a brief silence, then Milly said,

61

'Well, I haven't, but I was talking to Shirley Minogue this morning and she said she'd asked for credit at Huntly Pharmacy and at Newton King, and got it straight away, no questions asked.'

Lorna spoke up. 'Our HP at Farmers' comes due next Wednesday and, well, we haven't got the money, so I went in and explained and the clerk said not to worry about it for now. He just made a note that I'd been in.'

'Well, that's good news, isn't it?' Rhea said. 'I knew we'd be able to rely on the local businesses to help us out.'

Ellen had a cynical thought: if shopkeepers in and around Huntly didn't extend credit during the strike, when the men finally did go back to work their wives in retaliation would take their custom somewhere else, and in a town built on coal it would be commercial suicide to alienate the miners. But Huntly was a close-knit community and support for the strikers was strong, so a lot of shopkeepers and businessmen would help out where they could anyway. This was a relief, because the payment on her refrigerator was due soon and she wasn't sure she could come up with the money. She and Tom had a little put aside, but she didn't want to have to touch that yet.

'Don't worry,' she said to Lorna, 'I'll have to pay a visit to Farmers' myself. You probably weren't the first and I'm pretty sure you won't be the last.'

'But that's exactly the problem,' Rhea said. She removed her spectacles and let them fall on their fancy chain against her chest. 'The shame of having to ask for credit can do awful things to a family. They say it's a man's pride that suffers the most, but it's not easy for a woman either, having to go into the grocer's week after week charging up food and what have you, knowing that the bill is growing every time she steps through the door. It's humiliating and a terrible thing for the spirit.'

Lorna, Milly and Ellen stared.

Rhea stared back. 'It is, and I should know. Pat and I almost went to the wall in the strike of '26, and it took us a very long time to get back on our feet afterwards. We had nothing to fall back on. But the money wasn't the worst of it, it was what it did to us, as man and wife. It was a terrible strain.'

Nobody knew what to say.

Rhea flapped her hand. 'Oh, we came right, but the men don't think of that side of it when they're voting to go out. They don't, you know. This strike could go on for quite a while and if it does, marriages in this town will come under a huge strain, you mark my words. And that's when the trouble will really start. Children miss out and then wives start to blame their husbands. Oh, they won't to begin with, and they won't be proud of themselves when they do, but after a month or so of not enough food or money they'll start hinting about it, then accusing, then demanding. It's human nature — a mother has to take care of her children.'

The three young mothers in the room looked

at each other uneasily, knowing that Rhea was right.

'And if that happens,' she continued, 'then at least some of the men will give way. They're bound to. And if the miners fall, the other unions will too, and, in the end, so will the watersiders.'

Milly looked as if she wanted to say something; Ellen watched her open her mouth, then shut it again and frown.

'I know that would be bad, but exactly how bad?' she asked eventually. 'I mean, the watersiders might have to go back to work with less money than they wanted, but it's their pay rise, not ours. We're only out in support, aren't we?'

Rhea nodded. 'You're right, Milly, we are. But we're not just supporting the watersiders, we're fighting for the right of New Zealanders to belong to trade unions with enough power to make a difference. If we lose this one, it could be the end of all that.'

'Not of unions altogether?' Milly was startled.

'Of militant unions, perhaps. Oh, not tomorrow, probably not even next year, but eventually. If the government wins this time, it will keep on winning until there's nothing left of the unions worth having. The men — *our* men — can say goodbye to being able to negotiate decent pay rates, and to fair management, and probably even to safe working conditions. How are you going to feel when your sons leave school to go underground, and don't come back up one day because the union hasn't had the clout to make working in the mines safe?'

Ellen thought this was a mean shot, as all three of them had young sons, but she fully understood the reasoning behind Rhea's words, even if they were a bit over the top. 'I know it sounds dramatic,' she said, in support of Rhea's little speech, 'but it could even be the end of true democracy, if the Tories are allowed to get away with bringing in emergency regulations every time something slightly out of the ordinary happens.'

'You sound just like your father,' Lorna said, surprised.

Ellen was surprised herself. Alf never rammed his beliefs about trade unions down other people's throats, but he certainly made them public and he never minced his words. She was more inclined to keep her opinions to herself, although she had never made a secret of her support for the Puke miners' union and for trade unions in general, and it startled her to think that she might be starting to sound militant. She wasn't militant at all; she simply believed in sticking to her principles.

'Sorry,' she said, 'I didn't mean to sound all bolshie.'

'Well, why not?' Lorna said. 'You wouldn't be the only communist in town.'

Rhea clapped her hands together briskly. 'So, if we can get back on track, as well as the relief side of things we need to be able to offer support to the women of this town when the time comes. The enemy is at our gate, ladies, and we have to be prepared to go into battle.'

Rhea had been in the Women's War Service Auxiliary during the war, and it showed.

* * *

'Whew,' Milly said as they were walking up the street after the meeting. She wiped imaginary sweat off her brow. 'I thought we were only getting together to talk about recipes for turning half a pound of mince into ten nutritious meals, not planning a raid on Hitler's bunker.'

Ellen laughed. 'Well, you know Rhea, she never does anything by half. And you must admit she's very good at organising things.'

They trudged on up the hill in silence until Milly asked, 'Will we really have to go around telling women not to nag their husbands back to work? I don't think I really want to do that, Ellen — we could make ourselves very unpopular.'

'We could, yes, if we went at it like a bull at a gate. But I think what Rhea meant is that we should just suggest that staying out will do more good in the long run than going back too early. She wasn't saying we should pressure anyone. At least, I don't think she was.'

Milly looked at Ellen sideways. 'What did she mean about our boys being unsafe down the mine? I thought that was a bit below the belt.'

Ellen came to a halt and turned to face her friend. 'So did I, but what if she was right? Billy and Evan will probably go on the coal when they leave school, won't they? And so will Neil and Davey.'

Milly nodded resignedly. 'I expect so.'

Like many miners' wives, she didn't want her sons down the mine at all, she wanted them in nice, safe, clean jobs. But digging coal was where the money was, in this part of the country anyway, so down the mine they would probably go.

'So if the unions aren't as strong by then as they are now,' Ellen went on, 'who'll guarantee how safe it will be? It's bad enough now — imagine what it would be like if the unions had no clout at all, and they won't if Holland squashes the guts out of them.'

Milly pulled a face. 'It's just that, well, I can't really believe the government would do that, Ellen, I really can't.'

Ellen snorted. 'Of course they would, if it means saving a bit of money, and that's what it always comes down to.'

They both looked around as a truck pulled up beside them and Jack Vaughan climbed out. 'Can I give you ladies a lift anywhere?' he asked.

He was bare-headed, his shirtsleeves were rolled to above his elbows and his trousers rumpled but clean. Ellen caught herself thinking that if she could just get them off him she could give them a good iron, and her face reddened at the image the idea conjured.

Milly giggled. 'Nobody ever needs a lift in Pukemiro, it's too small!'

Ellen stifled the urge to roll her eyes. Milly might be happily married, but she wasn't immune to the twinkle in a good-looking man's eye. Neither, apparently, was Nora Bone, whose name had entertained several generations of Pukemiro children; Ellen could see the old lady peering through her front window across the street, her nets twitching and dropping back into place as she noticed she'd been spotted. Nora was seventy-five years old, however, and therefore not likely to be serious competition for the town's younger women.

And neither was she immune herself, Ellen noted with a rush of the same breathless, tingling discomfort she'd experienced the last two times she'd encountered Jack. 'We're fine, thank you,' she replied, more crossly than she had intended.

Jack looked at her for a moment, then nodded amiably. 'I know,' he said, 'you're only up the road — unless you've shifted since Saturday night.'

'No, we haven't shifted,' Ellen said.

Milly blurted, 'What did you think of the meeting on Monday?' She clearly didn't want Jack to go just yet.

'In town?'

'Mmm.'

'Good turnout.'

'As good as what you'd get at Ohura?' Ellen asked. For a reason she couldn't fathom, she wanted the local unions to measure up against their Taranaki counterparts, in terms of commitment and enthusiasm, at least. She didn't like the idea of Jack being anything less than impressed with his new colleagues.

He nodded. 'Good bunch of jokers, too. I haven't met many of the men from the other mines yet, but the Pukemiro blokes are top notch.'

Satisfied, Ellen looked at her watch. 'I'm sorry, but I've got a couple of things to do before the boys get home. Nice talking to you, Jack.'

He looked embarrassed. 'Er, actually, I saw Tom earlier today and he asked me around to your place tonight for a meal. Did he tell you? It's no problem if it's not convenient.'

Ellen forced a smile. It annoyed her when Tom did this; she usually enjoyed the company, but not the last-minute scramble to cobble together a decent dinner. And especially with Jack — something was bound to go wrong in the rush.

'No, he hasn't actually, but I've been out. We'd love to have you, will around six o'clock suit?'

'Be great, thanks,' Jack said. 'I'll see you then.'

He climbed back into his truck, tooted the horn once and drove off, leaving the two women staring after him.

'You lucky dog,' Milly said.

★   ★   ★

Ellen left Milly at her front gate and hurried home. Belting up the back steps — nobody ever used the front entrance except the Rawleigh's man, and the police during the war looking for conscription dodgers hiding on the coal — she banged open the back door and lunged for the refrigerator. On a plate sat five pork chops and two lonely sausages. She had planned to give three of the chops to Tom tonight, one each to the boys, and have the sausages herself, but looking at the plate she knew she wouldn't be able to feed two grown men with what she had. She snatched up her purse again and shot back down the steps.

Fortunately for her, Sid Pollard the butcher still had a reasonable selection left. She listened patiently to him extolling the virtues of a nice bolar roast, which required slow roasting and therefore would not be done in time, then fat sirloin steaks, which were far too expensive, and finally settled on five more chops: three for Jack and two for her so he wouldn't see she was eating leftover sausages. While Sid wrapped the chops in brown paper and tied the parcel with string, she dug into her purse; she hadn't budgeted for the extra meat, but this was an emergency.

The boys were home when she got back, eagerly eyeing her shopping in case she'd bought something interesting, like lollies. She hadn't, and they drifted off before she could rope them into helping her with the dinner.

She knew it was far too early, but she started on the vegetables anyway. Tom arrived home halfway through the beans. He came up behind her, slipped his arms around her waist and gave her a squeeze.

'Tea's early, isn't it?' he said. 'Oh, whoops, I forgot to tell you, I've invited Jack Vaughan around tonight. That's all right, isn't it?'

'Yes, but a little more notice might have been helpful,' Ellen said, extricating herself from his cuddle.

'Sorry, love, I forgot. Been a bit busy today.'

Ellen relented and gave him a smile. 'Milly and I saw Jack down the street. I think he was a bit embarrassed, actually, when he realised you hadn't told me.'

Tom looked sheepish. 'Well, you weren't home.' He gave her a quick kiss, and looked around. 'Is there anything to eat now?'

'Sandwiches,' Ellen said, pointing at the refrigerator.

Tom took out a plate of sandwiches made with thick slices of bread. He lifted the edge of the top one and pulled a face. 'Bloody cheese again. I'd rather have ham.'

Irritated, Ellen smothered a sigh. 'I know you would, and so would the boys, but there isn't any. We're a bit short at the moment, remember?'

Tom looked at her as if the complexities of housekeeping were not only beyond him, but beneath him as well, then shrugged, sat down and took a bite. 'Good pickle,' he said, and Ellen knew the comment was his way of apologising for complaining when he knew bloody well the grocery money wasn't going far enough.

He swallowed. 'How was your ladies' meeting? Get your order of battle from Colonel Wickham?'

'We did,' Ellen said, turning back to the bench. 'We're to help put together the food parcels and hand them out. She also wants us to 'encourage' the wives to stand behind their men while the strike's on.'

'I wouldn't have thought they'd need encouraging.'

Ellen contemplated the chopping board. Tom could be very naïve sometimes, when it came to understanding how people worked. Perhaps she'd spoiled him — she'd never once gone against his wishes or complained when money

71

was short when he was on strike. And she'd never really wanted to, either, because she'd always agreed with what the union was trying to achieve.

She said, 'Well, Rhea does. She says it's happened before and it'll happen this time, too.'

'What will happen?'

'That the women will start on at their husbands about getting back to work.'

'Bullshit,' Tom said. 'That's only when the stakes are low. This is different, we have to win this one, they all know that.'

'Do they?'

'Well, the miners all bloody well do.'

Ellen hesitated, then turned to face him. 'Are you sure about that?'

'Of course I'm sure. Christ, we all voted, every man at every pithead! An honest show of hands, too, not a gutless bloody secret ballot.'

'You don't think some of them were just putting their hands up for a couple of days off, or that they were swayed by what Pat and the others had to say? Do you think they all understand what's really at stake?'

Tom narrowed his eyes, but said nothing and resumed eating.

Ellen went on, although the last thing she wanted to do was annoy him. 'Perhaps it might have been an idea to take a secret ballot after all, then you would have got a better idea of how many of them genuinely wanted to go out.'

'They *all* wanted to go out,' Tom said through a mouthful of bread.

'Yes, but if you'd taken a secret ballot there'd

72

be a record of the exact numbers, wouldn't there, and you'd be able to remind them of that if any of them did start to waver. The result of a secret ballot always stands, doesn't it?'

'So does a show of hands.'

'Not if you have to have another one later on and not everyone puts their hands up.'

Tom leaned back in his chair and pushed his empty plate away. 'No one would dare, that'd imply they were prepared to scab.'

'Rhea says they might dare, if their wives are on at them to get back to work. A lot of them have kids to feed, Tom, and bills to pay. So do we.'

'What are you saying, Ellen?' Tom demanded. 'We've only been out a bloody fortnight.'

'Mum?'

Davey was standing at the kitchen door, his eyes big at the sound of his parents' raised voices. Ellen held out her arms, and he ran into them. She and Tom rarely argued, and when they did, she at least tried to make sure the boys weren't around.

'Are you and Dad having a fight?' Davey said into her skirt.

'Of course we're not,' Ellen said as she stroked his hair. 'We're having a discussion, that's all.'

'About the strike?'

'Sort of.'

Davey stepped back, the shine of tears in his eyes gone now. 'You know Kevin Insley at school? His mum and dad were having a discussion about the strike, and his mum belted his dad. A really good one, Kev said.'

73

Ellen refrained from glancing over at Tom. 'Well, I don't really think Kevin should be telling people about that sort of thing, do you? And you certainly shouldn't be telling anyone else, Davey. That's called gossip and it's not very nice.'

Davey gazed up at her. 'But why would Mrs Insley belt Mr Insley, Mum?'

Tom got to his feet and rummaged through his trouser pocket. 'Look, here's sixpence, why don't you and Neil run out and get yourself some lollies?'

Davey instantly forgot about Mr and Mrs Insley and whipped his hand out before his father could change his mind: being sent out with sixpence to spend solely on lollies was almost unprecedented.

Tom remained standing until his sons had galloped out the back door, then slowly subsided back into his chair. Ellen said nothing.

'The Insleys are always having a go at each other,' he said eventually, 'and they're always hard up. Barry Insley sits on his arse half the day down the pit so he never earns what he could.'

Ellen went back to preparing dinner, feeling that the tension had eased a little. It was unlike Tom to be short-tempered, and it worried her. She knew they would be all right, one way or another, but she also knew that Rhea Wickham was probably right too — sooner or later at least some of the men would find themselves under pressure from their wives, whether Tom wanted to believe it or not.

'Who'll be going up to Pukekohe for the veges?' she asked.

'Not me. Pat and I'll be at the watersiders' meetings once a week, I don't fancy going up twice.'

Ellen glanced at him over her shoulder. 'The meetings in Auckland?'

Tom nodded.

'Every week?'

'For as long as the strike's on, yeah.'

'Then why don't you get the veges on the way?'

Tom shook his head. 'Jack's doing that, since he's the one with the truck. And anyway the meetings are on a Friday, and the deal we've done with the market is for Mondays.'

Ellen sliced the ends off the last of the beans and tipped them off the chopping board into a pot. She rinsed the board then propped it behind the taps to drain, and sat down at the table.

'Tom?'

'Mmm?'

'How long is it likely to go on?'

Tom's eyes were suddenly serious and Ellen felt a worm of anxiety begin to uncurl in her stomach.

'I really don't know, love,' he said.

Ellen knew he wasn't quite telling the truth. 'But you know it won't be over soon, don't you?' she asked.

Tom looked as if he might be considering lying, which he had never been very good at, then thought better of it. 'No, it doesn't look like it. Pat says Barnes has no intention of giving Holland even an inch, and he'll never accept arbitration and that the watersiders are behind him one hundred per cent. And we won't go back until they do.'

'Just the Auckland lot, or the wharfies at all the ports?'

'All of them. They're all out and they'll stick together, and we'll stick with them. So will the other unions in the TUC, you can bank on that. And the Communist Party, of course,' he added, pulling a face.

Ellen nodded in commiseration. It was common knowledge that the communists openly supported the watersiders' strike, although neither Jock Barnes nor Toby Hill were party members themselves. But it wasn't much of a bonus because the papers were playing up the communist angle atrociously, accusing the watersiders of being agents of the Soviet Union and scaring the wits out of ordinary New Zealanders who didn't know any better because it was illegal to print anything in support of the strikers. The accusations didn't particularly bother anyone in Pukemiro because there were communists throughout the local mining community, and several high up in the unions, and nobody gave a toss. One of the shops down the street sold the *People's Voice* and quite a lot of people took it, but it didn't mean they were rabid reds about to invite Joseph Stalin around for afternoon tea any time soon. Tom read it himself and although he was appalled by what Stalin was doing in Russia, he liked some of the ideas the magazine espoused, and said it was very handy for lighting the coal range. But whatever people's views on communism, the idea that the strike

76

was being driven by the Soviet Union was laughable.

'So it all depends on Barnes and the watersiders?' Ellen asked.

'It depends on all of us. United we stand and all that.'

Ellen nodded. 'Well, as long as you and I are united. Rhea has asked us to keep an eye on the women, so we will. But there's no point you and I arguing about it, Tom, is there?'

He touched her hand. 'No, there isn't, love, so we won't, I promise.'

'Good,' Ellen said, relieved that they had cleared the air between them. 'Do you think it was wise giving the boys a whole sixpence just for lollies?'

Tom shrugged. 'I didn't want them to hear us.'

Ellen kissed the tip of his nose. 'No, neither did I.'

★ ★ ★

Tom went next door for a yarn with Bert Sisley, so Ellen made the pudding then tidied the kitchen and the sitting room, just in case Jack thought she was a slovenly housekeeper. She gave the outhouse a quick going over as well, even though the nightcart man had only been yesterday and it smelled quite fresh. It was absurd, really; they had electricity in the house and a refrigerator now, but the laundry still had to be done in the copper in the washhouse off the back porch, and their toilet was a long drop at the bottom of the garden because there was no town sewerage system, which was particularly hard going in the winter. Even Tom only took the newspaper in there with him during the summer months.

Jack arrived promptly at six o'clock, bearing half a dozen bottles of DB for Tom and a small bunch of flowers for Ellen. Neil and Davey tittered when he handed them to her and she shooed them out of the kitchen, trying not to let Jack see her red face. But they were back again within minutes, hanging about and making a production of sniffing the flowers which she'd placed in the centre of the table. She was very tempted to tell them to hop off outside until tea was dished up, but Tom seemed to be finding their antics amusing. Jack himself simply smiled at her, and at Tom, and at the boys. She wondered when he'd last had a decent, home-cooked meal.

The pudding was keeping warm in the oven, the vegetables were almost done and all she had to do was fry the chops. Tom, seated at the table which she'd laid with her best tablecloth and china, rolled a smoke while Jack flicked the lids off a couple of beers.

'Mum, can we have a beer?' Neil asked.

'No, you can't,' she said. 'Stop showing off.'

'I'm not showing off, I'm thirsty,' Neil said, punctuating this announcement with a theatrical clearing of his throat that sounded like gallons of water going down a plug hole.

Everyone laughed except Ellen. She put the chops in the frying pan and stood back as the heated fat sizzled and spat.

'Dinner will be in about ten minutes, Jack,' she said, glancing over at him.

'Anything I can do?' he asked.

There was a brief but profound silence as Tom, Neil and Davey all looked at each other in exaggerated amazement, and then across the table at Jack before they burst out laughing again.

Ellen ignored them. 'No thanks, Jack, I'm fine.'

Usually when Tom joked with the boys she joined in, even if it was at her own expense, but tonight she was feeling tense and unsettled, and wasn't finding their shenanigans funny at all.

She scooped the chops out of the pan and arranged them on a serving dish, then carried them over to the table. In honour of their guest the boys held back until Ellen had seated herself, looking at her expectantly. Even Tom kept his hands in his lap.

'Help yourself, please,' she urged Jack.

'Thank you,' he said, and speared a pork chop with his fork. To his plate he also added beans, peas and waxy yellow potatoes, while everyone watched intently.

Ellen nodded at a small jug on the table. 'There's apple sauce to go with the chops, if you'd like it.'

Neil said, 'But Mum, we never have apple sauce.'

'We do now,' Ellen said, feeling her nerves fray even further. She kept her head down so Jack wouldn't see the exasperation and embarrass-ment on her face, which she knew was flushed again from standing over the range.

Neil peered into the jug. 'It's got black bits in it.'

'Yes, it caught a little. I should have stirred it more.'

'Is it burnt?' Davey asked.

'Only slightly,' Ellen replied through gritted teeth. She could feel Jack's eyes on her.

Davey's bottom lip came out. 'I don't like burnt bits.'

Tom finally decided the boys had gone far enough. 'Then don't bloody eat it!' he snapped.

Neil and Davey froze. Jack reached for the sauce and dropped a great dollop onto his chop, then sampled it. His eyes closed in an expression of pure bliss. 'You lads'll kick yourselves if you don't try this. It's the best apple sauce I've ever tasted.'

Ellen smiled at her plate.

'Help yourself to more chops,' Tom urged, 'there's plenty to go around.'

Jack said apologetically, 'I wasn't sure . . . '

'It's all right, we're not on hard rations yet,' Tom said, glancing over at Ellen. He gave her a grin. 'This is a tremendous meal, love, well done.'

She smiled back, and then at Jack, absurdly grateful for his compliment about the sauce.

'She's a great cook, is Ellen,' Tom said, piling chops enthusiastically onto his own plate.

'I can see that,' Jack said, cutting a potato in half and plastering it with butter. 'Are these vegetables from your own garden, Ellen?'

Ellen, who had just taken a mouthful,

swallowed hastily and nodded. 'I grow as much as I can, depending on the season.'

'You've done well, these peas are lovely. What do you use for fertiliser?' He was looking at her intently, as if he really wanted to know.

Neil said, 'Chook shit.'

'Chook *manure*,' Ellen corrected, 'but not a lot, just a bucketful now and then.'

'I saw the chook run out the back,' Jack said.

Tom nodded. 'We've got vegetables and eggs,' he said, 'and Ellen can bake bread if she has to, and while the strike's on the meat will turn up as it's needed.' He tapped the side of his nose conspiratorially.

Startled, Ellen looked at him. She didn't at all fancy the idea of baking bread every day — it took absolute ages.

'Are you going out rustling, Dad?' Davey asked with barely contained glee.

'No, son, I'm not going out rustling. We made a deal with one or two of the cockies to send a couple of steers our way, as long as we do the butchering ourselves.'

'Not in my washhouse, you won't,' Ellen said.

'No, love, in Bert's shed. Lew can butcher, he was at Horotiu for a couple of years, and Sid said he'd give us a hand.'

'So can I, actually,' Jack said, 'but only sheep and pigs. I've never had a go at a steer.'

'Good,' Tom said, 'because we're expecting a few sheep as well and Lew reckons he never went on the mutton chain.'

There were oohs and aahs when Ellen produced the enormous blackberry and apple

81

pie she'd made for pudding. The pastry had puffed up beautifully and a thin, shiny rivulet of dark juice trickled from the vent in the centre.

At the end of the meal, Tom pushed his chair back from the table and sat with his hands over his stomach, replete. 'Another beer?' he suggested to Jack. 'We'll get out of Ellen's way while she cleans up.'

As they both stood and headed for the back porch, Ellen breathed a quiet sigh of relief. She'd been nervous about eating in front of Jack, and serving him with her cooking, and the boys had been little buggers for some reason. Why she'd been so on edge she didn't know; Jack Vaughan was just a man. A fascinating and very good-looking one, that was true, but just a man, and she already had one of those.

He and Tom came in an hour later when it was dark and the beer had gone.

'Jack's off now, and I'm just going down the back,' Tom announced. 'See you tomorrow, Jack.'

Jack nodded, and watched in silence as Tom went down the steps two at a time and disappeared into the shadows along the path that led to the outhouse.

When he was out of earshot, Jack said, 'Thanks for a lovely meal, Ellen, it was a cracker.'

She closed her eyes briefly as he spoke her name; it sounded so different when he said it, as though it had some special meaning, as though he really wanted her to hear what he was saying. She began to blush again and willed herself not to. She felt horribly awkward, just her and Jack standing on the porch by themselves, awkward and like a silly young girl.

'I'm sorry about the burnt sauce,' she said. 'And the boys — I don't know what got into them.'

Jack shrugged and smiled his slow smile. 'The sauce was lovely, and the boys were just being boys.'

'I expect so.'

'Thanks again for the meal.'

'My pleasure,' she said, and, flustered, held out her hand as if she were meeting him for the first time. She immediately felt even sillier, but it was too late to whip it back.

He reached out his own hand, and touched his middle finger to the pulse in her wrist. 'And mine,' he said.

4

'How did it go?'

Milly was sitting in Ellen's kitchen, drinking tea and eating the last of the blackberry pie from the night before.

'Pretty good,' Ellen said. 'The boys were little shites, though.'

Milly looked surprised. 'Were they? What did they do?'

'Neil made a fuss about the apple sauce . . . '

'Apple sauce! I say, how posh.'

'Don't you start. And then Davey complained because there were little tiny bits of black in it.'

'Oh dear, did you burn it?'

'Only very slightly, and I didn't have time, or the apples, to make any more.'

'You served burnt apple sauce to Jack Vaughan?'

Ellen nodded, then started to giggle. 'And Neil asked for a beer, and said 'chook shit' at the dinner table.'

'Yes, it's a worry, isn't it?' Milly shook her head. 'Evan dropped a cup of milk the other day and said the f-word and Frank didn't even pull him up. Didn't even notice, I don't think. Why were Neil and Davey acting up?'

Ellen shrugged. 'Because we had a visitor, perhaps. But they're usually pretty good with their manners, Tom makes sure of that.'

'Were they upset about something?'

'Like what?'

'I don't know. The strike?'

'I wouldn't think so. They've been running around on the lawn playing watersiders versus scabs all week. They think it's a great lark.'

Milly ran her spoon around the edge of her plate to collect the last of the blackberry and cream. 'How was Jack?' she asked, with a sly glance at Ellen.

'Jack? He was . . . Jack, I suppose.' Ellen looked at her friend quizzically, although she could feel her face heating up. 'How would I know? I hardly know him.'

'He looks like he'd like to know you,' Milly said, waggling her eyebrows.

Ellen, pouring herself another cup of tea, went still. 'How do you mean?'

'Well, he stares at you a lot, and he smiles at you all the time.'

'He smiles at everyone, Milly, he's that sort of person.' Ellen decided not to mention the flowers.

'Maybe, but when he smiles at you it's like it's just for you, no one else.'

'God, Milly, you do talk a lot of bloody rubbish sometimes.'

'Then why are you smirking?'

'I'm not smirking!' Ellen was mortified because she knew she was.

Milly laughed. 'Oh, for Christ's sake, girl, the man fancies you, be flattered. Just don't let Tom catch him at it, that's all.'

'God, no, there'd be hell to pay.' Ellen grimaced. 'But I wouldn't have thought Jack

85

Vaughan was the type, would you?'

'No, he seems too . . . well, honest. And you're not the type to stray, so just enjoy it until someone else catches his eye.'

'Like Andrea Trask, you mean?'

Milly made a rude noise. 'And the rest. Mind you, every bloke who isn't nailed down catches Andrea's eye.'

'She's only looking for a husband, Milly — she's young and unattached. We shouldn't knock her for that.'

Milly slurped the last of her tea and looked at her friend with genuine fondness. 'You can always find something nice to say about a person, can't you? Andrea can be a right little bitch sometimes — you've seen it yourself often enough.'

'She'll have her reasons.'

'I'm sure,' Milly said. 'Speaking of reasons, I didn't just come round to finish your pie, delicious though it was. Lorna's having a girls' get-together on Friday. Interested?'

'What time?'

'About twelve.'

'Well, I'll have to make Tom his lunch . . . ' Ellen stopped, then suddenly grinned. 'No, I won't, he and Pat are off to Auckland. So yes, I am interested. Are you going?'

'Try and keep me away.'

'Doesn't Frank mind?'

'Me getting on the booze? No, as long as I leave him something to eat and I'm home in time to get the tea on he couldn't care less.'

'Tom always has something to say when I come home tipsy.'

'But you hardly ever do, though, do you, Ellen? Except for that time when the kids were tiny. You're such a model wife, the *Woman's Weekly* should come and do an article on you.' Milly laughed at the look on Ellen's face. 'Anyway, Frank lets me do whatever I like — it's his way of making up for before. Unfortunately, I'm so boring I never get up to mischief. Not for want of trying, though!'

'You wouldn't, though, would you?' Ellen asked. 'Get up to mischief?'

'Depends on what sort of mischief you're talking about.'

'Well, you know, real mischief.'

'Of course I wouldn't. Frank's always been the man for me, regardless of his faults.' Milly patted Ellen's hand. 'And neither would you, and you know it.'

★   ★   ★

At midday on Friday, Ellen and Milly knocked on Lorna's back door, each carrying a plate. Milly had done egg sandwiches and Ellen cucumber and tomato on water crackers; neither had been able to scrape together anything more spectacular.

'Yoo-hoo!' Milly called, knocking again.

Lorna appeared in the kitchen, and beckoned them in. 'Oh, lovely,' she said, eyeing the plates. 'The others have all brought something too. Come through to the sitting room.'

From her bag Ellen withdrew a bottle of sparkling wine someone had given her at

Christmas, but neither she nor Tom drank wine, so it had remained untouched. She handed the bottle over to Lorna, who put it on the bench next to a bottle of medium sherry, one of Pimms and two of fizzy lemonade. To Ellen's surprise there was also a bottle of Johnnie Walker.

'Who brought the whisky?' she asked.

'Val,' Lorna said.

'How on earth did she wrestle it off Stan?' Valerie Mason's husband was extremely fond of his drink.

Lorna grinned.

In the sitting room, Dot Sisley was already seated on the couch along from Val; opposite them in an armchair lounged Avis Hale.

Ellen knew Val and Avis well; they were local miners' wives, of a similar age to her, and both with children of their own. She was surprised to see Dot, though, whom she hadn't seen out much lately.

She greeted the others and sat down on the couch. 'I didn't realise you were coming today!'

Dot nodded. 'Bert said I needed a change of scenery.'

'Is he minding the kids?'

'Just the little ones. He's taking them fishing in the creek.'

Ellen smiled at her, careful to hide her shock at her friend's appearance. She hadn't been over to see Dot in almost a week, and even in that short time she'd lost weight, a sure sign that her nerves were playing up, and there were deep shadows bruising the delicate skin beneath her eyes.

'How have you been keeping?'

'Not bad,' Dot said.

'You look a bit pale.'

'Just tired. I'm not sleeping very well at the moment.'

Lorna came in with the drinks on a tray. 'Right, who wants what?'

Ellen looked longingly at the whisky, but it was still unopened and she didn't want to be the one to start on it.

'Oh, go on,' Val urged, 'get the lid off it, Ellen, that's why I brought it.'

'What will Stan say when he finds out it's gone?' Milly asked.

'Nothing. I'll just tell him he drank it.'

There was a short silence while the others digested this.

'But won't he know he hasn't?' Avis said.

Val snorted. 'I doubt it. By the time he gets home tonight, he won't know what he's had to drink over the last couple of days, or when.'

The women suddenly all laughed at the image of big Stan Mason propping himself up at the kitchen cupboard, hanging onto the door, scratching his bristly head and trying to remember when exactly he'd polished off his whisky.

'It'll serve him right, too,' Val said. 'Too much of my grocery money's been going over the bar since this strike started, so to hell with him.'

Ellen poured herself a small whisky, feeling only slightly remiss at the thought of Stan searching in vain for it later on, and a sherry for Milly, who didn't like spirits. She slipped her shoes off, sat back and felt herself relax. They were her friends, these women, and had been for years. She'd grown up with most of them, had been at their weddings and they at hers, taken them little gifts when their babies had arrived, worked with them on school projects and stood beside them on cold winter Saturday mornings watching their kids playing soccer. Most importantly, perhaps, she'd lived through hard times with them — the Depression, the war, the strike of '42, and, worst of all, the communal darkness of accidents and deaths underground. She would never forget the day in 1939 when eleven good local men died from carbon-monoxide poisoning down the pit at Glen Afton.

She knew the histories of these women and many of their secrets, and they knew hers; it couldn't be any other way in a small, tight community. Sometimes she despaired of ever having any real privacy, and had learned a long time ago not to tell anyone anything she really didn't want to become public knowledge, but that was a small price to pay for the comfort of belonging and having friends and neighbours on whom she could always rely.

'Here's to us, the women of Pukemiro,' Milly announced, and they raised their glasses to each other.

'So,' Val said after downing a healthy gulp of her drink, 'how's everyone holding up?'

Lorna, ensconced in the other armchair, shrugged and folded her legs beneath her. 'We're doing all right, apart from the HP on what we're sitting on, and my mum's been helping us out.

Mind you, it's only been a couple of weeks.'

'We're not,' Avis said, lighting a cigarette. 'We're in the cart already. I haven't had to ask for credit yet, but I will by Monday. There's hardly anything in the house to eat and I'm buggered if I know what I'm going to feed them over the weekend.'

'The relief packages are starting on Tuesday,' Ellen said. 'We'll be giving them out at the hall from nine in the morning until about twelve.'

Avis breathed out a long, thin stream of smoke. 'Christ, that's a relief. I don't know about you girls, but I'm going to feel such a bloody fool asking for credit.'

'I know,' Val said, 'I already have. Me and Shirley Minogue went into Newton King last week, but they were good about it. I still felt stupid, though.'

'What sort of food will we get, do you know?' Dot asked.

Milly said, 'Rhea says it will be vegetables and a bit of meat, and basic stuff like butter and tea. Bread, maybe.'

Avis tapped the ash off her smoke into an ashtray. 'And Rhea would know, of course, the stuck-up old bag knows everything.'

'Oh, she's not so bad,' Lorna said.

'Yes, she is. Just because she's the president of the CWI she thinks she's the Queen of Pukemiro as well. And that husband of hers, stirring bastard. If it wasn't for him we wouldn't be in this mess.'

Ellen looked at poor Avis and thought, Oh yes we would, because Pat Wickham hadn't had to do much convincing to get the men to go out at all. And if Avis' husband Dennis didn't spend so much money on the horses it would be a few weeks yet before she was having to ask for credit. But nobody contradicted Avis; they all knew what she must be feeling.

'Vic reckons the men are getting a group together to go fishing,' Lorna said, neatly changing the subject. 'A fishing camp at Whangamata, I think he said.'

Avis perked up. 'Are they? That'd be good, I like a nice fresh bit of fish.'

'Although it won't be a nice fresh bit of fish if they stop off at every pub on the way back,' Val said.

'Why would they?' Milly asked innocently. 'Is Stan going with them?'

'Not if I have anything to do with it,' Val said, reaching for the sherry. 'No, bugger it, I'm having a whisky. It's come out of my grocery money, after all.'

It was at times like these that Ellen was extremely thankful that Tom didn't have any serious vices. Val was frequently having to dodge Stan's drunken tempers, and keep the kids out of his way as well, and a large portion of Avis' housekeeping money seemed to find its way to the tote week after week. It was true that Tom smoked, occasionally drank too much and swore like a trooper, but then most Pukemiro men did. Coalmining was brutal and demanding, and as far as Ellen was concerned that gave Tom the right to a bit of relaxation when he needed it.

She sighed. He was a good man, Tom. He

loved her and his boys, he worked very hard to support them, and they never went short of anything if he could possibly avoid it. He was a good father, too, helping Neil and Davey with their sports and taking them fishing and hunting. He had plans to buy a car one day, soon he hoped, then they would go for Sunday drives to Raglan, and maybe even to Hamilton.

He loved her very much, she knew that, and she loved him back. He was safe, solid and dependable. He seldom did anything out of the ordinary, she always knew how he would behave in certain situations and she had no cause to worry about him. Except for him working underground, of course, but that was the lot of a miner's wife.

He was a gentle and considerate lover, too, even if the passion they'd shared in their early days of marriage had gradually been replaced by the comfort of an easy, predictable and undemanding familiarity. They had sex once or twice a week, but not often more, not these days. Her mother had warned her it would go like that, that the physical excitement of the first year or so would ebb slowly but surely away, but Ellen hadn't believed her. Then, she'd simply been unable to foresee a time when she and Tom wouldn't snatch every possible moment to be together. But Gloria had been right, although Ellen had never admitted it to her.

She enjoyed Tom's lovemaking — it was comforting to be held in his strong arms and feel his warmth and know he desired her — but if she were to be rigorously honest about it, and she rarely was, sometimes it was boring. Sometimes she lay there while he grunted away on top of her, his eyes screwed shut and his jaw clenched with concentration, and thought about what she might need to buy from the grocer the following morning, or whether it was time to put the broad beans in yet. And whenever that happened she felt guilty, as if she were stealing something from Tom. Then, the next time they had sex, she would be extra attentive and loving to make up for it, and things would be all right again.

Unbidden, she thought about the dark hairs on Jack Vaughan's wrists and at the base of his throat, his strong white teeth and the toughness of him, and wondered what he would be like as a lover. And then she choked on her drink, because, with a spurt of excitement and fear churning in her belly, she suddenly knew what was going to happen.

'Ellen?' Milly was looking at her.

'Sorry, went down the wrong way.'

'Do you need a pat on the back?'

'No, thanks,' Ellen said, coughing until she was red in the face.

Content to be away from their coal ranges and children and husbands for a few hours, they gossiped and laughed, and drank. By two o'clock Ellen and Val had polished off almost half of the whisky. Ellen felt carefree, vital, almost airborne, and anything anyone said was unbearably funny. Val, who was a more seasoned drinker, was watching her with amusement. Dot had also had two small glasses of whisky, which was very unusual for her. She rarely drank much, and on top of the three sherries she'd already had, she was beginning to slur her words. At one point she missed the low coffee table with her glass entirely and it tumbled onto the floor.

Avis said, 'Steady on, love, we'll be taking you home in a wheelbarrow if you're not careful.'

Dot gazed at her with a startled expression, then started to laugh. She laughed so hard that the others joined in at the sight of her red cheeks and streaming eyes, but stopped abruptly when they realised that her hysterical laughter was turning into sobs.

Ellen blinked and shook her head slightly to clear it. 'Dot, love, what's the matter?'

Dot cried even harder.

Ellen moved closer and put her arm around her friend's jerking shoulders. 'Dot? What's wrong? What's the matter?'

'I don't know!' Dot wailed, doubled over now, her arms crossed tightly over her stomach.

The others looked on in sympathetic silence; Dot had come over like this before, the poor thing, and they'd all witnessed it at one time or another.

'Put the kettle on, Lorna,' Avis suggested.

As Lorna left the room, Milly moved to sit at Dot's feet. 'Are you not feeling well?' she asked.

'I . . . no, I'm not. I'm sorry.'

Milly patted her knee. 'Don't be sorry, love, it's all right.'

Dot made a noise halfway between a cough and a sob. A dribble of snot slid out of one nostril onto her upper lip, and Ellen reached into her bag for a handkerchief. Her own ebullient mood was gone now, flattened by the sight of her friend in such obvious pain.

'Here, it's clean,' she said, offering the handkerchief to Dot.

'I'm sorry, I don't know why I'm crying.'

'Has something happened?' Milly asked.

'No.' Dot blew her nose loudly and wiped her lip, then started crying again.

Milly said, 'Do you want me to walk you home?'

'No, thanks, I'm all right, Bert's coming for me after the fishing.'

Avis came over and sat on the arm of the couch next to Dot. Rough around the edges, and kind but always candid, she asked what everyone else was thinking. 'Is it your nerves again, do you think?'

Dot nodded.

'Because of the strike?'

Dot nodded again. 'I think it was starting before that, but it's got worse. It's just so hard already, so hopeless.' She hiccupped, and drew in a deep breath to calm herself. 'It's all coming down on me, the darkness is coming again.'

A shiver scuttled up Ellen's spine, because they were exactly the same words that Tom used when he had one of his buried-alive nightmares. She felt a fierce pang of guilt and regret; she'd been so busy rushing about thinking about the strike and food parcels and Jack bloody Vaughan that she hadn't even noticed what had been happening to her friend and closest neighbour.

96

Lorna came in with a cup of tea. 'Does anyone else want one?' she asked as she set it on the table in front of Dot. 'There's two teaspoons of sugar in it, so drink up, it'll make you feel better.'

It wouldn't, but Dot sipped at it anyway.

Nobody else wanted tea. Ellen, unsettled, ignored her own common sense and went back to the whisky.

To distract Dot, and to revive the party mood, Val launched into a story involving Stan's ill-fated trip home from the Waingaro pub. He'd been with a group of other blokes, two carloads of them, when the car in front had gone off the winding road at the bottom of a hill and into a creek. The vehicle Stan had been travelling in was only just cresting the hill, and they'd had a clear, heart-stopping view of the car some distance below them subsiding slowly into the swift-flowing water. They'd raced down the hill towards the spot where the car had gone over the bank, imagining the whole, winding, bush-screened way down the muffled screams of the men inside, the frantic scrabbling at windows and the desperate shoving to get doors open against the pressure of the water. At the bottom of the hill they'd come to a skidding halt in the gravel and leapt out, rushing to peer over the bank into the creek for any signs of life.

There, six feet below them, were their mates, waist-deep in the creek, wading around the overturned car with stricken and desperate expressions on their faces. Someone on the bank bellowed, 'Is someone missing?' and the would-be rescuers launched themselves into the

97

water to join the search.

Val paused, letting the tension of the story swell under its own momentum.

'Did anyone drown?' Milly asked.

Val delivered the punch line. 'No, but there was half a dozen on the backseat before the crash, and they could only find five.'

Even Dot smiled.

By the time Bert arrived half an hour later, with the youngest twins in tow, Ellen was well on her way again. She'd reached the stage where, after just one or two more drinks, she would plummet from inebriated elation into a pit of belligerence and remorse, but was too inexperienced to know it. It was the point where dedicated drinkers reached for the bottle again, and everyone else called it a day.

Avis was also the worse for wear, and Milly not much better, although she'd stopped drinking half an hour ago. Avis wasn't particularly bothered — Dennis probably wouldn't even look up from the racing pages when she got home — but Milly was starting to worry about Frank. He would no doubt smile at her and say, 'Come on, old girl, let's get a cup of tea down you,' and make a joke of it, but she was feeling guilty; it was unfair of her to rub his face in it.

Ellen took a sip from her glass, realised that it was empty and reached for the whisky. Upending the bottle, she waited for several seconds before she noticed that the lid was still on it.

'Are you all right, Ellen?' Bert said.

Carefully unscrewing the lid, she nodded.

Giving her a doubtful look, he went over to Dot and crouched down in front of her. 'You been crying, love?' he asked.

Dot touched his sleeve. 'A little bit.'

'Let's get you home then, eh?' Bert said. 'I'll make us something to eat and we'll have a nice cup of tea. We didn't catch any fish, but the kids had a good time.'

From the door, the two children, not identical but very similar, watched their mother with round, wary eyes. They looked apprehensive, as if they weren't sure of what she might be going to do next, but when she reached out her hand to them they trotted over and latched onto her skirt.

Bert announced, 'We'll be off then, ladies,' and began to shepherd his family out of the room.

Dot waggled her fingers. 'See you next time,' she said, and gave them all a sad little smile.

Bert turned back, and for a horrible moment Ellen thought he might be going to tell them off for getting Dot drunk and upsetting her. But all he said was, 'Dot hasn't been well again, what with one thing and another. She just needs a rest.' And then he was gone.

After several moments, enough time to let the Sisleys get outside and out of earshot, Lorna said, 'He must be a saint, Bert.'

'Christ, I'll say,' Milly agreed. 'Poor Dot.'

Avis reached for her drink. 'Poor bloody Bert.'

'It must be hard for him, having all those kids to look after, and Dot as well,' Lorna said, although not unkindly.

'I know,' Avis said. 'I bet he's made more

dinners and changed more nappies than all the men in this town put together.'

'Stan's never changed a bloody nappy in his life,' Val said with a hoot of laughter.

'Neither has Frank,' Milly agreed, 'but then it's not his job. He's a miner, not a baby's bum-wiper.'

They all laughed then, and Ellen tried to remember whether Tom had ever changed Neil and Davey's nappies. She thought he might have, just the once, but had refused to do it ever again, claiming that the stink was worse than anything he'd ever encountered down the mine.

She put her glass down on the arm of the couch, thought better of it and moved it to the coffee table. 'I'm off to the toilet,' she announced.

'Need a hand?' Lorna asked, thinking of the steps Ellen would have to negotiate to get out to the yard.

'No, I'm all right,' Ellen said, although when she got to her feet she discovered that actually she wasn't, and put out a hand to steady herself.

She held onto the rails on both sides going down the back steps, and raised her face to the breeze when she got to the bottom, feeling her hair lift away from her neck and the damp skin there cooling. This was better; she'd been starting to feel sick. She made her way across the lawn, taking care to step squarely on the paving stones that led past the clothesline and on to the outhouse, dimly remembering a rhyme they all used to chant in the playground when they were kids. Step on a crack, break your mother's back. But there weren't any cracks here, just the square lines of concrete pavers, blurring double then back into one again, and the faded green neatness of recently clipped, late-summer grass.

In the toilet she closed the door, hiked up her skirt and yanked her pants down, peeing almost before her bum was on the seat. She bent forward and put her elbows on her thighs and her face in her hands. The pee went on for ever, and she wondered dimly how she'd managed to hold it all in. What would Tom say if he came home and found her in this state? Perhaps she should head home herself; the boys would be in soon anyway.

She tore off some toilet paper, leaned over to wipe herself and nearly toppled off the seat, banging her elbow smartly on the wall. Giggling, she pulled her pants back up, stepped outside into the bright sunlight and headed for the house.

Her mood turned halfway through her next drink, and the room started spinning soon after that. When she dropped her glass on the floor and it broke, Avis announced, 'Right, girl, that's enough for you, time to go home.'

Ellen didn't disagree. She fumbled about looking for her handbag, which she'd kicked under the couch, and lurched unsteadily to her feet.

'Thanks for a lovely afternoon, Lorna,' she said, hearing herself making a mess of the words.

Milly stood too. 'I'll come with you. I'm not

101

sure you're safe to stagger up the street by yourself.'

'I am,' Ellen insisted. 'It's not far.'

Milly looked doubtful. 'Are you sure?'

'I'm all right.' Ellen was vaguely embarrassed now at the state she'd got herself into, and determined to salvage her pride by getting herself home. 'Have to stop off at the shop, anyway.' Except that it came out as 'stoff op'.

'No, Ellen,' Avis said. 'Come on, we'll walk you home.'

'No! I'll walk home my*self*!'

'Oh dear,' Val said.

Milly shrugged and sat down again. 'Well, if that's what you want.' Then her sunny smile reappeared. 'But if you're in the gutter by the time I come past, I'll get one of the stretchers from the rescue station, shall I?'

Ellen nodded, oblivious to the joke, and made her way to the door.

Milly watched her uneasily, wincing as Ellen put a hand out to stop herself from crashing into the wall in the hall.

'Oh, shit,' she said, 'we can't let her go up the street like that! What if someone sees her?'

'You won't stop her,' Val said, with the wisdom of someone who has spent years trying to manage the behaviour of a chronic drunk and has finally given up. 'Just let her go, she'll be all right.'

This time, the fresh air only made Ellen feel worse. Nothing she looked at would stay still. She went down the steps slowly, one at a time, clutching onto the rail with both hands, then made her way around to the front of the house. Lorna's place was at the very foot of Joseph Street, but all Ellen could see were two front gates where she dimly knew there should only have been one.

She lurched up the garden path, lost her balance and veered onto the grass. Another two steps, and then the ground raced up to meet her.

* * *

Jack was pulling away from the grocer's when he saw Ellen stagger across someone's front lawn, then fall over, hard.

He gunned the motor and roared down the street, the wheels of his truck throwing up little spurts of gravel and dust. Outside the house he stopped, jumped out and ran over to where Ellen lay sprawled on the grass.

'Ellen? Are you all right?'

She opened her eyes. 'I fell over.'

Leaning closer, he caught an eye-watering whiff of whisky coming off her, and swore. He sat her up, slid his arms under hers and hoisted her to her feet, holding her there until she found her balance.

'Sorry,' she moaned. 'Dunno what's wrong.'

'I do,' Jack said in her ear, 'you're pissed as a ferret. What the hell have you been doing?'

'Girls' getagether.'

Jack shook his head, then slipped his arm around her shoulders and steered her towards the gate. 'Come on, I'm taking you home.'

Ellen gasped. 'The boys!'

'Don't worry, they'll be all right.'

He led her over to his truck and propped her up with one arm while he opened the passenger door. The step up into the cab was high and she couldn't manage it, so he gave her a push; it was gentle enough, but she ended up on her face on the seat. By the time he'd gone around to the driver's side she'd righted herself and was scrabbling around looking for something.

'My bag!' she cried.

'You're sitting on it,' he said, hauling the leather straps out from under her backside and setting the bag in her lap.

At the top of Joseph Street he turned left into John Street and coasted along in first gear until he came to Ellen's house, wondering whether she would be able to get inside by herself. He thought not; she was pretty plonked.

'Do you need a hand?'

'No.'

He eyed her doubtfully. He wanted to pick her up in his arms and carry her inside and perhaps set her down gently on the couch or somewhere comfortable like that, but he'd spent enough time in pubs to know that whisky more often than not significantly increased the arsehole quotient in drinkers, and that his efforts would probably be rewarded with a fist in the face.

She rammed the door handle down, shoved the door open with her foot and fell out onto the grass verge at the side of the road.

Jack swore again, got out himself and went around to the passenger side. 'Come on,' he said, lifting her to her feet, 'let's get you inside.'

104

The steps up to the back door were daunting, but they managed, almost. Halfway up Ellen tripped and fell, banging her knee hard on the next step up, and said, 'Ow, fuck.'

Jack's eyebrows went up — he hadn't expected that from her, normally she seemed quite reserved.

The back door was open. Neil and Davey were sitting at the kitchen table eating Marmite sandwiches they'd made themselves.

'What's wrong with Mum?' Neil asked, his sandwich halfway to his mouth. He looked somewhat shocked at the sight of his mother, dishevelled and swaying at Jack's side.

'She's feeling a bit off,' Jack said. 'Why don't you lads take your feed outside while I get her sorted, eh?'

Neil and Davey seemed uncertain, but collected their plates and went out to sit on the steps.

Ellen collapsed in the chair Davey had just vacated. 'I feel sick,' she mumbled, and retched.

Jack looked around wildly for something she could spew into. There was the fruit bowl, but it was full of feijoas and anyway it was made of wicker. He dashed into the washhouse off the back porch, grabbed a bucket and darted back to the kitchen, where Ellen was leaning forward in her chair, her knees apart and her hand clamped over her mouth.

He set the bucket between her feet and stepped well back. She let go and an arc of vomit — pale orange, Jack noted — shot out of her mouth and into the bucket, making a dull

105

ringing sound as it hit the bottom. Then another lot came up, and he winced at the strangled groans coming from Ellen's throat. He moved behind her, collected up her hair and held it back off her face so it wouldn't get in the way.

'Mum?' Davey stood at the door, clutching a half-eaten sandwich in his grubby hand.

'It's all right,' Jack said, 'she's just having a bit of a spew.'

'Did she eat something yucky?'

'I'd say so. Outside now, there's a good boy.'

Davey retreated.

After a minute or two more of unproductive retching, Ellen stopped heaving and moved her head away from the bucket. Jack stayed where he was, stroking her hair and patting her shoulders, which felt slight and insubstantial under his big hands.

'I'm sorry,' Ellen said eventually, then she sniffed violently, coughed and spat into the bucket.

Jack pulled a face; it was a killer when spew went up the back of your nose. He called out to Neil, who appeared in the doorway.

'Where do you keep your towels, son?'

'In the hall cupboard.'

'Get a clean one for your mum, will you?'

Neil tiptoed past Ellen, giving her a wary look as he went. She didn't even look up, she was so ashamed of herself.

Jack moved over to the sink, filled the kettle and set it on the range. Neil came back as he was spooning tea leaves into the pot, silently handed his mother a fresh towel and went outside again.

After a moment Jack could hear the two boys running around on the lawn, kicking a ball and arguing about who was going to be the striker and who was the goalie.

By the time the kettle boiled, Ellen had shifted in her chair and had her arms on the table and her head down. Jack poured the water over the tea and sat down next to her.

'Feeling better?'

Ellen shook her head, her face obscured by her hair.

'Not used to the whisky?'

'No. I feel foul.'

Jack nodded in sympathy. He always felt bloody awful, too, after a heavy session on the whisky.

'Do you want to go to bed?' he asked, and almost smiled. He'd rehearsed asking her that question so many times in his head over the last fortnight, but never imagined she'd be half unconscious and stinking of vomit when he finally got up the nerve to do it.

When she said yes, he wasn't quite sure what to do. It was all very well helping out, but he didn't think Tom would appreciate him stripping his wife down to her underwear and tucking her up in bed.

He went to the back door. 'Neil! Come and give us a hand, will you?'

Neil turned away from the soccer ball he'd been lining up for the goal of the century between the feijoa tree and the lemon tree, and trotted up the steps.

Between them they got Ellen into the

107

bedroom. Jack resisted the urge to have a good look around, at the heavy dark furniture and the lace runner on Ellen's dressing table and the toiletries and trinket boxes scattered across it, and concentrated on sitting her upright on the edge of the bed.

'Pull the covers back,' he suggested, and waited while Neil folded back the quilted bedspread and the smooth cotton sheets beneath it.

'I'm sorry, love,' Ellen said to no one in particular.

'We should probably take her shoes off,' Jack said.

While Neil was crouching on the floor unfastening the buckles on his mother's sandals, Jack undid the belt at Ellen's waist, feeling disconcertingly guilty with the boy only inches away.

Satisfied now that she would at least be able to breathe, he urged Ellen to lie down. She rolled onto her side, facing away from him, and let her eyes close.

Neil pulled the blankets up and tucked them around her shoulders, as she'd done for him almost every night of his life, then stood back, unsure of what to do next. He looked upset and Jack felt sorry for him.

'I'll get the bucket,' Jack said, speaking from personal experience.

He took it out to the washhouse, emptied the contents into the tub, ran the tap to wash it away then rinsed the bucket thoroughly. On the way back to the bedroom he stopped to grab a fresh towel from the hall cupboard.

'That should do the trick,' he said to Neil as he put the bucket on the floor near the head of the bed, and arranged the towel over the blankets in case she missed. 'We'll leave her to it now, shall we? I'd better be off.'

Neil nodded, and followed him out into the kitchen. Awkwardly, he stuck out his hand. 'Thanks for your help, Mr Vaughan.'

Jack shook and said, 'She'll be right, son,' although he wasn't sure whether he meant Ellen, or things in general. He had no idea if he could guarantee this solemn-faced young boy either.

Outside in his truck, Jack sat with his hand resting on the keys in the ignition, trying to make some sort of sense out of how he was feeling. Normally a scene like that would have warned him very smartly off a woman.

But it hadn't. Not at all.

5

Tom refused to speak to Ellen until mid-morning the following day, even though she forced herself out of bed at seven as usual to cook breakfast for him and the boys. She'd gone through the motions while Tom deliberately ignored her and the boys snatched glances in her direction as she worked at the bench, too frightened by their father's stony silence to say anything. She'd almost vomited again over the fried eggs, but gritted her teeth and held it down. And, Jesus, her head hurt, and she'd had a terrible attack of the runs when she'd first got up.

Worse than that, though, was the absolute mortification she felt about having made such a spectacle of herself, more or less in front of the whole town. Thank God she hadn't staggered all the way up Joseph Street, weaving and lurching and probably throwing up all over herself on the way. Thank God Jack had come along.

After the dishes, she lay down on the couch in the sitting room and allowed herself to feel miserable. What on earth had he thought of her? He would probably never speak to her again, and she couldn't blame him. What a fool she'd made of herself. She had vague, fragmented recollections of him picking her up off the grass outside Lorna's house and bringing her home in his truck, and of sitting in the kitchen with her head in a bucket, but that was it. Had she actually been sick on him? She couldn't remember. And what the hell might she have said to him?

She slept then, for several hours, and woke only when sunlight began to burn into her eyelids. She whimpered and rolled over on the couch, moving a cushion so that it covered her face.

'Do you want me to close the curtains?'

It was Tom. She moved the cushion an inch and squinted up at him. The light was excruciatingly bright, but at least he'd finally said something to her. He was holding a cup of tea, with a piece of unbuttered toast cut in half and balanced on the saucer.

'Yes, please. Is that for me?'

'If you can keep it down,' he said.

She ignored the jibe, and sat up slowly while Tom went around the room closing the curtains. When he'd finished he sat down on the end of the couch and fixed her with a look.

'What the bloody hell did you think you were doing?'

Ellen felt herself going red, as she invariably did when he told her off.

'I don't know. I just . . . I got carried away, I suppose.'

It was on the tip of her tongue to ask him what he thought he was doing whenever he came home with a bit much under his belt, but she knew that would only make matters worse.

'I'm sorry, it won't happen again,' she said, aware that she'd never meant anything more sincerely in her life.

'I bloody well hope not,' Tom said. 'Who else was there?'

'Lorna, Milly, Avis and Val, and Dot, too, for a while.'

Tom frowned — he didn't approve of Valerie Mason. Stan was a reasonable sort of bloke, even if he did get a bit aggressive when he was on the booze, but Val could be a real shrew. 'I know,' he said, 'I was talking to Bert before.'

Ellen thought angrily, then why did you ask? She felt ghastly enough as it was without Tom interrogating her.

'Bloody lucky Jack came along and scraped you up,' he added, 'otherwise Christ knows what might have happened.'

They both knew nothing would have happened, apart from the possibility of her making an even bigger fool of herself, but that seemed beside the point as far as Tom was concerned.

'And as for the boys,' Tom went on, 'Neil was beside himself when I got home. Poor little bugger, having to pour his own mother into bed.'

Ellen winced; she would have to talk to Neil later on, on his own, and try to make it up to him. And Davey. She must have given them a hell of a fright.

They heard a knock then, and a familiar voice called out, 'Ellen? Thomas? Anybody home?'

Ellen closed her eyes in dismay — her mother.

Gloria marched into the sitting room and stood looking down at Ellen. Her mouth was doing its famous cat's-bum impersonation, and Ellen knew she was in for it.

'I hope you're proud of yourself, young lady,' Gloria said.

Ellen didn't respond, knowing from past experience that it would be useless to try to speak up for herself while her mother was winding up to one of her tirades.

'The whole town's talking about it, I've never felt so ashamed in my life!' Gloria went on loudly, her voice crashing into Ellen's skull like a hail of bullets.

'Probably not the whole town, Gloria,' Tom said. 'It's Saturday, not everyone will be up and about yet.'

Gloria turned on him. 'You know what the gossip's like out here, Thomas, they were talking about it at the shops just before.' She glared at Ellen. 'At the *shops*, Ellen!'

Ellen put her face in her hands; her headache was getting worse and she needed to go back to bed.

'Who was talking about it?' Tom demanded.

'Nora Bone, to start with.'

'Christ, it probably will be all over town, then, won't it?' Tom said, enjoying his mother-in-law's discomfort. 'Cup of tea? There's one in the pot.'

'Oh, go on then,' Gloria said, sighing ostentatiously and subsiding into a chair. 'I never thought I'd say this, Ellen, but this sort of behaviour suggests to me that you're turning out to be just like your father!'

'Oh, for God's sake, Mum, I am not.'

Tom headed for the kitchen.

'Yes, you are. What will everyone think?'

'How should I know, and why should I care?'

113

Ellen replied, borrowing one of Alf's favourite responses just to annoy her mother. She regarded her warily, waiting for what was sure to come next.

'You should care, Ellen. Where's your pride?'

'Still in Lorna's garden?'

There was the tiniest twitch at the corner of Gloria's mouth, but she stifled it before it could turn into a real smile.

Tom came back with Gloria's cup of tea.

'Ellen's having a lie-down now,' he said.

'Am I?' Ellen was surprised and grateful.

'Yes. And Gloria, the boys want you to go outside and have a look at their tree hut. You have to be impressed, it's taken them three weeks to build it.'

Gloria collected her cup and saucer and stood up. 'Your father's dropping in later, Ellen,' she said. 'He says he wants to congratulate you,' she added witheringly.

Unable to help himself, Tom laughed as he followed her out into the hall.

★ ★ ★

Grim news arrived several days later. Encouraged by the government, in particular Bill Sullivan, a scab port union had been organised at Whakatane. It was a blow to solidarity, and it sent ripples of unease and resentment through the heart of the TUC. On top of that Holland had come up with a plan, which he believed would tempt the striking unions in the FOL, at least, to return to work. He was desperate — the

114

unprecedented extent of this latest bout of industrial action was paralysing the country. He knew, too, that if the FOL accepted the conditions and went back, the watersiders would be more or less on their own. And so would the miners.

Against the recommendations of Labour Party leader Walter Nash, who was negotiating on behalf of the watersiders, Jock Barnes rejected the conditions. Fintan Walsh, Barnes' sworn rival, accepted them, and unions affiliated to the FOL began to return to work.

When Tom arrived home from his committee meeting and broke the news to Ellen, he was voicing the fears of thousands of strikers around the country: now that a crack had appeared in the dam, more and more unions would trickle back to work and the whole thing could eventually collapse.

He was still out of sorts on the following Saturday, as they walked down the street to the miners' hall for the St Patrick's Day dance. The boys were dressed from head to toe in green — or more correctly khaki, as the dye Ellen had used to transform their old shorts and shirts to a jaunty emerald hadn't taken very well. Ellen was also wearing green, but Tom had refused to join in and wore his usual white shirt and brown sports coat, saying he was buggered if he was prancing about like a bloody leprechaun after the government had done such a dirty on the Whakatane wharfies.

Ellen was wary about showing her face at the dance, worried that everyone might still be talking about her. They weren't, though, according to Milly, who had predicted that Ellen's fall from grace would be a one-day wonder. And apparently it was, because nobody had said anything about it when she'd arrived at the hall on Tuesday morning to pack and hand out the relief packages. She'd just got on with it, and so had everyone else.

But though the town might have forgotten about it, she hadn't. She hadn't seen Jack for an entire week, and had become convinced that he was avoiding her. She wouldn't be surprised if he was; she'd behaved terribly and her face still burned every time she thought about it. She would never, she'd decided, drink anything stronger than shandies again.

They were late, so the dance was well under way by the time they arrived. Vic Anscombe stood up and waved out to them, gesturing at the two empty chairs beside him. The boys raced off, looking for their friends. Everyone was here, except for Jack. And Lew Trask. Ellen's heart sank, and she told herself not to be such a fool.

When Bert offered to get her a shandy she accepted, then asked him where Dot was.

'At home, resting,' he said. 'She didn't want to come out. My mother's got the kids.'

Ellen looked at him, at his tired face and the dark bags under his eyes. 'She's really not well again, is she?'

Bert sat down. 'No, she's not.'

'Will it be a bad one, do you think?' Ellen asked.

Bert was silent for a moment. Then he said,

'She's not eating and she can't stop crying. It's been going on all week. It starts the minute she wakes up and goes on all day until she goes to bed again. She won't go out and she hides if anyone comes to the door.'

Ellen nodded; she'd gone over to visit two days ago and had seen Dot through the sitting room window sitting as still as a mouse on the couch, even though she'd knocked for ages.

'She won't even brush her hair any more,' Bert went on, 'or have a bath or get dressed. I had to wash her myself this morning, she was getting that whiffy.'

Shocked, Ellen looked at him as he fought back tears.

'But I had to come out tonight, Ellen. I can't sit and watch her like that twenty-four hours a day, I just can't.'

'Have you had the doctor in?' This was awful; she'd had no idea Dot was this bad.

'He was over yesterday.'

Ellen waited for him to go on, but he didn't. Finally, she asked, 'What did he say?'

Bert's mouth quivered, and for a moment she thought he might burst into tears in front of everyone. But instead he took a deep breath and looked her directly in the eye, the expression on his face a mixture of dignity, grief and resignation. 'He said she might have to go away, if she doesn't perk up soon.'

'Go away where?'

'Hospital. Tokanui, perhaps.'

Ellen drew in a sharp breath. Tokanui mental hospital?

'Just for a few months,' Bert said, 'just until she's back on her feet again. And only if she doesn't come right.'

'Oh, Bert.' Ellen felt tears stinging her own eyes. Suddenly, getting drunk and falling over in someone's garden didn't seem such a terrible thing to have to cope with after all. 'What can I do to help?'

He smiled gratefully. 'Nothing at the moment, thanks, Ellen, we're managing. Perhaps if we need someone to take the kids, say for a day or something like that? That would be good.'

'Oh, Bert, you know we'd have them. Overnight, too, if that's what you need.'

Bert patted her hand, as if she were the one needing consolation, not him. 'I know that, Ellen, you've always been a good friend to Dot. I'll get your shandy.'

As usual, the men were busy talking about the latest strike developments. Jack was conspicuous by his absence, to Ellen anyway. She wanted very much to ask where he was, but didn't. He wasn't at the dance, and that was that.

But half an hour later, suddenly he was there, sauntering casually up with his usual broad smile and his jacket slung over his shoulder. His hair was damp and curling up at the ends, as if he'd recently had a bath, and as he squeezed past her towards a vacant chair at the end of the table, she caught the faint smell of soap coming off him.

'You smell pretty,' Pat said as Jack sat down. 'Been having a nice long soak?'

'No, a short one. Needed it, though. Me and

118

Lew have just done that steer we got this morning. Big bastard it was, too, took us ages.'

Ellen had a sudden vision of Dot stumbling out to the toilet and being confronted with Lew and Jack up to their armpits in blood and animal parts.

'Not in Bert's shed!' she exclaimed.

'No,' Tom said, 'don't panic, at Lew's place.'

Ellen exhaled in relief, although she might have guessed that Bert wouldn't have allowed it.

She moved to sit with the women as the men talked on, raising their voices above the noise of the band — a three-piece this time, and evidently committed to playing Irish tunes. The children were making the most of the lively music, hurling themselves about in approximations of how they perceived Irish dancing should be done, and shrieking with laughter whenever one of them fell over, or let go during a hectic spin and went whirling out across the floor. Young Evan Paget banged into Nora Bone, who was almost sent flying, and received a clip across the ear from his father for it.

Ellen laughed at their antics along with everyone else, but all the time she was aware that Jack was sitting only feet away from her. And so was Tom. Was Jack watching her now? She dared not turn around to find out, and she knew she couldn't possibly summon the courage to move over and talk to him.

In the end he came to her, and asked her for a dance. He'd already been around the floor with Milly, and Lorna, and even Rhea, who was surprisingly graceful and light on her feet, and

119

Ellen wondered if he'd left her until last for a reason.

She accepted his hand and they moved onto the dance floor, keeping clear of the children who were still leaping about like dervishes.

'I thought you were avoiding me,' she said almost immediately, surprising herself.

He looked down at her. 'Why would I do that?'

'I haven't seen you all week. And I thought, after last Friday . . . '

'I've been out of town since Monday. I only got back this morning.'

Ellen stared at him; nobody had told her that. But then why would they?

'Where did you go?'

'Ohura. Pat decided it might be a good idea if I went down and had a yarn with the jokers I used to work with, find out what the story is with them, that sort of thing.'

'Oh,' Ellen said. She was such a conceited fool, thinking she mattered to him enough for him to deliberately avoid her. She looked down at the floor quickly, feeling her face grow hot.

'So why?' he said to the top of her head.

'Why what?'

'Why would I be avoiding you?'

Ellen hesitated, but only for a moment. 'Because I got drunk and you had to take me home and I vomited everywhere,' she said, glancing up at him. 'God, what on earth did you think of me?'

Jack threw back his head and laughed so hard that Ellen could see he had a back tooth missing.

Assuming he was laughing at her she pulled away, shrivelling inside with embarrassment.

He grasped her wrist and drew her back. 'No, Ellen, that didn't bother me. You were funny, though.'

'I'm glad you thought so. I, um, I didn't say anything to you, did I?'

'Such as?'

'Well, anything I shouldn't have said.'

'You did swear.'

'Did I?'

'Yes, quite impressively, too.'

'No, I didn't mean swearing. I meant anything, well, personal, about you. And me.' She flinched; this was *excruciating*.

He stopped dancing, and the couple behind them barrelled into him. With deliberate emphasis, he said, 'I think, Ellen, that if you had said anything like that, I would have remembered it.'

She stared at him, unable to break away from his gaze, and they stood toe-to-toe, motionless, while all around them couples danced and kids skittered about and the band bashed out a galloping version of 'The Banks of Roses'.

'Move,' she hissed.

'What?'

'Move! Keep dancing. Someone will notice.'

He took her meaning instantly, and stepped smoothly forward and into a turn. She let the pressure of his hand on her back guide her, but he was obviously distracted because they banged straight into someone else. Ellen turned to apologise and saw that it was Andrea Trask, glowering at her from beneath beautifully arched brows.

'I'm so sorry, Andrea,' she said. 'How clumsy of me.'

Andrea said nothing.

'It was my fault,' Jack insisted. 'I'm supposed to be leading. Sorry.'

Andrea smiled, a little soft one especially for Jack. 'I'll accept your apology if you promise to ask me for a dance,' she said, twirling a strand of her shining black hair around her finger so energetically that Ellen thought it might snap off.

Andrea's youthful dancing partner folded his arms and looked down at his shoes in resignation.

'I'd be delighted to dance with you, Andrea,' Jack replied, 'just as soon as I'm free.'

Andrea simpered at him again, shot a triumphant glance at Ellen and walked off, leaving her partner to trail along behind her.

Jack watched her go. 'Christ, she's a piece of work, that one.'

'You don't fancy her, then?'

'About as much as I fancy using my arm as a sprag.'

Ellen laughed; a sprag was a piece of timber used to jam into the spokes of a moving coal skip to slow it down.

When the next song ended he went off to fulfil his promise and Ellen sat down, her mood effervescent now with the knowledge that whatever she thought had gone wrong, or been ruined, or turned sour, hadn't.

'Have you just found a ten-pound note?' Milly asked.

'Sorry?'

'You look like the cat that got the cream.'

'Do I? No, it's just good to be out, that's all.'

Milly nodded. 'It is, isn't it? Everyone seems to be having a good time and to hell with the strike.'

'Well, St Patrick's Day only comes once a year.'

'Even though there's hardly any Paddies in Pukemiro,' Milly said with a giggle.

'Oh, I don't know, I think there's probably at least a drop of Irish blood in most of us. And what about the O'Malleys, they're first generation. And the Kennys. And anyway, does it matter? It's exactly what we need, don't you think? Everyone's letting their hair down.'

'Andrea Trask certainly is. Look at her over there with Jack.'

Ellen looked. Andrea had let her hair down, literally; it had been pinned up before but now it was swinging freely as she danced. But Ellen only smiled, because it didn't matter what Andrea Trask did now.

As usual she went home early with the boys, leaving Tom to sit with his mates and roar out the words to 'Dirty Old Town'.

He wasn't late home. She was still awake when he came in, and was pleased to see he was in a much better mood than the one he'd gone out in. She kissed him goodnight and lay beside him, listening to his breathing as it gradually slowed and he slid into sleep. But she remained awake

123

for some time, going over snatches of conversation, words and looks and touches, and trying to make some sense of what was happening to her.

★　★　★

The following fortnight brought nothing but more bad news. The emergency regulations were extended and Holland went on the radio appealing for scabs to join the proposed new unions at every port around the country. Worse, freezing workers at Westfield, Ocean Beach and Mataura went back to work, and so did drivers and cool-store workers in Dunedin.

Something else ominous was going on, too. After Barnes' refusal to accept Holland's plan, Prendiville and Crook had resigned from the negotiating committee of the United Mine Workers' Union and turned their backs on the watersiders. They'd refused, however, to step down from the miners' national council, despite rumblings from the rank and file that they should get out altogether, and were pushing for a secret ballot, which they maintained was official UMWU policy. Then Prendiville was spotted going around Huntly at night in a taxi, calling on opencast miners at their homes and talking to them, trying to get them to agree to vote in a secret ballot to return to work. Although the underground miners didn't think Prendiville's meddling would amount to much, it could potentially be quite dangerous and was something they would have to keep an eye on.

Then, on 29 March, the 1000 hydro workers

at Mangakino striking against the emergency regulations voted to go back to work, followed closely by most of the country's railwaymen. It was a devastating assault on the morale of the unions still standing firm.

But on the following evening, there was trouble much closer to home. Tom had returned from the Friday meeting in Auckland tired, short-tempered and despondent. The rain, which had been pelting down all day, had made his trip home miserable, and he'd eaten in silence, glaring through the kitchen window as if the wet were to blame for everything that was going bad.

Later, in bed, he lay on his back staring up at the ceiling until Ellen wondered if he would ever fall asleep. But he finally did, and then it started: the twitching and jerking, the mutterings and the sudden shouts that told her he was having one of his nightmares. A sharp smell began to come off him, and Ellen touched his chest to confirm what she already knew, that he was slippery with the sweat of pure fear. She sat up, wondering whether she should wake him, but sometimes it was best not to as hauling him out of his nightmares seemed to disorient him even more.

Then she heard the scream, short, sharp and eerily high-pitched, and it took her several seconds to realise that the sound hadn't come from Tom. It came again, and she turned her head to listen more closely. When it came a third time she threw back the covers, got out of bed and padded on bare feet across to the window. She pulled the curtain back. Outside the moon was half full and the rain looked like tiny pellets

125

of silver coming down from the sky.

And then she jerked back in shock — on Bert and Dot's back lawn lay a shape shrouded in white, like a bundle of soggy washing. It moved, and Ellen's hand flew to her mouth as she suddenly realised what it was. Dot was out there, in the rain, lying on the wet grass, screaming.

She ran back to the bed and shook Tom roughly. He yelled and lashed out at her, his forearm catching her across her neck and knocking her onto the floor. By the time she'd got back up he was sitting up and looking wildly around.

Dot screamed again.

Tom jumped. 'What the fuck was that?'

Ellen shoved her feet into a pair of shoes and yanked on a cardigan. 'It's Dot, she's outside in the rain.'

She hurried into the hall, stopping for a second to make sure the boys were still asleep, and ran through to the kitchen and out the back door. Lunging down the slippery steps, she crossed the soggy lawn to the narrow gap in the hedge that separated the Sisleys' property from their own. She turned sideways and scraped through.

Dot was on her hands and knees near the swing Bert had made for the kids when the second lot of twins had come along. Her cotton nightie was soaked and sticking to her thin body, and her hair was plastered to her scalp and across her face. Ellen thought she might be throwing up.

But when she got closer she saw that Dot

126

wasn't being sick; she was rocking backwards and forwards, her face only inches from the ground, sobbing with her mouth stretched wide open and her eyes staring wildly. Then she hurled herself down again and let out another scream, muffled this time by the wet grass.

Ellen crouched down and put her hand on Dot's sopping back, feeling the bones there beneath cold flesh, and a violent, spasmodic shaking.

'Dot, it's Ellen!'

There was no response. Then Tom was bending down beside her, rain running out of his hair and down his face. He hadn't stopped to put a shirt on and goosebumps dotted his wet skin.

'What's wrong with her?' He looked shocked.

'I don't know.'

Then Bert was suddenly there, in his pyjamas and bare feet. He fell on his knees beside his wife. 'I couldn't find her,' he cried, the panic in his voice raw. 'She wasn't in bed, and I couldn't find her. What's the matter with her? What's she *doing*?'

Tom pulled him away while Ellen remained crouching, stroking Dot's back over and over.

'Settle down, man,' Tom said, his hand on Bert's shoulder. 'Come on, we'll get the doctor.'

Bert didn't seem to hear. 'Is she hurt? Is she bleeding? I hid all the knives.'

Ellen felt her gorge rise at the thought that Dot might have harmed herself. Was she bleeding? It was so dark and wet she couldn't tell.

'Tom, help me turn her over.'

Dot didn't appear to be unconscious — she was whimpering and shaking her head slowly from side to side — but she didn't seem aware of what was happening, or even where she was.

While Bert stood watching, his face a picture of utter dismay, Tom rolled Dot gently over onto her back. Her nightie rode up and Ellen tugged it back down over her knees. As soon as Tom took his hands off her shoulders she curled into a tight little ball, but Ellen could see that there were no obvious dark patches on the whiteness of Dot's clothes or her skin. But she couldn't be sure; they would have to get her out of the rain for a good look.

A small voice called out, 'Dad?' and Bert looked up, covered his face with his hands and started to cry.

At the top of the steps to their house stood all five of his children, huddled close together, the bigger ones holding the hands of the little ones, their wan faces illuminated by the weak porch light.

Ellen swallowed around a hard, burning lump in her throat. This was terrible; even Tom, normally so practical and able, seemed stunned. And the children, she thought her heart might break at the sight of them.

'It's all right,' she called out. 'Go inside, go on!'

They stood staring a moment longer, then April began to shepherd them back into the house.

Ellen turned back to Bert. 'Help me get her inside. Can you go for the doctor, Tom?'

He nodded, and ducked back through the hedge to grab a shirt and his boots before he went down the street to bang on the doctor's door.

Bert lifted Dot in his arms and carried her up the steps, through the kitchen where the children stood in silence, and into the bedroom. He set her carefully on the rumpled bed and together he and Ellen began to strip off her soaked nightie, which was smeared with mud and covered with bits of grass. There was more mud caked under her fingernails, her skin was wet and cold and she was worryingly blue around the mouth, although she was still muttering incomprehensibly. Her eyes were closed now, as if she'd had enough of looking at whatever had finally pushed her over the edge, although beneath the lids her eyes were moving restlessly about. Ellen dried her off and pulled the covers up over her.

'Stay with her, Bert. I'll make us all a cup of tea.'

He nodded and sat down on the edge of the bed, one of Dot's limp hands between both of his, rubbing and rubbing the clammy skin as if he could somehow coax her back to normal just by doing that.

Dr Airey arrived ten minutes later, water dripping off his coat and the collar of his pyjama jacket poking out of the neck of his jumper. He removed his hat, tapped it briskly to get the last of the rainwater off, and set it on the table.

Tom asked April for a towel, and stood next to the coal range rubbing his wet hair vigorously as Dr Airey sat down and beckoned to the children.

The doctor knew the Sisley family well. The younger kids were probably too little to understand what was going on, although of course they were aware that their mother was often unwell, but he thought it important that they not feel frightened. Tom had told him they'd found Dot lying on the lawn in the rain screaming her head off, and in his books that would be enough to frighten anyone, child or adult.

The five of them shuffled over, April herding the others ahead of her, her hands protectively on the backs of the two youngest. Dr Airey sighed. Bert was a good man, a good provider and a caring father and husband, but it was clear that the eldest child, young though she was, had somewhere along the line taken upon herself the responsibility of looking after her siblings.

'Now,' he said, leaning forward in his chair. 'You know Mum's not feeling the best?'

They all nodded solemnly.

'She was in the rain, with no shoes on,' Robert, the boy from the younger set of twins, said. His thumb crept into his mouth.

'Was she? Fancy that!' the doctor said. 'Now, I need to have a little talk with Mum, to find out why she isn't feeling well, and then we'll decide what to do after that, shall we?'

Another round of nods.

Bert came out then, and stood waiting by the door into the hall.

Dr Airey said, 'In the meantime, why don't you ask Mrs McCabe to make you some hot cocoa?' He glanced at Ellen. 'Something to eat

130

wouldn't go amiss either. Something sweet.'

Ellen nodded and started looking through the kitchen cupboards for the baking tin.

'There aren't any,' Bert said, 'if it's biscuits you're looking for. Dot hasn't done any baking for a while.'

'Sugar or honey in the cocoa will do, and perhaps a sandwich,' the doctor said as he got to his feet.

Bert followed him out of the kitchen, and Ellen set about making hot drinks and jam sandwiches.

'Will you go and check on Neil and Davey?' she asked Tom. She inclined her head at the children, who had arranged themselves around the kitchen table. 'I think I should stay here for now.'

'Don't be long, though, will you?' he said.

'I'll try,' Ellen replied, although she was prepared to stay all night if she had to, and Tom knew it.

'Let me know what's happening, at least.'

She gave him a quick kiss. 'I will, don't worry.'

Bert was back out in less than fifteen minutes. He leaned against the bench and crossed his arms, and Ellen could see he was trying not to cry again. She said nothing, but simply waited until he was ready.

'He said there's nothing wrong with her physically as far as he can tell, except she's a bit thin,' he said finally. He drew in a deep breath, but even so his voice wobbled when he spoke again. 'He said she's had a major nervous breakdown.'

131

Ellen nodded, her hands warm around the cup of tea she was holding.

Bert turned around to stare through the darkened window at the rain. In a voice low enough for his children not to hear, he said, 'She has to go into hospital, tonight. Dr Airey says he doesn't think she's safe. He's going back to his house to ring an ambulance.'

'Bert, I'm so sorry. If there's anything we can do . . .'

'You've already done it. I don't know what would have happened if you and Tom hadn't been here.'

'You would have managed — you always do,' Ellen said.

Shaking his head slowly, like a man who can't quite believe what's happened to him, Bert said, 'I don't think so, not this time. She's never been this bad before. I just about shit myself when I woke up and found her gone. It's always been my worse nightmare, this.'

Ellen patted him on the shoulder. She wanted to give him a hug, but wasn't sure if it would be the right thing to do.

'They'll take good care of her, in the hospital.'

Bert looked at her. 'Will they? Do they really know how to fix this sort of thing?'

Ellen didn't have a clue. 'I know they'll look after her. They did last time, remember?'

'I know, but she was away for six months then. I don't want her gone that long again. Christ, I don't want her gone at all.'

'It's for the best, Bert. Dr Airey wouldn't send her there if he didn't think so,' Ellen said. She

132

tried to think of something else to say, something that would comfort him, but couldn't.

He blinked and wiped his nose on the back of his hand. 'I'll go with her tonight. I can't let her go all the way to Hamilton by herself. What if she wakes up and doesn't know where she is?' He looked over at his children. 'Christ, Ellen, what am I going to tell them?'

'The truth?'

He regarded her for a moment, then sat slowly down at the table. 'Kids?'

They waited expectantly, their faces filled with both trust and uncertainty.

'Mum has to go into hospital and I'm going with her.'

April put her finger in the bowl of her cocoa-stained teaspoon on the table and made the handle bob up and down. 'When?'

'Tonight, love. Soon.'

'Will she be home by the morning?'

Bert hesitated, and Ellen could see how much he wanted to say yes. 'No, I don't think so. Not tomorrow.'

Robert started to cry. Bert drew him onto his lap and rocked him in silence.

Ellen put her hand over her mouth to stifle her own tears, which she knew would only upset the kids even more. She dug the fingernails of her right hand into her palm to make doubly sure, then drew in a deep, steadying breath.

'I know!' she said. 'Why don't you kids all come and stay at our house tonight? You can bunk down in the sitting room, and then when Neil and Davey wake up in the morning you can

133

make pancakes for breakfast, with golden syrup. Would that be fun?'

Bert regarded her with such a look of gratitude that Ellen almost did cry. The four younger children perked up visibly, but April was watching her father.

'Is that what you want us to do, Dad?'

'I think it's for the best, love. For tonight anyway.'

'Can I come to the hospital?'

'No, love, hospital isn't the sort of place for little girls.'

For a moment April looked as though she was going to argue, then she turned away from him and said to the others, 'Come on, let's go and get our toothbrushes and some clothes.'

While they were getting ready, Ellen went in to see Dot. She was very pale and still, and for a heart-stopping second Ellen thought she might be dead. Then her chest rose and she realised she was sleeping.

'I gave her something to calm her down,' Dr Airey said. He was packing his bag. 'She should be out for quite a while.'

'Will she remember what happened tonight?'

The doctor shrugged. 'Possibly not. I don't know. I'm going home now to phone for an ambulance, then I'll come back. I'll go with them to the hospital and make sure she gets settled in properly.'

Ellen asked, 'How long do you think she might be in there?'

'I'm afraid I don't know that either. Arrangements will need to be made for someone

134

to look after the children.'

'Bert and his mother will do that. I suppose it's a good thing they're on strike at the moment and he's at home.' She bent down and tucked the covers more snugly around Dot's shoulders. 'Do you think . . . well, could it have been worry about the strike that brought it on?'

Dr Airey sighed and rubbed his chin. 'Perhaps. It's very difficult to say. Worry can do funny things to people, Ellen.' He regarded her wearily, as if he'd seen far too much of this sort of thing. 'And so can loneliness, and disappointment. And boredom.'

Ellen didn't meet his eyes.

6

Tom was chopping wood on the back lawn. Normally they used coal in the range, but there wasn't any at the moment — ironically because he and the other miners were refusing to dig it out. He was sweating beneath his singlet, and out of sorts, and worried.

Prendiville had had his secret ballot, but none of the local underground unions had taken part — they'd voted unanimously against it a few days ago at a meeting at the town hall. The opencasters had gone along with it, though, and unbelievably, they'd voted to go back. Or at least a lot of them had; there were still a few who were refusing to break the strike. It had been a huge shock, although they hadn't returned to work yet.

In the past, the opencast miners in the area had approached the Waikato Miners' Union several times and asked to join. But the central council had turned them down repeatedly, maintaining that most of them sat on their arses in trucks all day and weren't real miners anyway. So they'd formed their own Opencast Miners' Union, although they did have a couple of delegates on the central council. Like everyone else, Tom had always assumed that the opencasters would either stand loyal during any

136

industrial action, or if they didn't, that the underground unions would be able to knock them into line without too much trouble. But obviously they'd been wrong about that, badly wrong.

They'd overlooked one thing — opencast miners could be replaced much more readily than underground miners, because the levels of skill required were quite different, so the opencast men had more to lose, and would lose it sooner, if they refused to go back to work. And because they had their own union, they also had their own mandate, and they'd used it.

Tom swore and spat on the ground. He had good mates in the opencast mines, at Kimihia and around Rotowaro, and had no desire to fall out with them. But if they persisted with going back to work, he would hound them and harass them, and even beat the living shit out of them if he had to, because no honest union man tolerated a scab under any circumstances. Scabs were the scourge of militant unionism, wreckers of solidarity and thieves of workers' rights. And once a scab, always a scab.

He laid his axe on the ground and sat down on the chopping block; he was knackered too, after the business with Dot the other night. He'd been having one of his nightmares and had nearly crapped himself when Ellen had woken him up. He'd belted her one as well and still felt terrible about it, even though he'd apologised and she'd said not to worry. And he was sorry, because he'd never raised a hand to her before and couldn't understand why it had happened this time, even if he had been half asleep. He loved her dearly, although maybe he didn't tell her that quite as much as he should, and would rather cut his own arm off than deliberately hurt her. He'd worked bloody hard to make her his, and every day since had been worth it. She was beautiful and bright and soft and warm, she washed and cooked and cleaned for him, she'd given him two fine sons, she understood him and she didn't care that he wasn't perfect, like when he woke up screaming and sweating and crying out that he was shit-scared.

His nightmares were awful. The accident had happened in 1947, just after the Easter pay strike, but he was still dreaming about it as though it had only been last week. It drained him, and always set him thinking again about what had happened, which he dreaded. He'd discovered that he wasn't the man he'd always believed himself to be, and that had been worse than any of the rest of it put together.

★ ★ ★

1947

'Hey, Tom, where did we get?'

Tom was walking towards the pithead after the cavil, the drawing of lots every three months to determine where each pair of men would be working underground. It was a fair system, because it ensured that the bosses couldn't allocate the worst sections to the men they didn't like, and vice versa. And there were some fairly

138

shitty places: faces on slopes that meant you'd be shovelling uphill all day, or sections where the coal was harder than it was anywhere else.

He looked over his shoulder to see his partner, Johnno Batten, running to catch up, the battery and gas mask on his work belt bouncing, rucksack swinging over one shoulder, and his hard hat with the lamp on the front jammed low on his forehead. As usual he'd been stuck in the shithouse for ages, and had missed the cavil.

'North, that new section Doug and Wobbly started.'

'Shit,' Johnno said, and slowed down to a walk. 'Doug reckons it's been working a bit on and off.'

Tom shrugged. He and Johnno had been partners on the coal for nearly two years now, and both had been around long enough to know that when a section was 'working' — if the roof was creaking and moving — it didn't always mean it was going to come in.

He checked his watch: five to eight. There was no point going down five minutes early — their shift was from eight in the morning until three in the afternoon, and not a second longer, but, if they could get away with it, hopefully shorter — so he squatted down near the shadowed mouth of the mine and rolled a smoke. It would be his last until he came up again at the end of the day, as you couldn't smoke underground because of the gas. Johnno hunkered down and joined him.

The rest of the shift milled about the entrance smoking, laughing and coughing in the early

139

autumn air, until, exactly on the dot of eight, they headed into the drive, down into the warm dark throat of the mine towards the dimly gleaming coal.

It took them about twenty-five minutes to walk down to where they were currently working, each step taking them further and further away from the sunlight. Johnno whistled tunelessly almost the whole way, until someone finally told him to shut it.

Tom said, 'You're a box of birds today.'

Joe Takoko, a big Maori with the solid arms and shoulders of a seasoned miner, said, 'Yeah, all shit and feathers,' and everyone laughed.

'It's my birthday,' Johnno said. 'Donna's got a treat for me tonight.'

'Your annual root?' suggested Red Canning, Joe Takoko's partner.

More laughter.

'No, better than that,' Johnno said. 'Roast pork, with peas and roast potatoes and cabbage, and apple cobbler for pud.' He paused. 'With cream.'

Joe stopped and made a show of patting his pockets. 'Bugger, I seem to have misplaced my dinner invitation.'

'Fuck off,' Johnno said, laughing. 'It's *my* birthday.'

'Twenty-one again, eh?' Vic Anscombe said.

'Nearly. Thirty-three.'

Tom made a mental note to come up with some sort of prank to play on Johnno before the day was out, to mark the momentous occasion.

The tunnel gradually flattened out and they

came to the layby where they stored their heavy gear between shifts. Then, pair by pair, the men began to head off to their new sections.

Tom and Johnno's was at the furthest edge of the working face, and wrapped in total blackness except for the narrow, conical beams of yellow light from the lamps mounted on their hats. It was within hearing distance of adjacent sections, however, and as they settled down to start work they could hear the others doing the same.

The coal was mined using the bord and pillar method, and excavated in a pattern of grids about a chain square. Bords, or underground roads, were tunnelled into the solid coal and the coal removed, then cross-cuts driven at right angles to the bords, forming a pillar of coal in the centre. The pillar was then mined out as well, where possible, leaving the roof held up by nothing except the wooden props the miners put in as they excavated. It could be extremely dangerous work because the props didn't always hold.

The mine covered a large area underground, but only part of it was actively mined at any one time. On their way down to work every day the men passed the sealed entrances to goafs — areas that had been worked out and closed off permanently to stop gas leaking into the rest of the mine, and to minimise the risk and impact of fire. A barrier of brattice cloth nailed to boards divided the main tunnel, with fresh air travelling down into the mine on one side of the cloth, and the foul air being sucked out along the other side by an extractor fan on the surface.

141

The main tunnel also housed the endless rope, the mechanised, perpetually moving line that took empty skips into the mine and hauled full skips out, where they would be spragged at the surface to slow them down, unclipped and redirected to the screens. Underground, near the working coal faces, the empty skips were taken off the rope and pushed by hand by truckers along temporary rails to where the miners blasted and shovelled, to be filled then pushed back to the rope, clipped on again and sent back to the surface. Tom had done his time as a trucker, and still couldn't decide which was the harder job — shovelling coal or pushing the bloody skips.

He felt something strike his hat. He looked up and noted with satisfaction that the roof was dripping; good, they might be on wet time today and finish their shift a good hour earlier than normal.

'Water,' he said to Johnno, who glanced up and nodded.

Johnno cocked his head and listened for several seconds. 'Can you hear that?'

Tom stood still and closed his eyes. He could hear it, too; the constant creaking, scratching and faraway grinding that indicated that the fireclay above them was on the move. It was nothing to worry about, though — nothing solid was trickling down, and the faintness of the noise suggested that not much was shifting in their immediate area.

'She'll be right,' he said eventually. 'We'll put in some extra timbers before we blast.'

Johnno nodded. They'd both experienced this eerie shifting of the earth before and there'd always been plenty of time to get out before anything happened.

They erected three stout props, then used their pickaxes to chisel out a cut in the coal face six feet high, three feet deep and a foot wide, to give the coal somewhere to go when it was blown. Without the cut, nothing would move. Then, using three different-sized hand drills, Johnno carefully bored a six-foot hole at an angle into the cut where the powder and detonator would go. They couldn't fire their own shots because only the deputy had a shot-firer's ticket, and if it wasn't to his liking, if it was too tight or too short, he'd piss off again until it had been done properly and they'd get behind and lose that much of the day's pay. A mis-shot also wasted time. The good thing about being paid by the ton was that on a productive day you got good money, but on the other hand, on a slow day you didn't.

Tom opened his powder tin and pushed five plugs, plus one extra because the coal was so hard, into the back of the hole with the tip of the six-foot drill, then followed that with a detonator, making sure that the wires were left hanging out. Then he slid in the dummies — rolled-up newspapers filled with damp clay — which he tamped in firmly.

They were sitting down when the deputy arrived. Tom's singlet was soggy with sweat already, and he stank. So did Johnno. So did everyone working underground. The air and the temperature weren't too bad in the main tunnel, but beyond that, in the sections where the air didn't flow as readily, it was almost unbearably hot and stuffy. Tom was well used to it by now, but he was always grateful walking back up out of the mine at the end of a shift when he felt the first tickles of cool, fresh air on his face, drying the sweat there and setting the coal dust on his skin and in his ears and in the corners of his mouth and eyes.

'Happy birthday,' the deputy, Sean McGinty, said to Johnno.

'Ta.'

McGinty winked. 'No one played any nasty tricks on you yet?'

Johnno grinned. 'Not yet.'

'Well, don't worry, it's only half past nine.'

Johnno rolled his eyes. Without a doubt, something would be done to him today; miners were very keen on their practical jokes. And he should know, because he was responsible for a lot of them.

McGinty moved over to the hole in the cut, had a quick squint down it and nodded. 'That'll do.'

He attached the detonator wires to his cable and began backing away, playing out the cable as he went. 'Away you go,' he said to Tom and Johnno, and the three of them retreated along the bord until they were some distance away from the coal face and around a corner so they could no longer see it.

'Ready?' McGinty asked.

Tom and Johnno nodded, and jammed their

fingers in their ears. McGinty crouched over the battery and fired the shot. There was a muffled whump, felt rather than heard, and a moment later a haze of thick coal dust billowed from the direction of the face, settled silently over them and temporarily obscured even the light from their lamps.

When it cleared, McGinty hoicked and spat out a gob of dirty phlegm. 'Fucking hell, you jokers, how much powder did you put in?'

Tom shrugged. He and Johnno always put in as much as they could get away with; the more coal that came down the better, as far as they were concerned.

They trudged back to the face, and nodded in appreciation at the small mountain of coal that had spilled out onto the ground.

'Right,' McGinty said. 'I'll be back after crib time to do the next one.'

As he left, his boots squelching in the slurry of coal and mud underfoot, a trucker arrived pushing an empty skip and Tom and Johnno set about filling it with the loose coal.

They stopped for smoko, then worked solidly until five minutes to twelve, at which time they swapped their shovels for crib tins and headed back towards the layby in the main tunnel where they habitually ate their lunch.

Doug Walmsley and Wobbly Minogue, so named because of what happened to him whenever he consumed more than three bottles of beer, were already there, and Tom could see Joe Takoko and Red Canning also emerging from the gloom.

Tom dropped his crib tin on the filthy table with a clatter. Doug was reading the paper and Wobbly was opening his tin with extreme caution. Tom grinned. Poor old Wobbly still hadn't recovered from a recent incident when Johnno had nailed his crib tin to the table while he was off having a leak, one six-inch nail straight through the middle of his packet of sandwiches, another through his apple and a third through a slab of fly-cemetery cake lovingly baked by Mrs Wobbly. Johnno had declared it was revenge for the fact that every day without fail Wobbly had tinned sardines on his sandwiches, which, according to Johnno, stank out the entire mine.

It had been a good prank, but not as good as the one with Gerry Latimer's teeth. Old Gerry, retired now, had been the owner of a set of false teeth he couldn't eat with. One crib time he'd taken them out and left them on the table and, when he wasn't looking, Johnno pinched them. After several days of listening to Gerry moan on about his lost teeth, Johnno told him his uncle had died recently but had left behind a perfectly good, hardly used set of dentures. Did Gerry want to give them a go? Gerry, who didn't want to fork out for a new set if he didn't have to, said yes, and Johnno duly brought to work the teeth he'd pinched some days earlier. Gerry shoved them in his gob, moved his jaws around a bit, snapped them open and shut, and declared it a miracle because they fitted him even better than his old teeth. He was still telling people in the pub what an amazing coincidence it was that

Johnno Batten's uncle had had exactly the same-shaped mouth as he did.

Red Canning sat down and opened his own tin.

'What have you got?' Johnno asked.

Red peeked between two pieces of bread. 'Ham and mustard.'

'Not bad,' Johnno said. They did this every crib time, although they didn't need to ask; their sense of smell down the mine was so acute they could easily have guessed.

'What about you, Joe?'

'Boil-up.'

Another redundant question. Joe Takoko always had boil-up, which he brought in a thermos and ate with great hunks of buttered Maori bread.

They munched in silence for several minutes.

Johnno wiped his mouth on the back of his hand. 'The roof's still working in our new section.'

Doug nodded. 'Been doing that for weeks.'

'Anything solid come down when you were there?'

'No,' Doug replied, opening a stack of home-made peanut brownies wrapped in paper, 'just water. You want to be careful, though, eh?' he added. 'Keep your eyes and ears open.'

'Always do,' Tom said.

At twelve-thirty the men packed up and went back to work, making sure to leave nothing behind that might bring the rats. Tom wanted a leak but couldn't be bothered traipsing all the way back to the shithouse off the main tunnel. It

147

stank anyway and was enough to make a man spew, so he unbuttoned his flies and pissed against the wall. Up ahead of him in the darkness he could hear Johnno whistling again, then getting stuck into the loose coal.

It was the noise of Johnno's shovelling that prevented Tom, when he started work again himself, from picking up the steady whisper of a small trickle of coal and dirt coming down from the roof behind one of the props. There was another trickle three or four feet further along, and neither of them heard that one either.

Just before two o'clock Johnno stopped and leaned on his shovel.

'We aren't going to finish this lot before McGinty comes back.'

Tom straightened up. 'We might. We'll get another blast in before knock-off, anyway.'

Tom nodded, took his hat off and scratched vigorously at the itchy, sweaty skin on his scalp.

As he held the hat upside-down, a fist-sized lump of coal from the roof dropped neatly into it.

They both froze.

Another lump came down, then another, then a shower of it. They only managed a few panicked steps before the whole lot came in.

★   ★   ★

Tom cautiously tried to move his head, and found to his profound relief that he could. He still had his hat on, and the lamp was still going, but the hat felt like it was on sideways. There was

148

grit clogging his mouth and nostrils and something heavy across his back, but nothing hurt much, except for a vicious stinging above his left eye.

'Johnno?'

There was no answer, except for the final, uneasy whispers of the coal and rock slowly settling, and a deep, unpleasant rasping noise.

He was lying face down, with one arm folded beneath him. He got his elbow out, pushed himself up and rolled over as far as he could. The weight on his back slid off and he discovered that he could now turn himself all the way over. There was a hollow clang as his hat banged against something solid — the skip.

He turned his hat back the right way and saw in the light of his lamp that above him the roof had dropped about five feet, low enough now to prevent him from standing up straight. Some of the props had come down across the skip and were holding up sections of the roof, but surrounding him, within touching distance if he reached out with his boot, were nothing but walls of shattered coal and broken slabs of fireclay.

That liquid, rasping noise again. He sat up and as he did a trickle ran down his face and across his upper lip, and he tasted the warm tang of blood. He thought his nose might be bleeding too, and blew it into his hand. His lamp revealed a thick blob of dark blood made stringy with snot, and he wiped it off on his trousers.

'Johnno?' he said again.

This time there was a low grunt, slightly to his left.

Tom got to his knees and began to scrabble at the loose coal next to the skip until he found a boot, its toe pointing up.

It took him several minutes to very carefully clear the rubble and heavy timber off Johnno, who was lying on his back with his head under the skip, his shovel half-buried next to him. Tom ducked his own head and looked; Johnno's eyes beneath the brim of his hat were open and he was blinking slowly.

'Fucking hell, Johnno,' Tom said.

Johnno lifted his hand but didn't say anything.

'I'm going to pull you out, all right?' Tom said, and crawled on his knees back to Johnno's feet. 'Ready?'

There was no answer so he grabbed the other man's ankles and began to pull, gently at first, then with more urgency as he envisioned the roof suddenly dropping again and crushing the skip with Johnno's head still under it.

Johnno came out, his hat falling off and his trousers riding up as he slid forward, revealing pale hairy legs and a shallow cut across his right shin. He grunted, just once.

Tom shuffled closer again. There was bright red blood on Johnno's teeth and now his eyes were rolling back in his head.

Tom yelled in his face, 'Johnno, we'll be out in a minute! Stay awake!'

Johnno's eyes opened again. He focused on Tom, coughed wetly and licked his dusty, bloody lips. 'I've had it, Tom.'

'Fuck off, we'll be out of here soon, they're probably digging already.'

Johnno coughed again, and bloody spittle flew up into Tom's face.

'Where does it hurt?'

'Chest.'

Tom had already noticed the odd, flat shape of Johnno's front as he'd pulled him out from under the skip, although he'd tried not to. Reluctantly, he slowly pulled up his friend's singlet.

There was a deep depression in Johnno's chest all the way down almost to the base of his ribs. Three of his lower ribs were coming through the skin, but the rest was more or less intact. But it was purple, almost black, the whole lot, and Tom winced at the thought of the damage that must lie under it.

'I'm fucked, aren't I?' Johnno said.

'You're a bit flat, mate, but you're not fucked. They'll be here soon, don't you worry.'

Johnno coughed a third time, then let out a long, gargling burp followed by a gout of blood that surged out of his mouth and down over his chin and neck.

Tom leapt back in fright. Red bubbles were coming out of Johnno's nose now, as well, and it sounded like he was drowning.

Suddenly he gripped Tom's wrist, and in his eyes was a calm and terrible acceptance. 'Tell Donna I love her. Tell her I'm sorry about the birthday tea.'

And then his hand relaxed and let go.

Tom sat back on his heels, stunned.

'Hey!' he said, and gave Johnno's shoulder a gentle nudge.

Nothing.

He put his ear down to the ruined chest and listened for ages, but heard and felt nothing.

'Johnno, you bullshitter, wake up.'

But Johnno didn't wake up, and Tom suddenly knew he wasn't going to.

He remained sitting for some minutes, staring blankly at the body of his dead friend. Then an image slid into his mind of Johnno running to catch up, like he did almost every morning, his gear flapping and bouncing, a big smile on his face and a last-one-before-we-go-down smoke jammed behind his ear.

Tom lay down on his side in the coal. There was a roaring in his ears and he put his hands over them to try and stop it, but it wouldn't go away. It was getting louder and louder and it took him some moments to realise what it was. It was the sound of utter silence.

Then, suddenly, it was filled with the noise of his own weeping. He was glad there was no one to hear it because he was howling like a kid, real sobs that came wrenching up out of his chest and tore at his throat and made his nose bleed again.

He was crying for Johnno, and he was grateful for it, because now there was a sharp little worm of panic stirring deep in his belly, and he was starting to suspect that if it got out — if he let it out — he might not be able to squash it back down again. Being underground was one thing, and it had never particularly bothered him, but now he was beginning to feel as though he was *in* the ground, actually part of it, and that was something different altogether.

He didn't know how long he went on like that, but after a while he sat up, took several deep, shaky breaths and wiped his snotty face on his arm. He checked his watch but it had stopped, at six minutes before two. How long had it been since the roof had come in? Not long, surely. Or had it had been hours? Perhaps he'd been knocked out by the fall. But either way, he was sure someone would get to them soon — they would never just leave them down here.

Did Ellen know yet? Probably. Whenever there was an accident underground news of it spread straight away. She might even be standing up there now, not right at the mine entrance because she wouldn't want to get in the way, but not far away. Donna Batten was probably there too, and the wives and family of anyone else who might not have been accounted for.

Leaning over Johnno's body, Tom switched off the lamp on his hat. His eyes were still open. Tom closed them very gently and mouthed the first few lines of the Lord's Prayer, but he hadn't been to church for bloody years and couldn't remember most of it.

What the hell was he going to say to Donna?

A fresh trickle of sweat ran down his neck. It was getting stuffier and hotter and it occurred to him, for the first time, that he might not get the opportunity to say anything to Donna if he didn't get out soon, because the air in here wasn't going to last for ever.

153

He turned over onto his knees and began to crawl into a narrow gap beside the skip; unless it had moved drastically when the roof had come in, he was pretty sure he was moving along the floor of the bore that eventually led out to the main tunnel.

But before he'd even gone a yard he came up against another wall of coal and fireclay. And he'd known he would too, because he'd seen it in the light of his lamp, but he had to try. Unless he was going the wrong way and was looking at the rubble-covered coal face he and Johnno had been working before the roof had come in.

He thought for a moment — how the bloody hell could he tell? Then it came to him; there was always a big cross painted on one end of the skips, and it should be on the end pointing away from the coal face because of the way the truckers brought them in. Except this end of the skip was buried in bloody coal and rubbish.

The gap he was in was too small for him to turn around, so he crawled backwards to the other end of the skip, but there was nothing painted on it. Well, fuck, that was a relief, at least he was going in the right direction. He looked around and spotted Johnno's shovel. Right, he'd start digging himself out with that, and when he'd gone a reasonable distance he'd come back and get Johnno, and then dig some more and move him along and dig some more until they were both out.

Dragging the shovel between his knees he shuffled back to the other end of the skip. The roof was down here to the same height that it was near the coal face, so a couple of timbers were probably still holding it up. If he started digging at the rubble at the top of the heap, he should be able to go some distance forward without getting into any more trouble.

But he didn't have a hope in hell of swinging the shovel the way he normally did, so he held the handle with both hands down near the base and began scraping at the rubble. It occurred to him that he'd have to move everything he took out back into the bigger space at the other end of the skip, or he wouldn't be able to get past it to go back for Johnno, but that was all right; working out how best to do that would keep his mind busy.

It was while he was scraping away, steadily but slowly so he wouldn't use up more air than he needed to, that it also occurred to him that if the others were coming for them, why wasn't there any noise? Why couldn't he hear digging, or voices, on the other side?

Surely the whole fucking lot hadn't come in?

The absolute horror of the idea stopped him dead, and that was a mistake because the worm rushed out of him then, *burst* out, and he screamed so loudly he almost deafened himself. He screamed again until he thought he might faint, then bent over with his fists shoved against his mouth and little black dots floating before his eyes.

Abandoning the shovel, he started digging furiously with his hands, tearing his fingers until they bled and not even noticing, thinking that if he could just get a tiny bit closer they might be

155

able to hear him. He scraped and gouged and dug until his hands went numb, and when he uncovered a good-sized rock he wedged the shovel under it and leaned on it as hard as he could. The wooden handle creaked under the strain and the rock ground grittily against the rubble surrounding it, but it finally eased free and rolled out, coming to rest against Tom's knees.

There was another creaking noise then, but louder. He looked up and realised, too late, what he'd done.

The roof above him dropped another two feet, bringing with it a dislodged timber that crashed down onto his right arm with a sickening thud. He heard the bone snap, and then he felt it, a deep, slow burn of pain moving along the length of his arm. Cursing, he drew it against his chest and felt the broken ends of bone grinding together. But there were no bits poking through the skin, thank Christ.

And at least it had stopped his mad panic.

The pain drove everything from his mind for some minutes, but when it cleared he started to weep again with utter frustration and dismay. How the hell was he going to dig himself out with only one good arm?

Something bounced off his hat, and that gave him the impetus to shuffle slowly backwards on his knees towards the other end of the skip, holding his injured arm firmly against his chest. When he reached the space where Johnno lay, he turned around and settled himself in a sitting position with his back against the metal side of the skip, the safest place, he thought, if the roof dropped again.

He looked around for his rucksack but couldn't see it, and felt like crying about that, too; there had been a piece of cake in his crib tin, an apple and a bottle of water. Thinking about it, he was suddenly overwhelmed by a raging thirst. But there was nothing to drink down here, except his own piss and he didn't think he was quite that desperate yet.

He sat with his knees raised and the elbow of his broken arm cradled in his other hand. If he didn't move, it didn't hurt as much. He wondered whether he should take off his belt and strap the arm to his chest, but decided against it; if he had to move quickly for any reason he'd be buggered.

So he sat there, his head tilted back against the skip and his lamp illuminating the roof, staring at the rubble and coal balanced up there, waiting to crash down on him and bury him once and for all.

It was getting even warmer, and he fancied that the air in the small space was harder to breathe now, growing stale, running out. And was that methane or carbon monoxide he could smell? Couldn't be, they were both odourless by themselves. He tried to slow his breathing, counting ten seconds between each inhalation, but the dizziness it brought on panicked him and he reverted to breathing normally.

And all the time he was listening. For the telltale trickle that might signal another fall, but most of all for the sound of pickaxes and perhaps

157

even muffled calls, yelling out for him to hold on, they were coming, they would be there soon. But he heard nothing, only the faint whistling of air going in and out of his own blocked nose.

The panic rushed through him again, snatching him up and dragging him along mercilessly, and he bent over, willing himself not to scream. His heart was thudding and his brain felt as though it was inflating to a size that would any second now burst his skull. A scream was clawing its way up his throat and he clamped his good hand over his mouth, stifling the sound and squashing it back down to a series of sharp whimpers. The panic, he knew, would get him before anything else did, if he couldn't control it.

But, Christ, he was scared. He had never really been frightened of anything in his life and he'd taken pride in that, but he was shitting himself now. He was so scared he felt like vomiting. The realisation that he was capable of feeling such stark terror terrified him even more, and, under that was the niggling suspicion that he was a fool for having gone through his life ever thinking anything else. He wasn't Tom McCabe, tough coalminer and staunch union man, he was Tom McCabe, insubstantial, frightened and ordinary.

Tom McCabe, trapped in a small, airless hole deep underground.

★　★　★

He dozed. He dozed, and he thought he might have dreamed.

He saw his boys when they'd been born,

158

cuddly, milky-smelling little bundles with hair that stood straight up, and he saw them now: Neil with his bright, five-year-old face that was starting to look so much like Ellen's, and Davey with his chubby toddler's hands and legs, following him out the gate in the mornings clamouring to be allowed to go to work with him.

And he saw Ellen — his generous, sensible, thoughtful Ellen — standing at the kitchen sink up to her elbows in soap bubbles, tilting her cheek so he could kiss her goodbye. She'd been beautiful when they were courting. She had the sort of hair that picked up the sun and the most velvety dark-blue eyes that sparkled when she laughed, and even when she was only thinking about laughing. Her lovely firm body had given him aching balls for eighteen months until just before they were married and she'd finally let him go all the way, but the wait had been worth it. His mates had all said he was a lucky bastard, but he'd never needed to be told that.

And then the boys had come along, and he'd been so pleased and so proud he'd thought that nothing better could ever happen to him. Watching them growing up had almost made up for everything he feared he might have missed by not going off to war. And through all of it Ellen hadn't changed; she was just as beautiful now as she had ever been.

Tom woke up with a start, his arse numb, his arm throbbing and a dragging feeling deep in his guts. He grimaced as he realised what it was — he needed a crap. It stank in here, too. Was gas seeping in, or was it him?

He heard himself giggle. Ellen hated him farting, and she hated even more his response whenever either of the boys did it. 'Magnificent' he would say, with a short but heartfelt round of applause, and the boys would titter themselves silly. Ellen never did, though; she believed farting should be confined strictly to the outhouse or, but only if very short, outside the back door.

'Oh, Ellen,' he said out loud, 'I'll never fart again if I get out of here alive.'

His bowel cramped again, and he realised he was going to shit himself if he didn't do something about it soon.

Moving with exaggerated care to avoid bumping his arm, he leaned his weight on his left arm, drew his legs up and pushed himself onto his knees. He was getting very stiff now, and the pain in his arm seemed to be spreading. There was an almighty great bruise coming out from his shoulder to halfway down his forearm as well.

He fumbled with the buttons on his trousers and had them halfway down to his knees before he stopped; if he was destined to die down here, then the least he could do for himself was make sure he didn't have to share his last hours with a turd, even if it was his.

Hitching his pants back up, he shuffled on his knees as far away from the skip as he could get, which wasn't very far at all, and began to dig a hole in the loose coal and rubbish on the ground. When he judged it to be of a satisfactory depth, he pulled his trousers down and, his good hand out for support against the rubble that

160

made up the walls of his tomb, manoeuvred himself over it. As he crouched there, his bowels emptying, he reflected that this might be the last crap he ever had. In the confined space, the smell was terrible.

By the time he finished, he was laughing. There was no toilet paper, of course, so he yanked his pants up without wiping himself. He was still giggling as he scraped coal into the hole, covering it over completely.

Then he was crying again. He moved back to the skip and looked at his watch, seeing through the salty blur of his tears that it was still six minutes before two. He was unbearably thirsty, his throat raw with coal dust, and suddenly very, very tired.

He knew now that he was going to die down here, so there was no point in trying to keep the panic down any longer. But when he took a deep breath and relaxed, giving it ample opportunity to rise up, nothing happened. There was no wild lurching of his stomach, no uncontrollable racing of his heart, no ear-shattering screams. Instead, he stared at the opposite wall in the flickering, dying light of his lamp for a while, then drifted off to sleep again.

This time he dreamed about Johnno. Johnno with beer running down his chin as he raced to drink his last pints before the pub shut; Johnno dragging on one of his racehorse fags and adding to the fug in the workingmen's club room they called the Smoke Box because it had no windows; Johnno being Santa Claus at the last union Christmas party, giving out presents to all

161

the kids and little Willie Takoko complaining that his cotton-wool beard ponged of beer; Johnno sitting up, the shattered ribs in his caved-in chest crackling, and telling him he was going to die in this shitty little coal hole if he didn't pull his finger out and do something soon.

Tom sat up, the weight of his dreaming making his movements ponderous.

'What?'

Johnno's voice came again. A little clogged and muffled as though he'd just eaten several Weetbix without milk, or as if his mouth was filled with dried and flaking blood, but it was definitely his voice.

'I said pull your finger out, Tom, or you'll die in here. Come on, wake up.'

Feeling the bones in his own neck creaking, Tom turned his head very slowly in Johnno's direction.

Johnno was indeed sitting up, his broken ribs protruding forward and down over his lap, as if some sort of heavy, messy weight was pushing them out.

Tom sighed. 'I can't, Johnno, I'm too tired.'

Johnno pointed a dirty finger at him. 'I gave you a message for Donna.'

'I know, but I'm fucked.'

'Fucked, my arse,' Johnno rasped, and something dark flew out of his mouth. 'We're mates and you have to give Donna my message.'

'I'll do what I can,' Tom said. He sighed again and closed his eyes, but Johnno didn't go away.

'You'll do better than that, Tom,' he said,

louder now. 'You'll hang on until they get to you.'

'Yeah,' Tom mumbled, wishing Johnno would lie down and go back to being dead.

'*Wake up!*' Johnno bellowed. There was another dry snapping sound from his chest.

In his dream, Tom jerked upright again.

Johnno glared at him. 'If you don't stay awake I'll bring the roof in. I can do that, you know. I'm dead and when you're dead you can do what you fucking well like.'

'Oh, piss off,' Tom said. 'Leave me alone.'

'Right, I'm bringing the roof in,' Johnno said.

Three muffled thuds came one after the other, then an abrupt trickle of coal followed by the clatter of something bigger coming down. Tom woke up. The skip shuddered against his back, and he ducked his head under his good arm to shield himself.

There was a loud scraping noise and the skip moved again, then someone was shining a light in his face.

Tom raised his hand against the harsh glare.

It was Sean McGinty.

7

1951

Tom got to his feet again, positioned another piece of wood on the chopping block and spat on his hands.

He had given Johnno's message to Donna, and she'd cried so hard he hadn't known where to look. Ellen had said she was crying from gratitude, that he'd delivered the one final message from her husband she'd most wanted to hear, but it hadn't made Tom feel any better. Not at the time, anyway. Johnno's funeral had been huge, and the local mines had closed for the day to allow the miners to attend. Two weeks after he was buried, Donna Batten packed up her kids and moved to Te Awamutu to live with her parents, saying she would miss everyone in Pukemiro, but would never be coming back if it meant she could stop her sons from ever going to work on the coal.

Tom had had an almighty headache from the lack of oxygen for a couple of days after they'd dug him out, and a line of black stitches down his temple, and he'd been on the funds for six weeks until his arm mended, but he'd gone back to work after that. He didn't tell any of the other jokers, though, about how he'd almost turned and run that first day he went back into the main tunnel, how he'd had to force himself to put one

164

foot in front of the other until he'd made himself go right down to the coal face. The section where he and Johnno had been working had been closed off because it was too unstable, so he was spared having to go back there. But there was plenty more coal, and he'd been partnered with Frank Paget and had been working beside him ever since.

His fear in those first few weeks had been immense, and he'd told no one about it, except Ellen. She'd understood, or seemed to anyway, and had held him night after night in bed, stroking his back and his face and his arms, talking quietly and calmly until his fear started to ebb away, until he was finally able to go underground without his hands shaking as though he was an old man and his throat so dry he had to sip water almost constantly. She hadn't told anyone else, and she'd promised him she never would — not Milly, not Gloria (thank Christ) and not even Alf. And he loved her even more, for letting him keep his dignity.

Eventually his fear had subsided to not much more than a dull niggle, although it left him with a much greater respect for being underground, and a heightened awareness of his own safety and that of others. The experience had knocked the cockiness out of him but it had also made him a better miner, and subsequently a bloody determined union delegate. The nightmares still plagued him from time to time, especially when he was unsettled, but only he and Ellen knew about those.

He was unsettled now, although a lot calmer

than he had been; when he'd first heard that the opencasters had voted to go back to work, he'd been absolutely ropable. His heart thudded even now when he thought about it. Pack of scabbing bastards, even the blokes he'd counted as his mates. They hadn't actually gone back yet, but when they did, there'd be trouble.

He picked up his axe, swung it viciously and missed his piece of wood completely as someone yelled out to him.

It was Pat, trotting around the side of the house, looking as if he'd just sprinted all the way up Joseph Street. He bent over with his hands on his knees.

'What's happened?' Tom said, tensing.

'The opencasters — the cunts are going back tomorrow!'

'Back to work?'

'No, back to the bloody pub.' Pat straightened up, his face like thunder. 'Of course back to work!'

Tom put his axe down. 'Who said?'

'Lorna Anscombe was visiting in town this morning and Andy Sceats' mother was there . . . '

'Andy Sceats out at Kimihia opencast?'

Pat nodded. ' . . . and she told Lorna that Andy and the rest of them are going back tomorrow. There's bloody cops all over town, too. I've called a meeting at Bob Amon's place in an hour. We've got to stop them.'

Tom nodded. 'I'll let Bert and Frank know. What about the others?'

'I'll see them on my way home.' Pat checked

his watch. 'An hour, all right? Four o'clock.'

Tom reached for the shirt he'd draped over the hedge. There were seven surface mines in the Waikato, producing nearly half the district's coal, and the opencasters' return to work could bring the underground miners down in a matter of weeks.

'We'll be there.'

*   *   *

It was decided that they'd go out first thing the next morning to confront the delegates at each of the opencast mines, to try to talk them out of starting work. Tom and Pat were allocated Phil Burns, the union president out at Kimihia.

They arrived at the mine office at twenty to eight. Hardly anyone was in sight but it was clear that preparations were under way for resuming work. They spotted Phil Burns walking away from the office and nabbed him as he hurried over to one of the trucks waiting idle near the lip of the pit.

'Phil? Excuse me,' Pat called, 'can we have a word?'

Tom knew he was doing his best to be polite, because they'd agreed at yesterday's meeting that nothing would be gained by being aggressive, but it was clear that Pat was finding it bloody difficult.

Phil Burns stopped. His hands were jammed in his jacket pockets and Tom could see by the hunch of his shoulders he'd been expecting this,

167

but was perhaps hoping he might have got away with it. He turned slowly around.

'Look, Phil,' Pat said, moving closer, 'why don't we sit down over a cuppa and talk about this, eh?'

Phil's face was pale and his eyes had dark bags under them, as if he hadn't had much sleep in the last few days.

'I don't want a cuppa, Pat, and I don't want to talk,' he said. 'We've made our decision.'

Tom said, 'Just a couple of minutes, Phil, what harm can it do?'

'Bloody plenty,' Phil said.

Pat shrugged. 'We'll talk out here then,' he said, ferreting in his pocket for his smokes.

He offered the tin of rollies to Phil, who shook his head. Pat shrugged, handed one to Tom and lit one himself.

'We hear you're starting back today.'

'That's right,' Phil said.

Tom said, 'Have you thought about what that will mean, Phil?'

Phil took a step to the left. 'Of course we have — it means we'll be able to feed our kids again and pay the bloody rent.'

'That's right,' Pat said, smoke curling out of his mouth as he spoke. 'It also means you'll be scabbing, every bloody one of you.'

Phil stared at him.

'And that means,' Pat went on, his voice hard now, 'that you'll never work in this fucking town again.'

'Steady on,' Tom murmured. There was no point in winding Phil Burns up more than was

168

necessary; he knew full well what scabbing would mean.

Pat changed tack. 'You look like you need a decent night's kip. Conscience bothering you? Up a bit late last night, were you?'

'No.'

'That's not what we heard, Phil,' Tom said. 'We heard you had the cops at your place half the night.'

And so Phil had, according to the gossip.

'Have a nice chat, did you?' Pat asked.

Phil didn't reply. Instead, he turned and made a dash for the office and was up the steps and inside before Pat and Tom realised what he was doing. He shut the door behind him and Tom thought he might have locked it. They moved closer and watched him through the window, standing at the desk now and talking to someone on the telephone.

'Who do you think he's ringing?'

Tom said, 'One guess.'

Pat snorted. 'If it's only bloody old Sid Ballantyne it'll be a slap on the hand and a 'Now then, lads', and when he's buggered off we'll just come back and have another go.'

Inside the office Phil hung up the phone and came to the window. He opened it a fraction and announced, 'I've rung the police, they'll be here in a minute. I'd piss off if I were you.'

Pat raised his hands in bemusement. 'We aren't breaking any laws.'

'You're both trespassing.'

'Oh, for fuck's sake,' Pat said. He parked his backside on the office steps and got his cigarette tin out again. 'We're not going anywhere, Phil, until you've come to your senses.'

By this time a small crowd had gathered. Tom could see the faces of men he knew well, men he liked and had shared beers with in the pub and the workingmen's club. This morning, though, they wouldn't, or couldn't, look him in the eye.

Phil hung out of the window again and waved the crowd away. 'Go on, you lot, start work, show's over.'

As the men began to disperse, Pat leapt to his feet. 'The show is *not* over!' he barked. 'You'll regret this! You'll be branded as scabs for the rest of your lives, and then how will you feed your kids and pay your bills, eh, tell me that?'

Heads down, the men kept walking, but Pat and Tom didn't see them — they were too busy eyeing the three black Plymouth sedans driving at speed through the mine gates.

The front car stopped some yards from the office, and Sid Ballantyne, Huntly's sociable and generally lenient police sergeant of some years, got out. Pat relaxed visibly and took several steps towards him.

But before he could say anything, another policeman, his helmet under his arm, unfolded himself from the passenger seat, and three more climbed out of the back. Then the other two cars emptied. In all there were fourteen cops: Pat and Tom were outnumbered and they knew it.

The officer from the passenger seat called over

to Phil Burns, 'Is this them?'

Phil nodded, and Sid Ballantyne stepped back, giving Pat and Tom a look that was both resigned and regretful.

The officer wedged his helmet on his head and said, 'If you two don't get off this property in five minutes, I'll arrest you for trespass and jail you. Go on, hop it.'

Pat stared at the man for a long, tense moment, then turned away.

'Come on,' he said to Tom, 'there's not much else we can do here.' Then, to the onlookers who had gravitated back again as soon as the police cars arrived, he declared, 'We won't forget this, you know. Your cards are marked and we won't forget it.'

The cop took a step closer. 'Are you threatening these men?'

'No, officer,' Pat said, 'I'm just giving them some good advice.'

And he and Tom walked out through the mine gates, unaccompanied and with their heads held high, knowing in their hearts that this particular battle of the campaign had been lost.

★ ★ ★

Over the next ten days, the mood of the community changed.

The *People's Voice* issued a list of names of all the men who were scabbing, and more than one underground miner cut it out for future reference. The word scab was splashed across the homes of opencasters and on nearby telegraph

171

poles, and several families reported that their vehicles had been interfered with and livestock stolen.

Dozens of extra police had been brought into Huntly and were staying at the pub, and a twenty-four-hour police guard was placed on all opencast mines and the trains that serviced them. When they weren't doing that, the cops were patrolling the streets of Huntly day and night on foot or in their lumbering Plymouths, streets that remained lit throughout the hours of darkness. The big black cars were also seen cruising slowly around Pukemiro, and at Glen Afton and Rotowaro, all communities where known strike leaders lived. Twice now Ellen had had to pull Neil and Davey off the couch in the sitting room as they stood waving cheekily through the window at the police car parked across the street, its occupants watching and waiting in silence. The presence of the police was oppressive, and a miasma of gloom, resentment and bitterness was beginning to settle over the district.

But there was good news, too. Miners at Kamo finally joined the strike, and on 5 April a national strike committee was formed from the rank and file of the Waikato, Taranaki and West Coast coalminers' unions. The meeting was held in Wellington and although none of the Pukemiro union officials went, Bob Amon did and was elected onto the committee. Prendiville's fervent efforts to get the underground miners to take part in the secret ballot had been the final insult for many, and a new committee, divorced from the national council of the UMWU and therefore Prendiville and Crook, seemed the only solution. The old UMWU was now in tatters, but it was clear that the new committee had the mandate of the majority of the underground miners. It was a relief to regional union officials especially, as they were now back in a position of control and the strike looked certain to continue. They had held on now for six weeks, and still saw no reason to return to work before the watersiders had negotiated a satisfactory outcome, and while the emergency regulations were still in force.

But life was getting more and more difficult. Money was coming from various sources, including via a very convoluted and shady trans-Tasman arrangement with sympathetic trade unions in Australia, but it wasn't stretching far enough and most families had come to depend on the food parcels distributed every week. Ellen and Tom certainly had, in a desperate effort to conserve the little money they still possessed so they could pay their mortgage. It wasn't enough, though, what was in the parcels, certainly not for larger families anyway, and Ellen thanked God she had her vegetable garden. Each week they received six pounds of meat or fish, a variety of whatever vegetables came from the market, two pounds of butter, half a pound of tea, enough loaves of bread for the week and a portion of any fruit that might be available. Honey was also bought in bulk, as a substitute for sugar, which no one could get anywhere in the country because supplies had dried up as a result of the strike.

Tom had stopped complaining about getting cheese in his sandwiches as there wasn't any now, unless Ellen got a tiny bit on credit from Fred Hollis. But the boys never stopped moaning about the monotony of the meals she served up to them, and received several clips across the ear from Tom for doing so. From time to time she felt like smacking them herself; she made a real effort to prepare appetising food with what she had, but more often than not the result was uninspiring.

One morning at the breakfast table Tom lost his temper. It wasn't Davey's fault — none of this was the children's fault — but he did start it with his incessant whining. Unlike Neil, he wasn't quite old enough to read the signs from his father that he was going too far.

It started when Ellen put a plate of porridge in front of him. The oats had been a gift from Milly, whose mother had bought her a large sackful to help out, and Ellen had been very grateful for her friend's generosity.

Davey wasn't grateful at all.

'I don't like porridge,' he said, shoving the plate away so the milk on it slopped out onto the tablecloth.

Ellen moved the plate back in front of him, and blotted up the spilt milk with a tea towel. 'Come on, love, it's good for you.'

'I don't like it!'

'You have to eat something before school.'

'No, I don't.'

'Yes, you do. Come on, I'll put some honey on

174

it if you like. You like honey, don't you?'

Tom was looking up from his own plate of porridge now, watching Davey with eyes that were just beginning to narrow.

Davey blurted, 'I hate honey!' and put his hands over his face.

This wasn't true, and Ellen knew it: Davey would have honey on every single thing he ate if he could get away with it.

A silence developed that began to stretch on and on.

Ellen sighed. 'What do you want then?'

Davey's hands crept into his lap. 'Kornies.'

Tom very deliberately set his spoon down across his plate, perfectly balancing the handle on the edge so it wouldn't flip up and make a mess.

Neil lowered his own spoon and leaned as far back in his chair as he could get.

'You want Kornies, do you?' Tom said.

'Yes.'

'And why do you want Kornies, Davey? You've got perfectly good porridge right there in front of you.'

Ellen looked uneasily from Tom across to Davey, then back at Tom again.

'Kornies have got cards in,' Davey said.

Tom leaned forward. 'What sort of cards?'

'Colour ones, of dogs.'

'Really?' Tom said, as if this was the most interesting thing he'd heard all year.

Ellen could see what was coming, and for a moment she hated Tom for being so bloody cruel.

'Yes, and there's two cards in the big boxes, and you can get an album to put them in. You send away!' Davey's eyes were shining now.

'Mmm,' Tom said, pretending to consider the idea. 'And you think your mother should go down to the shop and get a box of these Kornies so you can have the dog cards?'

Davey nodded, but there was a hint of wariness in his face now. He looked quickly at Neil, and then at Ellen.

Neil got up from his chair and Tom snapped, 'Sit down, boy!'

'Tom,' Ellen warned, 'let it go.'

Tom ignored her. 'And what do you think your mother should use to pay for these Kornies, eh? Buttons? Marbles?' he demanded, his voice rising.

Davey said, 'Trevor Quinn's allowed them. He showed me at school. He's got an Alsatian and a husky.'

Ellen closed her eyes. This was the worst thing Davey could have said: Trevor Quinn's father was one of the opencast miners who had gone back to work.

Tom banged both hands down on the table, spilling everyone's porridge and making them all jump. 'Trevor Quinn's got them, has he? Well, fancy that! And do you know *why* he's got them?'

Davey shook his head from side to side, eyes wide with fright now.

'Well, I'll tell you why, Davey. It's because his father's a bloody scab, that's why! A disloyal, cheating, thieving bloody *scab*!'

'Tom! That's enough!' Ellen cried.

Tom picked up his spoon and shook it at Davey, so that drops of congealing porridge flew off it in all directions. 'And when you get to school this morning you can tell Trevor Quinn he can stick his dog cards up his arse, and after that you're not to speak to him ever again, do you hear me? Never!'

Davey burst into loud sobs. Ellen pulled his chair out from the table with him still on it, then took hold of his upper arm and steered him towards the back door.

As she gently pushed him outside, she said over her shoulder, 'Neil, take Davey over to Milly's. Tell her Dad and I are having a talk, then go to school when it's time, all right?'

Neil stood up smartly, more than happy to be getting away from his father, at least for now.

'What about our lunch?'

'I'll bring it to school. Go on, off you go.'

When they'd gone, Neil leading a still-bawling Davey by the hand down the steps, Ellen turned to face Tom. There were spots of bright colour high on her cheeks.

'You big bloody bully,' she said.

Tom put the heels of his palms in his eyes and rubbed. 'Oh, shut up, woman.'

'What a rotten thing to do, Tom!'

'He was getting on my nerves.'

'He only wants to collect something,' Ellen snapped. 'He's only a little boy, for God's sake.'

'He wants to collect something we can't fucking afford.'

'You didn't have to go on about the Quinn boy like that.'

'I did. Davey has to learn, Ellen. Sandy Quinn is a scab, and scabs don't deserve the time of day.'

'Yes, that's Sandy Quinn, but what have his kids got to do with it?'

Tom crossed his arms. 'Everything. An apple never falls far from the tree.'

Ellen shook her head in absolute frustration. 'Oh, for Christ's sake, Tom, I've never heard anything so bloody ridiculous in all my life!'

'Haven't you?'

'No, I haven't. They're just kids!'

'Then why are they punching the shit out of each other?'

'What?'

'At the school, there's fights just about every day, according to Ted Carlyle.'

Ellen sat down. Ted Carlyle was the headmaster at Pukemiro school, and he'd certainly never mentioned anything to her about fights.

'Involving our boys?' she asked.

'Well, Neil.'

'Neil's being beaten up?' Ellen was aghast.

Tom was quiet for a moment, then he said, 'No, Neil's doing the beating.'

Ellen looked at him properly then, and saw something she didn't like at all; across his face was an unmistakeable expression of pride.

'Our son's a bully?'

'No, our son's sticking up for his principles.'

'What principles? He's nine years old!'

178

'He knows a scab when he sees one.'

Ellen was so angry she couldn't sit still. She marched over to the sink and turned on the tap to fill the kettle, except that she turned it too hard and water exploded out of the sink and all over the bench and up the window.

She spun around. 'And you think that's all right, do you, our son beating up other children? I suppose you told him what a good little bloke he was for doing it?'

'No, I didn't. But I can't stop it if I'm not there, can I?'

Tears were brimming in Ellen's eyes now, and she blinked hard.

Tom saw, and relented slightly. 'Do you want me to go over to the school and see if I can sort it out?'

'Well, it certainly wouldn't do any harm. And talk to him about it, Tom, tell him it's wrong.'

'All right, if that's what you want.'

She nodded. She did want that, but she realised she wanted something else, too. She hadn't seen Jack for days and she had a sudden and overwhelming need to be near him. Not to touch him or anything like that, but just to see his smile and hear his voice. Jack didn't yell or bang tables or wave spoons around; Jack was calm and everything about him was soothing. And he listened.

She glanced apprehensively at Tom, who was stretched back in his chair now with his long legs thrust under the table, anger gone, waiting for his cup of tea. Was this the right time to tell him what she wanted to do? She put the kettle on the range and sat down.

'Tom?'

He raised his eyebrows.

'We won't be able to make the mortgage repayments next week,' she said. He didn't look surprised. 'So we'll have to get some money from somewhere else to cover it.'

'I know,' he said, 'I've been thinking about that.'

Her pulse raced as she allowed herself to think, just for a second, that he might have had the same idea as her.

But then he said, 'I think we should borrow the money off the mine, and pay the bank off.'

Her heart sank. 'From Pukemiro Collieries? With their interest rates?'

Tom plonked his elbows on the table. 'I know it's highway robbery, but we wouldn't have to pay anything at all then, until I go back to work.' She started to speak but he held up his hand. 'No, listen to me, Ellen, it would be better than losing the house, wouldn't it?'

'Yes, but why are we going to lose the house? Have you talked to the bank about what they might be able to do?'

'What, like put the payments on hold?'

'Something like that, yes.'

'No, I haven't.'

'Well, why not?'

He didn't answer, so she said it again. Then the kettle whistled and she got up to make the tea.

Eventually, he said, 'It would be like begging, like asking for credit but worse.'

Ellen didn't even turn around. She was the one who'd been asking for credit lately — Tom had never asked for credit in his life.

'If we went to the Collieries,' he went on, 'we could do it quietly. Bernie Tompkins in the pay office is a good bloke, he could sort it and then no one would even have to know, only him and us.'

'And all the Pukemiro Collieries bosses.'

'No, he said it doesn't work like that. He manages the loan details himself.'

Ellen did turn to look at him then. 'So you've already talked to him about it?'

'Only over a beer.'

'And what happens when you do go back to work? The repayments will be double, and so will the interest.'

'I'll do extra shifts.'

Ellen set the teapot on the table, but she didn't sit down this time.

'This is about your precious bloody pride, isn't it? You don't want anyone to know we can't pay our mortgage. Not unlike just about everyone else in this town at the moment, I might add.'

'You can add what you like, but no, it's not about my pride. It's business.'

'Then why can't I go to my parents for the money? Dad's already said to talk to him if we get stuck.'

'We're not borrowing money off your parents.'

Ellen knew that what Tom meant was he wasn't borrowing money off Gloria, because he couldn't bear her satisfaction at the fact that he

181

couldn't provide for her daughter and grandchildren.

'But Dad said we wouldn't even have to pay interest, that we could just pay them back when we could.'

Tom stood up. 'I said we're not borrowing money off your parents.'

'But Tom . . .'

'I said no, Ellen, and that's the end of it!' And he slammed out of the kitchen, banging the back door behind him.

★　★　★

He wanted sex that night, and Ellen suspected it might have been an attempt to say sorry for his obstinacy. But although she might have accepted an apology, she certainly didn't feel like having him grunting away on top of her, so she pleaded a headache, curled up and pretended to be asleep.

But by the following morning she was clear about one thing at least. Tom would hate it, but she would be the one doing the borrowing, so that was just too bad. She hadn't believed when the strike had first started that losing their home could be a real possibility, but things were different now. She was reasonably confident that the bank wouldn't foreclose on their mortgage, although she could be completely wrong about that, especially if the strike continued for much longer. But even if it only went on for another month or so, they still couldn't manage and she knew there would be financial penalties for postponing the repayments. They might even be as crippling as what the Collieries would charge. Tom was naïve to think that any deal he did with the mines would be any more of a secret than one with the bank, even if Bernie Tompkins was a good bloke, and she was still angry at him for letting his pride run off with his common sense.

She decided to visit her parents early, before her father had had a chance to disappear into town, and was glad she did, because Alf was sitting on the steps with his hat already on, having a last cup of tea before walking over to Pukemiro Junction to catch the train.

'Hello, petal,' he said, his weathered face lighting up. 'You're looking radiant as usual. How are those fine grandsons of mine?'

'Oh, they're good,' Ellen said as she sat down next to him. The wood was damp under her backside, but she didn't bother moving.

'Come to see your mum?'

'No, I've come to see both of you, actually.'

'Oh dear, that sounds ominous,' Alf replied, although his eyes were twinkling.

'Not really. Is Mum in?'

Alf shook his head solemnly. 'No, she's gone to Hamilton to order a new tiara for the next royal visit.'

Ellen looked at him, then burst into giggles. 'Oh, Dad, you're terrible.'

'I try, love. Yes, she's home.'

'Good. I wanted to talk to you both about . . . well, can you remember what you said about helping us out?'

She thought it wise to ask, because Alf didn't

always remember some of the things he said when he'd been drinking.

'Financially, you mean?'

Ellen nodded.

'Yes, petal, I do.'

'Well, I think we might need to take you up on the offer. If it's still open, that is.'

'Oh, it's still open, don't you worry about that. Hang on, I'll get your mother.'

Alf hoisted himself off the steps, wincing at the arthritic pain in his lower back — the curse of the retired miner — and went inside, yelling for Gloria. Ellen followed him into the kitchen.

Her mother appeared a minute later. 'Hello, dear,' she said as she pecked Ellen on the cheek.

'Our lovely daughter has come to talk to us about something,' Alf announced.

'Have you? Well, come through to the lounge, love, you know we don't receive visitors in here.'

Alf sat down deliberately at the kitchen table.

'Alf!' Gloria snapped.

'Gloria,' Alf said.

Ellen rolled her eyes. 'Stop it, you two.'

'Sit down, petal, and you too, Gloria,' Alf said. 'This is family business and we don't need any silly bloody airs for family business.'

Reluctantly, Gloria sat.

Without preliminary, Alf said, 'Ellen and Tom are in the shit.'

'Well, no, Dad, we're not in the shit, not quite.'

'It's your mortgage, isn't it?' Gloria said. 'I told you this strike would bring nothing but trouble.'

184

'Taiho, Gloria,' Alf said, 'let the girl speak.'

Ellen thought for a moment. She disagreed very much with what Tom wanted to do, but she didn't want to admit it to her mother because, his pride aside, she was convinced he thought he was doing the right thing for his family.

'We haven't got the money to pay it, Mum, and Tom thinks we'd be better off borrowing it from the mines then paying them back after he's gone back to work.'

Gloria snorted. 'Yes, that would be the financially sensible thing to do, wouldn't it, repay debt with even more debt?'

Ellen ignored her sarcasm. 'But I'm not sure that's the best way to go about it, so I was wondering if you and Dad might be able to give us a hand. Even a little bit would really help.'

Alf said, 'How much do you need?'

'I don't know,' Ellen said. She hadn't actually thought that far ahead.

Alf glanced across the table at Gloria. She nodded.

'Well, let's work it out, then, shall we?' he said.

He got up and rummaged through a drawer until he found a pencil and a writing pad, then returned to his chair.

'How much do you pay the bank a month?'

Ellen told him, and he jotted down a series of figures. When he'd finished he underlined the bottom number and pushed the pad over to Ellen.

'Will this be enough?'

She looked at it, then at him, then down at the pad again. 'But this is enough for six months!'

'Petal, you might need it for six months.'

'Oh, Christ, Dad, surely not!' Ellen exclaimed.

Alf and Gloria looked at each other, alarmed at the sudden note of desperation in their daughter's voice.

'Take it, dear, I'll write you a cheque now,' Gloria said, and patted Ellen's hand comfortingly. 'Then you can go into town and get it all sorted out today.'

Ellen felt like crying, so she did.

Alf looked on with tears in his own eyes. He cleared his throat. 'Does Tom know about this?'

'No, but I'll have to tell him, I suppose.'

'Why don't you bank it first, and then tell him?' Gloria suggested.

Ellen looked her mother for signs of sarcasm, but there weren't any.

'I mean it,' Gloria said. 'I know I've said often enough he's not the man I wanted you to marry, but you did marry him, and he does what he can, I know that. But he has his pride, like they all do,' she added, 'so just do it, then tell him afterwards when it's too late. Not a lot he can do about it then.'

She went off then to fetch the chequebook, which she hid from Alf so he wouldn't get any ideas about taking it into town on one of his jaunts.

When she came back, Ellen was laughing at another of his dreadful jokes. She stood quietly in the shadow of the hall and watched them, the father and the daughter, and wondered how a woman was ever supposed to know whether even half the decisions she made over her lifetime were the right ones.

Ellen went into town with Alf on the train, sitting next to him on the hard seat just as she had when she'd been a little girl. The whole family had been in the habit of going into town on Saturday mornings then, dressed up in their best clothes with her mother making a day of it, window-shopping and treating her and Hazel to a cake each in the tearooms, while her father invariably wandered off to the pub. Huntly had changed a lot since then, had grown and modernised, but it was still a coal town and that was exactly what Ellen loved about it.

There were no miners heading back into town as the day shift hadn't ended yet, so Ellen and Alf had the car almost to themselves. After three this afternoon, it would be packed with miners travelling home to Huntly, all smelling of soap from the mine bathhouses. But now there were only a handful of women going into town to do their shopping or run errands, or perhaps just to visit friends or family. Ellen was tempted to hang her head out the window to smell the bush and the coal smoke as the train rattled through the lush, green countryside, but knew from experience that she'd get smuts all over her face and have to spend ages trying to rub them off.

The train stopped several times, at Rotowaro then at the siding at Renown Collieries, then at Mahuta followed by Weaver's Crossing, then finally steamed over the rail and traffic bridge across the Waikato River into Huntly. They got off at the railway station, Alf kissing Ellen on the nose before heading for the pub, and Ellen went up the main street to the bank.

Now that she was in town with her parents' cheque folded carefully in her bag, she felt suddenly uneasy, worried about Tom. This was the first time she'd ever made a major decision concerning their financial affairs without him, and although she knew in her heart that she was doing the right thing, she was still worried about what he'd say. He'd be angry, and insulted too probably. But would he be hurt? The thought that he might be made her feel a little bit sick.

She paused in the doorway of the bank, smoothed her hair back nervously, took a deep breath and went inside.

8

Tom wasn't as angry as she'd imagined he might be — mainly, she suspected, because she'd only accepted enough money from her parents to cover six months, and not the entire sum of their mortgage. He vowed, however, that they would pay it all back to the last penny as soon as he started back at work.

And on the Friday, after his trip to Auckland, he came home in a good mood. He also brought home a present for Davey; probably, Ellen suspected, as a gesture to make up for scaring the wits out of him the other morning at the breakfast table.

She and the boys gathered around as Tom set the large box he was carrying on the table, opened it with a theatrical flourish and beckoned Neil and Davey to come closer and have a look.

They did, and Ellen couldn't help smiling as their eyes almost popped out of their heads, and at the look of delighted satisfaction on Tom's face.

'What is it?' she asked.

'A bird!' Davey exclaimed.

'And not just any bird,' Tom said, thoroughly enjoying himself. 'It's a parrot, an African Grey. Apparently.'

Ellen had to have a look. She peered into the box and there it was: a parrot about twelve inches high with a pale-grey head, a hooked black beak, dark-grey wings and startlingly crimson tail feathers. It was staring grumpily up at her through round, golden eyes, moving from foot to foot and looking as though it very much wanted to be somewhere else. It had also decorated the bottom of the box with a liberal carpet of droppings.

'How old is it?' she asked.

Tom had his hand in the box and was extending one finger towards the bird. 'Only young, about eighteen months, I think,' he said. The parrot snaked its head out and bit him. 'Ow, shit!' he yelped, and whipped his hand smartly out of the way. 'Little bastard!'

'Little bastard!' someone repeated.

'Neil,' Ellen warned.

'I didn't say it!' Neil said, aghast. 'It was the parrot!'

Ellen glanced at Tom, and they both looked down at the bird.

It gazed back at them, and said conversationally, 'Wanna root?'

Davey gasped, and clapped his hands over his mouth to stifle his giggles.

'Tom,' Ellen said after a moment, 'where, exactly, did you get it?'

'One of the jokers at the meeting was giving it away. I thought Davey might like it.'

'Is it mine?' Davey squealed in delight. He ran around the table and hugged Tom around the waist. 'Thanks, Dad, I've *always* wanted a parrot!'

Tom patted the top of his son's head, while at the same time avoiding Ellen's eye.

190

Oh, God, she thought, remembering reading somewhere that parrots could live for up to fifty years. 'Why was this joker giving it away, do you know?'

'Er, I'm not sure,' Tom said.

'Well, I don't know what it's going to live in.'

Tom brightened. 'No, I got a cage as well, it came with it. Hang on.' He went out to the porch and returned a moment later with a large metal birdcage complete with swing, a bell and two feeding dishes. 'The bloke I got it off said it was compliments of the house.'

'I'll bet he did,' Ellen said.

'Can we put it in?' Davey asked.

Tom reached into the box, carefully avoiding the parrot's beak this time, and grabbed it. 'Open the cage,' he ordered.

It was all going smoothly until he passed the bird through the door of the cage, but as soon as it realised what was happening, it began to scream at the top of its voice.

'Bloody hell,' Tom said, flicking the cage door shut and putting his hands over his ears.

'Bloody hell!' the parrot shrieked. 'Bloody hell, bloody hell!'

'I don't think it likes it in there,' Neil said.

As if to corroborate Neil's observation, the parrot backed up in the cage, stuck its tail through the bars and crapped copiously onto the table.

'Oh, for God's sake,' Ellen said. 'Davey, go and get some newspaper.'

'Why do I have to?'

'Because it's your parrot.'

Davey pulled a face but went off anyway. By the time he came back, the parrot had settled down. Ellen had discovered that if she moved slowly so she didn't startle it, she could put her finger through the bars and scratch the back of its head. It was leaning against the side of the cage now, extending its neck so she could reach better.

'Is it a boy or a girl?' Neil asked.

'A boy, I think,' Tom said, 'and I believe he's taken a fancy to you, Ellen.'

'No, I think he's just feeling more secure.' She leaned closer to the cage. 'How are you feeling now, parrot?'

'Not bad,' it replied.

They all looked at each other in amazement.

'Can it really understand what we're saying?' Davey asked, incredulous.

'I wouldn't think so, son,' Tom said. 'They're not the brightest, parrots, they just repeat what they hear.'

The parrot said, 'Cheeky bastard,' and moved to the opposite side of the cage.

Ellen burst out laughing. 'Are you sure about that?'

Tom shrugged. 'Rude little bugger,' he said. Then he smirked wickedly. 'I know, let's call him Fintan, shall we?'

Davey put his face close to the cage. 'Hello, Fintan the Parrot.'

'Fuck off,' Fintan said.

Davey recoiled. 'That wasn't very nice. Mum, he swore at me.'

'Right, he can go out on the back porch for

192

now, I think,' Ellen declared. 'At least until he's cleaned up his manners.'

Tom picked up the cage and carried it outside, Fintan squawking loudly. As he set the cage down on the porch, the parrot began to stamp his clawed feet and flap his wings vigorously, thrusting his beak through the bars.

'I think he wants to get out,' Davey said, recovered now from Fintan's grievous insult. 'He might want to stretch his legs, or go to the toilet again.'

'Well, he's not going to,' Tom said. 'He'll be off like a robber's dog.'

'No, he won't,' Neil insisted, 'not if we get some parrot food and hold it in front of him. Seeds and stuff like that.'

'What about vegetables?' Ellen suggested. 'Broccoli and cabbage, that sort of thing?'

But while they were discussing the finer details of parrot nutrition, Davey had crouched down and opened the cage. Fintan scuttled out, ran up his bare leg and settled on his shoulder. Davey looked terrified, and there were slight scratches on his skin where Fintan had dug his claws in.

'Stand still!' Tom commanded, and reached out to grab the bird's legs.

But it was too late; Fintan launched himself into the air and they watched helplessly as he flew over the porch rail, soared out across the back lawn, then banked and headed down the hill behind the McCabes' house, and almost out of sight until he landed in a stand of manuka some distance away.

'That's torn it, hasn't it?' a voice said.

It was Jack, standing on the lawn, shading his eyes with his hand as he squinted at Fintan's new bolt hole across the gully.

Tom went down to meet him. 'Bloody thing just took off,' he said, following Jack's gaze.

'They'll do that,' Jack said. 'My mother's got one, and a bad-tempered little bugger it is, too.'

'Can you catch them?'

'Oh, yeah, they're not as clever as they like to think they are.' Jack smiled up at Ellen. 'You wouldn't have any golden syrup, would you? Or even honey would do. And some sort of cereal?'

Ellen tensed as she waited for Davey to say something about not being allowed decent breakfast cereal, but he was hanging over the porch rail, calling out to the parrot, entreating him to come home and trying not to cry.

'We've got oats, and I think there's a tiny bit of golden syrup left. Hang on, I'll go and have a look.'

'And a spoon,' Jack called after her.

She came out a minute later with a handful of raw oats in the bottom of a bowl, the golden-syrup tin and a dessert spoon.

Jack trotted up the steps, sat down on the top one and prised the lid off the tin. He dipped the spoon into the last half-inch of sticky syrup at the bottom and scraped up a healthy dollop, then dribbled it over the oats.

Davey was hanging over his shoulder now. 'What's that for?'

'If I can get close enough, he'll . . . what is it, a him or a her?'

194

'It's a him. Dad's called him Fintan because he's rude.'

Jack grinned. 'That's a good name, isn't it? Very apt. If I can get close enough, he'll smell the syrup and hopefully he won't be able to resist climbing down and having a scoff. And when he does, I'll nab him!'

Neil made a disparaging noise. 'We could have done that.'

'I'm sure,' Jack replied, 'but can you make the special bird call that absolutely no parrot in the world can ignore?'

'No.'

'Well, come with me then, and I'll teach you how to do it.'

And off they went, Neil, Davey and Jack carrying the plate of oats, over the back fence, down the hill and across to the stand of manuka where Fintan was holed up. Tom and Ellen leaned on the porch rail watching them.

Several yards away from the manuka, Jack stopped and set the plate on the ground, then stepped back a couple of feet. He said something to the boys so that they crouched down, then put his hands to his mouth and made a piercing whistle that could be heard back at the house.

Fintan shuffled further out along the spindly branch under his feet, and looked down. Nobody moved. Jack whistled again. Then, after what felt like a very long couple of minutes, the parrot fluttered off his branch, circled Jack and the boys once, then alighted on the ground near the plate of oats. His head came out, as though he were having a good sniff, then he waddled over to the plate and poked his face into it. Jack pounced, grabbing him by the legs and flipping him upside down. Fintan's wings flapped madly for a second, then he relaxed and Jack turned him up the right way and shoved him inside his jacket.

The boys clapped delightedly, then the three of them trudged back up the hill. Jack returned Fintan to his cage immediately. Apparently satisfied with his little outing, the parrot hopped onto his swing, looked around and said, 'Where's the beer?'

Jack raised his eyebrows.

'Got it from a bloke at the meeting today, one of the wharfies,' Tom explained.

'That's what I came around about, actually,' Jack said, 'to see how you and Pat got on.'

'Well, it's good news and bad news,' Tom said, sitting down on the steps. 'Ellen, make us a cup of tea, will you, love?'

She went inside to put the kettle on, but could still hear what Tom was saying. The watersiders had evidently very firmly reiterated their decision to stay out, which meant that Davey wouldn't be getting his Kornies for a while yet. But at least the mortgage had been taken care of, for the moment.

She made the tea and took it outside, already poured.

'So what's next?' Jack asked Tom.

Tom shrugged. 'Barnes won't budge, I'd say.'

'And while he doesn't, neither do we.'

'That's right.'

Ellen sat down a few steps below them. 'Will you be going to the dance at Rotowaro tomorrow night, Jack?'

He took a sip of his tea, and smiled. 'You remembered, two sugars. Or is it honey?'

'Honey.'

'Perfect, just the right amount.' He put his cup down. 'Yes, I am going. I've, um, I've been invited by someone, actually.'

Ellen felt a spark of something very close to panic shoot through her.

'Andrea Trask has asked me.'

'Oh,' she said and looked away, overwhelmed with disappointment.

Tom gave Jack a sly nudge. 'About time you said yes, she's been after you since the day you got here.'

'I've got to get the dinner on,' Ellen said suddenly. She got to her feet, stepped between the two men and went inside.

Tom looked after her, then back at Jack. 'What did I say?'

But Jack wasn't listening.

★ ★ ★

Ellen took extra care getting ready for the dance. There was no money to have her hair done, so she set it in rollers, then brushed it out in a full, shining sweep that sat softly at the base of her neck.

She chose her blue dress, and under it her nearly new bra that gave her such a good contour. And although she didn't normally use much make-up, she paid special attention to her powder and lipstick. She took a final look in the mirror, put on the pearl ear studs Tom had given her as a wedding present, then removed them in favour of small gold hoops. Then, grabbing her good coat, she hurried out into the kitchen.

Tom whistled. 'You look nice, love. Should I go and change into my suit?'

'Don't be silly. Is Mum here yet?'

'She's in the sitting room. Oh, sorry, I mean the lounge.'

Ellen gave him a look. He'd already had a few beers at the Blue Room, and was in fine form — cheerful but cheeky, a combination she knew Gloria didn't appreciate, especially not from Tom. She said it reminded her too much of Alf.

They set off down to Frank and Milly's where the four of them were to be picked up by Frank's brother, who owned a car and had offered to drive the short distance to Rotowaro. Ellen thoroughly enjoyed the ride: she didn't often get the opportunity to swan about the countryside in a car. The hall was already crowded and noisy when they arrived. As they found themselves seats at a table with some of the Pukemiro crowd, Ellen noted that Jack was already there, although there was no sign of Andrea Trask.

He greeted Tom companionably, and pulled up a seat next to Ellen.

'You're wearing that dress again,' he said, his voice low. 'And your hair looks pretty.'

'Thank you,' she said, deliberately not meeting his eye. Her shoulders felt tense, and she made an effort to relax them. 'Did Andrea not come?' she asked, and instantly regretted it.

'She's in the ladies', I think.' He bent forward

so no one else could hear. 'I'm sorry, Ellen, I couldn't get out of it. She's asked me out four times now and I couldn't keep putting her off.'

'How persistent of her.'

The corners of Jack's mouth twitched. 'Did you just miaow then?'

Ellen felt suddenly ashamed of herself. 'Oh, look, I should be saying sorry, not you. It's none of my business who you go out with.'

Jack looked disappointed. 'I was hoping you'd think it was. I thought we had an understanding.'

Her heart began to thump wildly, and she felt her face growing hot. 'Do we?' she asked.

'Yes, and you know we do.' He moved even closer. 'So what are we going to do about it, Ellen? What do you want? Do you know?'

He was watching her intently, waiting, but before she could answer Tom turned around in his seat, and she almost passed out because she thought he might have heard them.

'What are you two whispering about?' he said.

Jack sat back. 'I'm teaching Ellen how to whistle parrots down from manuka trees.'

Ellen stared at him, almost shocked by the smoothness of the lie.

'That'll come in handy,' Tom said. 'I'm just shooting out to the car to grab a beer. Jack, do you want another one?'

'Thanks, but I've got a couple in the truck.'

As Tom negotiated his way outside, Andrea Trask appeared and sat down so close to Jack she was almost perched on his knee.

'Hello, Mrs McCabe,' she said, flicking her hair out over her shoulders and resting her hand possessively on Jack's arm. 'I love your frock. Isn't it the same one you wore to Dallas and Carol's wedding?'

Ellen smiled politely.

'Would you like a glass of beer, Andrea?' Jack asked.

'No, thank you, Jack. I prefer not to drink alcohol in public,' she replied, with a condescending smile at Ellen.

But before he could suggest something else, there was the sound of angrily raised voices.

'What is it?' Andrea asked.

'Hang on, I can't see,' Jack replied. He shook her hand off his arm and stood up. 'Oh Christ,' he said after a moment.

Ellen stood up herself and bumped into Tom, who had come up behind her. When she saw what was happening, her heart sank. Two men were being dragged towards the hall entrance by at least half a dozen others.

Ellen didn't recognise them. 'Who are they?' she asked Tom.

'Opencasters.'

Then, suddenly, a woman darted up and took a vicious swing at one of the pair with her handbag. He ducked, but it still clipped him soundly across the side of the head.

'That's for scabbing!' the woman shrieked. 'And for taking the food out of my kids' mouths! Bloody *scum*!'

Everyone in the hall was watching now, their expressions ranging from discomfort to indifference, but no one moved to help the two men.

After a little more scuffling, the pair were

punched several times by their evictors, then finally shoved out the door and onto the street. The chatter began again as everyone resumed their seats as if nothing had happened.

'Serves the bastards right,' Tom said. He took two bottles of beer out of his jacket pockets and set them on the table. 'Stupid bloody thing to try and do anyway.'

Ellen sat down, her legs rubbery and her heart beating wildly — not because of the violence, but because she had caught herself almost cheering when the woman had lashed out.

What was happening to them all? There were shocking, bitter rifts opening up everywhere: fathers aligned against sons, wives against husbands, miners against other miners. The very heartbeat of the community was changing, and when the strike finally ended, she wondered how they could ever go back to the way they had been.

And something in her was changing as well, a part of her she'd always believed could never be any other way, and it frightened her. But it was seductive, too, because it felt like the answer to something that had always been missing, only she'd never quite known it.

It felt like a breath of pure, sweet air.

Tom and Andrea had both gone off again, so now there was only her and Jack, sitting side by side, almost but not quite touching.

'Jack?' she said. She couldn't look at him, but she knew he was watching her. 'I do know what I want.'

He didn't hesitate at all. 'Then come and see me. Come on Friday.'

Over the next five days, Ellen went around feeling disconcertingly as though she were two different women in the same body: one a happily married housewife and mother, and the other the keeper of a dark and selfish little secret.

On Friday morning she was so sick with nerves she couldn't eat her breakfast and had to settle for just a cup of tea. She saw the boys off to school, then, hating herself for a moment, kissed Tom goodbye at the door before he went off to meet up with Pat.

She hurried through the dishes, made the beds, shoved some wood in the range, fed Fintan, then made herself wait another thirty minutes exactly, in case Tom came back, before she ran a hot bath.

Wrapped in a towel, she sat on the bed and dithered over what to wear, thinking she'd made her mind up during the week but realising now that she hadn't. She'd thought about something nice but casual, but not too nice, so that if anyone saw her on her way to Jack's house, they wouldn't wonder why she was all dressed up. And that had set her thinking about what horrendous gossip that alone would cause, her going to Jack Vaughan's house, on her own, in the middle of the morning, when everyone knew Tom was in Auckland.

The anxiety had convinced her that, rather than waltzing up to Jack's front door as though she were the Rawleigh's man, she should climb over her own back fence and walk along the gully at the bottom of the hill, away from prying eyes, then come back up at the end of Robert Street, where Jack lived. But if she did that, she would have to wear trousers because there was gorse and blackberry and cutty-grass all along the gully, and if she wore a skirt she'd be covered in scratches.

And then she'd thought, why not just bowl up to the front door exactly like the Rawleigh's man, with an armful of papers perhaps, to make it look like she was there on union business? That had been on Wednesday night, just as she was dishing up tea, and the awful realisation that she was going to such deliberate lengths to deceive Tom, and everyone else, had made her feel physically ill. She'd sat down, made herself eat something and decided on the spot that what she was thinking of doing was so terrible, so dishonest and disloyal, that she wouldn't go at all.

But by the next morning, she'd changed her mind again. She kept hearing Jack's low, gentle voice and smelling the faint muskiness that came off his skin, and that was enough to convince her that she would go and see him, but only to explain why there couldn't be anything between them.

So why had she just spent half an hour in the bath shaving her legs and thoroughly washing every bit of herself with her best rose-scented soap?

She had to go now anyway; it was too late not to, and his feelings might be hurt if she didn't turn up. Then she groaned and put her face in her hands — what about Tom's feelings? This was so awful and complicated and she hadn't even done anything yet. But she wanted to, very much, because Jack made her feel right. There was no other word for it.

She decided on her good pair of slacks, a light blouse and a soft, woollen jumper. Nothing that would suggest to Jack that she'd spent hours getting ready, but also not something so everyday that he might mistake her for the nightcart man. And she would go along the gully; if anyone spotted her she could always say she was looking for late blackberries.

She got off the bed and dried herself off, then looked at herself critically in the mirror, trying to imagine what Jack would see — although he wasn't going to get the chance. Her stomach was still flat and her waist neat, but since she'd had the boys her breasts had sagged a little. She breathed in deeply, expanding her rib cage and pushing her shoulders back, but it didn't make much difference. Her legs were still good, though. And there were faint silvery lines on her hips, and her bum was too broad for its own good — she wasn't a girl any more, that was very clear.

Oh God, she thought, what the hell was she doing?

★ ★ ★

She knocked timidly on the closed door and waited, glancing around nervously and hoping she wasn't being watched. There were no houses to the left of Jack's. There were some on the right, although it didn't look as though his neighbours, the Huriwais, were home. And his back porch was semi-enclosed, so she didn't think anyone could see her, if they hadn't already spotted her coming across the rather overgrown back yard.

She waited a minute, then knocked again, feeling relief as well as sharp disappointment at the thought that he might not be home after all. What if, after the beers had worn off, he'd decided he'd made a mistake?

She stood there a moment longer, feeling stupid, then turned to go.

Behind her, the door opened.

His hair looked freshly washed, he'd had a recent shave, and he was wearing a faded shirt tucked into old trousers, although his feet were bare.

'You did come,' he said, and gave her a little smile.

Now that she was here, she had no idea what to say.

He moved back and held the door open for her, and she stepped inside.

'It's not very flash, I'm afraid,' he said, indicating the small kitchen with a sweep of his arm.

It wasn't, either. The faded wallpaper was starting to peel, revealing the scrim beneath it, and the wooden floor was on a slight angle and completely bare of linoleum or rugs. It was warm, though.

He nodded at the rickety little table in the middle of the room. 'Have a seat.'

'Thanks,' Ellen said, and sat down.

'Tea? Or cocoa?'

'Tea, please.'

There was an awkward silence then, that Ellen was desperate to fill.

'Are you just renting?' she said, although she couldn't care less whether he was renting the house or had won it in a raffle at the pub — she just wanted something to say. Then she remembered he'd already told her that; he'd think she had a memory like a sieve.

Jack filled the kettle and put it on the range. 'It's cheap enough, so I thought why not? And it came furnished, sort of.'

'What about the single men's hostel, in Huntly West? A lot of the unmarried blokes stay there.'

'Closer to work here. Closer to a lot of things, really.'

He glanced up and smiled at her again.

Ellen felt herself blush. 'Can you afford it, with the strike on?' She winced at the nosiness of the question.

'I've got a bit put away, I'm all right. I send a bit down to my mum, but I haven't got much else to spend it on, being single. Except beer.'

He clattered about getting out cups and saucers and spooning tea into the pot. When the kettle boiled he brought everything over to the table, sat down, then got up again to get the milk.

'There's no biscuits or anything, sorry. I could make you a sandwich if you're hungry.'

Ellen shook her head; she wasn't hungry, and didn't think she'd be able to eat even if she was.

Her stomach felt fluttery and she kept having to suppress little shudders, even though she wasn't cold.

Jack sat down again and poured the tea. 'No sugar, either. You have milk, don't you?'

'Yes.'

He set a cup in front of her. The steam coming off it rose lazily into the air.

'So,' he said.

Ellen suddenly felt so nervous she thought she might faint. On her way along the gully she'd rehearsed what she was going to say: that she liked spending time with him and thought he was a very nice person but, unfortunately, there couldn't be anything else because she was a married woman. She was flattered, but she was married.

But her mouth wouldn't open to let the words out, and every time she glanced at him, her belly did a long, slow flip and the hairs on her arms stood up.

'Do you mind if I ask you a question?' he asked.

She held her breath: was this it?

'What do you think of the opencasters? Going back to work, I mean?'

Ellen almost laughed, although her heart was pounding madly. 'The opencasters?'

'They must have known what would happen.'

She felt on safer ground now. 'I'm sure they did, but, well, you know, you can understand it in a way, the ones with families, anyway.'

'Can you?'

She looked at him, her head cocked,

wondering what he meant. Then it occurred to her that she probably looked just like Fintan sitting on his swing, and sat up straighter.

'Yes, I can,' she said. 'That doesn't mean I agree with them, though.'

'You don't think they should have scabbed?'

'No. They voted to go out at the start and they should have stayed out. It's the only way to do it. There's no point having a bloody union if its members are going to throw in the towel the minute things get tough.'

Jack raised his eyebrows at her vehemence. 'I was talking to your dad in the pub the other day, and he said exactly the same thing.'

'Did he?'

'He did. You're a lot like him, you know.'

Ellen had an unwelcome vision of her father leaning against the bar in his tatty old sports coat, his nose red and his eyes watery with the booze. 'Thank you very much,' she said.

Jack realised what he'd just implied, and laughed. 'No, you have the same ideas. I don't mean you look like him.'

'Well, that's a relief.'

'He's not half as pretty as you, for a start.'

Ellen went very still.

Jack didn't take his eyes off her. 'He doesn't have your beautiful hair, or your extraordinary blue eyes or your lovely mouth, which I want to kiss every time I see you.'

Here it was, then. She took a deep breath; she had to tell him.

But before she could, he pushed back his chair and all of a sudden was standing over her.

'Can I kiss you, Ellen?'

She gazed up at the hunger in his eyes, and felt every one of her resolutions dissolve into nothing.

She nodded, and he did.

★ ★ ★

He took her by the hand and led her into his bedroom. It was as shabby as the kitchen, but the bed — an old, tarnished brass one with high head and footboards — was neatly made and topped with a woollen blanket.

'What a lovely old bed,' Ellen prattled. 'Is it yours?'

'Came with the house,' Jack said, sitting down on it. The mattress sagged visibly.

There were no chairs, only the bed and a chest of drawers. Ellen didn't know where to put herself.

'Come here,' Jack said.

Ellen hesitated, then moved a little closer.

He reached out, caught the ends of her sleeves and pulled her nearer still until she was standing between his legs.

She stared down at his hands, at the long fingers and the blunt fingernails, clean now from being off work, thinking how many times she'd imagined how they might feel on her bare skin.

'Ellen, are you happy about this?' he asked.

She felt herself trembling, and hoped he couldn't feel it. 'I'm not sure if happy's the right word.'

Jack lifted her hand to his mouth and kissed it. 'Do you want to do this? Because I don't want us to do anything you might regret.'

'I do want to.' The inside of his thighs felt warm and hard against her legs, and she leaned into him a little more. 'But I love Tom, I really do.'

'I know.'

'It's just that . . . '

He reached up and touched his fingers to her lips. 'Not now, we won't talk about that now.'

He slid his hands around her waist and drew her even closer. She could smell him now, clean and masculine.

'Lie down with me, Ellen.'

He took her hand and she climbed onto the bed beside him, awkward and shivering with anticipation. She kicked her shoes off in case they were dirty, wincing as they clattered loudly onto the wooden floor. Her heart was thumping so violently she was sure he'd hear that, too. She was stunned by what was happening to her, by her expectation and her desire; she hadn't felt like this in years.

No, she'd never felt like this.

He rolled over onto his side, propped himself up on one elbow and looked down at her.

'You're so lovely,' he said.

So are you, she thought.

He kissed her again, with more urgency this time. Her hand came up and she ran her fingers through his hair. It was thick and sleek and still far too long.

His lips were soft but insistent, and she felt herself responding with equal urgency, turning to meet him and pressing herself against him. He groaned, his hardness prodding her thigh.

She felt him smiling, and pulled back.

'What?' she whispered. 'What's so funny?'

'Nothing's funny,' he whispered back.

'You're smiling.'

'I know,' he said, and kissed her again.

Then his mouth moved off hers and trailed over her chin and down her throat, where he licked the delicate skin beneath her jaw, then bit. The sensation was electric, and her body jerked involuntarily.

She moaned then, too, unable to stop herself.

He rolled half on top of her, his leg settled between hers, and rested his weight on his elbows.

'Am I squashing you?'

She shook her head, then grunted softly as he shifted his leg so it pressed more firmly against her. The heaviness of him was erotic beyond belief, and her hips began to move in a gentle rhythm with his. Kissing her again, he slid one hand down and cupped her breast, and her back arched to meet his touch.

She was breathing harder now, and so was he; together, in the bare little room, they were beginning to sound like a pair of panting dogs, and she nearly giggled.

He groped behind her back and felt for her bra fastening.

'Can I?'

She nodded and lifted herself to give him access. But the hooks wouldn't open, and when he swore she rolled onto her side so he could see what he was doing. She pulled her jumper up and wriggled out of it, then undid the buttons on her blouse and slipped it off.

On her back again, she looked down at her breasts then quickly up at him. She felt herself blushing and turned her face away, unable to meet his eyes.

He gazed down at her. 'God, you're lovely,' he murmured.

He reached out and began to trace delicate patterns over and around her breasts, rubbing his thumbs over her nipples until they became so erect they ached. She shuddered again and a rash of goose bumps marched across her bare skin.

Jack sat up and pulled his shirt off over his head without even bothering to unbutton it. His arms and chest were muscled and the dark hair on his chest started at his throat but thinned below his nipples, converging in a line that ran down his hard, flat stomach and disappeared beneath the waistband of his trousers. Then he turned and settled himself gently on top of her, and the feel of his skin against hers came close to snatching Ellen's breath away.

Her knees came up around him and he began to move with a slow but powerful rhythm, the hardness of his erection almost hurting her. Turning her head to inhale the fresh sweat in his armpit, she savoured the sharpness and the tang of his maleness. She stuck out her tongue and tasted it.

He groaned and buried his face in her hair, his hips thrusting more urgently now.

Then, abruptly, he stopped and moved off her.

'Hang on a minute,' he said, grimacing. 'I'm getting carried away.'

Ellen reached for the buttons on her slacks and undid them, then slid them and her pants down to her knees, at which point Jack took over and pulled them the rest of the way off and tossed them onto the floor. Then Ellen waited with her thighs modestly together while Jack extricated himself from his own trousers.

'You'll have to forgive my lack of manners, it's been a while. It could be a bit quick, too, sorry,' he said as he rolled back towards her. 'My God, you've got a beautiful body.'

She laughed. 'So have you.'

He parted her knees and lowered himself, and she let out a small cry of pleasure and need as he slid into her. He found his rhythm immediately and she raised her legs and wrapped her arms tightly around his back, drawing him as close to her as she could. The strength of his thrusting increased, his hips driving her into the mattress and the muscles in his arms and back tensing.

She hung on, feeling her own, rather unexpected, climax begin to radiate out from the base of her belly, the delicious spasms jerking her limbs and contorting her spine.

Jack threw his head back and gasped, 'Oh God, oh shit,' and with an almighty groan, emptied himself into her.

Ellen cupped her hands around the back of his head as he shuddered once, then again, then collapsed on top of her, drained and sweaty, his heartbeat racing almost in time with hers.

'Oh Ellen,' he said, his face pressed into her

neck. 'Oh Ellen, my lovely girl.'

And she knew, then, that this was it, this was what had been missing.

⋆　⋆　⋆

The day before Ellen and Jack went to bed together, Jock Barnes had given Walter Nash a letter stating that the WWU was now prepared to accept Holland's plan, without any major qualifications. But only on the condition that the WWU was reregistered.

Nash passed the letter on to Holland, who went on the radio the same night declaring that he did not consider the watersiders' condition of reregistration to be a bar to 'an honourable settlement of the trouble'. All over the country, thousands of trade unionists began to believe that they might soon be heading back to work. Barnes had finally compromised, and all the government had to do was reregister the national watersiders' union.

But twenty-four hours later, Holland did a complete about-face and announced that he was adding an extra 'irrevocable condition' to his seven-point plan: new, separate port unions would have to be established and the national union broken up. Barnes withdrew his olive branch, and what had looked like a probable end to the strike skittered out of reach once again.

It was disappointing, but the unions still out remained stoic, not happy but willing to tighten their belts further if it meant victory in the end. Even Tom was disappointed, telling Ellen he saw

214

little sense in the miners staying out any longer than they needed to. But he was angry at Holland more than anything else.

When Pat came around on the Saturday for a yarn, Tom was still going on about how Holland didn't know his arse from his elbow and shouldn't be in charge of running a bath, never mind a country. But Ellen suspected that rather being dismayed by the prospect of the strike dragging on, Pat was almost pleased by Holland's turnaround.

'It wasn't right, Tom,' he said, sitting at the table with his hat balanced on his knee, 'and Barnes knew it. He's never been one for compromise.'

'I know it wasn't bloody well right,' Tom said, 'he's always been against conciliation and arbitration. So have we, otherwise we might as well have listened to Prendiville and Crook.'

'Yeah, well,' Pat said, 'Tony Prendiville's cashed in his chips, as far as I'm concerned.'

'It could have worked, though, if the watersiders had been allowed to reregister.'

'No, it couldn't,' Pat said.

'Then why did Holland near as buggery say they could, on the radio the other night?'

Pat shrugged. 'I'm buggered if I know. But it's better this way, we all still know where we stand. We're not going back until the watersiders do, and they're not going back until Holland agrees to a fair and reasonable settlement, end of story.'

But Ellen wasn't really listening now. She was thinking back to yesterday, to lying with Jack, sweaty and with her hair all over the place,

215

wishing she didn't have to get up and go home.

But she had, and in plenty of time before the boys arrived back from school. She'd had a thorough wash to remove every trace of Jack from her body, but hadn't been able to get even the tiniest little bit of him out of her mind. She'd also checked the mirror to see if she looked any different, because surely she must have changed somehow? She felt horribly guilty, and was sure that what she'd done must be written all over her face. She had just shattered her marriage vows, betrayed her husband and children and made love to a man she couldn't wait to see again.

Then she'd made tea in time for when Tom got home from Auckland, and he'd been so shitty about Holland's latest stunt that he hadn't even noticed he didn't have the same wife any more.

9

'Ellen, have you heard?'

'Heard what?' She took a jar of Marmite off the shelf and checked the price. No, she didn't have enough money for that.

Avis Hale moved closer. 'The railway bridge at Mahuta, somebody blew it up last night!'

Ellen gave her a look.

'The bridge? There isn't a bridge at Mahuta.'

'Well, the tracks over the culvert then. But somebody had a go at it last night with gelignite, and this morning the train nearly went straight over it. They could have been killed, the lot of them!'

Ellen assumed Avis meant the passengers, who at that hour would have been the opencast men travelling from Huntly out to work. But Avis was prone to exaggeration, and tended to enjoy a good story, so she wasn't unduly perturbed by the news. Something must have happened, though. She finished her shopping, asked Fred to please put it on credit and went home.

Tom was at the table, reading the newspaper and shaking his head.

'Avis Hale said someone had a go at the culvert at Mahuta,' Ellen said, setting her parcels down on the bench.

'I know,' Tom said, 'I'm reading about it.' He

217

tapped the copy of the *Herald* open in front of him and quoted, ''It is only by the grace of Providence that families in the Waikato coalfields are not mourning the loss of forty or more lives by violence.'' He shook the paper, folded it neatly and put it aside. 'What a lot of bullshit.'

Ellen sat down. 'But what happened?'

'Apparently — and this is only what Bert got off Vic this morning, who heard it off someone else — someone stuck six sticks of gelignite into the sleepers over the culvert and blew them.'

'Just before the train was due to go over?' Ellen was moderately shocked.

'No, during the night. But the charges were badly set, against the grain, and the sleepers only splintered. Sounds like someone who knows about dynamite.' Tom smirked. 'Sounds like an underground miner to me.'

'It's not funny, Tom, someone really could have been hurt.'

'I doubt it, because whoever did it also laid sleepers across the track and put up white flags on both sides of the culvert to warn the engine driver. Who hopped out, had a look, took the train over and hauled three hundred and fifty tons of coal across it on the way back in. So it can't have been that bad. But he already knew about the culvert before he got to it because he'd heard the blokes on the train talking about it.'

'How did they know?'

'I don't know, that's just what Bert told me. Is there any tea?'

'Yes, it's in the caddy, but I've got my women's auxiliary meeting and then I'm handing

218

out food parcels so you'll have to make it yourself. Did the police have a look?'

'They were all over the place, apparently.'

Ellen eyed him as he opened the paper again and turned to the sports pages. He hadn't gone out at all last night, so she knew it couldn't have been him.

'Who did it, do you know?' she asked.

He looked up. 'No, I don't, but when I find out I'll be buying him a pint.'

Ellen frowned. 'Holland will go to town with it, you know. We'll end up looking like a pack of complete anarchists.'

'Who will?'

'We will, the Waikato miners.'

'It was just a warning to the opencasters, that's all. Don't worry about it, love, it'll be a seven-day wonder then everyone will forget about it.'

★ ★ ★

There were no scones with cream and jam at Rhea's this time, and hadn't been for some weeks now. Ellen suspected that she and Pat were feeling the pinch as much as everyone else, even though they didn't have children still at home to feed. In fact, they were probably passing on any spare money to their sons, who were both miners themselves, and to their daughter who was married to one.

Rhea, as always, was smartly dressed and wearing her matching earrings and brooch: standards mustn't be allowed to slip just because there was a strike on. Ellen had always thought

Rhea and Gloria should have been good friends, but for some reason they weren't.

Rhea didn't want to discuss the Mahuta explosion, except to comment that the government had probably done it themselves to make the miners look bad. Instead, she wanted to talk about the petition that the Huntly Women's Auxiliary had collectively written and sent to Holland two weeks ago. There had been a fair bit of debate about what it should say, but agreement had eventually been reached.

We Women of the Huntly district, wives of the miners who are on strike against the Emergency Regulations, wish to associate ourselves wholeheartedly with our men in the struggle against these Regulations.

We demand the immediate repeal of the Regulations. We demand that freedom of speech be restored, and that our own men in the Miners' Union be given the right, along with the Watersiders and others to state their case freely over the publicly owned radio and in the press. We consider it a gross tyranny that your side of the case should be presented while the other side is suppressed.

We demand that trade union rights be restored immediately, and that police protection of the strike breakers cease.

, We demand that Parliament be called together. We consider that your Government should use the secret ballot you so ardently advocate for trade unionists and submit yourselves to a General Election.

No reply, official or unofficial, had been received yet, and Ellen wasn't the only woman on the auxiliary to think that there would not be one either, but Rhea wanted to tell them about the support for the petition they'd had from other women's auxiliaries around the country.

She held up a handwritten letter and beamed. 'This one is from Freda Barnes herself, saying she is very proud of us and hopes we can keep up the good work.'

Freda Barnes, Jock's wife, was co-ordinating the efforts of the watersiders' wives at ports around New Zealand, and Ellen suspected that Rhea saw herself as sort of a Waikato version of Freda. And why not? While Freda Barnes was working her fingers to the bone in Auckland and elsewhere, there was no denying that Rhea was doing the same thing here. But they'd all been working hard to assemble and distribute the food packages on Tuesdays, to take the time to chat to the local women about how they were getting on, and make sure that no one was about to crumble under the strain. Except for Dot, of course, who had been moved from Waikato Hospital to Tokanui three weeks ago.

But Dot aside, most of the women seemed to be bearing up reasonably well. It was very difficult, though, because unlike the bigger towns and cities, the Waikato could offer the strikers few work opportunities. The central council had decided a while ago that if any of the men wanted to go off and earn a few shillings on the quiet mending fences and digging the odd drain for farmers, then good on them, as long as they weren't back on the coal. And a few had done that, but there just wasn't enough casual work to go around.

Some of the men had taken to spending more and more time in the pub, which was causing problems in itself. God only knew where they found the money to do it, but they did, and there had been more than one loud, public scene as a result. Ellen could only imagine what happened behind closed doors.

There was trouble in the district with stealing, too. Several cockies had complained about missing sheep and pigs, and though the police — Sergeant Ballantyne himself, fortunately — had investigated, not much had been done about the charges because everyone knew that the meat from the pilfered stock was ending up in the weekly relief packages. It wasn't so much that the animals had gone, one cockie told the sergeant, it was more that no one had asked permission to take them. It was a matter of courtesy, more than anything else.

The bad feeling between people who held different views on the strike was also getting worse. And there were, in fact, increasing grumbles from the women about the lack of money coming in, because they were the ones who had to make ends meet, and tell their children there would be no treats, or new winter shoes, or special outings. But so far there had been no overt signs of wavering from the underground miners, and the women on the auxiliary took this to be a sign that the local wives were still prepared to stand behind their men.

But in spite of all this, the community was probably functioning together better than it ever had and there were plenty of examples of compassion and generosity. The local shopkeepers were extending as much credit as they could, and so were the businesses in town. Last week, one of the mine managers had turned up on Rhea's doorstep one night with several boxes of clothes and bits and pieces, all perfectly serviceable if not brand new, with strict instructions that they be passed on to a certain family known to be in dire straits. But the donation had to be made anonymously, or it wasn't going to be made at all, and Rhea had told only the women on the Pukemiro auxiliary.

It was this sort of thing that was keeping the community together, but only just, and they all knew it. Ellen wasn't the only one beginning to think that of all the unionists on strike throughout the country, the miners might be the worst off: coalmines were very rarely located close to big towns and cities.

And as the days passed, news of the strike's progress just hadn't got any better. Last week the FOL had announced that it had formally resolved to take no action against the emergency regulations. That had been a very bitter blow. Then the news had come that a scab union of almost 200 men was being organised to start work on the Auckland waterfront, right at the very heart of the strike. The following day the number had risen to 500, but everyone had had a good laugh when the Labour Department was forced to admit that at least half of the names put forward were fictitious. But now the newspapers were reporting that the number was rising again, and that the applicants were genuine this time. On Saturday, the day of the explosion at Mahuta, the government had gone through the public charade at the Auckland town hall of officially forming the new union, and thousands of the original watersiders had gathered outside to noisily register their protest.

And now Rhea was saying that overnight Holland had widened the scope of the emergency regulations. He'd also authorised the immediate formation of a voluntary emergency organisation to 'assist in the preservation of law and order', and was calling for every able-bodied man who might like to join in and 'serve his country in the present crisis'.

The women were stunned.

'Where did you hear that?' Milly asked.

'It was in the *Auckland Star*,' Rhea said, looking as dismayed as the others felt. 'The editorial says that the government should ban anyone from the WWU from going near the wharves, and that if they do show their faces they should be shot.'

'Shot!' Ellen was astounded.

'Yes, shot.'

'But that's absurd, this is New Zealand! Surely they can't print things like that in a public newspaper?'

'Well, they have.'

Ellen swallowed. Had Tom heard about this

yet? If not, she would have to tell him: they didn't take the *Auckland Star*.

Then, to her consternation, she realised that the person she really wanted to talk to about it was not Tom, but Jack. At the mere thought of him her stomach fluttered with excitement. But she made an enormous effort to put him out of her mind; she couldn't even think about him around anyone else, she was so afraid that her feelings would show.

Rhea went over what would be required of them during the coming week, plus confirmation of the details of a strike dance they were planning soon, then closed the meeting with the assurance that the moment she heard anything about a response to their petition, she would be sure to let them know.

Outside it was starting to rain, and Ellen turned up the collar of her coat.

'Bloody hell,' Milly said. 'My washing's still out.'

'I did all mine on Sunday,' Lorna said. 'I haven't had to do half as much since Vic's been off work.'

Milly snorted. 'You're lucky, Billy and Evan are even filthier than ever.' Then she said, 'Billy reckons he saw you the other day, Ellen, last Friday morning.'

Ellen forced herself to keep walking. 'Did he? Whereabouts?'

'That's the funny bit. He said you were walking along the gully at the bottom of the hill behind your house. So I said, 'Don't be a drongo Billy, what would Ellen be doing mucking about

225

in the gully?' And when I asked him what he was doing in the gully during school hours, the little bugger went bright red and it turns out he was down there having a quick smoke. Ten years old and he's smoking! That's Frank's fault, you know.' She paused. 'Still, if that's the only habit he gets off his father I suppose I should count my blessings. So, was it you?'

'Yes, it was, actually,' Ellen said, praying that her voice sounded normal.

'Oh. What were you doing?'

'Looking for Fintan.'

Milly frowned. 'Who?'

'Fintan, Davey's parrot. He got out.'

'Oh, yes, the parrot! Evan's being going on and on about it, he wants one too, now. He's not bloody getting one, though. Did you find it?'

Ellen nodded, feeling sick.

★　★　★

She couldn't stop thinking about Jack. It had been four days now since she had seen him, and it would be another agonising forty-eight hours before she might see him again.

There had been no dances on anywhere last Saturday night, so she and Tom had taken the boys to the pictures at the hall, but there'd been no sign of Jack. She told herself he was probably out drinking somewhere — Tom certainly had been, all afternoon at the pub, and fell asleep as soon as the film started. It was *A Streetcar Named Desire*, with Vivien Leigh and Marlon Brando, which Ellen had been wanting to see for weeks. Neil and Davey couldn't have cared less, much preferring cowboy or war films, but they'd insisted on coming anyway because it was better than sitting at home with Grandma Gloria, who always made them clean their teeth and get into their pyjamas at seven o'clock. But they'd amused themselves by yelling out 'Steeellaaaa!' at the tops of their voices all the way home after the picture finished, so she supposed they hadn't been too bored.

Ellen wondered why Jack hadn't been in touch. In fact, she was fretting. People always said that other people were fretting, and she'd never quite understood what they meant, but she did now. She couldn't concentrate on anything, she'd lost her appetite and she woke up during the night with her head filled with thoughts and images of him. It was almost as though her centre of gravity had been altered and she couldn't quite find her balance. It had been magical and perfect with him, but now, after not having seen him for four days, she felt completely bereft. And still appallingly guilty. She watched Neil and Davey and wanted to cry because they were her precious boys and they had no idea, and she saw Tom being grumpy and cheerful, annoying and familiar and loving all in the same day, and she wanted to cry even more because it was so unfair that all she could do was think about being with someone else. She wanted to reach out to Tom and tell him she loved him, because she did, but now there was Jack too.

She was being extraordinarily selfish, and

she knew it. She knew why, too. It was because Jack was more than what he seemed. He was a good-looking man, there was no denying that; he was physical and strong and had an easy confidence that made him very appealing. He was kind and thoughtful, too, but underneath there was a streak of something much tougher, a quiet danger that Ellen found irresistible. But it wasn't even that; it was something she couldn't define. He had something extra, something she wanted and needed and had to have. He made her feel whole — it was as simple as that.

So where was he? Surely he could have come around to talk to Tom about something. He needn't have said anything directly to her, but he could have caught her eye, given her some sort of silent message, and she would have known then that it was all right.

She sighed and cleared away the lunch things. Tom was next door helping Bert cut down a tree, and the boys were at school. There was the washing to do now, which she normally enjoyed, although it was always a bit of a chore. In the washhouse, she filled the copper and set the fire under it, then touched a match to the screwed-up newspaper she'd jammed between the kindling. She stayed crouching in front of it, watching the flame turn the edges of the paper black then creep over the kindling, catching the raw splinters and then the wood itself. The touch of heat was nice on her face; the washhouse was always cold and dank until the copper got

228

going, then it was far too hot, especially at the height of summer.

But it wouldn't get going for a while yet, so she straightened up and went out onto the porch, where Jack was standing with his hands in his pockets, watching Fintan in his cage.

'Jack!' she said. She smoothed her untidy hair behind her ears, wishing she wasn't wearing her tattiest old skirt and cardigan.

He turned around and gave her such a lovely smile she felt it in her bones.

'You shouldn't give parrots too much fruit, you know,' he said, 'it gives them a crook guts. And they waste it.'

Ellen glanced at the cage. Jack was right; she'd given Fintan a pear last night for his supper and he'd shat everywhere this morning, and the bits of fruit he hadn't eaten were glued to the bars of his cage.

Fintan glared at her and said, 'Jack!'

Jack said, 'I've missed you, Ellen.'

'Where have you been?' She felt such a flood of relief she thought she might have to sit down.

'Staying away.'

'But why?'

'In case you'd decided you might have made a mistake.'

'Jack, is that you?'

Ellen nearly jumped out of her skin. She looked across at Bert's house where Tom was hanging over the hedge, a pair of rusty loppers in his hand.

Jack said quickly, 'Will you come on Friday?'

'Yes.'

He turned and went down the steps, Ellen behind him.

'I've just seen Pat,' he called to Tom, who was sidling through the hedge, Bert close behind. 'More bad news.'

'Christ, now what?' Tom said.

'Scab union at Bluff, started work this morning.' Jack paused. 'And Timaru's gone back.'

'To work?'

'Yeah, they've accepted employer conditions.'

'The *union* jokers have gone back?'

Jack nodded.

Tom looked away in disgust.

Bert got out his tobacco and started to roll a smoke. 'Timaru always was rotten, right from the start.'

'There's more,' Jack said. 'The scab union's starting on the wharves at Auckland tomorrow.'

Tom snorted. 'They're only seagulls, though.'

'They'll do the work.'

'Then maybe we should all go up in the morning,' Tom said, 'show a bit of solidarity.'

'Could be trouble,' Bert said, tamping his smoke into shape.

Ellen thought so, too. If there was trouble, she didn't want Tom in the middle of it, and with Pat with him, he probably would be.

'What about it, Jack?' Tom said. 'We'll go up first thing tomorrow, doss down with some of the Auckland jokers overnight, and come back Friday afternoon after the meeting.'

Ellen held her breath.

'I can't, Tom,' Jack said. 'I've got something on.'

She shifted slightly, then settled her head back on Jack's damp chest. She had a couple of questions, but felt nervous about asking them in case she didn't get the answers she wanted. She'd wanted to ask him last Friday, but hadn't had the nerve.

She took a deep breath. 'The other day at our house, last week, why did you say you couldn't go up to Auckland?'

Tom hadn't gone either, in the end, because Pat had had a meeting with the central council he didn't want to miss, but they'd both set off this morning for Auckland as usual.

'I had enough of scrapping when I was overseas, and I had better things to do here.'

Ellen felt her heart lift, but it wasn't enough. 'What was better here?'

She cringed inwardly, squirmingly ashamed of herself. Her mother had warned her years ago that expecting a man to talk openly about how he felt was at best a waste of time, and at worst foolhardy. But she had to know what she meant to him; she had to hear him say it.

He made a pretence of careful consideration. 'Well, those porkers did need sorting out.'

And that was true: he had butchered two pigs last Friday morning, before spending two and a half hours in bed with her. Crushed by the brutality of his answer, Ellen willed herself not to react, but in the end she had to. She sat up and looked at him. He was grinning at the ceiling.

'Was that the only reason?'

231

He laughed, and she felt her disappointment sliding into anger. 'Well, if it was only bloody pigs, perhaps you should have gone,' she said.

Jack wrapped his arms around her, pulled her down and hugged her tightly. 'And miss out on being with you? Not a hope.'

Ellen wavered between absolute relief and the urge to remain insulted, but relief won and her heart soared. 'You wanted to see me?'

She felt him nod.

'Ellen, I'd rather be with you than just about anything.'

Savouring the words, she snuggled closer, rubbing her face across the hair on his chest, inhaling his scent and marvelling at how well their bodies fitted together.

But she hadn't finished yet. 'Jack?'

'Mmm?'

'You know how you took Andrea Trask to the dance at Rotowaro?'

'Mmm,' he replied, stroking her hair softly and rhythmically.

'Will you be seeing her again?'

'Well, she hasn't asked me out since, if that's what you mean.'

'Hasn't she?' Ellen tried not to sound too pleased. 'Why not, I wonder?'

'Is it important to you?'

'No.'

He shifted out from under her, propping himself on one elbow so he could see her face.

'You've gone red,' he said.

She willed the blood in her face to subside, but it wouldn't. It got worse. 'I'm hot,' she said.

'Are you?' Jack thoughtfully pulled the blankets down to her waist. 'I doubt she will ask me out again, actually.'

'Why not?'

'Because I told her I just wasn't interested in having a girlfriend at the moment.'

Ellen tried to keep the smile off her face. She struggled to turn it into a look of sympathy for poor Andrea, and failed.

Jack laughed out loud. 'There's that cat in you again.'

'Was she very annoyed?'

'Hell, yes. I thought she was going to haul off and belt me one.'

Ellen sat up and pulled the blankets up under her armpits. 'When did you tell her that?'

'After the dance, when I took her home.'

'Why then?'

'Because that was the night I asked you to come and see me. And I knew you would.'

'Did you? I didn't even know then. That was a bit presumptuous, wasn't it?'

'No, I don't think so. And you did, so I was right.' He reached out and swept a lock of hair behind her ear. 'I think it's a bit crook for a bloke to get tangled up with more than one woman at a time, so I had to tell her. I never fancied her anyway — too pushy.'

'Are we tangled up?'

He leaned down and kissed her. 'Yes, Mrs McCabe, we're very tangled up.'

She kissed him back, then forced herself to pull away. 'Just one more question, Jack. Please?'

He raised his eyebrows.

'It's nothing to do with us,' she said.

He waited.

'Who blew up the line at Mahuta?'

Jack bent over and whispered in her ear.

★   ★   ★

The following night, on his way home after a long afternoon at the pub, Alf fell on the steps leading up to his back door and knocked himself unconscious.

Gloria heard the crash from the sitting room, where she was working on a jumper for Neil, but didn't get up because Alf had fallen up the steps plenty of times before and hadn't done himself any lasting damage. But after some minutes, she realised that this time she wasn't hearing the loud swearing that usually accompanied such incidents, so she went out to see what he was doing.

He was lying face down halfway up the steps. His hat had fallen off and rolled all the way down to the bottom.

'Get up, you silly old bugger,' she said.

There was no answer and he didn't move, so she switched on the porch light and went down for a closer look. It was then that she saw he was bleeding from a gash on the side of his head, just behind his left ear. In the artificial light the blood trickling down his neck looked black. She also smelled alcohol fumes coming off him like an invisible fog.

'Alf?' she said. 'Alf, are you all right?'

Alarmed now, she put her hand on his

shoulder and shook him.

Still nothing, although she could see he was still breathing. She hesitated, wondering whether it was safe to leave him. Then she stepped over him and hurried down the steps and over to the Meehans', her neighbours, and banged loudly on their back door.

Len Meehan opened it. Behind him Gloria glimpsed Rose, his wife, standing at the sink and the three Meehan children sitting around the table, apparently finishing their tea.

'Len, Alf's had a fall and I can't get him up.'

'Oh, shit. Whereabouts?' Len said, jamming his feet into his boots.

'On the steps. I can't get him up, Len!' Gloria's voice was rising in panic.

'Hang on a tick,' he said, then spoke over his shoulder, 'Chris, run up the street and fetch Mrs McCabe. Tell her to hurry.'

Chris stood up. 'Neil and Davey's mum?'

'That's right, hurry up, off you go,' Len said as his son pushed past him.

Chris ran up Joseph Street, his bare feet immune to the gravel, then turned into John Street and didn't stop until he was knocking loudly on the McCabes' door.

Ellen answered. 'Hello, Christopher,' she said, surprised to see him there at that hour. 'The boys are just about to have their tea.'

Breathless, Chris said, 'Dad says you're to come quickly, Mr Powys has come a cropper.'

Ellen stared at him.

'On the steps. Mrs Powys can't get him up.'

'At their house?'

235

Chris nodded, his eyes big with the weighty but enormous excitement of it all.

Neil and Davey appeared, keen to see who was at the door.

Tom was out and Ellen couldn't wait for him. 'I'm just popping out for a minute, boys. Dad will be home soon. If I'm not back tell him to come down to Gran's. Neil, keep an eye on the potatoes.'

And then she was gone, running down the street in the semi-darkness, her slippers flapping and her apron flying and her heart inflating with dread.

By the time she arrived at her parents' house, Len, Rose and Gloria had managed to get Alf inside, where he was now lying on the kitchen floor. Gloria glanced up as she hurried in, her face white and her expression helpless and horrified.

Alf was on his back and Ellen could see where the blood had drenched the collar of his shirt. His face was as pale as Gloria's and his eyes were closed and he looked terrible.

'What happened? Is he all right?' she asked.

'He fell on the steps. I think he's unconscious,' Len said, chafing Alf's hands briskly. Rose was loosening Alf's belt and shirt buttons.

'I told him the bloody drink would kill him,' Gloria said, her voice shrill. 'I *told* him!'

Ellen laid a soothing hand on her mother's shoulder, although her own panic was increasing by the second. 'Mum, calm down, he's just had a bump, he'll come round.'

'No, he won't, I slapped his face a minute ago

and he didn't even stir. Help him, Ellen, help him!'

'Calm *down*, Mum. Has anyone gone for Dr Airey?'

Len shook his head.

Rose said, 'I'll go.' She got to her feet and pushed past Chris and Neil, standing bug-eyed at the door.

'Neil! I told you to stay at home and watch the potatoes!' Ellen said, fear making her snap.

'I made Davey to do it, I wanted to see Granddad,' Neil replied, unable to take his eyes off the still figure on the floor. 'There's blood on him, Mum.'

Ellen said, 'He's had a fall, love, but he'll be all right. The doctor's coming in a minute.'

Neil looked at her as though he didn't quite believe her.

'Now go home, sweetheart, and wait for Dad. You can't leave Davey by himself, you know he gets frightened.'

Reluctantly, Neil moved closer to the door.

'Granddad will be fine,' Ellen said again. She didn't want Neil to be here when Dr Airey arrived, just in case. 'Go on, I'll be home soon.'

Neil gave her a last, doubtful look and disappeared.

'You hop off too, eh?' Len said to Chris, anticipating that Dr Airey would need a bit of space.

He arrived five minutes later. Without preamble he crouched down next to Alf. 'What happened?'

'He fell on the steps and must have hit his

head,' Gloria said, very obviously trying not to cry now. Ellen put her arm around her.

Dr Airey leaned closer and wrinkled his nose. 'Been at the pub, has he?'

Gloria said, 'I told him it would be the death of him.'

'It's not been the death of him yet, Gloria, he's just out cold,' the doctor replied, although he definitely didn't like the blue tinge to Alf's lips. 'When did it happen?'

'About half an hour ago,' Gloria said. 'I heard him fall but I didn't . . . I didn't go outside straight away because I thought the silly old bugger had just fallen over. He's always doing it.' She burst into tears.

Dr Airey nodded. Thirty minutes was a long time to be unconscious, but he didn't think any earlier intervention on Gloria's part would have made a difference. He gently lifted Alf's eyelids and shone a small torch directly into each eye. The pupils were already fully dilated and didn't change in response to the light — another ominous sign.

Next he examined the gash behind Alf's ear. It was about three inches long and had bled copiously, as head wounds did, but it was what he discovered under it that bothered him. He looked away and focused solely on his sense of touch as he pressed his fingers delicately over and around the cut, wincing as he felt a spongy mass beneath it give sickeningly. When he detected what he suspected might be shards of bone, he stopped his examination immediately.

Wiping his bloodied hands on a tea towel, he

checked Alf's pulse, which was slow and erratic, then got to his feet, his heart sinking. He knew Alf Powys well, and was very fond of the easy-going old tosspot.

'I'm phoning for the ambulance,' he said to Gloria. 'He seems to have quite a serious head injury, I'm afraid.' At the stricken look on her face, he added, 'I can't say exactly how serious, but as he's been unconscious for half an hour I think we'd better get him through to the hospital.'

Gloria looked as though someone had just slapped her across the face. 'Hospital? The hospital in Hamilton?'

'Yes, they're properly equipped for this sort of thing.'

'He's going to die, isn't he?'

'Come on now, Gloria, I think it's far too premature to be thinking anything like that,' Dr Airey said. 'Let's just get him to the hospital, shall we?'

Gloria nodded. 'Yes,' she said, 'yes, let's get him to the hospital.'

She had stopped crying now, but her voice had taken on an eerie calm, and to Dr Airey that seemed somehow worse.

★ ★ ★

While Ellen sat on the floor with her father and Dr Airey checked his pulse every few minutes, Gloria changed into her good coat and shoes and collected her handbag. Alf still had not moved, although he had begun to groan sporadically. He

239

also wet himself, the dark stain of his urine spreading out across the front of his trousers as the others looked on helplessly. Ellen fetched a rug and put it over him, and a pillow for beneath his head.

Tom arrived, and sat down at the table with Gloria, stunned. Dr Airey observed them — Gloria with her hat on and her handbag balanced on her knee as though she were sitting at the Junction station waiting for the midday train into town, and Ellen on the floor gently and repeatedly stroking her father's limp hand — and sighed.

'There won't be room in the ambulance for everyone,' he said. 'I'm sure they'll let you travel with him, Gloria, but Ellen, I suspect you and Tom will have to make your own way to the hospital.'

'I'm not going,' Tom said.

Ellen looked at him in surprise.

'Well, one of us has to stay with the boys. We can't send them over to Bert's, he's already got his hands full.'

'What about Milly?' Ellen said. 'She'll take them.'

'I'm sure she would,' Tom said, 'but Ellen, love, do I really need to be there? He'll come right, you'll see, give it a couple of days and he'll be fine.'

He looked at her, wanting desperately to say what was bothering him, but he couldn't get the words out. He was a superstitious man, although he would never admit it, and was convinced that if they were to all sit around Alf's bed at the hospital weeping and being miserable as though he'd already died and it was simply a matter of the undertaker turning up with the coffin, then he actually might die.

'I'll come if you really need me,' he added, 'it's not that I don't want to.'

'No, you're right,' Ellen said, knowing full well that he really didn't want to. 'It would be better if you stayed with the boys,' she added, giving him a legitimate reason to stay behind.

'I'll ring Hazel first thing in the morning,' he said. 'She'll probably want to come down if Alf's going to be stuck in there for a few days.'

Dr Airey regarded Tom uneasily; the man was a miner so surely he'd seen the likely outcome of this sort of injury before? And then he realised — Tom was putting on a brave face for the women.

'Would you, Thomas?' Gloria said, sounding relieved and grateful. 'That would be a big help.'

'First thing,' Tom promised.

'But how will I get to the hospital?' Ellen asked. She looked at her watch. 'I'll have missed the train.'

Tom thought for a moment. 'Why don't I ask Jack if he'll run you through?'

Ellen opened her mouth to protest, then shut it again because it felt exactly right, the idea of being with Jack now. Guiltily, she realised that she very much needed to see him, to be close to his solid and reassuring presence. Then she looked at Tom, and remembered that not long ago he would have steadied her and given her

241

courage. She wanted both of them, but she needed Jack.

'Will he be home, do you think?'

Tom shrugged. 'I can soon find out.'

The ambulance arrived. Alf was lifted onto a stretcher and loaded into the back of it, with Gloria perched at his side, one hand clutching her handbag and the other resting proprietarily on his arm.

Ellen and Tom stood by the front gate and watched as the ambulance drove away, then went next door to tell Len and Rose what was happening. Rose offered to mind the boys if they wanted to follow Alf to the hospital, but Tom explained that he would be staying behind. He suggested then to Ellen that she go home, tell the boys some sort of half-truth about their grandfather, then get herself ready to go to Hamilton. While she was doing that he would go around to Jack's and sort out a ride for her.

As Tom headed off up the street, Ellen almost called out after him to tell him that she did want him to go with her after all, that it was really important that he did, but the words dried up before she could get them out, and by then he had disappeared around the corner and it was too late.

10

Ellen sat in silence, barely aware of the Waikato landscape flicking past in the darkness. She glanced over at Jack.

'All right?' he asked, his eyes on the road.

'Mmm.'

He'd arrived to pick her up so promptly she'd barely had time to change her shoes, run a brush through her hair and grab her bag and coat. She'd hugged the boys tightly, promising that their grandfather would be fine, then given Tom a quick kiss goodbye, feeling oddly self-conscious because Jack was standing in the kitchen with them, and then they were off. Lost in her own thoughts, she had said very little to Jack so far, and he'd seemed content to let her be.

But now he said, 'Penny for your thoughts, or don't you feel like talking?'

'No, it's not that,' she said after a moment. 'I've been thinking about Dad.'

'Banging his head like that?'

Ellen shifted in her seat to face Jack. 'No, just him in general. What a lovely father he's been. He is,' she corrected.

Jack nodded but didn't say anything. He'd been more than happy to bring Ellen through to Hamilton, although he had felt a shadow of guilty unease when Tom had turned up. If she wanted to talk, that was fine by him, but after what Tom had told him about Alf's condition, he doubted there was anything he could really say to ease her worry, or her fear.

'I can remember when I was tiny, I would have been about three I suppose, or maybe four,' she said, 'when he used to come up at the end of his shift and I'd wait for him at the mine entrance. And he'd always smile when he saw me and his teeth looked so white in his dirty face, and he'd pick me up and give me a cuddle and swing me up onto his shoulders on his way to the bathhouse. Then he'd put me down and tell me to play while he was in there, but not to sit on the concrete or I'd get piles. And by the time we got home I'd be covered in coal dust and Mum would always tell him off for getting my clothes dirty! But I loved it, Jack, I loved riding along way up high, hanging onto his ears so I wouldn't fall off. I felt like I owned the town when he did that, I really did.'

Jack smiled at the image.

Ellen did too. 'And he was always making things for us, for me and Hazel. Hazel's my sister, she's eleven years older than me and lives in Auckland with her husband and kids. Dad built us a swing, and a slide that used to give us splinters in our bums, and a playhouse.' She laughed. 'He pinched the wood for it from the Pukemiro Collieries sawmill, a couple of planks a night when it was dark. Took him about three months to get enough.'

'Sounds like the perfect dad,' Jack said.

'And he made us a canoe, for in the creek, with a pair of paddles, one each. That wasn't quite so successful, and Mum had a fit when she found out about it sinking, but Dad was there so we were all right. I don't think he told her half the things we got up to. She was always much more strict on us than Dad ever was. He took us down the mine a few times, too, and didn't tell her about that either. She would have gone berserk. She's always said thank Christ she never had sons, because there would have been hell to pay between her and Dad about letting them go on the coal.'

'Did he want boys, your Dad?'

'No, I don't think so. Well, if he ever did he never showed it. He always said Hazel and I were his little princesses, that he couldn't have asked for lovelier daughters if God had given him a pad and a pencil and told him to order exactly what he wanted. Mum spoiled us, making us all sorts of lovely little dresses so we'd be the best-dressed kids in Pukemiro, and spending no end of money on shoes and what have you for us, but Dad was always the one who gave us more of the things that didn't need money. Do you know what I mean?'

Jack nodded.

'He'd spend lots of time with us, especially when we were little, and taught us all about the weather and plants and animals and the coal and all that. Especially the coal. I could tell the difference between three different types of coal by the time I was five.'

Jack wasn't surprised. He already knew Ellen well enough to know that she was very bright, and had an appetite for the sort of knowledge a lot of women wouldn't be interested in, such as

245

how machinery worked and the different techniques used for mining. It delighted him, and he could see now that a lot of that had come from her father.

'I was jealous of Hazel, though,' Ellen confessed. 'She was so much older than me and was allowed to do more exciting things. Dad wouldn't take me underground until I was eight, he said it was too dangerous, so when he took her down when she was fifteen, which she didn't want to do anyway because she hated getting dirty but Dad said it was in her blood and she had to have at least one decent look, I remember sitting at home bawling my eyes out because it was so unfair. And she did come back filthy, too, and had to lie to Mum and say she'd fallen over on the railway track.' She shot Jack a guilty look. 'Actually, I was really pleased when Hazel got married and left home. She was twenty-one, and she'd met this lad Charlie Hammond the year before, boating on Hamilton Lake. Mum pushed and pushed her to get out of Pukemiro and 'meet a better class of boy', I think was how she put it, and anyway she'd gone through to Hamilton with some friends to go boating, and she did meet someone, and that was Charlie. Who Mum always insists on calling Charles, like she says Thomas. Charlie turned out to be from Auckland, and over the next year he came down to see Hazel quite a bit, then he asked her to marry him, which Mum thought was just wonderful, and I suppose Hazel did as well. I can't really remember because I was only ten. I do remember being a right little brat, though, following them around all the time and annoying them. Dad taught me to do this,' she said, slipping her left hand down the neck of her blouse and under her right armpit, and flapping her arm to make a farting noise. 'Dad and I thought it was hilarious, and I think Charlie might have, too, but Mum and Hazel were disgusted with me.'

Jack laughed out loud. 'I can imagine.'

'Anyway, they got married and Hazel went to live in Auckland, and I was absolutely chuffed because I had Dad all to myself for another ten years.'

'Has he always been a union man?' Jack asked.

He knew Alf had, but he wanted to keep Ellen talking about him because it seemed to be doing her some good. When he'd arrived to pick her up earlier, her face had been deathly pale and her eyes red and brimming, and it had been all he could do to stop himself from gathering her up in his arms and rocking her and telling her not to worry because he would fix everything.

'Ever since I can remember,' Ellen said. 'He was always going off to meetings all fired up, and coming home from work and chucking his bag down on the kitchen floor and declaring, 'Right, that's bloody it, we're out!' Poor Mum, she nearly died of shame when the Puke men went on strike during the war. I think she was convinced the Allies would be brought to their knees by any sort of industrial action in Huntly, and that Dad would get his name on the front page of newspapers all over the English-speaking world for being a saboteur.'

'I think the government thought that, too. About the industrial action, not your father,' Jack said.

'Probably. But he's always been a natural negotiator, Dad. He's got the gift of the gab and people listen to him. Except for Mum, she doesn't. I remember when Tom and I were going out together ... ' She stopped. 'Oh, you probably don't want to hear about that. Sorry.'

Jack shrugged. 'I don't mind, not if you don't mind telling me about it.'

Ellen looked thoughtful. 'No, I don't, because it's a story about Dad, not Tom. Turn right here.'

'What?'

'Turn right.' Ellen pointed to a road coming up at the north end of Victoria Street. 'We need to go around the edge of the lake to get to the hospital.'

'Oh, right,' Jack said, who for a moment had almost forgotten why they were driving to Hamilton.

'Tom was living at Rotowaro,' Ellen went on. 'His parents lived there, too, but they're out at Raglan now. I met him at one of the local dances. He was underground at Alison then. I knew Mum wouldn't approve of him, just because he was a miner, so I didn't take him home for months. It was tricky — whenever we went to the same functions as Mum and Dad I had to pretend I barely knew him. But then when we got serious we couldn't really avoid it. She knew anyway, of course. You can't do anything in Pukemiro without everyone else knowing your business.'

'I know, I've been worrying about that,' Jack said, bringing the conversation back to the present.

But Ellen ignored him, intent on her story. 'She was very nice to him when he finally did visit, and got the good tea service out and everything, but as soon as he'd gone she said, 'Don't get any ideas about marrying that one, young lady, because he's the wrong man for you.' And I said 'Yes, Mum' and took no notice, but then he did ask me to marry him and there was hell to pay when I finally told her.' Ellen shook her head as she recalled how relentlessly Gloria had gone on and on about the horrendous mistake she was about to make. 'She said Tom would never amount to anything, that he'd spend his entire working life underground and never earn enough money, that we'd be trapped forever living at Rotowaro, which she was wrong about because he moved to Pukemiro as soon as we were married . . . '

'That probably wasn't what she meant, though, was it?'

'No, but I'm happy living in a mining town, it's where I belong. It's where I'll always belong. In the end she said she'd see me marry Tom over her dead body.'

'Really? Christ, that was a bit steep, wasn't it?'

'I thought so, especially since I know that underneath she actually quite liked him, even then. And Dad really liked him, he thought he'd make a lovely son-in-law. Tom was a miner, he was moving up in the union, and he liked a beer. What could be better?'

'I think I can guess what came next,' Jack said.

'Yes, Mum and Dad had the most God-awful barney about it. I mean, they've always bickered and squabbled — well, Mum has, Dad's generally just ignored her and gone on his merry way — but I've never seen them at each other like they were then. They fought for days. Dad even yelled, which isn't like him at all. He got really angry and told Mum to stop interfering with my life because it just wasn't on. And Mum yelled back and said of all people he should know what she was going on about, and he said yes, he bloody well did know and wished to God he didn't. It got really nasty. It was awful.'

'Sounds it.'

'In the end, Dad put his foot down and said that Tom was a good man and if I wanted to marry him that was fine by him, and he didn't want to hear another word about it from Mum, ever.'

'And did he?'

'I'm sure he did, but she quietened down after that. Although she'll still have a little go now and then. She likes Tom, I know she does, but I think she still hasn't quite forgiven him for not being the man she wanted for me.'

'So what was your mother really worried about, do you know?'

Ellen felt herself blushing and was grateful for the darkness in the cab of Jack's truck. 'According to her, she wanted me to marry a man who wouldn't bore me, who had the ambition and the passion to keep the marriage going and keep me satisfied and happy. Those

250

are her words, not mine.'

There was a long minute of silence, while Jack pretended to concentrate on his driving and Ellen gazed out through the passenger window into the night.

'And did you?' he asked eventually.

Ellen closed her eyes. Up until very recently she would have said yes, but she couldn't now, not with any degree of conviction, and the realisation saddened and dismayed her. If she had only met Jack ten years ago, then her children would be his and not Tom's, and she wouldn't have to go around feeling as though she were being torn in half every minute of every day. Was it possible to love two men at the same time? Or did she only love one man, and was merely infatuated with the other? She didn't know, and didn't have the energy right now to try and work it out.

'I don't know, Jack,' she said. And then, with a truth that trickled through her veins like ice water, she added, 'No, I don't think I did.'

And there it was — out now, and out in front of Jack.

He reached across the seat and squeezed her hand gently, and she was grateful to him for not saying anything.

As they neared the hospital a few minutes later, the imposing line of buildings overlooking the lake lit brightly against the night, Jack said, 'Shall I drop you off and come and find you? Or would you rather I waited in the truck?'

'Oh, Jack, I could be hours, we could be here all night,' she said. 'It's lovely of you to offer but,

251

well, I wouldn't feel . . . '

'I know,' he said, 'I understand, it's not my place. I just don't like to think of you up here all night by yourself.'

'I'll have Mum.'

He looked at her sympathetically. 'What if I just come in and find out how he's getting on, then I can tell Tom and the boys when I get home? They'll be waiting for news.'

Ellen smiled at him gratefully. She didn't want him to go, not yet.

They parked the truck and walked together through the front doors of the main hospital building, and Ellen asked a passing nurse where she might find her father. The nurse indicated a nearby lift and told them the next floor and turn right.

Gloria was looking very lonely and bereft, sitting on a chair in what appeared to be a waiting room. Someone had given her a cup of tea, but she hadn't touched it. Her face was splotchy and her lipstick had come off, which looked odd to Ellen, who was so used to seeing her mother with her peach-coloured lips, even just around the house.

Ellen went over to her, while Jack hovered near the door.

'What's happening? Where's Dad?' she asked.

Gloria reached out a shaking hand. 'He's been taken into surgery, about twenty minutes ago. The doctor took one look at him and said he needed to go to theatre right away. Oh, Ellen, I'm so frightened.'

Ellen was startled. She had never heard her

252

mother say she was frightened, and certainly never in association with her father. Angry, insulted, embarrassed or exasperated, yes, but never frightened.

'Did he say anything else?' she asked.

'Your father?'

'The doctor.'

Gloria shook her head. 'He just asked if I had anyone to sit with me. I said you'd be along soon.'

Ellen beckoned to Jack, and sat down next to her mother.

He came over. 'Hello, Mrs Powys. Very sorry to hear about Alf. Let me know if there's anything I can do.'

'Thank you.'

'He's in surgery,' Ellen said, 'but Mum hasn't heard anything else, have you, Mum?'

'No, the doctor said he'd come and see me as soon as he's out.'

Jack stood before them, looking uncomfortable. 'Do you want me to stay?' he asked Ellen.

Even in her distraught state, Gloria caught the intensity of the look that passed between them.

Ellen shook her head, although she very much did want him to stay. 'We'll be all right. Thank you for bringing me though.'

'No problem,' Jack said.

'We'll phone Fred Hollis at the shop if there's any news,' Ellen added, 'and he can pass it on. Can you tell Tom?'

Jack nodded, and then he was gone.

Gloria and Ellen sat side by side for several minutes, both silenced by apprehension and fear.

Finally, Ellen said, 'Where did you get that cup of tea? Shall I get us another one?'

'A nice young nurse brought it to me.'

'Oh,' Ellen said. She was desperate for a drink.

'She went through there,' Gloria said, pointing to a set of double doors opposite the waiting room with a sign above them saying 'No Admittance'. Ellen went through them and found herself in a linoleumed, antiseptic-smelling corridor, turned left and kept walking until she saw a solid, middle-aged nurse, whose name tag said 'Sister Abernathy'.

'Excuse me,' Ellen said, 'I wonder if you could tell me where I could get a cup of tea?'

The nurse looked very put out. 'We don't allow the public in this part of the hospital, I'm afraid.'

'Well, my name's Ellen McCabe and I'm waiting with my mother, Mrs Gloria Powys. My father, Alf Powys, was brought in earlier and he's having surgery.'

Sister Abernathy's round face softened. 'Oh, yes, of course. I'm sorry, love, you're in the waiting room, aren't you?'

Ellen nodded.

'Well, I'll see what I can do. But this is the operating floor, and it's best if you stay where you were, I think.'

'Have you heard anything about my father?'

'Dr St John is still with him. But as soon as he's finished I'm sure he'll be along to see you.'

Ellen thanked her and went back the way she'd come. A few minutes later another nurse brought them a cup of tea each, and instructions

254

on how to find the public cafeteria if they wanted anything else.

They drank their tea. Occasionally someone would come bustling through the double doors, but no one stopped to talk to them.

Gloria said, 'I'll suppose I'll have to nurse him when he comes home.'

Ellen looked at her. 'You can do that, can't you?'

'I expect so. I'm just wondering how long he'll have to be off the beer. You know your father, he can get very snaky when he's deprived.'

'Mum, I've never seen Dad snaky in his life. Tetchy, perhaps, but never snaky.'

'Can you remember when he had that ulcer a few years ago, the one the doctor said was caused by too much booze?'

'The one Dad insisted he never had?'

'Yes. He was supposed to lay off the beer for three months while it healed, and do you know what I caught him doing?'

'No,' Ellen said, although she knew she was about to find out.

'Putting whisky on his porridge. And in his tea, and on his bread pudding after dinner. And when I had him up about it, he said he had a perfect right to put whisky in or on anything he liked, because the doctor only told him to lay off the beer.'

'You should have told me he was being difficult,' Ellen said. 'I could have talked to him about it.'

Gloria snorted. 'You wouldn't have been much

help. The pair of you have always been as thick as thieves.'

They looked up as a man came through the double doors.

Gloria took a deep breath. 'Dr St John, this is my daughter Ellen McCabe.'

'Hello, Mrs McCabe. Your husband is out of theatre, Mrs Powys. You can see him now.'

'How is he? Is he all right?' Gloria stood up.

'He hasn't regained consciousness yet,' the doctor said, 'but we think we've relieved a little of the pressure on his brain. He's had a very bad fall, Mrs Powys, and the outlook isn't terribly good.' At the shattered look on Gloria's face he added, 'I'm sorry to be so brutal, but there really isn't an easier way for me to say it.'

'Where is he now?' Ellen asked.

'We've taken him onto the ward, but he's in a room of his own so you're welcome to sit with him for as long as you like. I'll take you there now.'

Gloria and Ellen followed him up and down floors and through what seemed to be a rabbit warren of corridors until they reached a small room that already had 'Mr A. Powys' written on a piece of card on the door.

They went in, Gloria gripping Ellen's hand.

Alf's face was an ashen grey and a thick bandage covered his head and his left ear. His eyes were closed and he was breathing shallowly through his mouth. Sister Abernathy was already there, moving around the bed smoothing the sheets and tucking them in firmly.

'You can hold his hand and talk to him, if you

like,' she said. 'We're not completely sure, but he might be able to hear you.'

'I'll be checking on him regularly,' Dr St John said. 'We hope to see some improvement by the morning, but we may not. I'm sorry I can't give you any better news.'

Gloria nodded, pulled a chair up to the bed and sat down. 'Thank you, Doctor, I know you've done your best.'

He nodded, checked his watch and said, 'I'll be back at about eleven. We'll see how he's going then, shall we?'

*　*　*

Hazel and Charlie arrived at nine o'clock the next morning, later than they'd hoped because they'd made a detour out to Pukemiro to drop their two youngest children off with Tom.

Ellen had telephoned Fred Hollis an hour earlier, with a message for Tom telling him there had been no change, although Dr St John insisted that Alf was 'comfortable'. Fred had told Ellen that the whole town was thinking of them.

Ellen, Gloria, Hazel and Charlie took turns through the day sitting with Alf and talking to him, just in case what Sister Abernathy had said was true.

He may have heard them and he may not, but he never responded and at four-thirty on Sunday afternoon, Alf Powys died.

*　*　*

Gloria fell apart. She told Dr St John he'd made a mistake, then accused him of lying, and finally turned to the bed where Alf's body lay and berated him for being such a drunken old fool. Then she collapsed over him, sobbing hysterically, and Hazel and Ellen had to pull her off while the doctor went away to get something to calm her down.

Hazel seemed stunned into silence. Ellen herself could not quite comprehend what had happened, until Sister Abernathy drew the sheet up over her father's face. But she couldn't cry, not yet. Feeling as though she were trapped in some sort of ghastly, muffled nightmare, she went downstairs to the public telephone and rang Fred Hollis again to ask him to pass the awful news on to Tom.

'But tell him not to tell Neil and Davey, not yet. I want to be there,' she said.

'I'm so sorry, Ellen, I really am,' Fred said. 'If there's anything we can do, anything at all . . . '

'I know, Fred, thank you.'

'Do you have a lift back? Because I can organise someone to come and collect you.'

'No, thanks, Fred. Hazel and Charlie are here so we'll come back with them. We'll be leaving soon, I think.'

'How's Gloria bearing up?'

'She's not, she's sedated at the moment.'

'Oh, hell,' Fred said. 'And what about you, love?'

Ellen said nothing for a very long time, and then she started to cry.

On the other end of the telephone Fred felt his

258

own eyes filling with tears, and wished he'd never asked. 'There, there,' he said.

When Ellen was able to speak again, she said, 'I'm sorry, Fred, I have to go now. Please don't tell Neil and Davey yet.'

She hung up and wandered back to Alf's room.

Gloria was sitting with Charlie and Hazel on either side of her. She looked dazed, but she was quiet.

Hazel said, 'What do we do now?'

Charlie, his face pale, took a deep breath. 'We go back to Pukemiro and tell everyone we need to tell, then I suppose we'll have to arrange for the undertaker to come and get him. And then we'll need to sort out the funeral.'

★   ★   ★

Hundreds of people came, not just from Pukemiro but from Huntly and all the other mining communities as well. Many of them had to stand outside the church during the service, but no one seemed to mind.

The wake was held at the miners' hall. On the morning of the funeral it seemed that someone from just about every household in Pukemiro had turned up at Gloria's house bearing a plate, so there was no shortage of food, despite the strike.

Gloria had pulled herself together, with only a little help from the tablets Dr St John had sent home with her, and conducted herself with great dignity. She dressed in her smartest clothes and

259

applied her make-up impeccably, and only broke down when Alf was lowered into the ground at the cemetery.

Ellen and Hazel were in tears throughout the proceedings, but even they laughed when people began to get up at the hall and tell 'Alf stories', almost all of which involved alcohol and some of which had become legend over the years. Alf had been a drunk, but he'd been a happy drunk, and there wasn't a single person in the town who bore him any malice, not even the deputies and the mine managers he'd driven almost to distraction for decades with his incessant demands for better pay, better conditions and wet time so the jokers could catch the earlier train into town and have more time at the pub.

Charlie went back to Auckland the following day, taking the children with him, but Hazel decided to stay with Gloria for a week. Ellen spent much of every day with them, and when Friday came she couldn't find it within herself to meet Jack.

She saw him that afternoon, though, when he came to pay his respects to Gloria.

'I thought you'd be here,' he said, as she walked him to the door when he was ready to go.

Ellen touched his hand. 'I'm sorry I didn't come today. I just couldn't.'

They walked slowly down the steps.

'It's all right,' he said, 'I didn't expect you to. I did want to see you, though, to make sure you were all right. Are you?'

Ellen leaned against the rail at the bottom and sighed. 'Not really. It was such a shock, Jack, I

260

really thought Dad would last forever. I miss him so much it hurts.'

'How are the boys?'

'They were devastated. They still are. They thought the sun shone out of their granddad's backside.'

'They'll come right, though, kids always do,' Jack said.

'Do they?'

'I don't know, I just said that to make you feel better.'

Ellen smiled. 'You always try to say the right thing, don't you?'

'Only when it's not too far from the truth. So do you. And I think kids are fairly resilient.'

'I hope so, for their sake.'

She wanted to feel his arms around her, to be comforted and soothed. Tom was doing his best, but even as he cuddled her and told her that everything would be all right, it was Jack she was thinking about, and that only made her feel worse.

She would have dearly loved to have gone to him this morning — she felt she had no right to feel joy in the middle of such an awful time — and looking at Jack now, standing there with his hands in his pockets and his dark eyes regarding her with compassion, she wished she had.

'I'm sorry about this morning,' she said again.

'Will you come next week?' he asked, reaching out and touching her face.

'Yes.'

Hazel went home, and Ellen spent Sunday afternoon with her mother. Alf had been gone a week, but Gloria still didn't feel like leaving the house.

When Ellen arrived she found her mother in the kitchen, sitting at the table, with a decanter of sherry and two glasses in front of her.

Ellen was surprised. 'It's a bit early for sherry, isn't it, Mum?'

'No,' Gloria said. 'Would you like one?'

Ellen didn't particularly like the sort of sherry her mother drank, it was far too sweet for her taste, but accepted because she didn't want Gloria drinking alone.

'Have you had some lunch?' she asked. She was worried that with her father gone, her mother wouldn't bother cooking just for herself.

'Rose brought a shepherd's pie over this morning, I had some of that.'

'You have to look after yourself, Mum.'

Gloria pinched a roll of fat around her middle. 'I'll not fade away, dear, if that's what you're worried about.'

Ellen smiled. Had that been a hint of sarcasm? She hoped so — it would be a good sign.

They had a drink together, then another, and by the third, Ellen had decided that sweet sherry wasn't that undrinkable after all. But when her mother offered her a fourth, she shook her head.

'I've had enough, Mum. And so have you, I think.'

'Not quite,' Gloria said, pouring herself one

more. 'I need a bit of Dutch courage.'

'What for?'

Gloria stared into her glass for a long moment, then raised her eyes.

'Ellen, there's something I need to tell you. I should have told you long before this, but I haven't.'

Ellen waited, mystified.

'Your father was a good man, he was decent, kind, honest and hard-working. We didn't always see eye to eye and we were like chalk and cheese a lot of the time, but it wasn't always like that. When we first walked out together I thought I'd met the man of my dreams. He was good-looking, and he was funny, and he was quite good at, well, you know what I'm talking about.'

Ellen regarded her mother with something akin to shock. 'Before you were married?'

'Yes, before we were married. Your grand-mother always said you don't buy tomatoes without squeezing them first, so, well, let's just say I wasn't disappointed with the produce.'

'Mum!'

'Don't 'Mum' me, dear. You had a bit of a cheek wearing white at your own wedding, if I remember rightly.'

Ellen went red. 'You wouldn't have let me wear anything else.'

'No, I most certainly would not. Anyway, your father was doing well at work, bringing home plenty of money and working every shift he could get so we could buy this house and everything we needed for it.' Gloria sat back in her seat. 'Oh, I had such hopes for your father,

263

Ellen. He was clever as well, you see, and I thought with a little bit of application he could go for his tickets and work his way up to at least mine manager. Then we could go about town with our heads held high and be proud of everything he'd achieved.'

'All miners can hold their heads up, Mum, it's a good, honest job.'

'Yes, I knew you'd say that, and so unfortunately did your father. It took me a few years but I finally realised he had no intention of being anything other than what he was. He wasn't even interested in working up to under-deputy. All he cared about was that bloody union of his.'

Ellen knew all this. 'But, Mum, those were your dreams, not Dad's.'

'I know that now, dear, but for years I was so sure he'd want the same things as I did. I couldn't understand why he wouldn't.' Gloria took a long sip of her sherry. 'Are you sure you don't want another one?'

'Positive. But if you knew he didn't, and that he was never going to, why didn't you ever let up on him? Why couldn't you just let him be the way he was?'

'It was just our way. Your father loved me, Ellen, and I loved him, very much, in spite of the way it might have looked. We'd gone on like that for so long, what was the point of changing? What would we have gained?'

'A bit of peace and quiet?'

'We tried peace and quiet, dear, and we didn't like it. It was . . . boring.'

Ellen turned her empty glass around on the table, watching the tiny bit of sherry left in the bottom swirl from side to side. She was beginning to feel a little angry at her mother's admissions; what good were they now?

'Did you ever tell him?'

'Tell him what?'

'That your dreams were just that, Mum, dreams. Selfish ones, too, if you don't mind me saying so.'

Gloria regarded her daughter thoughtfully, glad to see the spark in her that Alf had so admired was still strong, even if he would never see it again. 'Oh, I know they were selfish. And yes, I did tell him, eventually.'

'Good.'

'Because I owed it to him.'

'I'll say you did. You didn't give them up, though, did you, your dreams?'

'No, we just agreed that he didn't have to listen to them any more. It was a good arrangement, it suited us both.'

Ellen frowned. 'Why did you owe him?'

There was a short pause, then Gloria said, 'Because he did something, and it was the kindest, most decent thing anyone has ever done for me. It was after I made a mistake.'

'What sort of mistake?'

'I left him.'

There was a stunned silence while Ellen gaped at her mother.

'You *left* him?'

Gloria nodded. 'When Hazel was nine.'

'But . . . she never said anything.' Ellen could

265

hardly believe what she was hearing.

'She wasn't there, she was staying with your grandmother. We were, well, we'd been having problems, your father and I, and we thought it would be better if she was somewhere that wasn't so . . . fraught.' Gloria finished her sherry and poured herself another one, although this time it was only half a glass. 'Just after she'd gone, I was in town one day at the bank and there was a new man there, behind the counter, showing something or other to one of the clerks. I'd never seen him before and I knew right away he wasn't from Huntly. He was wearing the most beautifully cut suit and his hair was all brilliantined and he looked so smart.'

Ellen wasn't sure now that she wanted to hear this.

'So I smiled at him,' Gloria went on, 'and he smiled back, and when he asked me would I meet him for lunch, I said yes. I can't explain why I said it, Ellen, so don't ask. And it started from that. He was from Hamilton and was only in Huntly for a week and when he went back I went through to see him. He had a little two-bedroom cottage in Collingwood Street and we met there.' She picked up her sherry glass, then put it back down without drinking. 'I thought your father and I were coming to a parting of the ways, and I just didn't have the energy left to keep on trying. I was so disappointed with him, Ellen, I just couldn't be bothered.'

'Because he wouldn't be a mine manager?'

'I suppose so, if you want to put it like that.

And Ray was everything I thought I wanted in a man. He was clever, he was educated, he had a good, professional job. There was just something about him, although I really couldn't tell you what it was. When I was with him he made me feel, oh, I don't know, that I was safe, that nothing bad would ever happen again. Something like that, anyway.'

Ellen avoided her mother's eyes. She wanted to keep on feeling angry at her but she couldn't, she felt too hypocritical.

'We met for about a month, then one day he told me he loved me and couldn't live without me. He said if I left Alf, he'd marry me as soon as my divorce came through. By then I was so besotted I would have done anything for him. So I did leave your father. I left Hazel, too, and by Christ that was hard, although she never really knew what was going on. I just walked out and went to live with Ray, and I was so happy, Ellen, I'd never known happiness like it. Then, about a month after that, he came home from work one day and told me he'd changed his mind, and could I please leave by the end of the week.'

'But why?' Ellen said, imagining how absolutely devastated her mother must have been.

'He told me he was married,' Gloria said, 'separated but still married, and that he and his wife had decided to try again. So I packed my things and I came back here and asked your father to take me back.'

'And did he?'

'Well, obviously.'

'Well, you're right, then, that was a very kind

and decent thing for him to do.'

Gloria lowered her eyes, took a very deep breath and placed her manicured hands flat on the table. Then she looked straight at Ellen. 'No, that wasn't the decent thing, not really. When I came back I was pregnant. With you.'

Ellen felt faint. 'What are you saying?'

'I'm saying, sweetheart, that your father wasn't really your father, although we told everyone you were his. That was his idea. I'm so sorry, Ellen, I should have told you long before this, but I just couldn't.'

Gloria watched as a succession of emotions flowed across her daughter's face — disbelief, anger, bewilderment and hurt, one after the other.

'I'm so sorry,' she said again. 'So you be very careful with that Jack Vaughan, Ellen, or you might just end up as sorry as I've been for the last thirty years.'

11

June 1951

Tom jammed his hat further down on his head and took a last deep drag on his cigarette. He was nervous, but it was more from anticipation than fear.

Lew was on his left, Vic on his right, and Pat and Frank were behind them. They were outside the Civic Theatre on Queen Street, waiting for the march to start. Bert had cried off, saying that if he was bashed on the head by a baton Christ only knew what might happen to his kids. The others understood, and there were no hard feelings. Jack was also missing, as he'd had to go out to the back of Waingaro first thing this morning with his truck to pick up a couple of sheep.

The crowd seemed huge to Tom, and the atmosphere crackled with tension and expectation. They were saying there were close to a thousand of them here today. There were even women taking part, members of the Auckland Women's Auxiliary, including Jack Barnes' wife; Tom could see them lining up at the front, carrying placards advertising a public meeting on Sunday at the Auckland Domain.

The word came to move and they started off, slowly but steadily, keeping four or five abreast on the left side of the street. Shoppers and bystanders stopped to look; some booed but the majority cheered, or so it seemed to Tom anyway. But they'd not gone far when the marchers at the front slowed and then came to a halt.

'What is it?' Vic said, craning his neck to see what the hold-up was.

Then the mutter filtered back through the marchers: it's the cops, the cops, the cops.

'Here we go,' Lew said, dropping his smoke on the ground and grinding it out with his boot heel.

Pat said, 'Fuck it, I'm going up for a look. Who's with me?'

Off they went, weaving through the column of stalled marchers and dodging individuals who'd had a good look at the wall of police blocking the street and turned around.

'Fucking hell,' Tom said when he finally saw them. There seemed to be hundreds of them, lined up in rows with their batons out and their cars blockading the road.

An officer near the front stepped forward and announced through a bullhorn that the marchers had five minutes to disperse.

For two long minutes almost nobody moved, and it seemed that Queen Street had fallen almost totally silent. Then suddenly there was an eruption of yelling and scuffling as the first row of about seventy police charged, raising their arms and swinging their batons down onto anyone within reach. Tom winced as he saw one of the women go down, falling to her knees and scrambling to get out of the way. Behind him he heard Pat roar, and felt him push past in his eagerness to have a go at the cops.

'Keep an eye on him,' Tom yelled to Frank, 'or he'll end up in the bloody paddy wagon!'

Then, heart thumping, he was level with them himself, a line of blue uniforms moving forward and laying into people right, left and centre. As the front line broke, the second wave surged forward. The marchers were all unarmed, but fighting back viciously with fists and boots. There were men on the ground already, and Tom saw one bloke stagger past holding his hands over a bleeding wound at the back of his head.

He was struck on the shoulder then, with such force he nearly went down, and he thanked God he was wearing his heavy overcoat. He righted himself and spun around, coming face to face with a cop raising his baton for another go. Tom ducked, and again the blow landed on his shoulder. The cop reached out and grabbed him by the lapel.

'Get your filthy fucking hands off me!' Tom swore, wrenching himself free.

He felt anger exploding out of him, anger and pent-up fear at all that had been happening over the last few months. He hit out, caught the cop a solid blow on the cheek and knocked his helmet off.

Then he was pushed from behind and almost went flat on his face, but on glancing over his shoulder saw he'd merely been collected by a knot of flailing, punching men. He looked quickly around for the other Pukemiro men, caught sight of Vic going hand to hand with a

271

cop, and elbowed his way over to him. He kicked out and caught the policeman a good one on the shin, then gave him another one as he reeled back, just for luck. It wasn't sporting, two men onto one, even if the one was a cop, but too bloody bad.

Some of the marchers were scattering onto the footpath now, or heading back down Queen Street, and Tom didn't blame them.

Then the paddy wagons started to arrive, sirens wailing and lights flashing.

Pat saw them too. 'Time to go,' he said.

Tom followed him as he shoved his way out of the melee, stepping over a cop on the ground, a young bloke with most of his front teeth missing and his nose smashed. He looked dazed and bewildered, and just for a moment Tom felt sick at what was happening. He thought about stopping to pull the boy up onto the footpath, but pushed the idea away and headed up the street for the rear of the town hall, where they had all agreed to rendezvous if they were split up.

He and Pat were the first there, but Vic and Frank soon appeared, Vic with a split lip and Frank with one sleeve completely missing from his coat.

'What a pack of bloody *thugs*,' Frank said. He surveyed his torn sleeve. 'Jesus H. Christ, Milly's going to kill me when she sees this.'

They all laughed a bit too heartily.

'Christ, did you see those bastards?' Pat said. 'I've never seen such brutality in all my life!' He stopped, remembering some of the other stoushes he'd witnessed, and been party to, in his lifetime. 'Well, not from the bloody cops, anyway.'

'Did you see that poor joker with the blood pouring down his face?' Vic said. 'He couldn't even see where he was going and they still kept having a go at him!'

'A couple of the women were knocked down, too,' Frank said. 'Did you see that?'

Pat spat. 'Yeah, bastards.'

Lew arrived fifteen minutes later, having gone the long way round to circumnavigate the police who, after successfully dispersing the marchers, were now roaming up and down the streets looking for likely suspects.

'Bloody hell,' he exclaimed as he hurried up to them. His hat had disappeared and there was blood on his coat.

'Did you cop one?' Tom asked, nodding at the stain.

'Eh? No, it's someone else's, I think,' Lew said. 'I hope,' he added, patting himself down theatrically and making a show of looking for wounds.

'You'd know, mate,' Tom said, flexing his aching shoulder. 'Those batons are fucking solid.'

He was sore, but elated. His heart was no longer thudding in his ribcage, but he still felt exhilarated, wondering whether it was like that when a bloke went into battle: the stomach-churning anticipation, the sharpness of sight and sound and the great rush of adrenaline.

Lew rolled himself a smoke, his hands shaking

273

slightly. 'What now?'

'Nearest pub for a beer, I reckon,' Vic said.

Pat shook his head. 'Cops'll be all over the place. Best if we just disappear, I'd say. We'll stop at Mercer for a couple on the way home.'

Frank's brother had lent Frank his car — on strict instructions that only Frank could drive it as he was the sole member of the group who didn't drink — so today they had the luxury of being able to make their way home in their own time.

Frank's brother was very wise.

* * *

Tom got home at half-past eight that night, reeking of beer and having a bit of trouble standing up.

Ellen was ropable. 'Where the hell have you been?' she demanded.

'Stopped off at Mercer,' he said, sitting down heavily at the table. He was knackered and his head was starting to ache. He looked around blearily. 'Where's the boys?'

'Next door.'

'Where's the boys?' mimicked Fintan, who had migrated back into the kitchen now that the weather had turned cold.

'Oh, shut up, you mouthy little shit,' Tom muttered.

'No, you shut up,' Ellen said, standing in front of the sink with her hands on her hips. 'Look at the state of you!'

'Don't nag, woman.'

'I'm not nagging, Tom McCabe, I was worried sick. You said you'd be home by four o'clock.'

'I said *about* four o'clock.'

Ellen tapped her watch hard enough to stop it. 'Well, is this about four o'clock? Is it?'

Tom's stomach rumbled, reminding him he hadn't eaten anything since breakfast.

'I suppose you couldn't cook me some eggs?' he said.

There was a brief pause before she walked over to him, bent down and shouted in his face, *'Cook your own bloody eggs!'*

They stared at each other for a moment, both shocked, then Ellen sat down and burst into tears. Tom moved to touch her, then thought better of it. He wished he'd brought some beer home.

'It's been on the radio all afternoon,' she said, fishing a handkerchief out of the sleeve of her cardigan. 'They said there was a riot, and that twenty-two demonstrators were treated for serious wounds.' She blew her nose. 'They said there were bottles being thrown and attacks with sticks!'

'Batons, more like,' Tom said.

'And when you didn't come home I had visions of you lying in the hospital with your head split open . . . ' She burst into fresh tears.

Tom closed his eyes, not too drunk to realise what had probably been going through her mind.

'I'm sorry, love, I didn't think.'

'No, you didn't, did you?'

'Ah, love, what can I say?' He pushed himself

unsteadily to his feet and put his arms around her, leaning down so his face was against her hair.

'You smell nice,' he said. 'Have you just had a bath?'

'No,' she said, pulling away.

'Well, you smell nice.'

'You smell like a brewery.'

He sat down again. He wanted to tell her about how it had felt, being right in the middle of the fight, the excitement and the adrenaline and the conviction that, after all these bloody weeks of being on strike, he was finally taking some sort of real stand against the government, even if it was only by having a go at the cops. But going over in his head how he might describe it to her, he realised it could easily sound quite stupid now, like a game of bull-rush for grown men. Perhaps it even had been. In fact, the more the booze wore off, the more it did seem like that.

He beckoned to her. 'Come and give me a proper cuddle.'

She came over reluctantly and he pulled her onto his lap and gave her a good squeeze. Normally this made her giggle, but tonight she just sat there, rigid and unmoving, so he let her go.

She patted his arm awkwardly and stood up. 'Your dinner's in the oven,' she said, then went into the hall.

★ ★ ★

Tom was as crook as a dog the next morning. He managed to get dressed, but his head was pounding and his mouth tasted like the bottom of Fintan's cage. Ellen put breakfast in front of him, but his stomach heaved at the sight of it and he decided he'd be better off going down the back first. Halfway down the path his guts cramped violently, and by the time he opened the toilet door he couldn't decide whether to put his head over the bog or his bum on it. With a hand clamped over his mouth he made a rushed detour to the shed for a bucket, then lurched back to the toilet, dropped his pants and sat down.

He felt marginally better when his bowel had emptied, but thought he should stay seated for a bit longer, just in case. He wouldn't be drinking Waikato again in a hurry.

He sat there, his trousers pooled around his ankles, his head in his hands and his arse on fire, feeling wrung out both physically and mentally. His elation from yesterday had dissolved, leaving him morose and with the certain realisation that he couldn't go on pretending that everything was all right between him and Ellen.

She had changed, there was no doubt about it. He'd caught her several times lately staring off vacantly, and when he'd asked her what was she thinking about, each time she'd said 'nothing'. But she was preoccupied and he knew it, and it was driving him around the bend. She usually did talk to him when she had something on her mind, but not this time, and he was feeling left out and increasingly anxious. No, not anxious, scared.

And it wasn't just Alf dying like that, either, or the revelation that he hadn't been her real father, although both of those things had knocked her all to the pack. The day she'd come home and told him about it he thought he was going to have to get Dr Airey in, she was that white and shaken. Bloody Gloria — all her airs and graces and her fancy furniture, and she had a secret like that! Alf must have been a saint, taking in a child that wasn't his. There weren't many blokes about who'd do something like that.

No, it was more than that, and it had started before Alf had his accident. He couldn't put his finger on it, but whatever it was, it had been there all right. Ellen had never been a short-tempered sort of woman, and she was nearly always reasonable even when he wasn't, but lately all sorts of things had been getting on her nerves. If he dropped his clothes on the floor in the bedroom, or left the paper spread out on the kitchen table, or came into the house with his boots on, he certainly knew about it these days. It wasn't that she nagged at him, she still very rarely did that, but her mouth would go all thin and she'd whip around tidying up and refusing to meet his eye.

And last night, shouting at him to cook his own eggs — she'd never in their married life done anything like that before. He'd been a bit pissed, it was true, and coming home drunk had never impressed her, but she'd always tolerated it. And it could have been a lot worse — he

278

hadn't been blind drunk, and he hadn't passed out or thrown up everywhere. It wasn't as if he did it regularly, either, just now and then; he wasn't another Alf, hardly ever at home, or Stan Mason, whom everyone knew regularly belted his wife after he'd been on the booze.

So why had she been so angry? He knew she'd been worried because he was late, but the way she'd looked at him, almost as though she despised him, had scared the hell out of him. Somewhere in the back of his mind he had the vague but terrifying sensation that she was slipping away from him, just a little bit each day, but slipping away nevertheless.

Sometimes he'd catch her watching the boys, sometimes with love, sometimes with sadness and sometimes as though she couldn't recognise them, as though someone had come along and plonked two kids she'd never met before at her kitchen table. And they knew something was up, too. Davey, who didn't often confide in him, he was ashamed to admit, had asked him last week if Mum was sick, and he hadn't known what to say. Finally he'd said no, she just had a lot on her mind at the moment. But he'd seen that even Davey was no longer satisfied with that answer.

And Neil had got worse at school. Tom still felt embarrassed about what had happened the last time they'd spoken to Ted Carlyle. He'd already been to see Ted once, but the second time — a meeting Ted had specifically requested a couple of weeks ago — Ellen had come too, apparently because she didn't trust him to get to the bottom of things by himself. Ted had said

Neil's behaviour was becoming more than a bit of a problem: he now appeared to be the ringleader of a small gang that was going around picking on other boys, kids of the opencast men who had gone back to work. The troublemakers had been reprimanded and given detention, and their desks moved as far away from the other boys as possible, but the bullying hadn't stopped. There were always two teachers on playground duty now, to keep an eye on the sixty or so kids at the school, but even then 'accidents' were still occurring. Ted had also informed them that he'd had to give Neil the strap last week, but even that hadn't solved the problem.

'It's as if he's persecuting those particular boys,' he'd said. 'Frankly, I find it extremely disturbing and disruptive. Where do you think he's got it from, this dislike for the opencast lads?' he'd added, looking straight at Tom.

Tom had stared straight back. 'Home, probably.' There had been no point in denying it. 'You know the feeling in the town about the opencasters.'

'Of course I know, but I won't condone it in my school.' Ted had crossed his arms then, and sighed. 'I understand how tough the strike has been on everyone, I really do, but I can't allow bullying among my pupils, for whatever reason. If the worst comes to the worst, you'll have to take Neil out of Pukemiro School and send him in on the train every day to Huntly Primary. Or to Rotowaro, perhaps, although he'd probably get into just as much trouble there.'

Ellen had said, 'But he's only ever gone to Pukemiro!'

'And why only Neil?' Tom had asked, irritated because Ted seemed to be singling his son out. 'What about the other boys in this . . . gang?'

'Because Neil is the ringleader,' Ted had replied, 'and he seems quite happy to admit to it. As I said, I find it really quite disturbing.' And then he'd looked down at his desk, as if he felt embarrassed. 'Tom, Ellen, I hope you don't mind me asking this, but is everything all right at home?'

'What do you mean?' Tom had said.

'Well, I'm not saying this is the case here, but sometimes when a child's home life is unstable, there are often problems at school.'

'Between me and Ellen?'

'Yes.'

'There's nothing wrong with us, is there, love?' Tom had reached for Ellen's hand; she'd taken it, but she hadn't said anything.

Ted hadn't said anything, either, for a minute. Then he'd leaned back in his chair. 'Well, I suggest you have a good long talk with Neil, because he can't go on the way he is, and if he does you really will have to think about moving him. I also suggest that you save your views about the opencasters for the pub, Tom, if you don't mind me saying so.'

Tom hadn't minded. Ted Carlyle knew the inside of the Huntly pub as well as anyone else, and he was right: that was the place for those sorts of discussions, not the family tea table.

If he was honest about it, even back then, early

in May, he'd known something was wrong between him and Ellen, but he wasn't going to discuss that with Ted Carlyle. After that meeting they'd told Neil he could end up going to Huntly Primary if he wasn't careful, which he would have hated, then Tom had given him a bloody good whack across the back of the legs with a willow cane, and so far there'd been no more complaints from the school about his behaviour.

But things with Ellen hadn't improved. In fact, they'd deteriorated. She didn't seem to be too keen on the physical side of things either, now. They hadn't had sex since before Alf's accident, although he couldn't blame her for that: she'd been shattered and so, in fact, had he. Alf had been a good bloke and losing him like that had been a hell of a shock.

Even before then, though, she'd seemed reluctant. Tom was accustomed to having sex at least once a week if not more. He knew she sometimes let him have what he wanted when she wasn't really that keen, but women were like that — they often weren't as interested in the physical side of things. Not that he'd had a huge amount of experience before he'd married Ellen, but he knew what was what. But it made him feel good that she was willing to accommodate him even if she didn't particularly fancy it. She did it for him, and he loved her for it. He'd never forced her, of course, that wouldn't have been on, and anyway he was confident she always got some pleasure, even if it was only from the really close cuddle. She liked those.

But they hadn't even had that sort of sex for a

while, and he was missing it. And it wasn't as though he hadn't tried. He stroked her and put his arms around her and said nice things when they went to bed at night, but she hadn't responded, except to say that she was sorry but she was too tired, or she had a headache, or didn't feel up to it.

But she wasn't grumpy and remote all of the time. Sometimes she could be in a very good mood, flitting about and laughing and having fun with the boys. You'd almost think she'd had a few, although he knew she hadn't. And she seemed to be in good form whenever they went out, except for when they'd gone to see that Marlon Brando film; she'd been pretty out of sorts that night. He loved it when she was bright and happy, because it was almost as though the old Ellen were back.

And she was still a battler. She was as staunch about the strike as she'd ever been — more so, in fact, since Alf had died. She'd said the other night that on top of everything else, she felt duty-bound to see it through to the end in honour of her dad's memory. He'd nearly had a heart attack when she'd come out with it, too, because it made what he was thinking about doing even more difficult. She wouldn't like it, not to start with anyway, but he'd be doing it for her, and for the boys, and he knew she'd understand in the end. He had his principles — he'd always have his principles — but the fear that had been creeping up on him over the past month, and which was now damn near suffocating him, was so bad he was ready to put all that aside if it meant that he and Ellen could get back on track again.

★ ★ ★

He decided to talk to her about it on Monday night, when the boys had gone off to Gloria's for their dinner and to keep her company, and he and Ellen had the house to themselves for a couple of hours.

They'd just finished their own meal of roast beef and vegetables. Normally Ellen enjoyed roast beef but this lot had been as tough as old boots; it obviously hadn't been hung long enough, but beggars can't be choosers, and there were a hell of a lot of beggars in Pukemiro these days.

'That was a bit tough,' she said as she started to clear the table.

Tom looked as though he wanted to agree but he kept quiet — probably, she suspected, because he thought she might take it as a criticism of her cooking. He'd been tiptoeing around her a lot lately. She felt him watching her for several minutes as she moved around the kitchen.

Then he said, 'Sit down, Ellen. I want to talk to you about something.'

She had her back to him, making a space on the bench for the meat platter, and she felt her shoulders tense. To her ears his words sounded harsh and accusatory.

'Can't it wait until I've done the dishes?' she asked.

'No, it can't. But put the kettle on, eh?'

While she was doing that, Tom got up and draped Fintan's blanket over his cage. He wasn't nearly so vocal if he was in the dark. Usually the things he came out with were funny, but obviously Tom wasn't in the mood for it tonight.

Ellen sat down hesitantly, noting that Tom looked wounded by her caution, as though he thought she didn't trust him any more.

He got out his tobacco tin and put it to one side, then set his elbows on the table. 'I've been thinking,' he said, 'and I think I know what's going on.'

She knew that her eyes were round and frightened and that her face had suddenly gone very pale. 'What do you mean?' she said.

'I know what's going on, and I know what to do about it.'

Her hands shook slightly, and she busied them doing up the buttons on her cardigan. Gloria had knitted it for her; it was pale lemon and she hated it, and only ever wore it around the house. 'I'm not sure I know what you mean, Tom,' she said, staring down at her hands. Had it finally come?

'With you and me,' he said. 'I know you're unhappy at the moment, and I know why. It's the strike, isn't it?'

Her head came up. 'What?'

'It's the strike, you're worrying yourself sick over it. I think it was all right at the start, but it's gone on for so long you've worn yourself out. It's the strain, isn't it, that's making us . . . well, making us the way we are at the moment?'

He'd never been very good with words and he wasn't making himself particularly clear now, but Ellen felt relief flood though her. She thought he'd found out about Jack, but obviously that wasn't it at all. Her eyes filled with sudden tears as she looked at him across the table and saw how pleased he was to have worked out what was troubling her.

He was gazing at her intently, and she wondered what he could see in her face.

'It's all right,' he said, 'I understand, I really do. The strike, and that business with Neil and then your dad, it's no wonder you're feeling blue.' He reached out and took her hand. 'I don't blame you, love, I don't blame you at all. You've been a real trooper through all of it.' Seeing more tears now, he rushed on to get it all out. 'So I've been thinking. I know how important the strike is, supporting the watersiders and all that, and I think we've done a great job, the miners and the freezing workers and everyone else. I'm really proud of what we've done and I'd do it all again if I needed to, there's no doubt about it.'

He seemed to run out of steam then, and sat back to roll a smoke. The thump of fear in her heart gradually subsiding, Ellen watched as he plucked a plug of tobacco from his tin and laid it along the crease of a paper. He rolled the paper expertly with his right hand, licked the edge, moulded the cigarette into shape and lit it. Apparently calmed by the ritual and ready to go on again, he took a deep drag and blew the smoke up towards the ceiling.

'But it's going to be over soon, Ellen,' he said.

She opened her mouth to speak, but he held up his hand to stop her.

'No, listen. We've been out for fourteen weeks now, and it's getting worse by the day. It is, love, and there's no denying it. We ran out of money weeks ago and so has just about everyone else around here, there's scab unions at nearly all the ports and most of the other unions have gone back to work. What we're doing, staying out, isn't making a hell of a lot of difference any more.' He paused. 'I think we should go back.'

Ellen was stunned. 'You mean, break the strike?'

Tom nodded. 'I was thinking of going around, just quietly, and talking to some of the other jokers about it, sounding out what they think of the idea. I know plenty of families are in just as much shit as we are.' He glanced up and caught sight of the look on Ellen's face. 'What? What's the matter?'

'You're thinking of scabbing?' she said, incredulous.

'No, not scabbing. Going back to work.'

'Well, if that's not scabbing, what the hell is it? Tom, can you hear what you're *saying*?'

He stared at her, dismayed at her response. He'd known she might not take to the idea straight away, but he hadn't expected this.

'We'd vote on it,' he said, 'I'd just be floating the idea. I know for a fact that a fair few of the jokers would be bloody relieved to get back.'

Ellen knew it too, but she said, 'You can't do that, that's inciting the men to scab! And only Pat and a majority of the committee can approve a vote, and only if Bob Amon and the central committee allow it, you know that.' She slammed the palms of her hands on the table in frustration. Her panic that Tom might have discovered her secret had gone, but this sudden announcement from him was almost as disturbing. 'Tom, what's got into you?'

'Nothing's got into me!' he said, his voice rising in desperation at her refusal to even consider what he was suggesting. 'I just think it's time we had a look at going back to work. Then if we did . . . ' He trailed off

'If you did, what?'

'If we did, then things between you and me would go back to normal.' His eyes pleaded with her. 'Things really aren't right between us, Ellen, are they? I can't do or say a bloody thing any more without you biting my head off. I can't seem to do anything right. You seem so, oh Christ, I don't know . . . ' He grappled for the right word. 'Distant, that's what you are, distant. You never used to be like this, we used to talk about everything, you and me. Now it seems like we've got nothing to say to each other at all, and I don't even know what you're thinking any more. I want us to be back the way we were before all of this started. For God's sake, Ellen, it's scaring the shit out of me!'

Ellen regarded his stricken face in horror: to make her happy he was offering to scab, to deliberately destroy his reputation as a union man in the Waikato, and quite possibly throughout the entire country, because everyone knew how that sort of thing followed a man around. If he did what he was suggesting, and it got out, which it would, he would never mine underground again. They would have to move away from the coal, to a place where he could find some other sort of work, where people wouldn't point them out as the family who had scabbed.

'Tom, no,' she said. 'No, you can't.'

He looked just as upset as she felt, and she knew it was costing him a great deal even to make such a suggestion. But he had made it, and for a moment she hated him for it, for his weakness and his desperation.

But then the flash of contempt passed, and she saw his proposal for what he clearly believed it was — a genuine attempt to fix what he thought had gone wrong.

Poor, dear Tom. She was flooded with guilt and remorse at the misery she was causing him. She had thought, over the past six weeks, that she had very carefully concealed her feelings from him: her elation after being with Jack, the anguish of having to wait until she could see him again, her awful guilt at what she was doing, her dismay at her growing suspicion that she had married the wrong man. But she knew now she'd been having herself on — he hadn't understood it, she was right about that, but he'd certainly seen it. He'd seen it all. And now he was willing to throw away one of the most important things in his life because of it.

She couldn't let him. She couldn't let him because he was wrong about her, but, more than that, she couldn't bear to see him brought so low. She had already cheated him of some of his dignity, even if he didn't know it; she wouldn't rob him of what he had left.

She stood up and went over to him. He had his head down, as though he didn't want her to see what was on his face. The light above the table shone down on his short, clean hair, and she felt a powerful surge of affection for him. She loved him still, she knew it, she just wasn't sure if she was in love with him. She put a finger under his chin and lifted his head, forcing him to look up.

'You're not doing any of that, Tom. It's not the answer, it wouldn't make anything better.'

'Why wouldn't it?'

'Because you couldn't live with yourself, that's why.'

'You don't seem to be able to live with me now.'

Ellen bit her lip. This was going to be the hard bit: more half-truths, more lies, more stealing from him. But he had to have something.

'It's not the strike, not entirely. You're right, it *has* been a long time and I *am* tired of living like this, scrimping and trying to make ends meet and worrying all the time. But I'm used to strikes, remember. This isn't the first and I'm bloody sure it won't be the last.'

'It could be, if we lose. And we are losing,' Tom said. He manoeuvered his legs so she was standing between them.

'No, we're not. They can dent the trade unions, but they'll never smash them completely.'

'So what is it then? Tell me, Ellen, please, I have to know. I feel so . . . oh, shit, I don't know what I feel.' His face reddened as he struggled to put his feelings into words, and failed.

Ellen smoothed his hair. 'It's everything. It's the strike, it's Dad going and what Mum had to say about him — it's just everything.'

It wasn't quite the truth, but it wasn't too far from it. Losing Alf so unexpectedly had devastated her: it still did, every time she thought about it, and she missed him so much. Finding out that he hadn't been her real father had been equally shattering but, to her surprise, she was no longer feeling quite so bad about it. She'd always considered Alf to be her dad in every sense of the word, and he'd certainly never behaved towards her as if he were anything else. He'd raised her and loved her and cared for her like a natural father — probably better than many natural fathers, she suspected — so she hadn't missed out. She'd had a lovely childhood, and she and Alf had always been the best of friends. She hadn't even asked Gloria much more about what her real father had been like, he mattered so little to her compared to what she felt for Alf. She had loved him then, and nothing had changed now.

'Is that really it?' Tom sounded as though he didn't quite believe her.

She made herself say, 'Yes, that really is it.'

'And will we be all right again, when the strike's over and you've got used to not having Alf around?'

He wanted reassurance, she could hear it in

291

his voice, and she couldn't give it to him. So she did the best she could: she bent down and kissed him.

He kissed her back with a passion that almost frightened her, then, trapping her between his legs, gazed up at her. She saw the look of need in his eyes and, to her surprise, felt the beginnings of sexual desire stirring within her.

Neither of them said anything for several long seconds, which seemed to stretch out and fill the kitchen.

Then Tom settled his hands tentatively on her hips, and pulled at the hem of her cardigan. 'This is horrible, isn't it?' he said.

She smiled at his silly, incongruous comment. 'It's one of Mum's efforts.' He knew that, of course; he'd seen it hundreds of times before and had suggested himself that it should be put out of its misery and chucked in the incinerator.

He moved forward, and rested the side of his face against her belly. Ellen lifted her hand and stroked his hair. She felt exceedingly strange. But Tom needed this, for reassurance and to make him feel better. What else could she give him? Surely not promises, not now, because she knew she'd never be able to keep them.

He stood up, undid the buttons of her ugly cardigan and slid it off. Her shoulders were bare underneath, and he pressed down on them to urge her onto the floor. She went easily, pulling him after her.

It only took him a couple of minutes, and even before he'd finished Ellen was crying. She clung to him tightly, feeling that everything had changed so fast and it was all so awful and Tom was her husband but she knew she wouldn't be able to give Jack up, no matter what.

Tom felt her breath hiccupping out of her chest and tried to wipe away the tears that were running across her temples and into her hair. 'Don't cry, love, please don't cry. It'll be all right.'

12

On 6 June, after a WWU rally at the Auckland Domain that had drawn 17,000 people and threatened to get out of hand, Holland reinstated the temporarily lifted ban on all public WWU meetings.

On the same day, across the Tasman in Sydney and Melbourne, police staged mass raids on the offices of the Australian Seamen's Union and the Australian Waterside Workers' Federation, tearing out drawers, ransacking cabinets and confiscating large numbers of records and files. No one was arrested, but 4000 Sydney watersiders walked off the job and congregated at their union hall to register their protest, and to send a cable pledging continued 'solidarity in the struggle' to their fellow wharfies in New Zealand. There were walk-offs in Queensland and at Fremantle as well. The industrial action wasn't a direct result of what was happening in New Zealand, but the enemy was the same, and when news filtered back to the New Zealand strikers, they took comfort from it.

But the following day the tide had turned again, a lot closer to home when the watersiders at Port Chalmers voted en masse to return to work. Not a band of scabs cobbled together by the government, but the original union members. Their president was quoted in the papers as saying that it was a decision between keeping the men together, or dragging them down even further into poverty and degradation. He had seen it as his duty to make the move, he was also quoted as saying, as somebody certainly had to.

Apart from the Timaru watersiders, who had accepted employer conditions at the beginning of May, this was the first port union to actually vote to return to work. It was a huge blow to the watersiders and to Jock Barnes in particular. Some thought — and others hoped — it was the beginning of the end for him. But a meeting of union representatives from the freezing workers, miners, seamen, drivers and labourers a week later resolved to continue fighting until there was an honourable settlement for the watersiders. There were now enormous cracks in the strikers' campaign, but they still weren't ready to give up.

But Ellen, walking down the street on the way to visit with her mother, wasn't thinking about the strike. It was almost halfway through June now, and the colder weather was definitely setting in. This morning, she had stood at the bend in John Street and watched the boys as they'd walked the hundred or so yards to the school, sighing as they'd jumped in the icy puddles in the shallow drain between the road and the grass verge, soaking their shorts with muddy water. Their socks and shoes were drenched as well, and no doubt they'd develop streaming colds by next week, which meant a trip to Dr Airey that she wouldn't be able to pay for.

Arriving at her mother's house, she saw that the lawns needed mowing and the hydrangeas could do with a trim, and made a mental note to ask Tom to come down when he got the chance. Her father had always done the lawns, his one concession to Gloria's obsessive need to have the smartest house in Pukemiro, and it was very unlikely that Gloria would ever get out and push the mower around. She cleaned and polished everything inside the house to within an inch of its life, but anything outside had always been Alf's domain. Which was why the shed at the back was almost falling down and the outhouse needed a good paint and the grapevine growing along the back fence a thorough prune, but no one could see those things from the street so Gloria had never been particularly bothered about them.

'Mum!' Ellen called out as she went inside.

The range had been stoked so the kitchen was nice and warm, and the cake tin was already on the table along with the tea caddy and a jug of milk. Gloria had finally given up insisting that all visitors be received in the lounge. It had been a silly and pretentious habit anyway, Ellen had always thought. Alf had always sat in the kitchen, and she suspected that her mother might now be taking comfort from adopting the same habit.

'Mum, where are you?'

'Coming, dear,' Gloria replied from the hall.

In the four weeks since Alf had died her mother had lost a lot of weight. She'd been a sturdy woman for many years — ever since Ellen could remember, in fact, although she'd seen pictures of Gloria when she was younger looking very slender and glamorous — but her clothes were hanging off her now. She did look better for it, but under her make-up her face was drawn and quite pale. Gloria liked to sew, however, and insisted that it gave her something to do, taking in her skirts and dresses. Ellen couldn't think of anything more boring, sitting around the house all day unpicking seams and sewing them back together again, but her mother seemed happy to do it. Gloria was a member of the Country Women's Institute, but there were only so many different types of preserves you could make and knitting patterns you could have a go at before you ran out of new things to try. Or got bored, as was the case with Ellen. She hadn't been to a CWI meeting for some weeks now, too busy with her relief work. That, and meeting up with Jack as often as she could.

A few hours at his house once a week on a Friday just wasn't enough any more, and over the last few weeks they'd come to an unspoken understanding that they would grab every possible second together. It was risky, even foolhardy, and they knew it, but they couldn't seem to stop themselves. There was a feeling between them that things could very well change soon, in ways beyond their control; rather than serving as a warning, it was drawing them closer.

It was difficult enough to find the time to be alone together, never mind coming up with suitable excuses. She was busy with relief work on Tuesdays, and with the boys and the housework; Jack was still going up to the Pukekohe markets on Mondays, and there were regular union meetings at the Huntly town hall that he wouldn't even contemplate missing, and she never asked him to. As a member of the union committee, he also put in a fair few hours just yarning with the rest of the men, taking note of the latest questions, grumbles and opinions, something that Pat insisted they all do. If there was anything in the wind, he wanted to know about it as soon as possible. And of course, Tom was often at home, and Ellen couldn't justify going into town more than once a week — there just wasn't the money for needless shopping trips any more.

But they had managed to get together yesterday. After her Tuesday morning stint at the relief depot, she'd walked over the hill from Pukemiro to the Junction, caught the train into town as far as Rotowaro, then got off and backtracked slightly to meet Jack, who was waiting for her up the road in his truck. They'd driven up Hangapipi Road, parked under a tree and spent a precious two hours alone.

She hadn't told Jack about what had happened with Tom, not about the sex and certainly not about his suggestion of going back to work. She was worried that it would make Jack think less of Tom — no matter what state their marriage was in, she couldn't do that to him.

It was odd; she believed now that she was hopelessly in love with Jack, yet she didn't want Tom to be hurt. What did that make her, she wondered? She had no idea. A naïve fool, probably. She had no idea about a lot of things any more. The strike had gone on for so long now that she'd given up trying to plan for anything, or even bothering to look beyond the end of each week. They were in debt to Gloria, they were in debt to Farmers', and to Fred and the Co-op in town, the boys needed new shoes and wouldn't be getting them unless Gloria offered to pay for them, which she probably would, and Neil had put his elbows through all of his jerseys and was growing so fast that his sleeves were halfway up his arms. Her hair looked like a bird's nest because she refused to go to the barber who was doing haircuts for free, she needed a new winter coat which was out of the question, and she'd been reduced to using old-fashioned rags when she had her period instead of the Modess sanitary pads she much preferred. It was revolting, washing out the bloodied squares of towelling and hanging them out on the line for the entire neighbourhood to see, but she'd noticed she wasn't the only woman doing it. Still, Tom might be back at work by the time her next period was due, and she might be able to afford to buy something decent.

'You're looking a bit brighter today,' Ellen said as her mother filled the kettle.

'I had a lovely night's sleep. I had a couple of sherries before I went to bed.'

'You want to watch out, Mum, you'll be turning into Dad soon.'

'I don't think so, dear,' Gloria said over her shoulder. She laughed. 'He had years of dedicated practice to get to the state he was in.'

Ellen was pleased to hear her making jokes; for the first couple of weeks she'd barely been able to say Alf's name without bursting into tears. She had seemed a little better lately, although Ellen expected it would take her mother a long time to get used to living by herself. She would be all right, financially, though. Alf had left a tidy sum in the bank from savings and his pension, which had startled everyone because they'd all assumed he'd drunk most of it away. Everyone except Gloria, who had apparently kept a very close eye on what he did and didn't spend. This had amazed Ellen even more, as she'd always had the impression that her father had done exactly what he'd wanted to do, and bugger the consequences. But it seemed he'd not been too bad with their money at all. It was true that on several occasions, when Gloria had sent him down the street to get groceries and to get him out from under her feet, he'd kept on going, hopped on the train and spent the lot in the Huntly pub, but that was just Alf.

'But still,' Ellen said, 'you don't want to become reliant on having to have a few drinks to get to sleep.'

'Don't worry, dear, it'll sort itself out in time,' Gloria said as she sat down. 'How are those little bugalugs of mine? Davey ate every one of his Brussels sprouts when they were here for their dinner the other night, even though I could see they were nearly choking him. Very proud of him, I was, for that.'

Ellen raised her eyebrows. 'How did you get him to do that? I have to just about force them down his throat with the kitchen plunger to get him to eat them at our house.'

Gloria tapped the side of her nose. 'I told him Brussels sprouts were his grandfather's favourite vegetable.'

'Were they?' Ellen hadn't known that.

'No, he hated them, said they were nature's very own little packets of vomit. But I thought Davey was looking a little peaky and could do with some extra iron. Are they all right, the boys? Are they getting enough to eat?'

Ellen nodded. 'They're getting enough, but they're not getting much variety.'

'Because if they aren't,' Gloria said, 'I can always help out.'

'No, Mum, we're fine. Only just, though, I have to say.'

'Well, for God's sake, have a piece of cake, it's sultana,' Gloria said, tapping the cake tin with the teaspoon. Squinting because she'd left her glasses on her bedside table, she peered across the table at her daughter, at the sag in the waistband of her skirt and the fragile narrowness of her wrists. 'You've lost weight.'

'So have you,' Ellen said.

'My beloved husband has just died, yours hasn't. What's going on, Ellen? Are you making sure everyone else gets fed and going short yourself? Because I know you, young lady, and that's exactly the sort of thing you'd do. Or is it something else? Is there something you're not telling me?'

Ellen took a moment to smooth a wrinkle out of the tablecloth. 'I do give the best bits of meat to Tom and the boys, you're right. And other things. But they need it, the boys are growing and, well, so does Tom.'

Gloria crossed her arms. 'And how are you going to cook for them and do their washing and get the shopping in while you're lying on the floor having fainted from hunger? Tell me that?'

'Oh, don't be silly, Mum, it's nothing like that.'

'Well, what is it like?'

Ellen kept her eyes down and her mouth closed.

Gloria sat forward; Ellen could feel her eyes boring into her. 'You're fretting and don't tell me you're not, because like I said, I know you. Come on, what is it?' she said, then added, 'As if I can't guess.'

Ellen forced herself to raise her eyes and look her mother in the face. But when she did, she saw not disapproval and recrimination as she had expected, but empathy.

'You are, aren't you? You're having an affair with Jack Vaughan.'

Ellen considered lying, but couldn't really see the point any more. 'Yes,' she said.

Gloria sighed. 'I thought you might be.'

Ellen thought she sounded sad, not angry, and that was worse. 'How did you know?'

'Because of the way you looked at him at Carol Henshaw's wedding when he was prancing around the dance floor with Andrea Trask . . . '

'It wasn't happening then,' Ellen said.

'I expect it wasn't, but it was coming, though, wasn't it?'

Ellen nodded.

'And the way the pair of you have been

carrying on whenever you're within a hundred yards of one another.'

'We haven't been carrying on.'

'Well, maybe not to that extent, but you only have to look at him looking at *you* to see something's going on. And if I can see it, then I'm sure plenty of other people can, too.'

Ellen's stomach lurched. 'Has somebody said something?'

'Not yet, but they will, you mark my words. You know what this town's like — if you change from strawberry jam to marmalade everybody knows by lunchtime.' Gloria got up to fetch the kettle. 'Do you know what really gave it away?' she said as she poured hot water into the teapot. 'Jack coming to the hospital. When I saw him I said to myself, 'Thomas, you bloody fool.''

Ellen knew Tom had let her down when he'd refused to come to the hospital, and the memory of it still hurt, but she still felt the need to defend him. 'But you know how much he hates hospitals.'

'Yes, and I hate hospitals too, especially when it's my man lying in one with his head split open,' Gloria said. 'He should have been there with you, Ellen, and he wasn't, but Jack was, and that told me all I needed to know. Not that I wanted to know, of course, not then. I had plenty of other things to think about.' She swirled the teapot gently so the leaves would settle before she poured. 'So how long has it being going on? Is that when it started?'

'Before that,' Ellen said.

'So how long?'

'About seven weeks.'

Gloria took her time pouring the tea before she asked her next question. 'How serious is it, Ellen?'

Feeling slightly insulted, she replied, 'Do you really think I would hop into bed with someone who wasn't my husband if it wasn't serious?'

'So you have slept with him?'

Now Ellen felt silly. 'Yes, I have.'

'So, is it serious?'

Ellen nodded.

'Well, then, what are you going to do about it? Because you can't go on like this. It just won't work, these sorts of arrangements never do, and I should know.'

Ellen put her finger against the handle of her cup and swivelled it around and around in its saucer. When it finally spilled, she said, 'I don't know, Mum. I don't know what to do.'

Gloria shook her head. 'I said you should never have married Thomas. I told you he wouldn't make you happy.'

'He did make me happy. He still does.'

'Clearly.'

'No, he does. He's a good man and a good provider and he always does his best for us, but . . . '

'But what?'

'He's not Jack.'

'Well, you'll have to make up your mind sooner or later. Or did you think you could have both of them? It won't work, Ellen, not in a town like this.'

'I don't want both of them,' Ellen said,

although that wasn't true. Then she said something she didn't really mean, but her shame was now turning into anger. 'I thought you'd be happy that Tom and I are having problems.'

Gloria looked at her sharply. 'Of course I'm not bloody well happy! And Thomas isn't having problems. Well, not yet anyway. You're the one with the problem. I like Thomas, you know that, he's just not the man I wanted for you. But you had to have him, though, didn't you? And now you've changed your mind. What about Neil and Davey, Ellen? What's going to happen to them when all this comes out?'

'It won't,' Ellen said.

'Oh, yes it will.'

Ellen knew her mother was right; she'd always known that, and resented Gloria for making her think about it.

'Well, what did you do with Hazel when you ran off?'

There was a short, brittle silence before Gloria replied icily, 'You know what I did. I chose to leave her behind, and a day hasn't gone by since that I haven't looked back and wondered what the hell I thought I was doing.'

'But what does it matter now? She doesn't even know you went away, does she?'

'Of course she does, but she thought I'd gone off for a rest because I wasn't well. It was your father's idea to tell her that, another thing I've always been grateful to him for, and don't you dare tell her otherwise!'

Ellen felt stung. 'Mum, I wouldn't, you know I wouldn't!'

'I hope not. I only told you because I thought you were owed the truth about your father. There's no need to upset Hazel as well.'

'Why, so you don't have to feel terrible all over again?' Ellen said. Then she closed her eyes in dismay, appalled at what had just come out of her mouth.

Gloria's eyes hardened. 'Listen to me, young lady, you brought this on yourself so don't get snaky at me about it. You've made your bed and now you're going to have to lie in it.'

Feeling so upset now that she thought she was going to be sick, Ellen half rose from her chair, but the nausea passed as suddenly as it had arrived and she sat down again. She pressed her hands over her face and gritted her teeth, but couldn't stop the tears.

Gloria let her cry for five minutes, then fetched her a handkerchief. The sight of Ellen in such distress was upsetting, even if her misery was of her own making, but she was hardly in a position to take the moral high ground. And there was no point the pair of them falling out over it; Ellen would find she had few enough allies when all this got out. No one admired a woman who cheated on her husband, especially when he'd done nothing to deserve it.

'Look,' she said, when Ellen's tears finally seemed to be subsiding, 'what is it about this fellow? Oh, I know he's a fine figure of a man and a charmer to boot, but there has to be more to it than that, love, and you know it. Yes, it'd be lovely for the first six months, or even the first year, but then the shine would wear off and

306

you'd be back to doing exactly what you're doing now — picking up someone's dirty socks and underpants, listening to him snoring and blowing off next to you in bed every night, putting up with him coming home from the pub smelling like a brewery and expecting his conjugals, complaining if his chips aren't crispy enough. Or do you think Jack Vaughan isn't going to do all those things? Because he will, you know, no matter how much you love him and he loves you. It's just the way it is, Ellen, and it's the way it always will be.'

Ellen blew her nose. 'I know all that, Mum,' she said, her voice muffled by the handkerchief. 'But I haven't thought that far, I really haven't.'

She hadn't either, and neither, she assumed, had Jack. He certainly hadn't said anything about it.

Gloria raised her eyebrows sceptically. 'Haven't you? You're not planning to run off with him, then?'

'No.' Ellen couldn't understand why her mother was making it all sound so sordid.

'So why are you risking your marriage for him?'

Ellen folded the handkerchief into a neat, damp square while she thought about her answer. 'You know the other day when you were telling me about my real father?'

Gloria nodded.

'Well, you said then that there was something about him, but not to ask what it was because you didn't know, but it was the one thing that made him so special, remember? Well, to me,

Jack is like that. He . . . well, he just feels right, Mum. In my mind and in my heart, he feels exactly right.' Ellen shrugged. 'I don't know. He doesn't tell me I'm the most wonderful thing that's ever happened to him, and he doesn't say all the time that he loves me . . . '

'They never do, men,' Gloria said. 'They're just not made like that.'

'It's more in the way he looks at me, and the way he touches me. And sometimes he'll say something, just something little, that tells me I really do matter to him, a lot, and when he does, it makes my heart just fly, and that's when I know.' Ellen shrugged. 'That's it, really. It doesn't sound much, but that really is it.'

'That's when you know what?'

'That he's the one.'

'Look, love, sometimes 'the one' isn't even the one. If that was the way it worked, you'd still be happy with Thomas, wouldn't you? I seem to remember you insisting that he was 'the one' when you told me and your father you would die if you couldn't marry him.'

'But this is different, Mum. You don't understand.'

Gloria snorted. 'Oh, yes I do. You're infatuated, Ellen. You're not in love with Jack Vaughan, you're in lust. And I'll bet you anything you like that if you did run off with him, you'd find that out a lot sooner than you bargained for. And lust isn't love, not by a long shot.' She sat back in her chair and crossed her arms again. 'No, I'm sorry, love, but you're going to have to put an end to it.'

Ellen knew her mother had been going to say that, but knowing it didn't make it any easier to bear.

'No,' she said, 'No, I won't, Mum, I can't.' She was surprised at how steady her voice sounded, when even the thought of it filled her with an intolerable sense of loss.

'Well, you're going to have to. It's not just you, Ellen, there are the boys to think about as well. And Thomas. You'll have to tell Jack soon, now, before it's too late, before somebody says something and lets the cat out of the bag. Because they will you know, you can't hide something like this for long. I thought I had, but of course I hadn't. Everyone knew what I'd done, that I'd gone off with a fancy man, in spite of what Alf told them all, and I still haven't lived it down, not as far as some people in this town are concerned.'

'I don't care, Mum, I don't care about that at all.'

Gloria regarded her daughter sadly. 'Oh, you will, dear, you will.'

★ ★ ★

Someone did let the cat out of the bag.

Tom went to Auckland as usual on Friday but the meeting didn't go well, and his mood was grim by the time he and Pat walked into the noisy, smoke-filled public bar of the Huntly pub at about half past three that afternoon. The only redeeming feature of the day was that they'd thumbed a ride with a bloke who'd brought

309

them all the way from Auckland to Huntly; usually it took them two or three rides to get home, with endless standing around on the side of the road in between.

The bar was full, as usual, and they headed over to their customary table. Or rather, their customary bench — there were no tables and chairs in the public bar, merely a collection of tall benches that the men leaned on while they drank. Bert, Vic and Lew were already there. Jack wasn't, Tom noticed, then he remembered he'd gone down to Ohura this afternoon for the latest gen on what was happening in Taranaki.

They'd had a bastard of a time at Ohura. In April they'd complied with Prendiville and Crook's order to hold a secret ballot but, all credit to them, had voted to stay out. But then Crook had sent them a suspiciously confusing telegram they interpreted to mean that all other miners in the country were going back to work, and because they were so isolated they didn't know any better and decided they might as well go back themselves. But when some of the jokers from the Benneydale pit up near Mangapehi had turned up to tell the Ohura men they'd got it wrong, the cops stepped in and refused to allow a meeting. This had annoyed the Ohura blokes so much that they'd decided to stay out after all, no matter what. But they were still isolated, and the Waikato central council had decided after that that it might be a good idea to keep in regular touch with them. And Jack had worked there for a few years, so it made sense that he'd be the one to do it.

'Just in time,' Bert said. 'I'm just getting a round in.'

'Not baby-sitting this afternoon?' Pat asked.

'My mother's got them for the night.'

Pat stowed his rucksack under the table and dug in his coat pocket for his tobacco. 'How is the wife?'

'She's coming right.' Bert didn't bother examining Pat's face for signs of sarcasm because he knew there wouldn't be any; Pat was a hard man but he'd always been sympathetic towards Bert's predicament. 'Doctor says she could be home soon.'

'That'd be good. Wouldn't it?'

'Don't know if it would, actually,' Bert said with his usual honesty, peering into his wallet to make sure he had enough money for his round. 'We're in worse shit now than we were when she went away. She might come home and end up having to go straight back again.'

Nobody said anything because he was probably right.

Tom watched Bert as he made his way over to the bar. Harry the barman lined up the handles and ran the beer hose over them, not even bothering to take his thumb off the button between glasses, because he knew the punters would drink gallons more than the amount that would end up going down the drain.

Bert carried the handles back, the beer frothing and spilling over the sides.

'Cheers,' Pat said as he raised his glass.

'Cheers,' everybody else said, and there was a

moment's silence as the beer went smoothly down.

'Anything happen at the meeting?' Vic asked as he wiped froth off his top lip.

Pat shrugged. 'Not much.'

'Not much that was good,' Tom added.

'There was talk that there might not be much more money from the watersiders in Aussie, because of that business with the ACTU telling them to pull their horns in.'

'Shit,' Lew said, 'that'll put a damper on things, won't it?'

There were nods all round. Although the miners' strike fund had run out a while ago, the Auckland watersiders had been managing to send a bit of money down now and then, which had been greatly appreciated, even if it wasn't very much. There was still the money that was coming more or less illegally from the Australian miners, but the funds donated by the Australian wharfies would be missed.

'Anything else?' Vic said.

'Just stuff about Barnes' wife being fined,' Pat replied, 'and the watersiders getting banned from the wharves for good. Don't know how the port employees think they're going to get any decent work done with those clowns they've got now.'

'The scab union?' Lew said.

'Yeah, and the military boys. They won't have the use of them forever.' Pat laughed. 'There might be another war, and then they'll be in the shit.'

'There is another war — in Korea,' Vic said.

'No, a proper war.'

'Korea is a proper war. Haven't you been reading the papers?'

'If it was a proper war,' Pat said, 'wouldn't all our blokes be over there already?'

Vic shrugged. 'How should I know? I'm only a coalminer.'

Tom let Pat and Vic's bickering wash over him, concentrating instead on how soothing the beer felt on his dry throat. He drained his handle and reached into his pocket for his wallet.

'My round,' he said, and nodded at Bert and Lew to drink up.

They went on like that for the next hour and a half and, by twenty minutes to closing time, were all well on their way.

It might have been all right if Tom had decided to wander down to the Bluebird for a parcel of chips before the booze train pulled out, but he didn't, he stayed in the pub for the last couple of rounds before the barman called time.

He was chatting to Vic when Red Canning materialised in front of him. Tom didn't like Canning; he'd known him and even worked next to him on occasion for years, and he was a belligerent bastard at the best of times. There had been a bit of trouble after Johnno Batten had died, too, and Canning had been at the bottom of it, going around saying that the roof had come in because Tom had used too much powder when he'd set up the blast. What came out of Canning's mouth normally wouldn't have bothered Tom, but the suggestion that his negligence had killed Johnno had, because he'd already been racked with guilt over what had happened. There'd been an inquiry at the time and the official verdict had been that no one had been to blame, but while Tom had been in hospital Red Canning had made a meal out of it until Pat had taken him to one side and told him that if he didn't shut the fuck up, he'd be out of the union, and therefore out of a job.

So Tom wasn't exactly pleased to see the man sidle up to him and set his beer down on the table.

'How's it going?' Canning said.

Tom regarded him warily. 'All right.'

'Good, good.' Canning took a long sip of his beer.

Tom could see he'd also had a few; under his bushy ginger brows his small eyes were bloodshot and bleary.

Vic glanced at Tom, who shrugged.

After a minute Canning said, 'Bad news about your father-in-law. He was a good bloke, Alf Powys.'

Tom nodded. 'He was.'

'It was a hell of a shock, wasn't it?'

'Yep.'

Canning took another leisurely sip. 'How's your missus now?'

Tom looked at him. 'My wife?'

'I imagine she was pretty much knocked all to the pack by it, losing her father like that.'

'Yeah, she was pretty upset. Still is. Why?'

'Just wondered.'

Tom didn't like the way the conversation was going. 'Why?' he said again, more sharply this time.

Canning smirked. 'Needing a fair bit of comfort, is she?'

There was a short silence.

'What the fuck are you talking about, Canning?' Tom said, feeling his shoulders beginning to tense. He put his glass down.

Canning swirled the beer around in his glass. 'It's just that the missus, well, she's good mates with Peggy Huriwai, that lives next to Jack Vaughan in Robert Street. And according to Peggy, your wife's been going in and out of Vaughan's house on a pretty regular basis. Every Friday, to be exact. When you're in Auckland.'

Tom didn't even think — his arm swung up and he punched Canning full in the face. It was a good one, too. Canning went flying and landed on his back on the dirty wooden floor, his glass following him and beer going everywhere. Nearby punters moved out of the way, but only far enough so they could still see what was going on. Tom stepped forward to put the boot in but Vic grabbed his sleeve and yanked him back.

'Steady,' he warned.

The last time there'd been a fight in here the cops had actually come in and arrested the blokes who'd started it. They'd been laying into a couple of scabs who'd thought they could sneak in unnoticed; Canning wasn't a scab, but that didn't mean the cops wouldn't turn up this time as well.

Canning got to his feet and wiped at the blood trickling from his nose. 'Ask her if you don't believe me. Or even better, ask Vaughan.' He looked around in an exaggerated manner. 'In

315

fact, where is he tonight, McCabe? I'd hurry home if I was you.'

Tom lunged again but didn't quite manage to connect because both Vic and Bert hauled him back this time.

'Fuck off, Canning,' Lew said. 'Go on, get out before we all have a go.'

Canning turned on his heel and went, his hand cupped protectively over his bloodied nose.

'Did you hear what he said, the lying cunt!' Tom roared. 'Did you hear what he *said*!'

The barman, who had been keeping a very close eye on what had just happened, checked his watch with relief. '*Time!*' he bellowed.

'Come on, boys, let's go,' Pat said, reaching for his bag. He was hoping Canning might still be outside. The bastard had had it coming for a long time.

But he wasn't.

'Must have scuttled off home,' Lew said. 'Bloody lucky he lives in town.'

'Don't worry,' Pat said, 'he'll keep.'

★ ★ ★

Tom sat in silence all the way home, brooding and massaging his bruised knuckles, thinking about Ellen's strange moods over the last few months, her apparent need to go out more than she normally did, her evasive answers to his questions.

The others glanced at him from time to time, but left him to it. They felt for him, but what could you say to a bloke who's just been told his

316

wife's cuckolded him? They all knew Canning was a prize bullshit artist, and a prick to boot, and none of them had believed what he'd said, but still, it wasn't a pleasant situation.

None of them, that was, except for Pat, who had heard a little rumour from Rhea recently. Rhea was a good woman, but she was partial to a bit of gossip, and she'd mentioned a few weeks ago that there might be trouble in the McCabe household before too long. When he'd asked her what she meant, she'd told him very disapprovingly that Ellen McCabe had been seen getting off the train at Rotowaro and walking back up the main road towards the Junction, at about the same time that Jack Vaughan had been spotted sitting up the very same road in his truck. She didn't want to put two and two together, Rhea had said, but you had to wonder. Pat hadn't said anything to anyone about it because it was none of his business, and in particular he hadn't said anything to Tom McCabe, whom he didn't want distracted from his union work.

They all got off when the train pulled into the station at Glen Afton, the end of the line. It was dark now and there was a fair bit of swearing and stumbling as they set off up the road to Pukemiro, a few miles further on. But they knew the road well, even after the sun was well down, and the walk was no hardship.

Still Tom said nothing. Bert was getting worried about his thunderous silence, and looked to the others for inspiration, but all they could do was shrug helplessly, except for Pat, who was marching on ahead. It just wasn't the

317

sort of thing they could do anything about. Even if there was a problem, Tom and Ellen would have to sort it out between themselves; matters like this always were best kept between a man and his wife. But Bert suspected he wasn't the only one relieved that Jack had gone down to Taranaki for the weekend. He wouldn't tell Dot about this, though, when he went to see her on Sunday; she was very fond of Ellen and would be devastated to hear that something might have gone wrong between her and Tom.

They reached the turn-off to Pukemiro and started trudging up the hill, Pat, Lew and Vic saying goodnight as they came to their front gates.

Halfway up Joseph Street, Bert tried for a bit of conversation, just to break the tension. 'Your lads playing football tomorrow?'

Tom's head jerked up. 'What? Yeah, I think so.'

'Who are they playing?' Bert asked, although he already knew because his eldest boy was playing as well. It was a home game at the school.

'Huntly Primary.'

Bert considered this response to be a reasonably good sign. 'You going along to watch?'

'I expect so.'

Silence again.

Then Tom suddenly blurted, 'Do you think what he said was true? What Canning said about Ellen?'

'Hell, no,' Bert said. 'Red Canning's full of shit and always has been, shit-stirring bastard. It's

318

either a load of rubbish or he's got his wires crossed, that's all.'

Tom grunted, but didn't say anything else.

As they parted at Bert's gate, Bert said, 'I'll see you tomorrow at the school then?' but Tom didn't reply.

Bert stood and watched for a moment as the big, dark shape of his friend disappeared into the shadows on the other side of the hedge, then went inside himself.

★ ★ ★

Ellen poked a knife into the meat, testing to see if the mutton was cooked properly yet. It was stewed chops, which no one really liked, with potatoes and cabbage. Fortunately for the boys, they wouldn't have to eat it; Milly had been over earlier, and had decided to take Neil and Davey back to her house for tea. Her mother had given her a big pork roast, and she'd insisted that her lot wouldn't be able to manage it all by themselves.

'Save the leftovers for sandwiches for tomorrow, or for a shepherd's pie tomorrow night. Don't waste it on these two gannets,' Ellen had said, laughing and inclining her head towards Neil and Davey, who were sitting at the table playing a very noisy game of Snap.

'Gannet! Gannet!' Fintan had squawked, and Milly had shrieked with laughter. She thought Fintan was the funniest thing she'd ever seen, especially when he swore.

'It's not a waste,' she'd replied, ruffling the

boys' hair, making them giggle and squirm away from her. 'You've got two growing boys here.'

'And you've got two growing boys as well.'

'But it's a very big roast. I'll send them back just before they're too stuffed to walk, all right?'

So off the boys had gone, delighted to be having roast pork for tea instead of stinky old mutton chops.

To be honest, Ellen was glad of the peace and quiet. Tom would be home soon, and she wanted a few minutes to herself. The three hours she'd spent with Jack this morning had been wonderful, but what Gloria had said to her on Wednesday had given her an almighty fright. She'd almost decided to tell Jack about it, then changed her mind in case he'd thought she was fishing for some sort of promise or assurance. He was on his way to Taranaki now, anyway, so she wouldn't see him for a couple of days.

She heard Tom coming up the steps and gave the chops one last poke; another ten minutes should do it. She wiped her hands on her apron and turned to greet him, then felt her heart sink because it was obvious he'd had quite a few at the pub. There was something else, too, something dark and closed-off about him. Perhaps the meeting in Auckland hadn't gone well.

'Hello, love,' she said, making an effort to make her voice sound bright. 'Tea's nearly ready. Mutton chops, unfortunately.'

'Where are the boys?' Tom asked as he pulled two bottles of beer out of his pockets and sat down heavily at the table.

'Milly's, they're having their tea there.' Ellen eyed the bottles, but didn't comment. 'Her mother gave her a big pork roast.'

'Hip hip hooray.'

Ellen frowned. What was wrong with him? He wasn't usually sarcastic like this.

'Did you have a bad day?' she asked.

'Yes and no,' he said, flipping the lid off one of the beer bottles with a knife.

'Well, tell me about it then.'

He looked at her levelly. 'No, why don't you tell me about your day?'

'My day?' She was unpleasantly surprised; he hardly ever asked what she'd been up to. 'Well, just the usual. After you went, I made the boys their lunches then saw them off to school. Then I did the breakfast dishes and made the beds and did a bit of ironing. Oh, and Milly came over later this afternoon for a cup of tea.'

Tom took a long swig straight from the bottle.

'Do you want a glass?' she asked.

'No,' he said, and burped without excusing himself. 'Did you do anything else?'

'No, not really.'

Ellen felt a bubble of dread begin to inflate in her chest, and turned away from him, moving the pots off the range and onto the bench. Then she stopped because she could feel him staring at her.

'Are you sure?'

She spun around, sudden fear making her shrill. 'Of course I'm sure! Why would I not remember what I did today?'

'No reason.' His voice was ominously steady

but she could hear something welling beneath it. 'What about all the other Fridays I've been away?'

Ellen looked at Tom's narrowed eyes and the dark flush that was spreading across his face, and felt as if her legs might go from under her. She put a steadying hand on the bench.

'No, I can't remember every minute of every Friday!'

'I'll jog your memory then. You weren't, by chance, visiting someone who lives in Robert Street?'

'Who?' she asked, then immediately realised it was probably the worst thing she could have said, because now Tom would say his name and she wouldn't be able to hide any of it from him.

'Jack Vaughan,' he said.

And in that instant, in less than a heartbeat, Ellen saw that he knew.

'Jack?' she said, with as much surprise in her voice as she could muster.

Then she panicked. Perhaps she could convince him that whatever he'd heard was wrong, just gossip or the wrong end of the stick, anything that would steer him away from the truth. Because it was too soon for this to be happening. She wasn't ready, and she suddenly realised with a nauseating rush of dismay that she might never be.

Then another voice said, 'Jack!'

They both turned and stared at Fintan in his cage.

'Jack!' the parrot trumpeted again. 'I miss you, Ellen!'

The blood drained from Ellen's face. 'Oh, God,' she whispered. 'Tom, it's not what you think.'

He banged his bottle down so hard that the beer frothed up and spewed out all over the table. 'I bet it fucking well is,' he hissed, 'I bet it's exactly what I think.'

'He's a parrot, he doesn't . . . '

'Fuck the parrot. Why, Ellen? *Why?*'

'I don't know,' she said. 'I don't know! I'm so sorry.'

'You will be,' Tom said, and stood up.

He crossed the room, raised his hand and hit her a solid blow across the side of the head that knocked her sprawling. A grunt was forced out of her as her face scraped along the floor, but she didn't scream — if it was the last thing she did, she would not scream. And then, with stoic resignation, she covered her head with her arms.

13

But he didn't hit her again, and neither did he say anything else before he slammed out. She lay there for nearly ten minutes, weeping, before deciding she should move, just in case Neil and Davey came back early. There was the tea to sort out, too; it was unlikely to be eaten tonight but there was no point in wasting good food. She sat up, wiped her tear-stained face on her cardigan, then got to her feet.

She transferred the chops and the vegetables into bowls and put them in the refrigerator, washed and dried the cooking pots, then went down the street to Milly's house and asked her if the boys could stay with her for the weekend.

Milly knew straight away that something was wrong.

'You've been crying,' she said. 'What's the matter?'

Frank, who was reading the paper at the table, took one look at Ellen, then got up and went out, leaving the women alone.

'What are the boys doing?' Ellen asked.

'Barricading themselves into Billy's bedroom. It's a fort, apparently. Did you need to see them?'

'No, I just wanted to know they're all right.'

'They're fine. Ellen, what's wrong?'

Ellen bit her lip. Then she took a deep breath and said in a wobbly voice, 'Tom and I are having a bit of trouble. We . . . we've had an argument and he's gone off somewhere.'

'Obviously that was after he took a swing at you,' Milly said, nodding at Ellen's reddened cheek.

'So I was wondering if Neil and Davey could stay here for the weekend. There might be . . . well, I'd rather they were here, if that's all right with you. I'll bring their things over in the morning.'

'Of course it's all right, love.'

Ellen knew her friend wouldn't pry, but she felt she deserved some sort of explanation. An honest one.

'It's, well, it's Jack. Jack Vaughan.'

Understanding began to cross Milly's face.

'I've been seeing him. And Tom has found out.'

Milly sighed. 'Why am I not surprised?'

'What, that Tom found out?' Ellen felt a stab of alarm. Did the whole town know about it?

'No, that you've been seeing Jack. It's been coming for a while, hasn't it?'

'I never thought so, Milly, I really didn't, until it actually happened. I never thought I'd cheat on Tom, but I have.' She looked at her friend with infinite sadness. 'I've hurt him so badly, Milly.'

Milly nodded, but said nothing.

'You're not angry at me?' Ellen asked.

'Come here,' Milly said, and held out her arms.

Ellen stepped into them for a comforting moment, absurdly grateful, then pulled back and

325

started to cry. She dug in her pocket for a handkerchief.

Milly waited patiently until Ellen had herself under control. 'What will you do? Does Jack know what's happened?'

'He's away until Sunday.'

'What do you think he'll say?'

'When he finds out that Tom knows?'

'No, love, when you tell him it's over.'

Ellen stared at Milly, then her eyes brimmed with tears again. 'I don't think I can tell him that,' she said.

'I know, love, it'll be hard, but you can do it. You'll have to.'

'No, you don't understand, Milly. I don't want to tell him, I don't want it to be over.'

For the first time since Ellen had arrived, Milly finally looked doubtful. 'You can't just up and leave Tom, Ellen. It wouldn't be right. Shouldn't you try and patch things up? It might not be too late.'

'I don't know if I can, not after this.'

Milly gave Ellen a long, searching look. She reached out and touched her hand. 'Look, I know Tom isn't normally a violent man, but if you need to, you come down here, all right?'

Ellen nodded.

'And the boys can stay here as long as they need to, don't worry about that.'

Overcome by Milly's kindness, Ellen could only nod again. Then she left.

As she walked back home the night was sharp and cold even though a layer of cloud obscured the moon. She thought rain might be on the way and pulled her cardigan across her front. She felt numb and detached, as though she were trudging through a soundless dream in which everything was motionless except for her, and wondered abstractly if she was in shock. Her ear still buzzed from Tom's blow and when a cat yowled from behind a fence it seemed to take ages for her to register what the sound was, and when she finally did it nearly gave her a heart attack. She half expected Tom to appear, but he didn't. She had no idea where he'd gone.

She was on the back steps to her house when someone called out, 'Ellen?'

'Bert?' She stopped and peered into the darkness, just able to make him out standing on the other side of the hedge.

'Is everything all right? I thought I heard . . . ' He trailed off.

Ellen's heart swelled with affection for him. 'No, things aren't all right, Bert, but thanks for asking.'

She watched as he nodded hesitantly, then he merged back into the shadows shrouding his back lawn. He climbed the steps and a moment later his porch light went off.

She went inside, changed into her nightie, then got into the empty bed where she curled up on her side and began to cry again.

★ ★ ★

She woke early the next morning. Her neck was very stiff, and there was a graze on her cheek where she'd connected with the kitchen lino.

When she moved her fingers tentatively over the side of her head, she found a painful lump there.

The house was silent, but she went in to every room to see if Tom had come home during the night. He was asleep on the couch in the sitting room, a blanket from one of the boys' beds thrown over him. Ellen watched him for several minutes then crept away, thinking it would be best to leave him to sleep for as long as possible. Anything to put off what she knew would be coming.

She got dressed, went outside and began to work in her garden, systematically weeding from one end of a row to another, pulling out the odd vegetable plant that wasn't doing so well and tamping down the soil around the ones that were. The cabbages were coming along, and so was the silverbeet. The cool, damp dirt felt good on her hands, soothing and reassuring. She worked mindlessly and repetitively until it occurred to her that she should take the boys' football gear along to Milly's.

She washed the dirt off her hands under the outside tap, then went inside. Tom was sitting at the table, still in yesterday's clothes, unshaven and bleary-eyed. He regarded her in silence.

She stoked the range, filled the kettle and set it on the heat.

'I asked Milly if she would take the boys for the weekend,' she said eventually. 'I thought it would be better if they weren't here at the moment.'

'I'm surprised you thought about them at all.'

Stung, Ellen turned away and busied herself

getting the frying pan out of the cupboard.

Tom said, 'I don't want anything to eat.'

Ellen put the pan back; neither did she. She sat down, and waited.

Tom rubbed his face wearily. 'How long has it been going on?'

She knew he would ask that, just as she also knew she couldn't lie to him any more. 'Nearly two months,' she said, aware that there was no way she could answer the question honestly without hurting him.

Tom winced as though he'd been punched in the stomach, and Ellen had to look away.

He was quiet for a long time, and she could see that he was thinking back over all the Fridays he'd been away, the dances at which he'd left her to entertain herself, the times that Jack had been around to the house — any occasions when the pair of them might have been together.

He seemed almost paralysed by the awful finality of her admission, and she saw that they wouldn't be able to talk, not yet. And what was there to say anyway? Sorry, it won't happen again? Because she knew that it would. She felt as lost and as hopeless as Tom looked, although in a way he was lucky that he had his rage and his self-righteousness to buffer him from his pain. All she had was the cold, selfish reality of what she'd done, and Jack wasn't even here to tell her it would be all right.

A small noise made her look up, and to her horror she saw that Tom was working hard to control the trembling muscles in his face and his tensed jaw. A tear trickled down one unshaven cheek and he swiped it angrily away with the palm of his hand.

Automatically, she reached out to touch him.

'Get off me!' he snarled, and whacked her hand away.

She jerked back, shocked.

He shoved his chair back from the table and stood up. 'I'm going out.'

She wanted to ask when he would be back, or even if he would be back, but couldn't seem to get the words out. It was only half past nine on a Saturday morning, and she wondered numbly where he would go at this hour.

As he jammed his feet into his boots and clumped down the steps, she heard someone coming up the other way.

Tom uttered a curt, 'Gloria,' then she heard her mother reply, 'Good morning, Thomas.'

Then she was in the kitchen, standing with her hands on her hips and her face flushed with anger. 'Well, you've done it now, young lady, haven't you?'

Ellen looked away, her heart plummeting.

'Nora Bone just accosted me in the street. Nora bloody Bone, of all the nosy bloody parkers in this godforsaken little town!' Gloria said. 'You might at least have had the decency to tell me what was going on.'

'I was going to, Mum, as soon as . . . ' Ellen trailed off. 'I don't know how Mrs Bone found out.'

Gloria dumped her handbag on the table and sat down. 'Everyone's found out, according to Nora. You knew this would happen, Ellen, I warned you. I'm surprised Tom is still here, I really am. I'm surprised you're still here. Plenty of husbands would have thrown you out in the street by now, and chucked your bags out after you!'

Ellen didn't know what to say, because Gloria was right.

Her mother took her hat off. 'Are Neil and Davey all right? Where are they?'

'At Milly's, they stayed the night. I'm taking their gear along soon, they're playing today.'

'I know they are, Ellen, that's why I came out — to see my grandsons play football, not to be told by a nosy old bitch what a terrible tragedy it is that my daughter has felt the need to lead her poor, blameless husband up the garden path and therefore ruin a perfectly good marriage.'

Ellen could almost hear Nora Bone saying all that, and felt her face burn at just the thought of it.

'I'm sorry, Mum, I was going to tell you.'

'Well, it's too late now, isn't it? So come on, get dressed, you're not going out looking like that,' Gloria said, waving her hand distastefully at Ellen's mud-stained trousers and old gardening jumper.

'What?'

'I said get dressed, go and put something presentable on.'

'I'm only going down to Milly's.'

'No, you're not. You and I are going to watch the boys play football.'

Ellen was horrified. 'Mum, I can't!'

'Why not?'

331

'Everyone will be . . . talking.'

'So? Your father made a fool of himself on many an occasion, and he wasn't afraid to show his face in public. My God, if he had been, he'd never have set foot outside the door! Go on, go and get changed.'

Gloria waited while Ellen reluctantly went to her bedroom to put on something more presentable. She was convinced that if she let her daughter hide away while all this was going on she'd lose her nerve, and that would put an end to any chance she might have of ever holding her head up in Pukemiro again. Alf had told her the same thing when she'd come back to him all those years ago. After watching her mope around the house feeling sorry for herself, he'd sat her down and pointed out to her that people could only make her feel bad if she let them.

Ellen reappeared wearing her good slacks, a jumper and her winter coat. They set out for Milly's, Ellen carrying the boys' football gear in a duffel bag slung over her shoulder. The school didn't have a real strip, just old shorts and shirts, but her boys both had proper football boots, bought for them by Tom last Christmas, and she knew they'd be very put out if they had to run around the pitch in their bare feet.

They were waiting for her at Milly's back door, and she knew by their happy, bright faces that they had no idea of what was going on.

'Have you had a good time?' she asked, forcing herself to sound jolly.

'Evan farted all night,' Davey said, pulling a face.

Evan said, 'No, it was you.'

'No, it wasn't!'

'That's enough, boys,' Gloria warned. 'And don't say that word, it's vulgar.'

'What, fart?' Neil said.

'Yes. You refer to it as 'passing wind', if you have to refer to it at all.'

'Mum says 'parp',' Billy said.

'Yeah,' agreed Evan, 'or 'poot'.'

'Georgie Takoko says 'patero',' Neil said, making a great production of the Maori pronunciation.

Milly bustled into the kitchen, also dressed for the cool weather. 'Cut it out, you lot. Right, are we ready?'

The boys galloped outside and took off up the street towards the school playing fields, where a crowd had already started to congregate. The bus had disgorged the Huntly Primary team and its supporters, who were also standing about, eyeing up the Pukemiro boys warily. There was a healthy rivalry among school sports teams in the district, and soccer was one of the most fiercely contested games.

Davey came running back for his boots. 'Where's Dad?' he asked, as he sat down on the damp ground and tugged them on.

'Socks as well,' Ellen said automatically. She passed him a pair from the duffel bag while she thought about how she was going to explain Tom's absence.

But then Davey yelled, 'There he is!' and pointed across to the other side of the playing field. He jumped up and raced off.

Ellen looked over and saw Tom standing under a tree with Vic Anscombe and Bert Sisley, all of them smoking and stamping their feet against the cold. He must have ducked back home because he was wearing his coat and hat now. Bert waved, but Tom seemed to make a deliberate point of not acknowledging her at all.

★ ★ ★

After the game, which the Pukemiro boys won, Tom went into town with Vic and a few of the other jokers and spent the afternoon in the pub. He was reasonably pissed by closing time, and bought himself a dozen DB to ward off any likelihood of sobering up. On the train on the way home, Vic asked him if he was going to the dance that night at the miners' hall.

Tom had forgotten all about it.

He shrugged. 'Dunno. Yeah, probably, but it'll be by myself.' The idea that he and Ellen would go along like a happily married couple was laughable; the whole bloody town must know by now.

'You going home first?' Vic asked. The current state of play in the McCabe household must be pretty dire. He'd heard Red Canning's accusations, Tom and Ellen hadn't even stood together during the game this morning, and Tom had spent the afternoon alternating between sullen moping over his beer, and mouthing off angrily about anything and everything.

Tom shrugged again, as if he neither knew nor cared.

'Well, why don't you come back to ours for your tea?' Vic said.

'I can't see Lorna wanting a pissed bastard in her kitchen.'

Vic laughed. 'She's used to it, don't worry.'

So Tom went back to Vic's. If Ellen was wondering where he'd got to, that was her bad luck.

He wasn't a very charming dinner guest, but then Vic hadn't expected he would be. Lorna rounded on him when Tom left the table to go out to the toilet.

'For God's sake, Vic, why did you have to bring him here?'

She was angry at not being consulted about the extra mouth to feed, and at Tom for spilling beer all over the tablecloth and for swearing his head off at the table. Fortunately, she'd told the kids to go and eat their meals in the sitting room before he'd started in with it.

'Jesus, Lorna, look at the state of the poor bastard,' Vic replied. 'I couldn't leave him to stagger up and down Joseph Street all night.'

'Why couldn't he just go home?'

'You know as well as I do: they're having a bit of trouble.'

Lorna's mouth compressed into a narrow, self-righteous line. 'Well, it's none of our business if they are.'

Vic snorted. 'You seemed to think it was when you were having a bloody good gossip with Rhea Wickham at the game this morning. And don't bother denying it because I saw you. You want to learn to keep your nose out of things that don't concern you.'

Lorna went red. 'Well, it's disgusting, her and Jack Vaughan carrying on like that.'

Vic's hand flew to his mouth. 'Don't tell me he's been getting a leg over Rhea as well. The dirty dog!'

'Oh, stop it, you know what I mean.'

'Yes, I know exactly what you mean, and if you're that concerned about the injustice of it, have a heart for poor Tom. He's the one who's been hoodwinked.'

'You know, I've always had my doubts about Ellen McCabe,' Lorna said.

'That's enough, Lorna,' Vic said, suddenly angry. He pointed his knife at her. 'You have *not* had doubts about Ellen McCabe. She's been a good friend to you over the years and don't you forget it. Whatever's going on will get sorted out one way or another, and they don't need you making high and mighty judgements about it, all right?'

'I really don't think . . . ' Lorna began.

'No, you don't think at all, do you? Now shut up, here he comes.'

Tom had heard the raised voices from outside. 'Is something wrong? Is it my swearing? Sorry, Lorna, I'll fuck off if it is.'

Vic shook his head. 'No, mate, you're all right, sit down before you fall down.'

So Tom did, and knocked his beer over again.

Lorna took her husband's advice and kept her mouth closed. She stood up and began to clear the table around the pair of them.

★ ★ ★

Tom had sobered up marginally by the time he got to the dance, mainly because Vic had taken his beer off him. There had been an uncomfortable moment when Vic thought his friend might take a swing at him for it, but in the end he'd just sat there and nodded resignedly.

The hall was almost full when they arrived at a little past eight o'clock. Tom looked around to see if Ellen had had the cheek to come herself, but to his relief he couldn't see her anywhere. He did, however, catch the furtive glances of people unable to stop themselves. They'd been giving him sympathetic — and curious — looks all morning at the game, too. It should have been gratifying to know he had their commiseration, but it was humiliating because it felt like pity, not sympathy.

He felt Vic's hand on his elbow, steering him firmly towards a table where Pat and Rhea, Frank and Milly, and Lew and Andrea Trask were already sitting. Rhea, done up to the nines as usual, gave him a long, cool look as he sat down.

'Is Ellen not with you tonight?' she asked.

Tom regarded her steadily. He might be pissed, but he knew when someone was having a go at him.

'Pinny pains,' he said, and watched with satisfaction as she blushed furiously. That'll teach you, he thought, as she heaved her backside around in her chair and presented her back to him.

'That was a bit naughty,' Milly said, trying not to laugh.

Tom ignored the comment. 'Who's looking after the boys? Have they gone home?'

Milly shook her head, making her curls bounce. 'Gloria's taken them, and Evan and Billy. They're camping out in her *lounge*, apparently.'

'Oh.'

So what was Ellen doing? He very much wanted to know, but wasn't going to ask Milly. He hoped she was sitting at home as miserable as he was, although she probably wouldn't be drunk. But then a truly ghastly thought occurred to him: what if Jack had come home early, and was at this very moment sitting on the couch with her?

He lurched to his feet, but in an instant Milly had grabbed his sleeve and yanked him back down.

'Sit down,' she said, reading his mind. 'She's at home, by herself. She said she wanted to think about things. And if I were you, Tom, I'd go home myself and have a go at sorting it out before it's too late.'

But Tom didn't hear the deliberate emphasis Milly put on the last four words. 'That'll be the day,' he said, 'there's nothing to sort out. If she wants a backdoor man she can have him.'

Milly frowned. She was very worried because Jack Vaughan was obviously much more than just a backdoor man to Ellen, although Tom hadn't seemed to realise that yet. And if he didn't do something soon, he could lose her altogether.

'You don't mean that, Tom, I know you don't. Look, you're a bit worse for wear. Why don't you

338

go and sleep it off? Go back to ours if you don't want to go home.'

'I'm all right,' Tom said. He reached for a beer. 'I think I'll stay a while.'

Milly suggested to Frank that the men should keep an eye on Tom, and although they did what they could he somehow managed to get even drunker, alternating rapidly between rowdy high spirits and bursts of anger and gloom.

Then, very uncharacteristically, he decided he felt like dancing. He dragged Milly up first, and she managed two songs to humour him before she had to sit down again because her toes were so badly trampled. Next he asked Andrea Trask, who was delighted as she saw it as a blow against Ellen McCabe, who was obviously the reason Jack had dumped her. But even she sat down fairly quickly: Tom was a big, heavy man. Then he approached Rhea Wickham, who made a great show of ignoring him, which only made him laugh his head off.

It was then that Vic suggested seriously that Tom go home, or anywhere really, for a bit of a kip before he got himself into real trouble. He seemed to be having a high old time, but there was something very nasty brewing behind his eyes, and Vic could see it.

But Tom refused, declaring at the top of his voice that if it was good enough for Jack Vaughan to whizz the ladies around the dance floor like Fred fucking Astaire, then why shouldn't he?

'Because Fred Astaire isn't built like a brick shithouse, he can actually dance and he isn't usually full of DB when he does,' Vic replied.

'Now go on, Tom, go and get your head down.'

But instead Tom asked Meg Thomasson if she would care to cut a rug. Giggling, she agreed and off they went, banging indiscriminately into couples as they swept through the crowd.

As Tom looked down at her big, brown eyes and wide smile, he realised that Meg really was quite pretty. He'd never really noticed that before. She was also rather drunk, but he decided that that was neither here nor there. She felt nice, too, and he appreciated the way that her breasts — much bigger than Ellen's — were pressing against his chest. In fact, all of her was bigger than Ellen, although she stood no taller and came up to about the same place at his shoulder. Her body, warm and soft, was sort of melting into his and although he wasn't a very good dancer, a social impediment of which he was usually very conscious, they seemed to be doing pretty well together tonight. Perhaps it's who you dance with, not how good you are. But then that reminded him of Ellen dancing with Jack, the pair of them whirling elegantly around the floor as though they were made to be together, and his mood plummeted.

He stopped suddenly, and Meg almost went over backwards.

'Christ!' she said as she teetered, then found her balance again. The silk flower in her bright, blonde hair had almost fallen out, and she raised both hands to adjust the hair pins securing it. 'A bit of warning wouldn't be a bad thing.'

'Sorry,' Tom said.

But she didn't stay put out for long. 'Where's

your wife tonight?' she asked, smiling up at him with an expression that Tom couldn't fathom. She must have heard, surely?

'Ellen?'

'Yes, unless you've got more than one wife.'

'No, I've just got the one.'

'Is that 'just' as in only one wife, or 'just' as in you're only just hanging onto her?' Meg said.

Tom shook his head to clear it; she couldn't be that drunk, she was talking rings around him. Or perhaps it was him who was really drunk.

He nodded his head at the couples going past. 'Do you want to keep going?'

'Why not?' she said.

And they started off again, unsteadily at first, but were soon spinning around and around until Tom began to feel quite giddy, and then sick. Near the door he called another halt and dabbed at his sweaty brow with his sleeve. 'I think I need some fresh air.'

'Want some company?' Meg asked, slipping her arm through his.

Tom thought about it for a moment. He knew he was drunk, but not drunk enough to claim insensibility as a defence against what he suspected was going to happen next. And that was good, because then it couldn't be classed as an accident, one of those things that just happened when a bloke had a few too many beers and got carried away. Not that he'd ever been carried away like that himself, not since he'd been married, and certainly not like Ellen and Jack Vaughan, not by a long shot. But perhaps it was time he did.

'Yeah, I do,' he said, 'that'd be nice.'

Outside it had been raining, and heavy mist shrouded the hills surrounding the town. Clouds drifted across the night sky, letting the moon show through and turn the raindrops on the grass and in the trees into dull diamonds.

Tom felt a lot better in the fresh air, the nausea that had swamped him inside receding. He got out his tobacco and rolled a smoke.

'Want one?' he asked Meg.

She nodded.

They stood on the steps for several minutes, smoking in silence as people ducked past them in and out of the hall.

Tom was starting to feel a flutter of nervousness in his belly at the thought of having sex with a woman who wasn't Ellen, as well as an unpleasant sense of unease and wrongness, which he bludgeoned away with deliberate images of Ellen and Jack, together. He held out his hand to Meg.

'Coming?' he asked.

'Where?'

'For a walk.'

She smiled coyly, then said, 'As long it isn't far, I've got my good shoes on.'

'No, it won't be far.'

He took her hand and led her down the steps and around to the back of the hall. He saw that she gave the dingy shadows there a weary and disappointed look, as if she'd been there before and nothing much had changed.

'Here?' she asked.

'No, not here, further back, by the shed.'

She followed him through the long damp grass across the overgrown section at the rear of the hall to an old shed tucked beneath a row of pines, and waited patiently as he shook the rickety wooden door. It rattled but didn't open. Tom swore. He gave it a last belligerent shove, then towed Meg around to the side of the shed, out of sight of prying eyes where the shadows were deepest. He thought she must know what was coming next, because she leaned back against the flaking weatherboards and relaxed.

Tom set his hands on her shoulders and lowered his face to kiss her. Her mouth tasted of beer and cigarettes, and something waxy and slightly scented — her lipstick, he supposed. But her lips were soft and welcoming, and he felt himself stir at her response. Her arms came up around him and she moved her ample hips against his groin.

'I knew you'd be a big man,' she murmured in his ear, and Tom felt his erection spring to full attention.

He pushed a cold hand down the top of her blouse, not bothering to caress and take his time as he usually did with Ellen. He didn't think he needed to, because this wasn't Ellen, this was just going to be a root, and he assumed Meg knew that as well as he did. He was very aroused, though, in spite of the amount he'd had to drink. It was exciting to caress the skin of a woman he shouldn't be touching, and the more he did it the more he felt he was clawing back a measure of dignity and confirmation that he was still a desirable and attractive man, regardless of what Ellen obviously thought.

Meg raised a leg and he felt her heel stroking rhythmically up and down over the back of his knee. The gesture encouraged him to undo the small buttons on her blouse and slide a hand up her back. The hooks of her bra defeated him, however, and after a minute Meg reached around and undid them herself. Her breasts dropped heavily, her nipples dark in the expanse of soft, pale skin. He bent his head to kiss them and she sighed, her hands resting on his shoulders.

But he didn't stay there for long. Sliding her skirt up her legs, he slipped his hand between them and felt his pulse thud as his fingers moved past the nylon of her stockings to the warmer silkiness of her skin. He inched his way further up and was pleased to note that she had her pants on over her girdle — good, that would save a lot of mucking around.

She pulled them down herself, wriggling her hips as she did in a manner that made him squirm. She stepped out of them and popped them neatly into her handbag in the grass at her feet, then raised her skirt, giving him unobstructed access to her. He looked down hopefully but couldn't see much: it was too dark to make out more than the shadowed triangle at the top of her thighs.

She reached out and rubbed the bulge in his trousers. 'Ready?' she asked.

'Hell, yes,' he said, anticipating the heat and slipperiness of her.

But when he slid his fingers between her legs

she was dry, not ready at all. He felt his mood, and his erection, begin to deflate.

'What's the matter?' he asked.

Meg brushed a hand tenderly across his cheek. It felt strange and he pulled back.

'It's not you, Tom, it's being out here. But I can't take you home because of the kids.' She spat tidily onto her fingers and ran them between her legs. 'There, that should help,' she said, and guided his hand back down.

The sensation revived him and he unbuttoned his trousers, let them fall around his ankles and shoved his underpants down to his knees. But he was too tall for her, and very conscious of the fact that if he bent his knees far enough to ease himself into her, he'd be crippled within minutes. So he lifted one of her legs up to his hip, set his hands under her buttocks and hoisted her up, but had to let her go again almost immediately.

'Christ, woman, you weigh a ton.'

'And you could charm the birds out of the trees with comments like that.'

'Sorry, I didn't mean it like that. Shall we lie down?'

Meg obliged and lay down on her back in the long grass. Tom settled himself between her legs, then pushed himself into her, groaning as her warm flesh enveloped him. She raised her knees and he settled into an urgent rhythm, his face brushed by stalks of paspalum as he supported himself on his elbows above her.

It only took him a minute or two, minutes punctuated by his grunting, a couple of squeaks from her as he squashed the breath out of her, and the hoots of a morepork in the trees above them. Afterwards, as he lay collapsed on top of her breathing heavily, he thought about asking how it had been for her. But he suspected he knew the answer, and didn't want to hear her telling a lie, so he stayed quiet.

When his pulse had returned to normal, he rolled off and pulled his underpants and trousers back up. He felt hollow now, and somehow cheated, the confidence he'd experienced only a few minutes earlier gone. He buckled his belt, then held out a hand and helped her up off the ground.

'Is there grass stuck to my back?' she asked.

'Turn around.'

Tom methodically picked off every blade of grass and pine needle adhering to her. It took him longer than the sex had and, for some reason, felt infinitely more intimate.

'There you are,' he said, turning her around to face him again. 'You look as good as new.'

'I doubt that,' she said, and Tom saw in her eyes, hard and sad at the same time, that whatever she'd thought she was going to get from him, it hadn't eventuated.

He hadn't got what he'd wanted, either. He'd thought that having sex with Meg would go some way towards evening the score, that it would make him feel better, less humiliated and powerless, but now he felt even worse. He didn't even have the moral high ground now.

He waited for Meg to put her pants back on

and apply fresh lipstick, then followed her back to the hall.

'Are you coming back in?' she asked.

Tom shook his head; he was still drunk but didn't feel like being sociable any more. What he really wanted was a good spew to get rid of the beer still sloshing around in his stomach, then to find somewhere dark and quiet where he could lie down and sleep off the booze, and the hangover that would undoubtedly arrive in a few hours' time.

'No,' he said, 'I think I've had enough.'

Meg shrugged. 'Up to you,' she said, and walked up the steps, her heels clacking on the concrete as she went.

Tom waited a second, then called out, 'Meg?'

She stopped and turned around.

'I'm sorry,' he said.

She stared down at him for a moment, then went inside.

14

When Ellen got up the next morning, she found Tom on the couch again, but awake this time. She stood in her dressing gown and watched him as he struggled to sit up, then lean forward with his face in his hands. His eyes were bloodshot and his skin a pasty grey, and she could smell him from the doorway.

'Do you want a bucket?'

'No,' he mumbled. 'A cup of tea though.'

Ellen went out to the kitchen. He'd clearly been to the dance the night before and drunk himself silly, and she supposed she couldn't blame him for that. She'd had an awful night's sleep herself, tossing and turning in the big empty bed, wondering whether he would come home, wondering whether anything would ever be the same between them again, if in fact she even wanted things to be the same.

She took the lid off the tea caddy and sighed when she saw it was nearly empty. In the bedroom she got dressed, ran a brush through her hair, then ducked into the bathroom to clean her teeth.

'I'm going down to the shop,' she said to Tom, who was still slumped on the couch. 'We're out of tea.'

Fred Hollis greeted her cordially enough from behind the counter, but when Andrea Trask came into the shop a few minutes later, Ellen was sure she felt the temperature drop several degrees. She selected her tea, asked Fred to put it on credit and was on her way out when she felt a sharp tap on her shoulder.

'Thanks very much, Ellen McCabe!' Andrea said, as Ellen turned to face her.

'I'm sorry?'

Andrea thrust her arm through the handles of her shopping basket and hitched it up over her shoulder. 'Thanks for stealing Jack Vaughan off me,' she said. 'I was wondering why he dumped me like a hot potato. But why wouldn't he, if he was getting what he wanted on a plate?'

Ellen was shocked at the vehemence of her outburst. 'I'm sorry, Andrea, I didn't mean it to happen that way.'

'What way *did* you mean it to happen, then? I really liked Jack and he thought the world of me.'

'Andrea . . . '

But Andrea charged on, her voice getting shriller by the second. 'I just don't understand it, why would he pick you over me? You're old. And it's not fair, you've already got a husband and two kids and a house of your own, and a bloody refrigerator, why couldn't you be happy with that? What's wrong with you?'

Ellen wished she knew the answer to that, but she didn't. 'You don't understand, Andrea.'

'Oh, I understand, all right. I know about women like you. Your mother was the same, wasn't she? That sort of thing must run in the family, does it?'

Fred came up behind Andrea, wiping his hands on his grocer's apron. 'That's enough,

Andrea Trask. Either keep a civil tongue in your head or take it home.'

'You leave my mother out of this, Andrea,' Ellen warned, finally losing her temper. 'And grow up. Jack Vaughan was never really interested in you. You'd still be going out with him if he was.'

'Ladies, ladies,' Fred cautioned, flapping his hands. If there was one thing worse than women fighting, it was women fighting in his shop.

For a moment, Andrea looked as though she might take a swing at Ellen with her shopping basket, but she didn't. Instead, she said, 'Don't worry, Mr Hollis, I'm going.' Then, to Ellen, she added, 'You can't have everything, you know. Why don't you ask your husband what he was doing with Meg Thomasson last night? Hand in hand they were, apparently, disappearing behind the hall.' And with a satisfied smirk at the expression on Ellen's face, she flounced off.

Fred stared after her, then nervously cleared his throat. 'Ellen, I'm sorry but I can't have that sort of thing in my shop. If it happens again, I'll have to ask you to take your custom somewhere else.'

Ellen regarded him for a moment, and realised with a dull shock that the esteem and affection that Fred had had for her for as long as she could remember was no longer there. She imagined she saw disappointment in his face instead, disappointment and a measure of censure.

'I understand, Fred, I'm really sorry.'

Fred nodded, embarrassed. 'I can't have my

regular customers upset.'

Ellen thought Fred's regular customers would probably be delighted to be entertained by cat fights while they were doing their shopping, but she didn't say so.

Instead, she said, 'Well, thanks for the tea.'

She marched back up the street, her shoes crunching on the gravel, blind to everything around her as she forced herself to confront Andrea's last poisonous little barb.

Tom was still on the couch in the sitting room, although he didn't look up when she paused at the door. He looked terrible.

'I just saw Andrea Trask at the shop,' Ellen said.

Tom didn't respond.

'She said you were with Meg Thomasson last night.'

He did look up then, and scowled, guiltily and belligerently. Ellen suddenly knew that it was true.

'You bloody bastard!' she yelled, and hurled the packet of tea at his head.

It hit him in the centre of his forehead, bounced off and sprayed a shower of tea leaves everywhere as the packet burst. The aroma that suddenly filled the room reminded her of cosy, steamy winter mornings in the kitchen, and it made her want to cry.

'Why, Tom?'

He sat up straighter, rubbing his forehead. 'Why do you think? Why did you do it?'

'Because I love Jack. Do you hear me, Tom? I *love* him!'

It was the first time she had admitted it to him, and the awful power of her words almost knocked him backwards.

'I don't care if you love him or not,' he said, 'you still cheated on me.'

Ellen ignored him. 'And I know you're not in love with Meg Thomasson, so what was your excuse?' She was standing over him now, so angry she could feel herself quivering from head to toe.

'She was there, she was keen. It didn't mean anything.'

Ellen raised her hand and slapped him across the face as hard as she could. 'How could you, you selfish bloody bastard! How could you take advantage of her like that?'

Tom gazed up at her, startled and thoroughly confused. She could see in his face that he didn't know what she meant, and for the first time in her life she despised him.

She bent down, so close to him she could smell his stale breath. 'I never thought I'd say this about you, Tom, but using Meg like that is the weakest, most pathetic and selfish thing you've ever done.'

'And you opening your legs for Jack Vaughan wasn't selfish?'

'No, it was a bloody escape.'

His mouth opened then closed again in anguish and impotent rage. She stepped out of range because she could see he wanted to hit out at her again: his hands had clenched into fists, but, for the moment, he kept them tight against his belly.

'Stop that this minute!' It was Gloria, standing in the doorway, glaring at them. 'Stop it, the pair of you, the boys will hear.'

'Are they home?' Ellen asked, her heart pounding even harder in case they'd heard.

'They're outside, playing in the tree hut. They wanted to come home, they know bloody well something's wrong.' She sat down in an armchair, the look on her face suggesting that she was prepared to sit there for ever if she had to. 'For God's sake, you two, you have to sort this out. So, Ellen, go and put the kettle on.'

Tom said, 'There's no tea.'

Gloria eyed the tea leaves scattered across the couch, on the floor and in his hair. 'Then get a spoon and scrape some up. And while you're at it, go and wash your face, you're a disgrace. Then we'll talk.'

★ ★ ★

The boys came in to say hello, then were sent outside again with jam sandwiches and mugs of cocoa to have as a picnic in the tree hut. Neil wanted to know what was going on, but Gloria shooed him away with a promise of sixpence to spend at the lolly shop if he could keep Davey entertained for the next hour or so.

'I don't want sixpence,' he said, 'I want to know what's going on.'

'Well, you can't, it's grown-up business,' Gloria said. 'Go on, be a good man and look after your brother. Everything will be all right, I promise.'

353

Neil trudged outside, dragging his feet and looking back over his shoulder at her, eyes filled with confusion.

When he'd gone, Gloria didn't actually do much of the talking, in the end. Tom didn't want her to do any of it, and when he'd cleaned himself up and changed out of yesterday's smelly and crumpled clothes, he said so.

'I know you want to help, Gloria, but this is between me and Ellen.'

They were sitting around the table, the three of them.

'No it's not, Thomas, it's my business too,' Gloria said. 'Anything to do with my grandsons is my business. And I'm warning both of you that if you can't get this mess sorted out without upsetting those poor little mites even more, then I'm taking them. They can come and live with me until you've come to your senses.'

Tom said, 'Gloria, I said I don't want anyone else involved.'

'Well, too bad,' Gloria replied, 'because they already are. I am, Neil and Davey are, Jack Vaughan is, and I'm damn sure at least half of the town would love to be as well, if they could. Everyone's gossiping about it, particularly after your performance last night, Thomas.'

He had the grace to blush, but at the same time looked thoroughly appalled at the fact that she'd mentioned it in front of Ellen.

'What?' Gloria went on. 'It isn't as if she doesn't know — you were both going hammer and tongs over it ten minutes ago.' She stood up and reached for her bag. 'I've brought my

354

knitting and I'm going into the lounge to finish a set of sleeves, and I'm not leaving until you've worked something out. And if I hear even a hint of a raised voice, I'll be straight back in here, you mark my words.'

When she'd gone, Tom and Ellen sat on opposite sides of the table, eyeing each other warily. The emotional distance between them felt like a bottomless pit, and neither of them knew where to start.

Tom said eventually, 'She's right, we have to look out for Neil and Davey.'

'I know we do.'

'Then why didn't you think about that when you decided to take your knickers off for Jack?'

Ellen closed her eyes against the bitterness in his voice. She didn't feel resentment about what he'd done with Meg, only anger because he'd done it so casually and selfishly. She believed him when he said it had meant nothing, and she wondered desolately whether she would have cared if he'd told her that it had. She suspected not, and it was breaking her heart.

'Can we not snipe at each other, Tom, please?'

He rubbed his face wearily and exhaled. 'I can't help it. This is killing me, Ellen. I just don't understand what's happened.' He pulled at a loose thread on the cuff of his jumper. 'I don't understand why it's happened, either. I thought we were all right, you and I.'

'We were.'

'So what went wrong?'

Ellen didn't know what to say. Her earlier anger was ebbing away, and now she just felt sad

355

and empty. The truth was, it had gone wrong simply because Jack Vaughan had come along, and Jack Vaughan had turned out to be the finest thing that had ever happened to her. But she couldn't say that to Tom while he was looking at her with eyes that were so bewildered and hurt.

'Would it have gone wrong if Jack hadn't moved here?' he asked.

'I really don't know.'

And she didn't, either, but Jack had come to Pukemiro, and talking about what might have happened if he hadn't was pointless.

'I thought it was the strike upsetting you,' Tom said in a tone that implied he couldn't believe how stupid he'd been. 'I thought if I could make it so we went back to work, you'd be happy again and everything would be all right. But it wasn't the strike, was it? It was Jack. I made a complete fucking idiot of myself with that one, didn't I?'

Ellen said, 'No, you didn't. And you wouldn't have done it anyway. You're not a scab, Tom, and you never will be.'

She could see that he was faintly mollified by her words, but also that they weren't enough; he needed to have the upper hand, which saddened her, because he'd never had it at any time during their marriage.

'You accused me of being weak and gutless before,' he said, 'and you're right. I shouldn't be sitting here having a nice chat with you about all this, I should have chucked you out days ago. Other blokes wouldn't put up with it.' He pulled at the loose thread again until the bottom of his sleeve began to unravel. Then, with obvious reluctance, he asked, 'Did you think about going away with him?'

Ellen noted that he was referring to the idea in the past tense, as if the possibility would now never eventuate.

'He never asked me,' she said, and felt her heart ache at the sudden flare of hope in Tom's eyes.

'I don't want you to see him any more.'

She had known he would say that: any man with an ounce of pride would have to say it.

'He won't be coming around here,' Tom went on, sitting up straighter now that he was laying down the law, 'you won't go to his house, and when we're out you won't speak to him. You're not to go anywhere near him.' Then he played his best card. 'It's for the best, Ellen, it's for the boys.'

He was blackmailing her. She knew it and she forgave him for it immediately, because she knew he loved his sons dearly. But the relief that often comes with forgiveness didn't make her feel any better, because she knew in her heart that she wouldn't be able to abide by his demands.

With impeccable timing there was a timid knock on the door and Davey pushed it open. 'Mum, can I have another sandwich?'

His socks were sagging around his ankles, one of his pockets was turned inside out and there was a smear of dirt on his cheek. Ellen held out her arms and he ran into them and buried his face in her breasts. She prayed that no one had said anything to either him or Neil, but it was

357

clear that they knew that something was badly wrong.

She held him at arms' length and gazed into his small face. He had a cold and there was a trickle of snot glistening on his top lip. She wiped it gently away with the hem of her cardigan.

'Did Grandma not feed you at her house?'

'Yes, but I'm hungry again. Mum?'

'What, love?'

'I don't want to go back there.'

'To Grandma's?'

'Mmm.'

'Why not? Don't you like it there?'

'I do, but it's better here. I missed you.'

Ellen glanced over Davey's fair head at Tom, who was staring back at her, the expression on his face making it very clear that he thought she was to blame for the boy's sudden clingyness. And she supposed she was.

'I want you here too, love, I missed you too.' She gave him a quick cuddle then got up to make him another sandwich.

'Ellen?'

Alerted by the tone in Tom's voice, she turned slowly around to face him. 'What?'

'Did you hear what I said before?'

'Yes.'

'Then say it. Say 'I won't see him again'.'

'See who?' Davey asked, looking from his mother to his father, then back to his mother again. They both ignored him.

Ellen stood very still for a moment, feeling rage and a sudden, sharp panic thumping in her

358

chest. The bastard — he knew that with Davey in the room, there was only one thing she could say.

'I won't see him again,' she said.

★   ★   ★

But she saw him two days later. She simply walked out of the house, down Joseph Street and into Robert Street, through his gate and up to the front door.

He opened it before she'd even knocked and pulled her into his arms, kicking the door shut behind them. He hugged her so hard she almost couldn't breathe. 'I saw you coming up the path,' he said into her hair. 'Christ, I've been so worried. I wanted to come and see you but I didn't want to make it worse. Did you get my note?'

She stepped back from him, nearly in tears from the relief of seeing him. 'No, the only note I've had is one from Rhea Wickham telling me I'm suddenly not needed on the women's auxiliary any more. Did you leave me one?'

Jack nodded. 'I came around on Sunday night, really late, and stuck it in the copper in your washhouse. Haven't you done any washing since then?'

Ellen giggled at the incongruity of his question. 'No, I haven't. I've had rather a lot on my mind lately. How did you find out?'

'The woman from next door came over about two minutes after I got home on Sunday evening, bursting to tell me to watch my back because someone had told Tom you've been

359

coming to see me. Does he know you're here?'

'No, he's down the street seeing Pat at the moment. He'll be home soon so I can't stay long, but I had to see you.'

'How was he?' Jack asked.

Ellen tilted her face so he could see the faint mark on her cheek. 'He was a bit free with his fists,' she confessed, although she felt strangely uneasy saying it. There was no satisfaction in it at all. 'I don't blame him, though.'

Jack wrapped her in his arms again. 'My poor girl, what have I done to you?'

'You? You haven't done anything to me, except make me happy. This isn't your fault, Jack. I made the decision to start seeing you, and I'm making the decision to carry on seeing you.' She hesitated. 'If you want that, I mean.'

'Christ, of course I want it.' He smoothed a strand of hair back off her face and regarded her seriously for a moment. 'That's you all over, isn't it? Tom belts you and you don't blame him. I seduce you and get you into all sorts of trouble, and you say it isn't my fault.'

'You didn't seduce me, I wanted it to happen. And I'm so pleased it did,' she said, resting her cheek against his chest. 'I'm just not that keen to blame it on anyone else.'

'You're a bloody hard woman, Ellen.'

'Sorry?' She raised her head, startled.

'It's a compliment. You're strong and you're stubborn. You're a real coalminer's wife.'

'I'm a coalminer's daughter, too, Jack, don't forget that. It's bred into me.'

'I know, it's part of why I love you.'

360

'I love you too, Jack.'

He bent his head and kissed her, a long, lingering kiss, but, with a huge effort, she pulled away from him.

'We can't, Jack. Tom will be back soon and when he finds out I'm not there he'll be straight down here. And anyway, I can't go home to him all . . . well, without having a wash.'

'Have one here,' Jack said.

'I can't, not today.'

'When, then?'

'I don't know, I don't know when I can get away.'

'Is Tom going up to Auckland on Friday?'

'No, he's staying here for the big meeting in town, and he's quite happy to go to it because he knows you'll be there too. Otherwise he'd be at home, making sure I don't leave his sight.'

'Do you really think so?'

'No. I don't know. Maybe. Probably.'

'Poor bugger, this must be driving him mental,' Jack said.

'You like Tom, don't you?'

Jack nodded. 'He's a good bloke and I've got nothing against him. I feel like a prize bloody bastard, actually.'

'But not enough of one to stop what we're doing?'

'No, not enough to stop.'

They stared at each other for a moment.

'But when can we meet?' she said, frustrated because she couldn't think of a single opportunity.

'There's a committee meeting on Thursday, to

361

sort things out before the Friday meeting.'

'But won't you have to go?'

'No, I resigned.'

'From the union?' Ellen was stunned.

'No, just from the committee. Well, I can't stay on it, can I? Tom's the secretary.'

'What did Pat say?'

'He said it was a bugger, but if that's the way it was, so be it.'

'I thought you were his golden-haired boy, the new blood rising up through the ranks of the union and all that.'

'You've got a sarcastic tongue on you sometimes, haven't you?'

'No, I mean it, I thought Pat had his eye on you.'

'No, it's Tom he wants. I think Pat was happy to sacrifice me. He'll do anything to keep the union steady, especially at the moment, and one of the committee members sleeping with the secretary's wife doesn't quite fit in with his plans.'

'He always was a bit of a mercenary bastard, Pat.'

'Has to be, though, doesn't he? I don't begrudge him. It's a tough job, union leader.'

'Yes, it is,' Ellen said, thinking about Tom's ambition to one day take Pat's place. 'You're not bothered, stepping down?'

'No, there's plenty of other committees around the country.'

A nasty little prickle of fear hooked its claws into Ellen's spine. 'Would you go somewhere else?'

'I might have to, after this.'

She looked at him helplessly, and saw that he knew exactly what she was thinking. 'What are we going to do?'

He enfolded her in his arms and rocked her gently. 'Don't worry, love, we'll work something out.'

She leaned into his warmth and the solidness of his chest, her eyes closed, willing herself not to cry. A sharp, painful lump had formed in her throat and she didn't trust herself to speak.

'So, could we meet on Thursday?' he asked.

She cleared her throat. 'Are you free?'

'Of course I'm bloody free, and it's no problem for me, but what if Tom catches on? He'll be even more suspicious when he finds out I've resigned. He might not even go to the meeting himself when he does find out.'

'He'll go. He won't miss it.'

★   ★   ★

Tom did go to the Thursday meeting, and he went knowing that, before he was even halfway down the street, Ellen would be slipping off to meet Jack. He knew she'd been with him on Tuesday, because he'd seen it in her face when she'd come home; he'd been waiting for her and neither of them had said anything, but he'd known.

They hadn't said much to each other at all since then, and had spent the last two days stepping around one another in the house, being civil in front of the boys but only just. He slept on the couch and spoke to her only when he absolutely had to. He was being childish, he knew that, but as he couldn't decide whether to throw himself on his knees and beg her to stop what she was doing, or to wring her neck, he thought it best if he just kept his mouth shut. There didn't seem to be a lot to say any more anyway. The strike was disintegrating, his beloved wife was having an affair, his life was crashing down around his ears, and there didn't seem to be a bloody thing he could do about any of it.

He also went to the meeting on Friday in Huntly, with almost a thousand miners jammed into the town hall. He didn't know whether to take that as a good sign or not. Some of the mass meetings called by the Waikato central council over the past few months had been poorly attended, which had suggested an alarming level of apathy from the rank and file. But this one was different because today they would be discussing whether they would accept the Minister of Labour's terms for a return to work, terms that Sullivan had issued after the miners had approached him, independent of the watersiders, about what conditions might be imposed should they decide to go back.

Tom sat down next to Bert near the front, and had a good look around but couldn't spot the one face he desperately wanted to see.

'Good turnout,' he said.

On the stage was a trestle table where the central council would sit. Tom could see Bob Amon standing to one side, talking animatedly to someone and smacking a rolled-up sheaf of papers into the palm of his hand.

'Depends how you look at it,' Bert replied, rolling a smoke. 'If we vote and the hall's full of jokers who've had enough of the strike no matter what, we're buggered. If they're pissed off with Sullivan's conditions and happy to stay out, we'll be home and hosed.' He licked the edge of his paper, pressed the smoke into shape, and lit it. 'You getting on all right now, you and Ellen?'

'No, I think we've had it.'

'Sorry to hear that,' Bert said, 'I really am. Anything I can do?'

'You could put a bullet through the back of Jack Vaughan's head for me.'

Bert looked at him, one eye closed against the smoke from his cigarette. 'You mean it?'

'No, but it would make things a lot simpler.'

'You got on well with Jack, didn't you?'

'For a while there, yeah.'

Knowing Tom well enough to be sure he wouldn't mind the question, Bert asked, 'Does that make it worse?'

Tom thought about it. 'Yeah, it does. It might be slightly easier to stomach if it was some bastard I didn't know, if it had to be anyone at all, but bloody Jack, Christ. What a fuck-up.'

He turned around again to scan the crowd, and froze. There he was now, coming into the hall and slipping into a seat near the back. Tom exhaled, angry and relieved at the same time. Bert turned to follow his gaze and spotted Jack himself.

'You want to keep out of his way, Tom, just to

be on the safe side.'

'He wants to keep out of my fucking way!' Tom said, making heads around him turn sharply.

'That's what I meant,' Bert said. 'It might be an idea to go straight home after the meeting's finished.'

It was good advice, but Tom didn't take it.

There was a lot of talking during the meeting from Bob Amon, and some more depressing news about the weakening resolve of strikers around the country, including some miners at pits in other areas, but when it came time to vote, a good majority rejected Sullivan's terms for a return to work. They were dictatorial and, as Amon pointed out, would almost certainly lead to victimisation and the loss of former favourable working conditions. The men weren't tempted to break their strike. The atmosphere of solidarity in the hall was strong after that, and there was talk of declaring the entire Waikato coalfields permanently black, and of reducing Huntly to a ghost town.

A good majority also headed for the pub the minute the meeting concluded, and Tom went with them. He walked the short distance from the town hall along the main street with Vic and Bert, all the time with an eye open for Jack, hoping that he was off to the pub as well, but knowing at the same time that they would both be a lot better off if he wasn't.

But he was there already when they arrived, standing at a table with Pat and Lew. He nodded amicably as they approached, collected his beer and casually moved off to another table. It was an uncomfortable situation for the Pukemiro men, who didn't know where to look and didn't want to get involved, but it was far worse for Tom, who knew he wouldn't be leaving the pub that night without taking at least one swing at Jack.

He got stuck into the beer straight away, buying the first round and an extra one to keep him going. By five o'clock he was in a fine state, drunk and mean with it. Knowing that something was brewing, the others kept a wary eye on him to make sure he didn't cause any trouble with the wrong people. Jack stayed away, at a table in the far corner, although anyone observing the two men, and that was almost everyone in the bar, was aware that they were eyeing each other up. The occasional visitor to Jack's table suggested, just quietly, that it might be a good idea if he left now, while he still could, but Jack wouldn't budge.

'He's bigger than you, lad,' Wobbly Minogue pointed out, 'and he's got a skinful. He'll do you like a dog's dinner.'

Jack just nodded, calm and stoic; he knew what was coming and was quite relieved that it finally was. He would much rather it was this way than what had gone on all week, the two of them skulking around Pukemiro like a pair of dirty old tomcats, both bristlingly aware of each other's presence but neither quite willing to encroach on the other's territory.

'No, he won't,' Doug Walmsley said. 'Jack here's got more weight behind him, given his height. It affects the centre of gravity with the punches.'

Wobbly stared, blinking slowly. 'Who made you a boxing expert all of a sudden?'

'I don't need to be a bloody expert, I've got eyes.'

'Bloody red ones tonight, too,' Wobbly said. 'No, Tom'll have him.' He turned to Jack. 'Sorry, lad, nothing personal.'

Jack shrugged and took another sip of his beer.

'He bloody won't,' Doug said, banging his glass down on the table, but not emphatically enough to spill the contents.

'He will, you know,' Wobbly said, refusing to be swayed. 'Tom McCabe's got bloody long arms.'

'He won't.'

'He will, and I'll put a quid on that.'

'You haven't got a quid.'

'Yes, I have, and if I don't bet it I'll only drink it by six o'clock.'

Jack shook his head at the pair of them, then risked a glance across the room at Tom, but he wasn't where he had been a few minutes ago. Jack looked quickly over his shoulder to make sure he wasn't coming up behind him, then relaxed as he saw Tom's big form moving through the smoke away from the bar, four handles gripped in his hands. If he kept going like that, Jack thought, he wouldn't have to fight him: Tom would be out cold on the floor all by himself.

Tom looked up then, and saw Jack watching him. He gave the other man a small nod, not in

368

greeting, but in acknowledgement that it wouldn't be long now. He made his way back to his table and set the handles down, spilling beer as he did, then rolled himself a smoke, pleased to see that his hands weren't shaking. He felt steady, if steady was the right word for it. He was pissed but he was angry, and he knew that every man in the bar was waiting for him to do what they would all do themselves, given the same circumstances.

But something was missing. He was waiting for the feeling that had raged through him that day in Queen Street just before the coppers charged, that wild, exhilarating sensation of being truly alive and that nothing else mattered except being part of the fight. But he didn't have it and, deep in his belly, Tom thought he knew why: Jack wasn't the enemy. And it was a gut-wrenching revelation, because he would have to fight him anyway or he'd never be able to hold his head up again.

'All right, son?' Pat asked.

Tom looked at him. 'I'm going over there,' he said, putting his unlit cigarette back into his tobacco tin. 'I want to get this over with.'

Pat nodded, knowing exactly what Tom meant. He emptied his glass and reached for another, then leaned his elbow comfortably on the table, settling himself in for the show.

But Jack had already made a move. He'd been watching Tom and feeling so sorry for the poor bastard that he'd decided to make it easy for him: he was already walking away, across the room towards the door, as if to slip out while

Tom had his back turned.

Tom moved immediately, barging his way through the crowd towards Jack, who was now only a yard or so from the door.

'Oi!' he yelled, catching up and shoving Jack's shoulder hard.

Jack spun around and took Tom's first blow full in the face, his head snapping back and his legs going out from under him. But he was up again straight away, oblivious to the trickle of blood coming out of his nose.

He feinted with his left hand, then hit out with his right, catching Tom a solid thump on the side of the head. Tom staggered but didn't fall, and then they were circling each other, fists up and heads down.

The crowd, most with beers still in hand, swarmed around them, forming a wide circle with Tom and Jack in the centre; others sat up on the tall tables and three or four jokers got up on the bar for a better view until Harry the barman told them to get the hell off it. There was a roar of approval at every punch thrown, not in favour of one man or the other, but in simple acknowledgement of each bloke's skill.

Jack let go with another swing that took Tom by surprise and knocked him sideways, but he recovered and lurched back, delivering another blow to Jack's face. For the first time, Jack looked annoyed, and hit out with a punch so heavy it split Tom's eyebrow. Both men were bleeding now, and breathing raggedly as they stepped around each other.

Then the boxing stopped and the real fighting

began, with a barrage of blows that had the crowd yelling and hooting wildly. Tom hooked his leg behind Jack's knees and tried to shove him down, but Jack hung on and took Tom with him, the pair of them crashing into a table and sending glasses and beer everywhere.

Behind the bar, Harry swore.

Tom and Jack rolled around on the floor until Jack finally tore himself away and staggered to his feet. Tom, caught on his knees, prepared to duck in anticipation of Jack's boot. But the kick didn't come, and when he glanced up at Jack's face, streaming with blood now, he saw in the other man's eyes that it never would. But he wasn't going to put out his hand to let Jack help him up — neither of them could ever claim to be that gentlemanly.

Then he was up and they were at it again, moving more ponderously now, lurching instead of sidestepping, their swings wilder and less calculated. They'd been fighting solidly for nearly ten minutes and both were flagging, the sweat on their faces mixing with the blood and their clothes dishevelled and ripped. With a colossal effort they launched themselves yet again, but instead of hitting out they held on to each other, staggering around like a drunken couple on the dance floor at the end of a very long night.

'Jack,' Tom gasped as he clung to the other man's shirt.

Exhausted, battered and sore, they swayed against each other, faces barely inches apart. Jack blinked at him through eyes bleary with sweat and blood.

'Jack, man, leave her alone. Please,' Tom whispered, his voice hoarse.

Panting and hoicking back blood and snot, Jack slowly shook his head. 'I can't, Tom. I just can't.'

They stared at each other for several long heartbeats. Then, dredging up the last of his strength, Tom shoved Jack as hard as he could; again Jack hung on and another table crashed onto its side.

Behind the bar, Harry muttered, 'Right, that's it,' opened his little hatch and marched over to the crowd.

'Break it up, break it up!' he roared, shoving spectators out of the way. 'Come on, the pair of you, on your bikes, you're wrecking my pub.' He grabbed Tom by his already torn collar and dragged him to his feet. 'And you're banned for a month, Tom McCabe, this is the second time you've done this in as many weeks. Now go on, bugger off, both of you.'

★　★　★

Tom was in considerable pain over the next twenty-four hours, once the effects of the beer wore off. His right eye was black and swollen shut, his eyebrow was split and he'd lost one of his back teeth. In frosty silence, Ellen made him ice packs for the bruises and dabbed iodine on his cuts, but she never once asked him how he'd come to be in such a state. She didn't have to:

372

news of the fight was all over Pukemiro almost before the Friday night train had pulled into the Junction. She wouldn't have asked him anyway, she was so irate at what he'd done. Irate and ashamed, because everyone must have known bloody well what he and Jack were fighting about, and it made her feel like some sort of chattel being bickered over in a shabby little public dispute. It was humiliating, for all of them.

Tom was still sleeping on the couch, and the atmosphere in the house was colder than the winter air outside. But Ellen continued to cook and clean and look after the boys, she worked almost obsessively in her vegetable garden and she slipped out of the house to see Jack at every opportunity she could grab. Tom knew exactly where she was going, but said nothing. He neither told her to pack her bags, nor did he make the decision to leave himself. It was a situation that was almost intolerable, for both of them.

Then, on 26 June, the day that the swelling in Tom's eye finally started to recede, news came that the Seamen's Union had advised the WWU to return to work on the government's terms, and had confirmed their own decision of some days earlier to go back themselves. It was an almighty blow to the strikers who still held out hope, although their numbers were dwindling by the day.

But then good news followed. Thoroughly rattled by the town's crumbling economy after more than eighteen weeks of strike, and even more by talk of ghost towns and of blacking the coalfields for ever, fifty of Huntly's businessmen petitioned the mayor, who urgently telegraphed the government asking that the miners' standing working agreement be honoured should they return to work. If it wasn't, if Sullivan insisted on applying his own terms and the miners refused to go back and went further afield for work instead, then the town could very well turn to dust, and with it the coal that until very recently had fuelled half of New Zealand.

Two days later, Sullivan announced that he would modify his conditions after all.

National officers of the UMWU recommended immediately that Sullivan's new terms be accepted. As soon as they were informed of the decision, the two Waikato delegates to the national council of the UMWU boarded the train for Wellington.

15

Ellen sat at the kitchen table, waiting and glancing anxiously at her watch; the meeting should be over by now. Yesterday, the UMWU had officially accepted Sullivan's conditions, and Tom, in sullen silence, had oiled his boots and hung his work clothes out to air. Today he'd gone with the rest of the men to the Pukemiro pithead to vote by secret ballot on whether they would finally return to work, although the result was more or less a foregone conclusion. The Renown miners had started back yesterday.

She tensed as she heard someone coming up the steps, but a discreet knock told her that it wasn't Tom.

She opened the door — it was Jack.

'Tom will be home in a minute,' she said, before he even had a chance to open his mouth.

'No, he won't, he's gone down to Pat's with the others, but I'd better be quick.'

Ellen stepped back. 'Come inside, it's cold.'

Jack followed her into the kitchen; he didn't sit down but propped himself against the bench instead. He seemed preoccupied and on edge.

Ellen asked, 'What happened at the meeting?'

'Back to work tomorrow morning. It wasn't quite unanimous but they're all going back.'

'And the other pits?'

375

'Alison and McDonald tomorrow, Glen Afton and Rotowaro on Monday. Not sure about Glen Massey, or the rest of the opencasters.' He moved closer and grasped her hands. They were cold, and he rubbed them gently.

Her eyes were shut: he had said 'they' were going back. Not 'we', but 'they'.

'Ellen, there's something I have to tell you.'

She nodded, her eyes still tightly closed against the words she knew she was about to hear.

'I'm leaving, Ellen. I can't stay here after everything that's happened, it wouldn't work.' He squeezed her hands. 'Come on, love, open your eyes, look at me.'

She forced herself to do as he asked.

'That's better,' he said. 'I'm going back down to the West Coast, they're hiring at Strongman at the moment.' The look of desolation in her eyes almost broke his heart. He cupped her face in his hands, and wiped a tear away with his thumb. 'No, Ellen, don't cry, please. I want you to come with me. Will you?'

Ellen stared at him, at the now familiar and comforting angles of his handsome face, the healing cut on his brow from Tom's fist, his bright, dark eyes and the laugh lines that fanned out from them. And, slowly, she nodded.

Jack exhaled in relief and gave her a quick but passionate kiss that almost bruised her lips. 'Thank Christ,' he said. 'I've been dreading what I'd do if you said no.'

'Did you think I might?' Ellen said, incredulous, then burst into tears. 'My babies!' she

376

blurted, her hand pressed over her heart, struggling to contain the pain there that was already almost too much to bear.

'Bring them,' Jack said.

'Take them with us?' Ellen thought of Tom, and how his life would be without her or his sons, and shook her head. 'Oh God, I couldn't, I couldn't do that to him.'

'You could send for them, when we're settled. You don't have to leave them for ever.'

She rested her forehead against his chest. 'I don't want to leave them at all.'

'I know.'

They held each other, not saying anything.

In his cage, Fintan had a scratch so violent that his swing rattled wildly, and said to no one in particular, 'Cold out there?'

'When will we go?' Ellen asked.

'Tomorrow morning, after they've started back.'

Ellen was jolted by the suddenness of it, but knew that there was no other way they could do it.

'I'll come and pick you up,' Jack said, in case she changed her mind. 'You don't have to bring much, I'll get you anything you need.'

Ellen's gaze moved around the kitchen over her beautiful white refrigerator, the wooden flour scoop that Neil had made for her in its special place on the windowsill, the curtains she'd sewn when they'd first moved into the house, and the crooked shelves at the end of the bench her father had put up when Tom's arm had been in a plaster cast.

'No, Jack. Thanks, but I'll meet you in town. I'll come in on the morning train and meet you at the station.'

'Do you want to say goodbye by yourself?'

She nodded, grateful that he understood.

'But you will be there?' he asked.

'I will.'

He lifted her chin so he could see exactly what was in her eyes. 'Promise?'

'I promise.'

★　★　★

That afternoon, while Tom was mowing the lawn, she prepared the tastiest meal she could manage from what was in the cupboards and the fridge, and opened the last jar of preserves to make a fruit cobbler, a family winter favourite. Then she cried her eyes out as she kneaded the mixture with her hands, thinking how bloody stupid she was imagining that the memory of a pudding would make everything all right when the boys arrived home from school tomorrow afternoon to find she'd walked out on them.

Every time she thought about what would be happening in the morning, she felt like being sick. She'd learned a lot about herself over the last few months, and not all of it pleasant, but she'd never imagined she would ever find it within herself to abandon her children. But here she was, on the eve of doing exactly that. She was determined to send for them as soon as she could, there was absolutely no doubt in her mind about it, and she clung to that resolution

378

desperately because it was the only thing stopping her from drowning in her own guilt. That, and the image of Jack waiting for her at the railway station tomorrow morning.

She thought about Tom, too, and how he would feel when he realised she'd gone. It wouldn't kill him, he was far too strong for that, but it would change him for ever and she would always carry the responsibility for that. For a moment she tried to tell herself he'd be better off without her, but she knew she was having herself on. If he still loved her, her leaving would hurt him terribly.

They ate their meal that night in the same stony silence that had enveloped them over the past two weeks. It was agonising. The disillusion and despair rolling off Tom was palpable, Davey knocked his milk over and burst into frightened tears, and Neil got up and walked away from the table halfway through the meal and slammed into his bedroom. A few weeks ago he would have been given a swift clip across the ear for such bad manners, but now no one even commented on it. The atmosphere was unbearable and for a moment Ellen wished it was tomorrow morning already.

But when she went into the boys' bedroom later to tuck them in, she was overwhelmed with such love for them that she thought her legs might buckle from the force of it. She stood holding onto the door handle, gazing at them, her eyes prickling with tears she hoped they couldn't see, then moved over to sit on the edge of Neil's bed.

She bent down to give him a cuddle, but he turned his head away.

'Neil, love, don't. What's the matter?'

'Nothing,' he said.

'Come on, sweetheart, I want to know.'

'Why?' he said to the wall. 'You don't care about us any more.'

She recoiled as though he had punched her in the face. 'Oh, I do, Neil, so much. Why are you saying that?'

He turned his head back towards her. In the semi-darkness, his eyes were flat and distant. 'Trevor Quinn says you're a slut. He says you've got a fancy man and you don't love us any more.'

'Oh, Neil, sweetheart!' Ellen reached for him, but he batted her hand away exactly as Tom had done.

He rolled over to face the wall again. 'Go away, Mum, I'm tired,' he said, and closed his eyes.

She watched him, her heart breaking. When she couldn't stand it any longer, she moved over to Davey's bed. He was on his back with his arms out, on top of the covers.

'Davey, love?'

He didn't answer, although she knew he wasn't asleep because he was holding his breath.

'Davey?'

He stayed still a few seconds longer, then suddenly sat up, leaning into her and beginning to cry. She sat there for some time, stroking his hair and wiping tears and snot off his face. When he'd finally cried himself to sleep, she laid him back down and tucked him in.

She went back to Neil's bed, but he didn't stir.

Finally, she went out and shut the door behind her.

Tom wasn't in the kitchen but she saw him through the window, sitting on the steps next door having a smoke and talking to Bert. Dot would be home soon but she would miss her, Ellen thought with a deep pang of regret. She could write to her, though, she could write to everyone she wouldn't be saying goodbye to, and perhaps try to explain why she'd gone. If she could. She'd already decided not to say goodbye to her mother, or Milly, because she knew they both would try to stop her, and she wouldn't be able to bear what they'd say to her about Neil and Davey. She thought about the advice Alf might have given her. She wanted to think he'd have told her to follow her heart, because he'd always told her that, but now she suspected he might have told her something completely different.

And she wouldn't have wanted to hear that, because she'd made up her mind.

★ ★ ★

In the morning she got up early, washed and dressed quickly, and packed a small carrybag with two changes of underwear, a clean blouse and the basic toiletries she would need. Then she shoved the bag under the bed and went into the kitchen to start breakfast.

No one spoke at the breakfast table, and when

381

it was time for Tom to leave for work, she sent the boys to the bathroom to clean their teeth. While Tom packed his crib tin in his rucksack, she watched in silence, trying to decide what she wanted to say to him.

He went out to the porch and she followed him, watching as he bent over to tug on his boots.

'Tom?'

He stopped, but didn't turn around. She moved closer, wanting to reach out and touch his broad back, but knowing it was far too late for that now.

'You've always been a good husband.'

'I wanted to be,' he said. Then he straightened up, picked up his rucksack and went down the steps, not once turning back to look at her.

She stood there listening to his boots crunching up the path at the side of the house then, when the sound had faded completely, she went inside again and shut the door.

She hugged the boys as hard as she could when it was time for them to go to school. Davey clung to her, but Neil stood rigid and unresponsive. She walked with them to the front gate and watched them until they turned the corner and disappeared from sight.

Then she gave Fintan his breakfast, stoked the range, changed into her walking shoes and put her coat on. She picked up her bag, stepped out onto the porch and closed the back door behind her for the last time.

★　★　★

382

She sat by herself on the train, but no one she knew was in her carriage anyway, which was an immense relief. She was sick of talking, and especially of lying. She'd had enough of lying to last her a lifetime.

The small, dirty coal towns she loved so much rolled past as the train lumbered across the damp countryside towards Huntly, but she didn't see them; they were part of the old Ellen and there was no room in her heart for them any more. There would be new towns soon, and a new life.

As the train pulled into the Huntly railway station, she collected her bag from the seat beside her and moved to stand by the carriage door, anxious to be off the train as quickly as possible. She could see him already, leaning against the side of his truck, waiting for her.

The door opened and she stepped down onto the platform and walked towards him, not hurrying now but moving confidently and with her head held high. He saw her then, and the special smile he kept just for her spread across his lovely, welcoming face. He stepped forward, his arms opening to embrace her.

She was barely six feet away from him when she heard it, a small, panicky voice behind her.

'Mum! Don't leave me!'

She spun around. Near the wooden bench that ran along the side of the station building, a little boy was stamping his feet, his face red and wet with tears. A harassed-looking woman stood glaring down at him.

'Oh, for God's sake, I'm only going to the

toilet,' she said. 'You'll be all right for five minutes, surely!'

In an instant Ellen knew it was too late, for her and for Jack. She felt something inside her shift, and she knew it with a clarity that almost knocked her off her feet.

She turned back to Jack and his smile had gone because he'd seen it too — he'd seen in those few echoing moments everything that was in her heart.

'Oh, Ellen,' he said.

She dropped her bag on the platform, feeling as though she wanted to collapse beside it.

'I can't come with you, Jack,' she said. 'I can't leave them. I'm so sorry.'

He stepped forward and so did she, wrapping her arms around his neck and pressing herself against him as hard as she could to capture the feel of his body, his warm strength and the precious smell of him.

'I love you, Jack Vaughan,' she whispered.

'I love you too, Ellen McCabe,' he whispered back. 'You know where I'll be. I'll wait for you, for as long as it takes.'

The pain in Ellen's heart was so terrible she felt as though she were burning. She nodded and stepped back, then picked up her bag and walked away from him, back the way she'd come.

Epilogue

The cat has moved out from under the coffee table, and is lying stretched out on the floor in front of the gas heater. In the sudden, thick silence of Ellen McCabe's sitting room, Cathy can hear it making funny little snoring noises.

Overwhelmed by the magnitude of the old lady's story, she feels like crying, but can't because historians aren't supposed to do that sort of thing, not even inexperienced students.

She clears her throat. 'Can I ask, Mrs McCabe, did Tom take you back?'

The old lady nods. 'He did.'

Cathy is surprised at the extent of her relief, and then smiles, because she likes a happy ending.

Then Mrs McCabe says, 'Would you turn the tape off now, dear?' It's an order, not a request. 'The rest of this isn't for anyone else's ears, but I might as well tell you, you've come this far.'

'Oh, OK, no problem.' Cathy presses the button and settles back to hear the end of the story.

'He took the baby too,' Mrs McCabe says, her timing perfect.

Cathy's jaw drops.

Mrs McCabe laughs, a surprisingly loud and hearty sound for such a frail old woman. 'I knew

385

that would get you, dear,' she says.

Even Matt smiles; he's back now, sitting quietly on the couch, listening but saying nothing.

'You were pregnant?'

'Only just. About four weeks, give or take.'

'And Jack was the father?' It's an extremely rude question to ask, but Cathy can't stop herself. She's glad the tape isn't running.

'Oh, no question, and when she was born she was the spitting image of him. Dark curls, black eyes, the lot. It was hard for Tom, her looking so different from him and from the boys, but he loved her anyway, he really did. Well, you couldn't not, really, she was such a lovely child. We called her Sarah.'

Cathy says, 'So you got your little girl after all?'

'I did, although she's not a little girl any more. She's Matt's mother.'

Cathy gives Matt a quick sideways glance, and suddenly sees in him the face of the man Ellen McCabe fell in love with more than fifty years ago. A shiver of something both eerie and sad scuttles up her spine.

'And were things . . . was it all right between you and Tom in the end?' she asks after a moment.

'In the end they were, but it took a while. It was very hard for him, it was hard for both of us. Half the town wouldn't speak to me for quite some time.' But Mrs McCabe shrugs, as if to say it didn't really matter then and it certainly doesn't now. 'He was a good man, Tom, and a

386

forgiving one. Things came right eventually. We had a good life.' She laughs again. 'I suppose we did become my mother and father, really, me with my illegitimate daughter and him with his wayward wife. They say history never repeats, but it does, love, it does. Although Tom didn't turn into an alcoholic and I never insisted on having the newest and best of everything, so I suppose we weren't exactly the same. I still appreciate a nice fridge, though. Davey buys me a new one every couple of years. I don't know why, but he does.'

'What did happen to the boys?' Cathy asks.

A shadow crosses the old lady's lined face. 'They both went on the coal as soon as they left school. Neil went to Australia a year after that, to work in the mines at Illawarra, and never really came back. He's retired now, with a grown-up family of his own. I don't think he ever quite forgave me for what happened.' Then she brightens. 'But Davey's still here. His boys are both miners up at Huntly East.'

'And Sarah?'

'Sarah's in Hamilton, but she comes through at least once a week. Matt's at Huntly East too, and flats with a group of rowdy boys in Hakanoa Street, don't you, love?'

'Yes, Gran.'

Cathy says, 'You said earlier that Tom died quite a while ago.'

'Yes, he did. In 1977, from lung cancer.'

'From smoking?'

Mrs McCabe shakes her head. 'Silicosis, from the coal dust.'

'That must have been very hard for you.'

'It was, but it wasn't unusual. Not then, anyway.'

Then Cathy asks the question she most wants to hear the answer to. 'And did you ever see Jack again?'

Ellen McCabe gives Cathy a long, contemplative look. She's clearly tired now and Cathy wonders whether she's finally asked a question the old lady doesn't want to answer.

But, eventually, she says, 'Matt, bring me the letter, will you?'

Matt gets up and crosses the sitting room to a china cabinet with a large cut-crystal bowl on top of it. Under the bowl is tucked a yellowed envelope. He draws it out and hands it to his grandmother.

She opens it carefully, making sure not to tear the fragile papers inside.

'I was sent this in 1967,' she says. She puts on a pair of glasses, clears her throat and begins to read:

Dear Ellen McCabe,

You don't know me, but I know who you are. I married Jack Vaughan in 1959, and a day never went past that I didn't know he was still in love with you. He married me because he got me pregnant, and I believe that was the only reason he did.

But Jack died recently. He was killed with the other fifteen men in the explosion at Strongman Mine. I would not have got in touch with you, because your ghost did nothing but blight my life with Jack, but he left instructions that I send this note to you in the event that anything ever happened to him, and because he was a decent man I am doing this.

I don't know you personally, and I hate how you came between Jack and me, but I wish to God I knew what it was you had over him, because I never saw a man who loved a woman more than he loved you.

Yours faithfully,
Mrs Gina Vaughan

* * *

Cathy stares at Ellen, stunned.

The old lady retrieves another slip of paper from the envelope. 'This is the one from Jack.' She takes a deep, measured breath and bends her head again.

Dear Ellen,

This note is just in case anything ever happens to me, and if you are reading it, then something has. At the time I am writing it, I am still waiting for you, and if you never receive it then I will still be waiting.

I love you more than anything, and the months we had together were the best of my life. I have never met anyone like you, and I expect I never will again.

So no matter what happens, Ellen, remember that I loved you then, I love you now, and I will love you always.

Yours always and for ever,
Jack

As Cathy presses the heel of her palm against her eyes to blot the moisture there, she sees that Mrs McCabe has tears coursing down her own face.

For a second the two women, one at the end of her life and the other only starting out, are united.

'My God,' Cathy says, 'how did you feel when you read that?'

Mrs McCabe stares down at her hands for a long time, then slowly looks up. 'Just for a minute, I felt as though I was with him again,' she says. 'Yes. That's how I felt.' Then she clears her throat again, and sits up straighter in her La-Z-Boy. 'I'm sorry, love, but I'm very tired now. Do you think you've got everything you wanted to know?'

Matt gets to his feet and comes to stand protectively behind her.

'There's just one more question, Mrs McCabe, if you can manage it.'

The old lady nods.

'Was it worth it? The strike?'

Mrs McCabe's head sinks onto her chest and her eyes close, and Cathy wonders if she's fallen asleep. But, finally, she speaks.

'You can turn your tape recorder back on for this bit.'

Cathy does.

'No, in a lot of ways it wasn't worth it. We all stood strong in the end, one way or another, and we still all lost something. When I was young I thought there was no battle in the world that couldn't be fought and won. I thought we could take on the government and beat it, and I thought that the love of a wonderful man would give me the strength to walk away from my children. But I was wrong, on both counts.'

'Would you do it all again?'

'All of it?'

'Yes.'

Ellen McCabe smiles. 'Yes, love, I would.'

TAMAR

Deborah Challinor

The first volume in a three-volume family saga.

When Tamar Deane is orphaned at seventeen in a small Cornish village, she seizes the chance for a new life and emigrates to New Zealand. In March 1879, alone and frightened on the Plymouth quay, she is befriended by an extraordinary woman. Myrna McTaggert is travelling to Auckland with plans to establish the finest brothel in the southern hemisphere and her unconventional friendship proves invaluable when Tamar makes disastrous choices in the new colony. Tragedy and scandal befall her, but unexpected good fortune brings vast changes to Tamar's life. As the century draws to a close, uncertainty looms when a distant war lures her loved ones to South Africa.

WHITE FEATHERS

Deborah Challinor

The second volume in a three-volume family saga.

In 1914, Tamar Murdoch's life is one of ease and contentment at Kenmore, a prosperous estate in Hawkes Bay, as storm clouds over Europe begin casting long shadows. Tamar's love for her children is sorely tested as one by one they are called, or driven, into the living hell of World War One. During the Boer War, Joseph, her illegitimate eldest son, fought as a European, but this time he is determined to enlist in the Maori Battalion. As loyalties within the Murdoch clan are divided, and the war takes Tamar and Andrew's only daughter far from her sheltered upbringing, the people and experiences their children encounter will shape the destiny of the Murdoch clan for generations to come.

BLUE SMOKE

Deborah Challinor

The final volume in a three-volume family saga.

On 3 February 1931, Napier is devastated by a powerful earthquake — and Tamar Murdoch, beloved matriarch of Kenmore, is seriously injured. As she recovers, Tamar is preoccupied with the ongoing effects of the Great Depression. When her grandson threatens to leave for Spain to join the International Brigade, she feels a familiar dread — once again her family is threatened by war and heartbreak, as Hitler's armies march.

FIRST IMPRESSIONS

Jude Deveraux

Eden Palmer, a single mother, has worked hard to raise her daughter — now twenty-seven, and recently married. The offspring of a terrible event, Eden's daughter, Melissa, has been the jewel of her life. But now, feeling the need to build a separate life on her own, Eden moves to Arundel, North Carolina, to take ownership of Farrington Manor, an old house filled with charm and memories. Arriving in Arundel, Eden is pursued by two eligible bachelors, Jared McBride and Braddon Granville. Eden soon finds that juggling the attentions of two men is hard enough, but her bid to start over plunges her into a mystery that threatens not only her plans, but also her very life.